It was hard to place one foot in front of the other for his legs would no longer obey the command of his will. He tried counting his paces, but he was so cold, so exhausted, that his mind refused to keep a tally.

'Ready to give up yet, boy?'

'Not while there's breath in my body,' he gasped through his teeth.

'Won't be long then,' said his father's spectre cheerfully.

His garments were as wet as Nicholas's own and he wore a shimmering necklace of seaweed. There was a huge, sea-washed wound in his side. 'Listen, they are tolling your death knell.'

In the distance Nicholas thought he heard a church bell, as loud and real as his father's voice.

Then he thought nothing at all as his legs gave way and the ground rose up to welcome him in the dark grave of its embrace.

Also by Elizabeth Chadwick

THE CONQUEST
THE CHAMPION
THE LOVE KNOT

THE MARSH KING'S DAUGHTER

Elizabeth Chadwick

A *Warner* Book

First published in Great Britain in 1999
by Little, Brown and Company
This edition published by Warner Books in 2000

*All characters in this publication are fictitious
and any resemblance to real persons, living or dead,
is purely coincidental.*

A CIP catalogue record for this book
is available from the British Library.

ISBN 0 7515 2410 7

Typeset in Horley OS by
Palimpsest Book Production Limited,
Polmont, Stirlingshire
Printed and bound in Great Britain by
Clays Ltd, St Ives plc

Warner Books
A Division of
Little, Brown and Company (UK)
Brettenham House
Lancaster Place
London WC2E 7EN

Acknowledgements

I would like to thank the many people who have helped me along the way in one form or another while writing this novel. On the publishing front, my gratitude goes out to Barbara Boote for being a wonderful editor and fighting my corner at every turn and to Filomena Wood for her efforts on my behalf each time publication day comes around. Copy editors are a frequently vilified breed, but I am delighted by mine, Richenda Todd, and would like to say thank you very much for her help with freeboards, halyards, furling and clewing! Any mistakes remaining in the terminology and techniques of Medieval shipping, I acknowledge as mine. I would also like to thank everyone at Blake Friedmann for their tireless endeavours on my behalf, especially Isobel Dixon and Carole Blake. I am much more knowledgeable about geography these days because I have to get out my atlas to look up the whereabouts of the myriad countries in which they sell my books and stories! My thanks for their interest and support also goes out to Richard Lee and Towse Harrison of the Historical Novel Society.

On the domestic front I could not do without the love and support of my husband Roger and our sons Ian and Simon. My parents, Robert and Joan Chadwick, are always there to back me up and I would like to thank Alison King for her interest and long-standing friendship.

In the research category, I want to say a huge thank you to members of Regia Anglorum and Conquest for extending my knowledge and giving me the opportunity to expand my Norman culinary expertise (never ever cook in a posh frock with hanging sleeves!). My appreciation goes out to Gary Golding, Lyn Mcquaid, Patrick O'Connel, Steve, Joe and Daniel Wibberly, Sharon Goode, Sarah and Mike Doyle, Jon Preston, Simon Carter, Ivor and Simone Lawton, Rosemary and Trevor Watson – and anyone else who knows me!

Finally, for the inspiration, I would like to extend my gratitude to Bruce Springsteen, Jim Steinman, Runrig and Tori Amos among a host of others. Thank you for the music.

CHAPTER 1

LINCOLN, SPRING 1216

It was a glorious May morning in the world at large – soft, balmy and harmonious. At the home of Edward Weaver in Lincoln, however, a violent storm was raging.

'I won't go!' Miriel shrieked at her stepfather. 'You can't force me into a nunnery. I'll run away; I swear I will!'

Nigel Fuller's light eyes bulged with fury. Planting his legs wide, he adopted a dominant stance. 'I'm the head of this household now and you'll yield me obedience. Your shameless headstrong ways have been indulged for too long!'

'You've wanted rid of me ever since you married my mother!' Miriel spat. 'My grandfather's been buried less than a season and already you're at your schemes.' She tossed her head in contempt. 'You'll never match up to him. They'll still be calling this Edwin's house long after they've shovelled you into your grave.'

She realised that she had bated him too far. With a roar he swung his fist. Miriel side-stepped the blow and seized a distaff of raw wool from a basket by the hearth. 'Don't you dare lay a finger on me!' She tried to swallow, but her throat was dry with fear. Now that her grandfather was no longer here to shield her from Nigel's rage, a whipping seemed inevitable. She jabbed the distaff at his soft belly and, as he leaped aside, she darted for the door. Despite his bulk, Nigel was fast. Before she could raise the latch, he caught her by her thick tawny braid and jerked her back into the middle of the room.

Miriel struck at him with the distaff pole, but he wrenched it from her grasp and hurled it aside. The fleshy side of his hand clouted her on the temple and his gold seal ring opened a jagged cut. Held fast by her hair, Miriel fought back, gouging with her nails, biting like a dog until she tasted salt blood between her teeth. Nigel bellowed and struck her again. She lost her vision; her knees buckled and only the twisting, vicious grip on her braid held her upright.

'You will obey me!' he panted. 'Whether you will it or not, tomorrow you go to the nuns at St Catherine's!'

'Never!' Miriel refuted in blind litany. Her defiance was all she had left. Let him murder her first; she would rather break than bend.

A crackling sound of small flames growing bigger and the stench of burning wool filled the room. The flung distaff had landed half in and half out of the hearth and now fire was licking along its length and devouring the nearby basket of raw wool. There was a belch of air as the door opened and suddenly the room was full of choking, greasy smoke. Fire lashed towards the rafters.

Cursing, roaring like a goaded bear, Nigel threw Miriel to the ground, kicked her brutally in the ribs and, grabbing the flagon from the coffer, dashed wine at the blazing remnants of the wool basket.

The woman who had opened the door screamed the alarm and sped to fetch a water pail. Other household members came running with cloaks and besoms to smother and beat the flames from existence.

Miriel closed her eyes and willed her awareness, already blurred, to vanish, but as with the rest of her life, she could not have the things she desired even for the fiercest of willing. It was true that her stepfather had almost vanished just now in a puff of smoke, but almost was not good enough.

'It is all your daughter's fault!' she heard Nigel snarling at her mother. 'She's as disrespectful and wild as a vixen. Now you see the fruit of Edward's indulgence and pampering. She should have been put in a nunnery at birth!'

'Yes, Nigel.'

The dutiful murmur caused Miriel's closed eyelids to twitch with irritation and pain. Even to save her own life, she doubted her mother would gainsay a man. As far as

Annet Fuller was concerned, they were the masters, their orders and opinions all that mattered in the world.

'She's not spending another night under this roof. She can sleep in the warehouse with a bolt on the door, and at dawn she leaves.'

Miriel wondered if she heard the briefest hesitation before the next placatory 'Yes, Nigel', but decided it was just wishful thinking. Then she heard Nigel's harsh breathing as he stood over her. 'I hope for your sake that those nuns can find something worth saving in your soul. God knows, they have a thankless task before them.' He gave her a vicious nudge with his toe. 'It's no use to play dead, you deceitful wench, I know you can hear me.'

Miriel had an urge to poke out her tongue, but resisted it and lay unresponding. Even if she could not defeat him in battle, she would not give him the satisfaction of being right.

The floor rushes crackled as he strode to the door. His fingers clicked. 'Get this mess cleared up before I return.'

'Yes, Nigel.'

'And I don't want to see her again.'

The door banged. There was a brief silence which was swiftly overtaken by the serving women who commenced chattering and clucking over the state of the room like a pair of disturbed hens. Miriel groaned and opened her eyes. Blood stung in one of them, making her squint and blink. Huge, sooty fireprints had made violent patterns on the lime-washed walls. The wicker wool basket was a skeleton fretwork of blackened strands and the stink of charred wool was almost overpowering.

'Oh, Miriel, what have you done?' Her mother shook her head in exasperation. Annet Fuller was three and thirty years old with a swirl of golden-tawny hair like her daughter's, although hers was decently tucked within a housewife's wimple. She had clear grey eyes and fine, thin features which were seldom brightened by a smile.

'Nothing.' Miriel sniffed and sat up. Her head was throbbing and her ribs ached sharply with each breath. 'He started the fire. I always get the blame; he hates me.'

'Oh, he doesn't,' Annet said in her mild voice. Going to a water pail near the charred basket, she soaked a linen cloth and wrung it out. 'Your father only wants what is best for you.'

'He's not my father.' Miriel's own voice was hard and tight. No one had ever said much about the man who had begotten her. All she knew, and that gleaned from servants' gossip and the occasional stray remark of her grandfather's, was that he had been a minstrel, an itinerant singer who had taken advantage of the wealthy weaver's virgin fourteen-year-old daughter and moved on long before her belly began to swell. It was from him that Miriel had inherited her slender height and honey-brown eyes.

Annet sighed and her knuckles tightened on the wringing until they were white. 'He is in the eyes of the law.' She knelt by Miriel and laid the cloth against the jagged cut on her temple. 'You gainsay him at every turn, child. A man has to know he is master in his own house. I am surprised that he has not taken his belt to you before now.'

Miriel's teeth chattered with shock and revulsion. 'My grandfather was master here and he never beat me once.' The tightness in her voice grew and strangled her. Suddenly she was choking on tears. She didn't want to cry, and clenched her fists in her gown, fighting herself. It was the mention of her grandfather that had caused the damage. The image of his creased, dour features filled her mind. He had been harsh and stern, but never unfair – and he had loved her. That was what made the world's difference.

Her mother's lips compressed as she continued to dab with the cloth. 'Your grandfather was an old man.'

'You mean he would have beaten me if he'd been younger?' Miriel said with scornful flippancy.

Annet ceased dabbing and sat back on her heels. 'I mean that his judgement was impaired.' Her voice remained level, but it was no longer soft. 'He indulged you when he should have been strict. He let you wrap him around your little finger. Whatever you wanted, you received.'

The envy and resentment in her mother's words came as no surprise to Miriel; the emotions had always been there, unspoken, but until this moment she had not realised how deep and bitter. Being the favoured one, there had been no reason to probe.

'You want to send me to the nunnery too,' she whispered, and the terrible notion rose in her mind that perhaps it had been her mother's idea from the beginning.

Annet looked away. 'It is for the best,' she said stiffly. 'You should have been given to St Catherine's long ago, before you became too wild.'

'But I don't want to be a nun!' Miriel clutched her aching ribs and rocked her body in anguish.

'Then what do you want?' The grey stare was as cold as frost. 'To stay here?'

Miriel shook her head miserably. Three months ago, with her grandfather in good health and head of the household, it would have been a different matter.

'No,' Annet agreed grimly. 'None of us could bear it. Nigel would kill you in the end and I would not blame him.' She looked at the cloth and folded it in a precise, neat square. 'We could seek you a husband, but the way you behave, who would want you unless you came with a great dowry?' She gave a disapproving sniff. 'Even if some man did take you in marriage, we would dwell in constant fear of you shaming this household by being a bad wife.'

'As you shamed it by bearing me?' Miriel hit out, then flinched as Annet made an abrupt movement. The slap, however, did not descend. Annet lowered her hand and clenched it in her lap. Her eyes fastened on the dull gleam of her wedding ring and she tightened her jaw, emphasising the delicate lines of first ageing between nose and mouth.

'Yes,' she said, 'as I shamed it by bearing you. I was too young, too innocent to see your father for the thief in the night that he was. He stole my life from me in begetting yours. Now, by God's grace and the passage of years, I have found a good man and won back the right to hold my head high.' She gave Miriel a bright stare, the suspicion of a glitter on her lashes. 'I'll not have you jeopardising my future with your tantrums.' She made an abrupt gesture. 'Enough of this. I am wasting time that could be better spent.' Her glance flickered to the sooty mess around the hearth and the two women who were sweeping up the blackened floor rushes. Their backs were turned, but that did not mean they had lost their hearing. The scandal would be all over town by dusk.

'Can you stand?'

Miriel nodded and struggled to her feet. Her head was pounding fit to burst and she felt sick. She shook out the folds of her gown. It was made of the finest English wool, woven and clipped on her grandfather's Flemish loom and dyed the colour of ripe, dark plums. The thought of exchanging such luxury for the scratchy drab folds of a novice's habit appalled her. As Edward Weaver's granddaughter, she was accustomed to wearing the most stylish of garments fashioned from the best fabric.

'Come.' Taking Miriel's arm, her mother drew her towards the door. 'You heard what your stepfather said. He doesn't want you in this house.'

'And you don't either.' Miriel's voice quivered.

'Not at the moment,' Annet said without compassion.

The warehouse, where sacks of wool were stored before being sorted, carded and spun, stood across the yard from the main house. It was a sturdy stone dwelling with solid oak doors and a shuttered gable window. Just now it was almost empty, for the shearing season had not long begun, and only a few raw fleeces were piled in the far corner.

Miriel heard the wooden bar shoot into place across the doors, and then the large iron key grinding in the lock. Rubbing her arms, she walked slowly to the middle of the room. Threads of light filtered through gaps in the shutters and sparsely illuminated the beaten earth floor. Although there were few fleeces in store, thirty years of use had saturated the walls with their ammoniac, fatty smell. To Miriel, the pungency was comforting and poignant. Her grandfather's white beard had been like a fleece and his clothing had always held the aroma of sheep in its creases.

Leaving the centre of the room, she paced its walls, running her fingers along the flinty stone and remembering herself doing just the same as a small child in her grandfather's shadow. Following him, asking interminable questions until he was jolted from his taciturn disapproval to laugh and answer. Her fascination had flattered him and through the years, first at his knee and then at his shoulder, she had learned the weaving trade until she knew as much as he did, albeit without the seasoning of maturity and experience. Much good it had done her.

Her throat tightened. She plucked a snag of wool from the stone and teased it between her fingers, recognising by the length of the staple that it had come from a lowland breed. Edwin Weaver her grandfather was dead, and Nigel Fuller ruled the household like a cockerel on a dunghill. He would no more tolerate her presence in the weaving sheds or at the fulling mill than he would contemplate sweeping the floor or washing his own dish after he had eaten. Men and women had their place in the world and never the twain should blend, except at night in the bedchamber, and even there man was the master.

Miriel wandered over to the pile of fleeces in the corner. Five hundred of them from the abbey at St Catherine's, the nunnery where she was to be imprisoned, out of sight, out of mind and, more to the point, out of trouble. They always sheared their flocks early. Her grandfather, with a twinkle of amusement, had called the start of the shearing season St Catherine's Day, although the saint did not celebrate her feast until November.

The family's association with the abbey was a long and profitable one. Her grandfather's twin sister had been the sacrist there until her death two years ago, and a distant cousin had taken her vows at St Catherine's before becoming a prioress at a Benedictine house near Lincoln. A new oblate from the Weaver household would be welcomed with open arms. Indeed, there had been hints from the Abbess on several occasions. Aided by Miriel's pleading, her grandfather had stolidly ignored them, but Nigel was of a different mind. Her mother was young enough to bear a complete generation of Fuller children. What need of a troublesome bastard daughter?

Miriel made herself a nest among the pungent, foamy

fleeces and curled herself into a foetal ball. If she was going to be forced to callus her knees in a freezing chapel at all hours of the day and night, she would spend the time praying for God to visit a murrain on her stepfather.

'A murrain, a murrain, a murrain,' she chanted through her teeth like a holy song, until the words broke on a sob and the tears came.

The light ceased to glimmer through the shutters as dusk fell and darkness encroached. No one came to bring Miriel food or water or comfort. Only once did the heavy wooden draw-bar rattle as someone checked that it was solidly in place. Then the footsteps trod away in the direction of the house. A small figure, lost in the vastness of the warehouse, Miriel closed her eyes and sought oblivion in sleep.

CHAPTER 2

EAST COAST OF ENGLAND, OCTOBER 1216

There was nothing to see over the sides of the cart but white, clinging mist. Nicholas de Caen knew that if only he could rid himself of the tough hemp cords binding his wrists and ankles, he could evade his captors in its thickness like a flea in a blanket. They would not spend precious time searching for him. Despite his bonds, he was to them a minor fish in the game, trapped in the net and kept in case he was useful.

He was going to disappoint them for they had already taken the only items of value he possessed – his elderly horse, his rusty mail shirt, and a rather fine old sword that had belonged to his father. Stripped of these, all that remained was a young man of three and twenty with no living relatives to pay his ransom and nothing to yield but hatred for King John who had beggared and destroyed the de Caen family.

Nicholas tested the knotted rope with his teeth, but his captors had been thorough and there was no give in the hemp. Undeterred, having naught better to do, he persisted. Around him the hazy shapes of other baggage carts and lines of roped pack ponies loomed in the thick sea-mist. Although he could see neither water nor beach, the salt tang of the muddy foreshore filled his nostrils.

They had camped the previous evening on the banks of the Wellstream at the hamlet of Cross Keys. This morning they were preparing to traverse the murky bay of The Wash at the inlet while the tide was out.

'Ye'll not loosen them ropes, lad,' said Alaric the cart-driver not unkindly as he appeared out of the mist, his woollen hood dewed in hoar and clear water droplets sparkling in his beard. 'I've trussed enough chickens in me time to know me trade.' He made sure the back of the cart was secure, then climbed on to the driving board and lifted the reins.

'I can but try,' Nicholas replied wryly. There was no profit in being sullen with his gaoler who was decent enough in his way. He had let Nicholas keep his cloak against the cold, and had not stinted to give him hot gruel and ale from the supplies that morning, although he had not been obliged to feed him at all.

'Then you're a fool.' Alaric glanced at Nicholas and scrubbed his nose on his sleeve. 'We'd not need to chase you with crossbows and dogs; you'd be sucked into them quicksands yonder faster than a wink.'

Nicholas shrugged. 'If it is so dangerous, then what is the baggage train doing here? Why didn't we take the long road with King John and the rest of the troops?'

''Tain't dangerous if you knows what you're doing,' Alaric said gruffly. 'There's a causeway straight across and we've got a guide. This way, although we're slower moving, we'll make up the distance. We should reach Swineshead Abbey by dusk, about the same time as the vanguard.' Facing forward, he clicked his tongue to the horse, and the cart lurched forward.

Nicholas was jolted against the sacks of grain which, apart from himself, were the wain's cargo. If he focused hard and concentrated, he could just make out a string of pack ponies following, their sides laden with chests and panniers. Their breath added to the drifting mist, and their keeper was a dark shape swathed in a broad-brimmed hat and heavy mantle.

If there were other prisoners in the baggage train, Nicholas had not seen them, but then his own capture had been a matter of pure mischance. If his horse had not cast a shoe, he would not have been at the smithy on the Lincoln road, where John's soldiers had seen and seized upon him as one of the escaping rebels from the aborted siege of Lincoln. They had brought him to Lynn where John was staying. By the time they arrived, the King had moved on to Wisbech, heading for Swineshead, so they had tossed

Nicholas in with the baggage until they had time to interrogate him.

Nicholas had no intention of being present when that moment arrived. He had heard far too much about the techniques employed by the King's mercenaries. As far as Nicholas was concerned, red-hot pokers belonged at the hearth and nowhere near a human orifice. Besides, he had sworn a vow to live until he was ninety and die in his bed.

He worked at the knot, but the tough fibres only cut further into his skin, making angry weals. The cart rumbled on to the causeway, which was little more than a narrow path raised above the surrounding mud. When the tide turned, that path would be obliterated by the freezing North Sea.

Nicholas tried not to think of the vast sheet of grey water lurking out beyond the horizon. He had been born to the sound of waves crashing against a harbour wall, had learned to sail almost before he could walk. The sea-surge was within him, blood and bone. There was love, and above that love was a deep, deep respect.

The mist cleared a little, a haze of white sun glimmering through somewhere in the region of noon, but Nicholas could see that it was a temporary respite. Come mid-afternoon, the faery wisps and veils would thicken into true, hobgoblin fog.

Alaric was whistling through his teeth, as much to keep his spirits up, Nicholas suspected, as from natural good humour. The young man knelt up to glance over the side of the cart, but even though the sun had thinned the cloud there was little enough to see: a glistening brown expanse of shore populated by gulls and oyster catchers probing the mud for crabs. The landward side was dun-coloured marshland, fading into a grey, vaporous haze.

John's baggage train was slightly more interesting. Neither the beginning nor end of the procession could be seen although, from what he had observed earlier, Nicholas judged that it must extend for about two miles. Not only were general supplies being transported across the estuary, but also the entire contents of John's household, including coin to pay his troops, and the personal treasures and trappings of the royal household.

Nicholas looked down at his bound wrists and grimaced. It was the closest he was ever going to come these days to wealth of any kind. All he had to his name were the clothes on his back and the prospect of being hanged for a traitor – although it was King John who had committed treason, not the de Caen family.

They were perhaps halfway across the causeway and the mist was gathering like a murky fleece when the cart jolted to an abrupt halt and Alaric swore roundly. The impact flung Nicholas on to his side. He rolled over and pushed against the sacks of grain to right himself. Behind the cart, the pack ponies crowded to a standstill, their breath smoking like witches' hair. Beyond them again, a cursing cart-driver hauled his wagon out of line to avoid a collision.

'What's happening?' Nicholas craned his neck. Confused bellows of anger and command drifted to them from further up the convoy.

'Buggered if I know.' Alaric leaped down from the cart and disappeared into the gathering fog.

Nicholas stared around. The cold air prickled his nape. Christ Jesu, this was dangerous. They were full out in the estuary on a narrow causeway with the turn of the tide due far too soon. They couldn't afford a delay.

A sudden, terrified bellow for help came from the seaward side where the cart-driver had pulled his team out of line. Nicholas jumped at the sound and narrowed his gaze into the mist. Shadowy forms struggled and twisted, but the quicksand had snared them and was rapidly sucking them down. The driver danced on top of his cart, crying for help in a voice raw with panic. Men threw ropes but they slapped on the mud, falling far short. The driver jumped down on to one of the half-sunk wheels, reaching, pleading. The ropes were cast again, but they grew no longer. Finally, the stranded man's desperation burst. Leaping from the safety of the cart, he made a grab for the nearest lifeline. He missed by yards, floundering and clawing at a safety that was so close and yet beyond his reach. The quicksand slowly drank him, swallowing him down its long, voracious maw until his screams were smothered.

All down the line, the tragedy was re-enacted as drivers and pony-keepers tried to by-pass the blockage and only realised how narrow their margin of safety was when they found themselves out on the quicksand.

Alaric returned. He was still whistling through his teeth, but now they were bared and there was fear in his eyes. 'There's a cart up front cast a wheel,' he told Nicholas. 'Axle's split and it's beyond repair. They're going to try and drag the entire thing off the causeway, but it's heavy laden.'

'How long before the tide turns?'

Alaric shrugged. 'Not long enough.' He went to the end of the cart and gave his news to the pony-keeper behind. Together both men started back up the line.

'Wait!' Nicholas cried, his voice choking with the horror that they were just going to leave him. Out on the sands, concealed in cloud but pitilessly within hearing, the cries of men and horses sounded like a knell as they were sucked into the sludge. He held out his wrists as Alaric turned. 'For God's pity, cut my bonds. I'm another pair of hands!'

Alaric studied him narrowly, then drew the knife from his belt. 'Aye,' he said grimly. 'You'll not be running anywhere, will you?'

The blade sliced through the cords at wrist and ankle and Nicholas shook them away with disgust as if they were snakes. Fortunately the binding, although skin-tight, had not robbed him of feeling. Apart from minor cramp and stiffness, he was able to jump from the cart and walk without difficulty. Flexing his hands, he followed Alaric and the pony-man to the head of the line.

The broken wain was one of the most heavily laden in the convoy. It heeled to one side, the shattered wheel thrusting at an awkward angle and half jammed under the strakes of the base. As Nicholas and the men arrived, sections of the royal bed were being disgorged from its bowels and passed down the line to be distributed among the other carts. Nicholas eyed a gorgeously painted chest as it followed a feather mattress through the ranks and thought sourly that however short of funds John claimed to be, he still lived in luxury unknown to most men.

'Here, you, take this.' One of the soldiers emptying the stricken wain shoved a glass container into Nicholas's startled hands. He gaped at the object in astonishment. If he had been told a week ago that he would be standing in the middle of the Wellstream estuary holding King John's piss-flask while the North Sea gathered beyond the horizon, he would have dismissed the prediction with an incredulous guffaw. Now, although he laughed, there was more despair in the sound than disbelief.

'Don't just stand there, dolt!' the soldier snapped. 'Pass the things down the line.'

A silk pouch arrived in Nicholas's other hand. Through the fabric he could feel several long-stemmed objects with small scoops at the end, and a tiny pair of shears. The royal ear spoons and beard trimmer, he surmised, laughing harder until tears squeezed through his lashes.

It took the best part of an hour to unload the broken wain. There were sheets and bed hangings, tapestries and curtains; there were more painted chests with brass hasps and heavy barrel locks. One in particular caught Nicholas's eye. It was slightly smaller than the other coffers, being of a size that one man could manage alone if he were strong. The sides were fashioned of blue and gold enamelled copper, and a decoration of crosses in contrasting red outlined the lid and edges. Unlike the piss-flask and ear spoons, this particular item remained firmly in the custody of the royal guards who divested a pony of its panniers and strapped the chest to its pack-saddle instead.

'Don't get any ideas.' Alaric gave Nicholas a sharp nudge. 'They'd have your head off your shoulders faster than slicing a cabbage in the garden.'

Nicholas rubbed his elbowed ribs. 'I've never been this close to a fortune before.'

Alaric snorted. 'Bad fortune if you ask me. Do you think the King's any happier for owning it?'

'I would be.'

'Shows how much of a fool you are then. A man's own heart

makes him what he is, not cold yellow metal.' He thumped his concave chest to emphasise the point.

'But having two coins to rub together helps.' Nicholas looked sidelong at the older man's scowl. 'You're not going to tie me up again, are you?'

Alaric sucked his teeth and shook his head. 'No reason to,' he said brusquely. 'We're all prisoners for the nonce.'

The horses had been left harnessed to the broken wain and now their driver straddled the leading one, urging with whip and voice. As the animals strained, the cart began to move, lurching like a clawless crab on to the sands beyond, some of it quick, some of it firm, but no telling until it was too late. The cart gouged a deep, muddy track through the foreshore. The ground rippled like some great beast twitching its hide at the irritation of lice, and the rear wheels started to sink. Wide-eyed with effort and terror, the driver cut the traces and whirled the horses for the safety of the causeway.

'Safe!' he cried triumphantly as he reached solid ground in a churn of muddy sand. But as the other carters and soldiers cheered him, the joyous expression froze on his face, for he could see what they had yet to turn and notice. 'The tide,' he gasped. 'Christ, the tide, it's here!'

Beyond the causeway, the soft roar of moving water was like a beast returning to its lair.

'God help us,' Alaric said harshly and delved inside his tunic for the small cross he wore around his neck.

Knowing from bitter experience that God was seldom so charitable, Nicholas said nothing. The only help was that which they gave themselves.

Men ran to tend their animals and carts, but in the time it took the supply train to start on its cumbersome way, the sea had already covered the causeway in an inch of water. Panicking, some tried to cross the foreshore, hoping to find solid ground, but it was too treacherous, the firm channels too narrow, and as before, the horses and wains quickly became stuck. And the sea poured in, foaming, brown, relentless.

Nicholas unpinned his cloak and threw it away. He tore his woollen tunic over his head and unwound his hose bindings.

Alaric stared at him. 'Have you run mad?'

'When the water's deep enough, I can swim a horse to shore,' he said. 'If you have any sense, you'll do the same. There is no other hope.'

The old man chewed his underlip and continued to finger his cross with work-worn hands. Then he made a brusque gesture at the bay cob in the cart's traces. 'Unhitch him,' he commanded and, shivering, began removing his own surplus garments.

The sea-water washed around Nicholas's thighs as he struggled with straps and buckles. Men's entreaties to God were louder now and filled with panic. The convoy ceased to move, except by command of the heaving buffet of the waves.

'Here.' Nicholas turned the cob in a tight circle and gave the reins to Alaric. 'I'll find my own mount.'

Despite his cold and fear, the old man's eyes sharpened. 'And even if we should both survive, I doubt I'll be seeing you at Swineshead Abbey,' he said tartly.

'I doubt it too.' Nicholas extended his hand, the wrist branded with a faint red line where he had been tied. 'God be with you.'

Alaric clasped his leather palm to the younger man's. 'And you,' he replied with a brusque nod.

Nicholas waded away up the line. He needed a horse, but not just any horse.

By the time he reached the front of the line, the sea was above his waist and he could scarcely control the chattering of his jaw. Men had clambered on top of their carts, thus prolonging their lives by the length of a quarter candle. Soldiers were desperately shedding their armour, but many had left it too late. There was no possibility of removing a heavy mail shirt and sodden quilted undertunic when more than the half was beneath the waves. They were the first to drown.

Horses panicked, rolling their eyes, plunging and splashing as the freezing brown water lapped their bellies. Nicholas sought for the pack pony with the enamelled coffer strapped to its saddle. He knew he must be close when he saw a little bay beast with the royal piss-flask gleaming in one of its panniers, the fluted glass cushioned by embroidered linen towels. The pony was unattended. Others, all laden with mundane articles, milled nearby, jittery, kicking out in fear. But there was no sign amongst them of the horse he sought.

In resignation, Nicholas reached to the bay's bridle and hauled himself out of the chest-deep water and across its back. 'Hah!' he cried and splashed his heels against its flanks. The pony plunged forward and Nicholas tasted murky salt spray on his lips.

A huge wave wallowed over the struggling baggage train, spinning carts sideways, engulfing men. Nicholas's pony was knocked off its feet by the surge and threshed in panic. Nicholas was swiped from its back and washed under. Gritty salt-water filled his mouth. He surfaced spluttering, saw the pony and made a grab for its tail as it started to swim for the shore.

The choked cries of drowning men rose in the fog, joining the flotsam from John's doomed supply train. A wooden ladle bobbed past Nicholas and a section of oak box chair, exquisitely carved with leafy scrollwork.

Suddenly he saw the pony with the treasure chest swimming strongly on his right, head up, ears flat, and there were no guards accompanying it now.

Without pausing to think, Nicholas released his own beast's tail and launched himself across the gap between the ponies. He caught the rein, lost it, grabbed again, and his fingers curled around the girth strap. The pony rolled its eyes and tried to lash out. A wave crashed over Nicholas's head, filling his eyes, ears and mouth. His throat burned and he came up choking. He relinquished his grip on the leather and seized the animal's tail instead, winding hanks of the thick, black hair around his fists. And then, having helped himself as much as he could, he prayed to a God with whom he was on uneasy terms to do the rest and let them not come ashore on quicksand.

It seemed an eternity but could have been no more than a matter of minutes before he felt ground beneath his feet, soft, yielding ground under the brown thunder of the waves, but it swallowed him no further than his ankles. The pony bunched its muscles and leaped through the surf, almost jerking Nicholas's arms from their sockets as he strove to keep a grip on its tail. He was not going to lose that coffer now.

The pony lurched on to the muddy beach, Nicholas staggering after. His breath sobbed and rattled in his lungs and his limbs felt like wet rope. Pure, stubborn will held him on his feet. Still clinging to the pack pony he fumbled along to the headstall and, with a final effort, dragged himself across its back. It staggered beneath the extra weight, but then it rallied and, at a tottering plod, wove towards the fawn expanse of reeds and marsh grass bordering the estuary.

At first it was enough to be alive, to know that he had outwitted both tide and quicksand. He was too exhausted for euphoria, too cold and numb and shocked. Even though he could no longer hear the cries of the dying, the sounds still rang in his head.

The horse wandered its own track through the marsh, finally halting with drooping head and trembling legs. Nicholas slid from its back, fell to the ground and lay unmoving for a moment. He was desperate to close his eyes and sleep, but knew that if he did, he would not awaken. Warmth was what he needed, and food and shelter.

Forcing himself to rise, he gazed at the bleak, mist-shrouded scenery. To his right he could hear the distant bleating of sheep, which suggested the likelihood of a shepherd's hut and perhaps even a shepherd. The alternative was to think that he was going to die of exposure and become just another bleached skeleton on the fenland wilderness.

If he was to find people, then first he had to hide the chest. Too many questions would be asked, and the answers, or lack of them, would be his downfall. He had not survived this far only to be cast in prison and executed for theft.

Grasping the pony's tough black mane, he dragged himself across its withers and urged it with heels, hands and voice to make another effort. With great unwillingness, its head came up and it began a desultory plod. At this pace they covered perhaps another half-mile before the pony stopped again and, this time, despite all Nicholas's persuasion, refused to move. Nicholas dismounted again, and his legs almost gave way. The tussocky grass beneath his feet was suddenly the most inviting bed he had ever seen – and his last if he lay down on it.

He set his teeth and braced his muscles. But it was the effort of his will rather than his body that unstrapped the chest and eased it down the pony's flank to the ground. The weight nearly felled him, and he knew that carrying the thing further than a few yards was impossible. It could perhaps be dragged, but not for any distance.

He began casting around for a hiding place. His father, during sword practice, had been wont to say that Nicholas never knew when he was beaten, that he was unable to accept defeat with grace. It had been intended as a criticism, but Nicholas had always taken a perverse pride in his sire's exasperation.

Now, because of that lack of grace, he removed the pony's bridle with fumbling red hands and painstakingly strapped it around the coffer. Winding the reins around his fists, he started to haul it towards a small stand of stunted alder and willow trees surrounding a small mere.

A root, rising from the poor soil like a swollen vein, tripped his faltering steps and sent him sprawling full length. He lay stunned, exhaustion screaming in every limb. A leaden weight settled across his eyelids.

'Do you yield at last then?' his father demanded, a grin parting his golden beard as he pointed a sword at Nicholas's throat.

Nicholas swallowed. The tip of the blade swallowed with him. His father's smile was that of a skull. 'Do you, boy, do you?'

'No!' Nicholas's eyes snapped open and he scrambled to his feet, his heart thundering. 'God's bones,' he muttered and rubbed his hands over his face. With a shuddering breath he collected his wits and looked down at the place where he had tumbled. The root belonged to an ancient crab apple tree that leaned against a neighbouring alder like a drunkard clinging to a companion. Where the two trees met, they formed a low arch leading to a natural chamber filled with brambles and dead white grass. A wild pig might force its way through, or a fox slide around the perimeter, but neither had done so this year at least.

Grunting with effort, Nicholas pushed and pulled the painted coffer through the arch and into the midst of the bramble thicket beyond so that no glimmer of blue or gold would reveal the secret to a passer-by. The thorns scratched his hands and drew tiny beads of blood, but he was too cold to feel the pain. He concealed the entrance with more sheaves of dead grass plucked from the surroundings and secured them with several dead branches. Then, wiping his hands and smearing the blood, he stood back to consider the effect.

It would do. To the casual observer there was nothing to see but a windblown thicket of trees winding back from the poolside, and he would be back on the morrow to claim his prize. He glanced around, to make sure of his bearings, and then began to walk towards the sound of bleating.

It was hard to place one foot in front of the other for his legs would no longer obey the command of his will. He tried counting his paces, but he was so cold, so exhausted, that his mind refused to keep a tally.

'Ready to give up yet, boy?'

'Not while there's breath in my body,' he gasped through his teeth.

'Won't be long then,' said his father's spectre cheerfully. His garments were as wet as Nicholas's own and he wore a shimmering necklace of seaweed. There was a huge, sea-washed wound in his side. 'Listen, they are tolling your death knell.'

In the distance Nicholas thought he heard a church bell, as loud and real as his father's voice.

Then he thought nothing at all as his legs gave way and the ground rose up to welcome him in the dark grave of its embrace.

Chapter 3

'Child, you do naught but harm by this wayward behaviour.'

Mother Hillary, Abbess of St Catherine's-in-the-Marsh, sighed wearily and folded her gnarled hands on the trestle before her. At her back, the open shutters admitted misty October light to her private chamber. A grey cat, the abbey's prize mouser, was coiled around the heavy candelabra on the table.

Miriel bit her lip. A trace of defiance lingered in her honey-brown eyes. 'I did not mean to cross Sister Euphemia. I was angry and the words came out by themselves.' Which was only half true. There was no doubt in Miriel's mind that Sister Euphemia was a carping hag whom no one with half a wit would have put in charge of the novices, but that was where the opinion should have remained – in her mind, not blurted out in front of the other five horrified but delighted young oblates.

'No, child, the words came out by your will. You have to take the responsibility.' Mother Hillary bestowed a stern glance. 'You must learn to curb your anger and submit to the rule.'

Miriel lowered her gaze from the Abbess's severe expression and stared at the handsome tiled floor. Asking why was not advisable. In the five months since arriving at St Catherine's, she had learned that questioning the rule led to harsh bread and water penances, supervised with relish by Sister Euphemia, who was so padded with flesh that it was obvious she had never done a penance in her life. 'Yes, Mother Hillary,' she murmured, with a detectable lack of grace.

'Your life would be much easier if you would only try.' The nun leaned forward to emphasise her point. Although she was approaching her seventieth winter, her light blue eyes were sharp and clear. 'You came to us in the spring, Miriel, and we welcomed you with open arms. Now autumn is upon us and you have scarce progressed at all. You fidget at prayers when your mind should be upon Our Lord; you shout in the cloister and disturb the other sisters with your worldliness. You say that you "do not mean" these things, that you will strive to improve, but I have seen little evidence in your attitude.'

Miriel gazed at the painted clay tiles. They bore the armorial device of the Earls of Lincoln in red and white slip. It was easier to look at them than meet Mother Hillary's incisive gaze, for Miriel knew that once again she had failed the senior nun's expectations.

Despite her hatred of convent life, Miriel liked and respected the Abbess. Mother Hillary was strict, but generally fair, and behind the stern façade lay a softening of kindness. If all the others had been cast in her mould, Miriel might have been more tractable, but greedy sows like Sister Euphemia only fuelled her rebellion. Miriel always left the Abbess's chamber with a boosted determination to rise above the petty niggles of daily routine, but the mood and her patience never lasted beyond a few days of Euphemia's persecution.

'Well, daughter, have you nothing to say?'

Miriel continued to gnaw her lip. The problem was that she had too much to say and all of it stoppered up inside her, churning and fermenting.

Mother Hillary sighed again. 'What am I going to do with you, child? If you cannot fit into our community, then you must leave it. I know that you came to us without vocation, but I had hoped that one would grow.'

Miriel raised her head at the word 'leave', and a spark lit in her brown eyes.

The Abbess was not slow to see it. She pursed her lips and shook her head. 'I have my duty to God and I am not prepared to relinquish you so soon. Your family has entrusted me with your welfare and I must do my best for all concerned.'

Her family had also entrusted Mother Abbess with a considerable amount of silver in payment of her dowry to Christ, Miriel thought cynically. St Catherine's would not be prepared to relinquish that too soon either. Strict and fair Mother Hillary might be, but she was also a woman of shrewd business sense.

'Then take me away from Sister Euphemia,' Miriel said. 'We are each a thorn in the other's side.'

Mother Hillary arched her thin, silvery brows. 'Sister Euphemia has charge of all the novices. It is her duty to ensure that they learn obedience to the rules of our house.'

'Then she appears to be failing,' Miriel retorted with a toss of her head, then compressed her lips as the Abbess's brows remained aloft and the blue eyes grew cold.

'Do you answer me with your quick tongue also?'

Miriel clenched her fists in the coarse cloth of her habit. The pressure of tears gathered at the back of her eyes. 'No, mother, I did not mean . . .'

'No, you did not mean,' said the Abbess, emphasising each word to make her point. 'And that in turn makes your life meaningless, does it not?'

Miriel said nothing because Mother Hillary was right. Her life was meaningless and only the fight gave her some faded sense of being alive.

The nun clicked her tongue against the roof of her mouth. 'I doubt that shutting you in a cell to contemplate the error of your ways on rations of bread and water for a month will make the slightest morsel of difference. Your spirit will break before it bends and I have no wish to see that happen.'

'Nor I, mother.' Miriel's voice was tight. She sniffed hard and swallowed.

The cat woke, stretched, and curled up again. Abbess Hillary reached to stroke the rich blue-grey fur and a rumbling purr filled the chamber.

'For the good of both yourself and St Catherine's, I will grant you a month's leave from Sister Euphemia's care. But' – she raised and wagged an admonishing forefinger as Miriel's expression blazed on the instant from despair to utter joy – 'you will still sit with the other novices for the services in church and receive instruction as appropriate.'

Well, that was a penance, but at least it was bearable. 'Yes, mother, thank you!'

The Abbess's lips twitched, then with effort straightened. 'At the end of the month we will review your position. Despite your reluctance, your family harbour firm hopes that you will make your life with us.'

'They do not want me back, that much is true,' Miriel said with contempt. 'They would have to arrange a marriage for me and that would mean yet more expense. If I stayed at home, there would be no peace. I hate my stepfather and he hates me. That's why he put me here.'

Mother Hillary looked at her thoughtfully. Having negotiated the terms of the girl's entry into St Catherine's with Nigel Fuller, she could imagine the friction between the two . . . indeed, more than friction on the man's part. She had recognised, even if he did not, the violence of suppressed lust. The girl irked his loins as much as his temper.

'I did try to be dutiful.' Miriel's voice was filled with grievance. 'But he wouldn't let me near the workshops, let alone inside, and I wasn't allowed to meet with any of the other traders and merchants.'

'And you did all this before?'

Miriel nodded. 'My grandfather treated me as his apprentice. He took me everywhere with him and taught me all he knew. I went to the great summer fair at Boston with him, and twice to Flanders. I watched him haggle the price of fleeces with wool merchants, I kept tallies for him, and mingled with his clients and customers.' Her breathing grew swift with passion.

'So it is the power you miss, child?'

Miriel shook her head. 'It is being powerless,' she said. 'It is being told that to help the business prosper I must bridle my tongue and stay at home like a good and modest daughter, not "gad about playing the hoyden". I should know my proper place.' She made an abrupt gesture of disgust.

'A proper place,' Mother Hillary murmured and her lips twitched again as if at some inner amusement. 'I have always wondered about that myself.' She scratched the cat between the ears and the purring rose to a crescendo.

Miriel eyed the Abbess warily. 'Mother?'

The nun shook her head. 'A proper place to me is a niche that fits,' she said, meeting Miriel's puzzled stare. 'For the nonce you can help Sister Godefe and Sister Margaret in the infirmary. Sister Margaret has the gout and cannot move far for the pain, and Sister Godefe will need a companion when she rides out to tend Wynstan Shepherd's leg.'

A queasy feeling of joy and the fear that she had misunderstood turned in Miriel's stomach. 'You want me to go with Sister Godefe?' The prospect of open air and freedom for no matter how short a time was almost too wonderful to be true.

'Have I not just said so?' Now an open smile creased Mother Hillary's cheeks.

'But . . . but what about my punishment for insulting Sister Euphemia?'

The Abbess tilted her head. 'If you can perform your new duties without incurring my displeasure, then I consider the matter closed. Sister Euphemia will do the same once you have made your apology to her. Now, go and bring Sister Godefe to me, then wait in the cloister until she comes for you.'

'Yes, mother.' Miriel dipped another curtsey and, with flushed cheek and sparkling eye, left the room. Although as a novice nun she was supposed to move with a decorous glide in the eyes of God, she could not prevent herself from skipping like a spring lamb.

Mother Hillary shook her head, and not for the first time wished a little blasphemously that she could change places with the cat.

Sister Godefe had entered St Catherine's as a ten-year-old orphan, and unlike Miriel had taken to the life as if she had never known any other. The community was her family and she truly saw the other thirty-five nuns as her 'sisters'.

As assistant to the ageing infirmaress Sister Margaret, she was currently tending an ulcerous wound on the senior shepherd's leg, which had to be dressed and anointed daily.

'Although it is mending well,' she said to Miriel in her earnest, anxious voice as they rode out from the convent on mules. 'By the week's end I shall not need to come again.' The words carried a note of relief, for she hated forays outside St Catherine's walls.

Miriel nodded for the sake of politeness, but she was not really listening. Although the mist enclosed her vision, she could still breathe the freedom of the open air. It was as if she had been constricted in a small, airless box and then suddenly set free. The day could have been lashing a storm and it would still have been glorious. The praise to God, which she had no inclination to sing in the dark enclosure of the chapel, swelled in her heart now.

Sister Godefe glanced at her sidelong. 'Mother Abbess says that you are to help in the infirmary.' She sounded doubtful.

Miriel concealed a grimace. As always her reputation seemed to have gone before her. 'I have a little knowledge of nursing. When my grandfather was sick, I was the one who cared for him.'

The nun relaxed slightly, although the anxious expression did not entirely leave her face.

'I won't cause trouble,' Miriel added.

'With Sister Margaret off her feet, you'll have so much work that you won't have time for trouble,' Godefe sniffed.

'I am not afraid of hard work,' Miriel said stoutly.

Godefe pursed her lips. 'We shall see.'

They rode on in silence, each attending to her own thoughts. The mist clung to their garments like air-spun cobwebs and the landscape was a dull, autumnal brown. In summer the fenland had glittered under the sky, each feature reflecting the other to a never-ending horizon. Now it seemed as if they were on the edge of the world. With each sway of the mule, Miriel half expected to be presented with a sudden precipice.

'Not far now,' Godefe announced with relief in her voice.

Miriel nodded. She could hear the clonk of the collar bell on a leading ewe and the disembodied bleating of sheep. She was also aware of a muted roaring sound, like the wind through the trees, but that was impossible on a day of heavy mist like this one.

'The sea.' Godefe cocked her own head to listen. 'Tide's new in.' She gave a little shiver and tightened her cloak around her body in a protective gesture.

Miriel lifted her head, seeking the elusive salt tang of the ocean. She had caught glimpses of its grey vastness from the convent bell tower on a clear summer day, but she had never been down to the shore. It was not permitted unless for a very good reason, wistful attraction not being one. 'Have you ever been on a ship?' she asked her companion.

Godefe looked at Miriel as if she thought her mad. 'No, and I wouldn't want to either. All that water with naught but a plank of wood between me and drowning.' She made the sign of the Cross.

Miriel smiled, her eyes full of distant remembering. 'I was thirteen years old when I went with my grandfather to the fair at Antwerp. We sailed on a Boston nef with her timbers painted red and her hold full of our cloth. Some folk were sick when the sea grew choppy, but I loved every moment.' She licked her lips, imagining the taste of spray on her tongue and saw again the green-blue glitter of fast, sunlit waves. The wildness, the sheer exhilaration.

It must have shown on her face, for Sister Godefe clicked her tongue with disapproval. 'You should not be talking of worldly matters,' she admonished. 'You're a nun now. It is not seemly.'

'I have taken no vows,' Miriel retorted. 'And is the sea not God's creation?'

Godefe opened her mouth. At the same time, Miriel's mount tossed its head and with an alarmed snort, shied into the other mule which brayed and lashed out with sharp hooves.

Uttering an oath that would have earned her a beating had Sister Euphemia been within earshot, Miriel wrenched her mule to one side, controlling him with the strength of her hands and the tight grip of her thighs. Then she stared at what had frightened him, and her heart lurched.

A man was sprawled in the dying brown grass. He wore

naught but a torn shirt and linen braies, the garments clinging to his body in saturated outline. Sister Godefe let out an involuntary shriek, one hand rising to cup the sound against her mouth.

Dismounting, Miriel thrust her reins at Godefe and hastened to kneel at the man's side.

'Is he dead?' Godefe's voice was watery with fear.

Miriel touched his throat with tentative fingers. His flesh was cold and clammy, but she could feel a thready pulse. Against the dark spikes of his hair, his skin was corpse-white.

'No, he's still alive,' she reported, 'but he soon won't be if he continues to lie here; he's chilled to the bone.'

Godefe chewed her lip. 'What are we going to do?' Her voice was tearful with panic.

Miriel nearly snapped at her not to be such a milksop, but reminded herself just in time that the nun had dwelt in the convent for more than twenty years. Although Godefe was accustomed to tending the ailments of the other sisters and administering occasional potions and ointments to the abbey's lay servants, injured young men in a state of near nudity must be a horrifying prospect.

'Well, we can't let him die,' she said tartly. 'You must return to the abbey and fetch help.'

'And leave you alone with him?' Godefe's voice rose in distress.

'You know the way back, I've never been on this path before,' Miriel snapped. 'He is hardly going to ravish me, is he? If you are concerned for my modesty, then know that after nursing my grandfather, there is no part of a man's body that is a mystery to me.'

Godefe made a shocked little sound in her throat.

Miriel unpinned her cloak and tucked it around the young man. 'Give me yours too,' she commanded. 'We have to keep him warm.'

Dominated by Miriel's more forceful personality, Godefe unfastened her cloak and handed it down. 'Who can he be?' she whispered. 'What is he doing here?'

'We'll never know if he dies.' Miriel gestured pointedly

in the direction they had come. 'Ask Mother Hillary for her litter and make haste.'

Huge-eyed and white-faced with anxiety, the nun reined the mule about and clopped off through the mist.

Miriel tucked the second cloak around the first, drawing Godefe's hood up around the young man's face. The dark wool made him look paler than ever. She too wondered from whence he came. Travellers on the marshes were few. Those they received in St Catherine's guest house were usually on their way from Lynn to Cambridge and Lincoln and they did not come from this direction. All that lay beyond the sheep pasture were mud flats and the grey North Sea.

Frowning, Miriel reached beneath the hood of the cloak and touched his hair. Then she licked her fingertips and her memory of the sea was fulfilled in the taste of the salt. He must have fallen overboard from a fishing vessel or Lynn trader, she thought. Perhaps he was a poor sailor, which would explain the sparse state of his clothing.

She took one of his frozen hands to chafe in her own. The palm was work-blistered as she had expected, but there were narrow bands of white skin at the base of some fingers, suggesting that rings had recently been worn. There were also scratches on the backs of his hands as if he had been fighting his way through thick undergrowth. Pin-pricks of dark bronze stubble outlined his jaw and rimmed his mouth. There was bruising on one cheekbone, fading to yellow. Miriel touched the mark, but he neither moved nor made a sound.

'Whoever you are,' she murmured, 'you are going to create an unholy stir at St Catherine's.' The thought made her smile with relish.

Chapter 4

The church bell which Nicholas had heard as he collapsed, was still tolling as he opened his eyes. For a moment he thought that he had died and gone to hell, for he was naked and his limbs felt as if they were on fire. By smoky candle-light a black-robed demon was embalming him with a pungent lotion that stung like nettle burn.

He yelled a protest, but it emerged as little more than a croak, and when he tried to move, his limbs would not obey his will.

The demon turned its head. A face, double-chinned and whiskery, loomed over his own and he inhaled a waft of garlicky breath.

'He's waking at last,' it announced.

More of the demons crowded around him. One of them made a disapproving sound and covered his loins with a linen towel. 'Will he live?'

'Too early to tell,' said the first demon. 'I have rubbed his body with warming herbs and now he must be well wrapped to help them do their work. If he survives the night, then his chances will improve.'

So he wasn't dead, and these were not demons. 'Where am I?' he asked weakly.

'In the convent of St Catherine's-in-the-Marsh,' said the looming face. 'You were discovered lying on the sheep pasture by two of the sisters.'

Nicholas nodded. He seemed to remember a young woman's voice saying something about his creating an unholy stir at St Catherine's. That must be where his notion of demons had originated. The dark robes were habits and he was obviously lying on a bed in the convent's infirmary.

'Can you tell us who you are and what happened to you?'

The question came from an elderly nun. She was tiny and thin as a twig, but her gaze was a piercing pale blue and she had an air of authority that dwarfed her size.

'The tide,' he said and swallowed.

'You perhaps fell overboard from a ship?'

Nicholas shook his head. The looming faces swam out of focus and all he could see was water, all he could hear were the screams of drowning men and horses. And cutting through that sound, the incessant tolling of a bell. He closed his eyes and wished he had not woken.

A rim was set against his lips and warm liquid flowed over his tongue. He fought to push it aside, imagining it was sea-water, but his head was held in an inexorable grip, his nose was pinched and when he opened his mouth to breathe, the brew was forced down his throat, not salty, but bitter as aloes. Then he was parcelled up like a fly in a web and left.

The bell ceased to ring and silence descended. Behind his lids, the darkness was shot with lightning flashes of nightmare. He was swimming in glutinous, liquid mud, his arms hampered by a bulky wooden coffer that grew heavier and heavier as he tried to kick for the shore. Every time he looked at the beach to see how much progress he had made, he discovered that he had gained no distance at all. From below, the hands of those already drowned began pulling him down.

A loud crash jerked him into awareness, and he gulped with desperate greed at the cool, herb-scented air.

A young nun was swearing to herself as she crawled around on her hands and knees, picking up the pieces of a broken clay pitcher. A white wimple framed her face, sapping her complexion, but not the strength of her features. Her language would have done justice to a fishwife. Had he possessed the strength, Nicholas would have laughed, but he was too weak and stupefied with exhaustion to do anything but stare.

She must have sensed his attention for she swung round, the shattered pieces in her hands. Their eyes met and for a moment he saw blind panic in her expression before she schooled it to a nun-like impassivity. Dropping the shards in a wicker basket, she dusted her palms. 'It shouldn't have been left so close to the trestle edge – what else do they expect?' She shrugged defensively. 'They'll blame me just the same when they return from prayers.' She came and stood over him, one hand on her hip, the other cupping her chin in a curiously masculine gesture. He could not know that she was aping the stance of a sixty-year-old weaver.

Her eyes were gold-brown, her nose thin and aquiline. She reminded Nicholas of a falcon he had once owned.

'Don't you have a name?' she demanded.

'Nicholas,' he said weakly, and a shiver ran through him. He wondered if he was wise to tell her, but in the same thought decided that it did not matter. Other survivors, if they existed, would have more on their minds than pursuing him.

She continued to rub her chin and a slight frown appeared between her sharp brows. 'You had been in the sea.'

'Crossing the causeway – caught by the tide.' He closed his eyes, feeling nauseous and drained. The shivering began again and he could not stop.

'Then you are more than lucky to be alive,' she murmured and once more a cup was pressed to his lips. Nicholas turned his head from the bitter taste.

'Drink,' she commanded. 'It will give you ease.'

He did not have the strength to thrust her away. The touch of her hands and her closeness as she leaned over him were as recently familiar as her voice.

'You found me, didn't you?' he asked hoarsely.

She removed the cup. 'Yes, fortunately for you. Sister Margaret says another hour and you would have died.'

'I thought I had.' He gave her a bleak smile. 'When I woke up, I believed I was in hell.'

Her eyes widened, and for an instant he thought that he had shocked her, but that notion vanished as she burst out laughing.

'I have the same experience every day when the matins bell rings,' she said, and the laughter left her face. 'But I don't think I'm in hell – I know.'

The door opened, its squeaky hinge giving a spare second of warning. She jumped and whirled guiltily to face it, her fists clenched.

'Do my ears deceive me, or did I hear laughter just now?' demanded a slack-jowled nun who was hobbling very slowly with the aid of a stick. Nicholas recognised her as the one with the whiskery chin whom he had thought a demon. Another nun, thin as a rake and anxious of brow, hastened before the older one to smooth the covering of an upright box chair and stand ready with a footstool.

Nicholas watched the young nun's fists tighten behind her back. 'Yes, Sister Margaret, you did.' Now definite uncertainty marred the clear, low-pitched voice.

'May I ask why?' The sound of the walking stick punctuated each step with a heavy thump. Once again Nicholas found himself the object of narrow scrutiny.

'He said he thought he was in hell.'

'And you think that cause for mirth?'

'No, sister. I was just pleased that he seemed a little better. His name is Nicholas and he was caught out on the estuary when the tide came in.'

'Hmph,' said Sister Margaret, glancing from one to the other with suspicious eyes. 'Pleased enough to laugh seems to me an excess of concern, Sister Miriel. I doubt I would have discovered you thus had our patient been one of us.'

'I found him, I saved his life. It is no more than that.'

The nun drew herself up. 'God led you to him, and his life is in God's hands. To say anything else is to show lack of respect.'

'Yes, Sister. I didn't mean to be disrespectful.'

Her stance was so rigid that she was trembling almost as much as Nicholas. He wanted to snap at old whisker-chin to leave her alone, but he was too weak, his eyelids too heavy. Whatever she had given him in the drink, it was flooding through his body, bringing warmth and deep lassitude.

'Aye, well, keep a close rein on that tongue of yours. You know I'll be reporting on your progress to Mother Abbess and Sister Euphemia.'

Nicholas heard the walking stick stump away across the

floor and then the creak of overburdened chair timbers as the nun sat down from a height. 'And come away from that bed. He's asleep now. There's nothing more you can do for him, and plenty you can do for me, Sister Miriel.'

'Yes, Sister Margaret.' Nicholas felt the vibration of the young woman's unuttered sigh as she left him. Miriel. The name twined like a ribbon through his fading consciousness and he clung to it as the dreams of drowning encroached.

There was a stone sink in the infirmary with a drain. Having been thoroughly castigated by Sister Margaret for smashing the clay pot yesterday, Miriel was now washing and drying dozens of the things ready for reuse. Sister Margaret herself was snoring in her chair, her swollen legs resting on the footstool, and Sister Godefe was away on an errand to the cellaress.

Their patient had spent a restless night, tossing and muttering, now and then crying aloud in his sleep. His rapid French bore the accent of Normandy and the curses he rained upon King John made him guilty of treason. Sister Margaret had taken the duty of watching him during the night when Miriel and Godefe were at prayers and had continued to make of herself a bulwark between the young man and Miriel as if suspecting the worst of them both.

Miriel rinsed the last jar and let the water drain into the gutter below. His name was Nicholas and he had been caught by the tide. That was all they knew for sure of his circumstances, but there was much more she could guess. His manner of speech, coupled with the evidence that he had worn rings, marked him out as nobly born, as did his railing against King John. Ordinary folk had little enough to fear from their sovereign; it was the barons and magnates who had suffered – and rebelled. Their patient also had a soldier's physique: lean, muscular and honed. Miriel had an inkling that whatever he had been doing on the estuary, he was probably part of the rebel force that had recently been ravaging Lincolnshire. As such, he ought to be chained up in prison and was doubly fortunate to have literally washed up on St Catherine's threshold.

Taking a linen square from a pile on a nearby shelf, she began drying a container and tiptoed past the slumbering dragon to look at the young man.

He was asleep, but when his eyes were open they were a dark blue-green. His hair had dried to the hue of dark oak polished with a hint of bronze, and was in dire need of barbering. Since last night his jaw had grown a crop of strong, golden stubble. His mouth was tender; his nose had a slight kink in profile as if it had once been broken. Miriel slowly rotated the jar in her hand and gazed upon him while a warm glow spread through her body.

'What are you doing?'

Miriel jumped and spun so swiftly that she almost smashed a second clay jar. Sister Margaret was sitting up in her chair, her eyes narrow and suspicious.

'I was just making sure he was all right, Sister.' Miriel hastened from the bedside and setting the dried pot on a trestle, collected the next one. 'His breathing is swift and he's a little flushed.' The same could be said of herself, she thought wryly. Jesu, the woman had eyes in the back of her wimple.

'Well, in future leave that duty to myself or Sister Godefe.' The infirmaress gave a convulsive heave. 'Hand me my stick and I will look now.'

Dutifully, Miriel did as she was bid. Arguing would only cause aggravation and at the moment she was full of fresh resolve to keep her tongue behind her teeth. Sister Margaret might be grumpy with gout and out of sorts because the young man had interrupted their routine, but she was still a thousand times better than that harridan Euphemia.

Sister Margaret struggled out of her chair and hobbled over to the bed to study the patient. 'Aye,' she said grudgingly, 'he's a mite feverish. Most likely he's taken a chill on the lungs.' She sucked her teeth and gave an infinitesimal shake of her head.

'What's to be done?'

The nun shrugged. 'Dose him with feverfew and put a mustard plaster on his chest to draw out the evil humours.

Wrap him well and keep him warm.' She looked sidelong at Miriel. 'And pray.'

Miriel swallowed, misliking the tone of Sister Margaret's answer. 'Will he recover?'

'That is in the hands of God.'

After yesterday's discussion, Miriel had arrived at the conclusion that God's hands must be enormous to encompass all that they did, and human endeavour so small that some things must surely slip through the gaps between his fingers. Gazing at Nicholas, she began to understand why prayers held so much value to some people – as reminders to the Almighty.

Sister Godefe returned from her errand to the cellaress, and within the quarter candle she and Miriel departed to tend the ailing shepherd whom they had missed in yesterday's excitement.

Today a stiff breeze had rolled away the fog and the land stretched uninterrupted to the coast in dull shades of green and brown and grey. Stabs of sunlight between the scuds of cloud edged the colours in bright gilding and filled Miriel with pleasure, even while she worried about Nicholas. She had paused in the chapel to say a quick prayer on her way out, which had earned her a suspicious glance from a passing Sister Euphemia. But Euphemia's distrust was nothing compared to the necessity of calling God's attention to the young man's plight and entering a plea for his safe deliverance. It was a test of faith. He had to survive.

There was no sign of old Wynstan the shepherd at his hut, nor of his wife or dogs. Miriel dismounted and pushed open the dwelling door. Inside it was warm, but the peat fire was covered by a metal curfew lid, denoting that the occupants expected to be gone some time. Smoked mutton sausages dangled from the beams side by side with skeins of homespun wool dyed in rich shades of honey and copper. The bed bench was neatly made up with a striped cover. Cooking pots and utensils were stacked in an orderly fashion on the trestle under the hut's single window space. Strangely out of place amongst them, Miriel recognised a piss-flask fashioned of clear glass with a design of fluted rays. She wondered how a common rural shepherd came to own such a thing. Her grandfather had possessed one but his had been of thicker glass without the fluting; even that had cost a small fortune.

Returning outside, she closed the door behind her. 'They can't be far away,' she said.

Godefe frowned and gave an irritated click of her tongue. 'I didn't see them out on the pasture with the sheep, nor their herd boy.'

Miriel shrugged and went round to the garden enclosure. Leeks, cabbages and swedes adorned the dark soil in well-tended rows. A sow and five fat weaners squealed at her over the mud wall of the pigsty. Draped over a hemp drying line were several exquisite linen shirts and embroidered towels. Miriel blinked at the sight and began to reassess her ideas on the way that humble shepherds lived.

Tethered by the house were two sturdy bay pack ponies. One was bright-eyed with a lively swish to its tail; the other, head down, slept on its feet.

Godefe joined her and she too stared at the line of clothes and the ponies in utter astonishment. 'They're not Wynstan's, that's for sure,' she said.

'Do you think they're connected with the man we found? Perhaps they're his linen and ponies.'

'Mayhap.' Godefe nodded at the possibility. 'But Wynstan's an honest man. He must have come on them by chance.'

The women remounted. Torn between returning to the convent to see how Nicholas was faring, and enjoying her freedom for a little longer, Miriel circled her mule while she deliberated.

'Wynstan might be down at the estuary,' she said. 'It's probably where he found the ponies.'

'I don't think we should . . .' Godefe began, but Miriel had already set her heels to the mule's flanks and was trotting down the narrow track that led to the shore.

'It won't take long,' she called over her shoulder.

Filled with misgiving, Godefe followed her.

As they neared the beach, it swiftly became clear that something was afoot. The foreshore was busy with people. Walkways across the treacherous mud had been improvised out of wattle hurdles, and it appeared that the entire populations of Sutton and Cross Keys were out on the sands, poking and prodding with long poles, broom handles and spears. There were soldiers amongst them too, their presence marked by bright surcoats and the silver glint of link mail and weapons. Piled on the beach were the battered remnants of several covered wains.

Miriel and Godefe stared in amazement. 'Something terrible must have happened here yesterday,' Miriel said, her notion of Nicholas as a man alone now destroyed. 'Look at all the debris.' Even as she spoke, a cry went up and a knot of people clustered around something in the mud. Ropes were fetched and, as the women watched in horror, a bedraggled corpse was heaved out of the slime and laid along one of the hurdles. The hands reached, fingers curled in rigid claws and the throat was stretched in extremity.

'God have mercy.' The older nun crossed herself and suppressed a heave.

Thinking of Nicholas, Miriel had to swallow her own gorge.

They heard another shout closer to hand. A man dressed in homespun wool and sheepskins was limping towards them from the search party. He carried a shepherd's crook, slick with mud for over half its length. Two shaggy grey and white dogs trotted at his heels, their tongues lolling.

'Sisters,' he greeted Godefe and Miriel. The wind had whipped a flush into his leathery cheeks and he was breathing hard from his walk.

Godefe inclined her head stiffly in return. 'We have come to treat your leg,' she said, frowning. 'You are supposed to be resting it.'

'Not today I'm not.' He turned to view the activity on the foreshore. 'Course, they'll not find much. I've had sheep drown out there and you seldom recover the bodies. Lucky to have found what they have.'

'What exactly are they looking for?' Miriel asked.

The shepherd cocked her a sharp look. 'You've not heard the news then?'

Miriel shook her head.

He fixed the women with a bright stare, paused for a moment to extract the final drop of drama, then said, 'King John's baggage train got bogged down out there in the mist yesterday on the way to Swineshead Abbey. The mud and the tide swallowed it up in less than an hour. Lost everything, so it's said – including his crown.' He winked at the nuns. 'Be a huge reward for anyone as finds it.'

'King John's baggage train,' Miriel repeated and gazed at the people busy on the sands. 'Were there any survivors?'

The shepherd spread his hands. 'A few reached Sutton and raised the alarm, so one o' the soldiers told us, but the rest of them's out there, buried wi' the King's gold. All we found so far are two bodies and a broken candlestick.'

Miriel pursed her lips. 'We saw the ponies tethered behind your cot, and your linens blowing in the wind.'

He met her gaze squarely. 'I discovered them ponies wandering on the sheep pasture; I haven't stolen nothing. If they wants them back, they can come and get them – aye and the laundry too, providing they pay my wife for the washing of it all.'

'Of course,' Miriel said. It was an effort not to laugh at his burst of righteous indignation. Whatever Godefe said about old Wynstan's honesty, Miriel doubted that King John would ever see the return of his ponies, linens, or piss-flask.

The shepherd cleared his throat and looked at Godefe. 'You may as well tend my leg here. I'll be staying awhile yet.'

'Even though there's nothing to find?' Miriel asked innocently.

'You got to show willing, haven't you?' He sat down and began unwrapping his hose binding.

Leaving Godefe to deal with the shepherd, Miriel turned her mule and rode him down closer to the shoreline. The wind bustled off the sea, watering her eyes and almost dislodging her white novice's wimple. A strong salt tang filled her lungs. On the raised causeway above the mud, nobles wearing fur-lined cloaks and jewel-bright colours were supervising the operation. Miriel imagined the tide rolling up behind and engulfing them as it must have done to the baggage train yesterday. She gave an involuntary shudder and thrust the thought to the back of her mind, wondering instead how much treasure had been lost.

If someone found it, then it would literally be a King's ransom. In her mind's eye, she saw herself scooping a crown from the muddy sand and holding it aloft, soft pinpoints of light catching exposed areas of gold. How much would it be worth? More than enough to buy her freedom from the cloister and begin a new life. A house of her own, good food and fine clothes. She would be able to do as she pleased with no one to tell her nay. A smile curved her lips. She would build her own weaving business and become the best in all the Midland shires. She would—

'Sister Miriel!' Godefe's insistent voice jolted her from her daydream. The crown vanished, leaving her the plain view of windswept shoreline and the villagers working methodically across the estuary with their hurdle fences and prods.

'I'm coming.' She turned the mule.

'You shouldn't have ridden off like that.'

'I wanted to see what was happening.'

'Yes, but you—'

'Mother Abbess will want to know the details,' Miriel interrupted quickly before Godefe started to lecture in earnest. 'We can give a better account from what we have seen for ourselves.'

Godefe narrowed her eyes, but conceded the point with a sniff as she tugged on her mule's bridle. 'Even so, it is time we returned. They will be ringing the bell for nones soon.'

Then vespers, then compline, Miriel thought grimly, and nothing for sustenance but a piece of dry bread and a small cup of weak, herbal tisane. Concealing a grimace, she followed the older nun.

The shepherd, his leg anointed and rebandaged, touched his forelock to her in passing, and limped back towards the shore and the illusion of royal gold.

CHAPTER 5

Stifling a yawn, Miriel shifted her buttocks on the hard wood of the choir stall and repeated the words of the service after the priest. She knew them by rote. Even if her mind was unwilling, her memory had absorbed the chants with ease. Each phrase intoned was a step closer to the end of the night's prayer in the chapel and the first of two welcome visits to the refectory. Even though breakfast was only barley porridge made with water, and ale to drink, her stomach growled ravenously. There was never enough to eat.

She glanced towards the east window above the altar, but the jewelled tints of the glass were dark, as yet unlit by the dawn. The prospect of her first winter at St Catherine's filled her with dread. Already the threat of chilblains prickled her toes and her voice rose toward the rafters on clouds of misty breath.

Beside her, one of the other novices, Sister Adela, had fallen asleep, her head lolling sideways. Before Miriel could nudge her, the girl was noticed by Sister Euphemia. Instead of a dig in the ribs, Sister Adela received a stinging rap across the knuckles from Euphemia's willow switch. The young novice jerked upright, stifling a cry between her teeth. Tears brimmed in her eyes.

Miriel felt a surge of anger and sympathy. On numerous occasions she had been the victim of that switch. The smallest misdemeanour was cause enough for Euphemia to bring it whistling down. Now that the nun no longer had Miriel for a scapegoat, she was testing out the other novices to find a fresh victim.

Euphemia met Miriel's disgusted stare with one of malice and challenge. The wand twitched in her hand, but she did not lean over to use it. As of two days ago, the Abbess's intervention had given Miriel a certain immunity.

A reluctant dawn brightened the window above the high altar and St Catherine was martyred on her wheel in the gemstone colours of the glass stainer's art. Less than exalted, but feeling sympathy for the saint's plight, Miriel raised her voice and joined the chants. As the service ended, the priest exhorted the nuns to pray for the souls of the wayfarers lost on the estuary and for the recovery of the young man lying sick with fever in their infirmary.

Miriel bowed her head, clasped her hands and prayed. The previous evening, after vespers, she had tried to speak with Nicholas, but there had been no opportunity. Sister Margaret had kept her busy with errands and other patients, and when finally there had been a brief moment, he had been lost in feverish sleep, his brow as hot as a coal to her touch.

'Please, by Your great mercy, let him live,' she entreated, but was answered by nothing more than the hollow voice of the priest echoing against the painted stone columns.

The service completed, the nuns departed the choir stalls and walked in procession to the lavatorium to wash before they breakfasted.

'I'll get you some salve for your knuckles from the infirmary cupboard,' Miriel murmured to Adela as they stood side by side at the long stone trough.

Adela steeped her hands in the icy water and shook her head. 'It was my own fault; I sinned in falling asleep. Sister Euphemia was right to chastise me.'

Miriel rolled her eyes. 'She was just looking for an opportunity. She can't keep that stick to herself. One day I'm going to snatch it out of her hands and shove it—' Miriel broke off as Sister Euphemia herself bore down on the two young women like a large black crow.

'No unnecessary talk,' she hissed. The stick jerked in her grasp.

'No, sister.' Adela hung her head and swished the water with trembling hands.

Miriel said nothing, knowing that her reply would likely result in a sharp rap across her own knuckles and yet another bitter confrontation.

With chewing jaw, Euphemia moved on. Adela's breath escaped on a furtive gasp of relief.

'Shove it up her fat backside,' Miriel concluded, watching the nun waddle down the line. 'No one ever strikes her with a switch for filching provisions from the store rooms to fill her fat belly!'

'Hush, oh hush!' Adela squeaked like an agitated mouse. 'She'll hear you!'

'Oh yes, she's certainly got better ears than God,' Miriel said viciously, but heeded Adela's warning and finished her ablutions in jerky silence. Uppermost in her mind was the sure knowledge that she did not fit in here and never would.

Following the silent breaking of fast in the refectory, Miriel collected a stone costrel of wine and a basket of loaves from the cellaress and crossed the courtyard to the infirmary. Owing to her own disability and her duty to the sick, Sister Margaret had been excused the long, nocturnal hours of prayer in the chapel. The bread and wine were for her patients. There was also a hearth in the infirmary where nourishing meals could be cooked to tempt ailing appetites. Sister Margaret, although not afflicted by the latter, had availed herself of the frying pan and was devouring the last of a mushroom omelette as Miriel entered, staggering a little beneath her burden.

The delicious smell of the food made Miriel's half-empty stomach churn with longing, but she was not so foolish as to hope that there was any left. She would have to wait for the midday meal several hours hence and hope that the cellaress was feeling generous.

Setting the bread and wine on the trestle, she threw a glance in the direction of the curtain screening the man's bed from the three sick nuns occupying the main part of the infirmary. She could hear a constant low muttering and the swish of bedclothes tossed by a restless body.

'We said a prayer for the young man in chapel, sister,' she ventured. 'How does he fare?'

Leaning on her stick, dabbing her lips with a napkin, the infirmaress heaved to her feet. 'He is in need of prayers for certain,' she said. 'There is nothing more that we can do for him.' She hobbled to the curtain, and drawing it a little to one side, beckoned to the girl.

The gesture surprised Miriel. For the past day and a half she had been kept well away from the patient. She was not, however, going to look a gift horse in the mouth, and hastened to Sister Margaret's side.

'See the red spots on his cheekbones?' the nun said with a grim nod. 'First they will darken until they are the colour of pig's blood, and then the tips of his fingers and the soles of his feet will blacken and he will die.'

Miriel swallowed and stared, filled with horror and pity. She did not doubt the nun's word for such a death had happened to a neighbour in Lincoln two years ago after he caught a winter ague.

As if aware of their scrutiny, the patient tossed and groaned. Sweat plastered his hair to his skull in dark spikes and shone in the hollow of his throat, as if he had just been pulled anew from the sea. His eyes were open but blind as unpolished stones. The irises flickered, following some inner vision, and he licked his lips.

'The tide,' he panted. 'Christ Jesu, the tide!' His body threshed and fought.

Without thinking Miriel darted to the bedside. There was a bowl of lavender water on the coffer with a cloth soaking in it. She wrung out the linen and laid it on his brow, then set her arm behind his shoulders and gave him a drink from the cup that also stood on the coffer.

'Surely there is something that can be done for him?' She fixed Sister Margaret with a pleading stare.

The infirmaress shook her head. 'Save for washing him down to cool his body and giving him willow bark in wine, we are powerless. It will be as God wills.'

'But if God had wanted him to die, he would have let him drown out on the estuary, not here with us,' Miriel protested.

'The ways of God are not ours to fathom, only to obey.'

Miriel bit her lip on an unsuitable retort concerning the ways of God. 'Then may I perform those tasks and pray for him?' she requested.

Sister Margaret frowned at her. 'It would not be seemly, a young girl like you.'

'More than half the "young girls like me" are already married with a baby in the cradle,' Miriel pointed out. 'And I am no shrinking innocent to balk at what must be done,' adding quickly as the sister's frown deepened, 'I nursed my grandfather through his final sickness. I had to do everything for him – everything,' she emphasised. 'My mother refused to go near the sick room.'

The infirmaress conceded the point, but her brow remained furrowed. 'Why the interest in this one?' she asked suspiciously. 'I wonder if you are tempted by the devil's trap of his youth and comeliness?'

Miriel breathed out hard, forcing control upon herself. It was all she could do not to shriek at the old nun. 'He is not comely at the moment,' she said. 'I hate being helpless. I want to feel that I am doing something – that even if he dies we have tried our best.'

The patient tossed, threw out his arm, and knocked the watered wine from her hands, splashing the bedclothes with a blood-red stain. Miriel swiftly retrieved the cup and pulled back the sheet.

'Hide it,' he muttered. 'Have to hide it.' His chest rose and fell with the rapidity of his breathing. They had dressed him in a spare chemise from the linen coffer and it clung to his body in wet creases.

Miriel took his hand. 'Hide what?'

He turned his eyes to her, frowning, struggling to focus. For a moment they glimmered with lucidity. The semblance of a grin parted his lips. 'Pandora's box,' he gasped, and fell back, shuddering.

The nun waved her stick. 'Do as you will with him,' she snorted and turned away, plainly deciding that she had wasted enough of her time. 'I doubt he is long for this world anyway.'

'Thank you, sister,' Miriel said with a rush of relief. She

was powerfully aware of how easily the infirmaress could have refused. 'Who's Pandora, do you think?'

Sister Margaret shrugged indifferently. 'People in the grip of fever babble all manner of nonsense.'

'I just wondered if he was trying to say something about the King's treasure.'

The infirmaress stopped and gave Miriel a severe look over her shoulder, but then her lips twitched. 'Now who is babbling nonsense?' she asked. 'Keep your mind on your prayers, not the lure of material things.'

'Yes, sister.' Miriel lowered her eyes and pretended to be chastened. But her curiosity was too great for that. She thought of what he had said and the way they had found him on the sheep pasture. If only she knew more. 'You're not going to die,' she muttered fiercely. 'I won't let you.'

Nicholas felt as if he had been swimming for days in a hot and salty sea. Many times he had almost drowned beneath its waves, surfacing at the last moment, choking and gulping in extremity. He was aware of someone swimming with him, trying to buoy him above the waves, pleading with him to continue when all he wanted to do was let go and have peace.

Occasionally his father appeared, but for once the spectre said little, except to make the tart observation that while Nicholas appeared to be fulfilling his vow to die in his bed, he was almost seventy years too soon.

Nicholas ignored him for he did not have the strength and the current was too strong for him to turn and answer. Doggedly he continued to swim while the mist around him thickened into something resembling soup and scarcely breathable. Then he heard voices and saw the ship looming at him through the mist. Her strakes glistened and a scarlet dragon's head snarled at her prow. She was called *Miriel* and even at first sighting, even before he had seen the treasure chest in her open hold, he knew instinctively that she belonged to him.

Firm hands reached down and hauled him aboard. Above his head a striped sail billowed, and the mist shredded away to clear blue sky before the strengthening wind. Beneath him the ship's deck rocked on the swell. The air was cold, clean and sharp. He drew a great lungful and opened his eyes.

A young nun whose brown gaze and thin nose he vaguely remembered was leaning over him, a linen cloth in her hand. The fragrance of woodsmoke clung to the coarse fibres of her habit and a plain wooden cross on a leather cord swung at her neck. She looked at him narrowly and passed her hand back and forth in front of his face.

'Are you awake?'

Nicholas started to say of course he was, and discovered that his voice had disappeared. When he tried to speak, he was seized by a paroxysm of violent coughing. The nun exchanged her cloth for a goblet and swiftly set it to his lips.

As Nicholas drank, the spasm eased, leaving him breathless and weak. Subsiding against the bolsters, he nodded his thanks to her.

'They were all certain that you were going to die. Father Gundulf gave you the last rites and prayers were said for your soul in the chapel.' Tilting her head to one side, she gave him a considering look. 'Either the prayers are working, or I am a good nurse and you are stronger than you look.'

Nicholas grimaced and shook his head. Just now a newborn child could have defeated him in a fist fight.

She offered him the drink again. Out of pride he raised a shaking hand to the cup and his fingers clumsily covered hers. The young nun gave a little start at the move and colour flushed across her cheekbones. Studying her as she set the cup aside and arranged the bedclothes, he remembered that her name was Sister Miriel. And then he thought of the gleaming ship in his dreams. The mind had a strange world and language of its own.

'You are in the convent of St Catherine's-in-the-Marsh,' she told him as she smoothed and tucked. 'We found you out on the sheep pasture, but you told us that you had come from the estuary.'

Nicholas frowned. It was difficult to sort the reality from his fevered dreams. All that came to him were images of churning mud and water, of desperation, terror, and the grim struggle to survive.

'I suppose,' she said, 'that you were a member of King John's baggage train.'

Nicholas looked at the woven stripes on the coverlet and nodded warily. An unwilling member, it was true, but nevertheless a witness to the doom.

'The soldiers have been searching the shore every day since it happened, but they have recovered naught but a few bodies and broken pieces of wood. It is said that the entire royal treasure was lost beneath the waves.' There was a sudden vibrancy in her tone at the mention of the treasure, which sat ill-at-ease with the image of a nun dedicated to the pure service of God. Nicholas had not missed the glow in her voice, but he was too tired to examine its reason. He thought it fortunate that the loss of his own voice meant that he did not have to explain anything.

She studied him and pursed her lips, which were as full and sensual as her nose was thin and austere. 'We had to say prayers in chapel for King John too,' she remarked, 'although not because he lost his baggage train. We heard the news yesterday that he has been stricken with gripes in the belly and is sick unto death.'

Nicholas's gaze sharpened and he formed a question with raised eyebrows.

'It is true, I swear it.' She placed her hand on the little wooden cross at her breast. 'He was first taken ill at Lynn, but his condition has worsened apace. Mother Abbess says that his sins are coming home to roost.'

Nicholas nodded and closed his eyes again so that she would not see the leap of joy in them. It might be wrong to exult at such news, but he would go to confession with a light heart. To the devil his own – and in very short order, he hoped. Perhaps then he could close the door on his past.

Gradually Nicholas recovered the use of his voice. His strength returned too as he devoured the nourishing broths and tisanes that were prepared for him. Although he much preferred the ministrations of Sister Miriel who would talk to him and was easy on the eye, she was seldom in attendance. Usually it was a nervous biddy called Godefe, skinny as a punt-pole, who treated him as if he was going to spring from his pallet and ravish her at the slightest opportunity. On the occasions when Godefe was not in attendance, he was left to the tender mercies of Sister Margaret. She, it seemed, had not the slightest fear of being ravished – all she would have to do to render him *hors de combat* would be to sit on him – but her irritation at having a man in the infirmary was made known at every turn.

One evening in late October, however, his fortune changed. Instead of the intimidated Godefe, or the intimidating infirmaress, Sister Miriel came to him with a bowl of chicken broth and a bulky bundle tucked under her arm. A blue dusk had fallen outside. Her cheeks were flushed with cold and the keen smell of impending frost clung to her habit. Outside a bell was tolling in solemn, resounding strokes, but he was not aware of any religious office being due.

'King John has died,' she said as she gave him the broth and seated herself on the curule chair at his bedside. 'We heard the news not an hour ago from a merchant on his way to Lynn.'

Nicholas dipped the horn spoon in the broth and stirred the surface, but he did not eat. He knew that he should feel triumphant, but strangely there was only a great numbness where emotion should be. He had hated and feared John for more than ten years, and it was impossible to let it go in an instant.

'I am sorry, were you one of his men?' she asked with concern.

Nicholas laughed grimly. 'One of his men,' he repeated and shook his head. 'Christ, if only you knew.'

She rested her elbows on the bundle in her lap and leaned forward. 'If only I did.'

Nicholas started to eat the broth; with his mouth full he could not answer.

Her lips twitched. 'But you're not going to tell me, are you?'

Nicholas swallowed and raised his eyes to meet the intelligent humour in hers. Keeping his own counsel had become second nature, the difference between life and death. Yet he sensed a kindred spirit in the young nun seated at his bedside, and she too had made the difference between his life and death. 'I wasn't one of John's men,' he said. 'It was pure mischance that I came to be travelling with the royal baggage train.'

'You mean you were with them because of safety in numbers after all the trouble in Lincoln?'

He drank some more broth and she watched him in waiting silence, her chin cupped in her hand.

'I was one of the rebels causing the trouble at Lincoln,' he risked finally. 'They caught me trying to escape and brought me with them for interrogation. If John had realised that he had me in his possession, he would have strung me higher than the man in the moon.'

Her eyes widened in shock. 'But why?'

'Reasons,' he said grimly. 'My family is not the first to fall foul of John's dark nature.' He contemplated the spoon. 'Actually John would not have cared how I died, just that it was quick and quiet.'

She gave a delicate shudder. 'We used to hear tales in Lincoln and roundabout,' she said. 'He hanged some tiny children who were hostages in his care, and I remember a terrible tale about a woman he starved to death.'

'That woman's knowledge is mine, and it was my father's too.' No longer hungry, he put the broth aside unfinished. 'He died while crossing the Narrow Sea. Both he and his ship vanished. No trace of him or the *Péronnelle* was ever found, yet he was an experienced sailor and navigator, and the night was as calm as glass.'

'You are saying that he was killed?' Her eyes by now were huge.

'How can I when there is only suspicion and no proof?' He waved his hand. 'I should not be speaking of this; it is too dangerous.'

She sat upright in her chair and looked affronted. 'I won't tell anyone.'

'Mayhap not, but I am a rebel and even if John is dead, the war is not over. Word of my presence here is bound to leak out.'

'But I am the only one who knows more about you than your name,' she said practically. 'And I won't say anything, I swear.' She clutched her wooden cross as she spoke.

Nicholas smiled without humour. 'Like the law of the confessional, you mean. But that still does not stop the other nuns from speculation and gossip. Women are the same the world over.'

'If not for me and my fellow nuns you would not be here now,' she said indignantly.

He inclined his head. 'For which I would not have you think me ungrateful. But it is not safe for me to remain here much longer.'

'You are not yet strong enough to leave.' She spoke quickly, almost as if panicking, he thought, and her hand gripped the bundle on her lap. He saw that it was a garment of some sort with lozenge-patterned braid on the cuffs.

'No, but I will be soon.'

'Where will you go?'

'Wherever the road takes me.' He pointed at the clothing. 'Is that for me, or are you on an errand elsewhere?'

She sighed and placed the bundle on the bed. 'Mother Abbess says that since you are feeling stronger, you might soon want to move to the guest house. As you have no garments of your own save shirt and braies, of her charity she has provided you with a tunic and chausses.'

'That is most generous of her.' Nicholas picked up the tunic and shook it out. It was fashioned of soft, tawny wool that had been both fulled and napped – a rich man's garment, finer than he had owned in a long time. The chausses were of serviceable brown linen and there was a green hood with a short shoulder cape.

'We keep spare apparel in the guest house,' she explained to his look of surprised question. 'Travellers often arrive in foul weather and it is miserable to spend the night in wet clothes.'

'I pray you give her my deepest gratitude, and I will do so again myself when I have risen from my sick-bed,' he said with genuine sincerity, and rubbed his fingers over the luxury of the fine cloth. Then he glanced at her. 'You said that you heard tales of John in Lincoln. Was that your home before you became a nun?'

She gave him a small, bleak smile. 'I lived there,' she said, 'but I am not sure that it was ever my home.' With a sudden look of revulsion, she stood up and shook out the folds of her habit, the weave coarse and uneven in contrast to the finery he held between his hands. 'And I belong to this benighted place even less.'

Nicholas frowned. 'But I thought that . . .'

'That I had a vocation?' She laughed bitterly and raised one hand to her head. 'This is the wimple of a novice, not a full-fledged nun, and if I had my choice, it never would be.' In a single movement, she jerked the linen covering from her head and her braid tumbled down, strands of hair wisping free of the thick tawny plait.

Nicholas stared, his jaw dropping. He knew that nuns wore their hair short as a mark of respect to God and a rejection of vanity, but he had never thought for one moment that she was so recent a novice as to be unshorn. Without the prim folds of her wimple, her face was much younger and softer, and the blend of honey-bronze hair and golden-brown eyes was striking.

'My family desired to be rid of me,' she said succinctly, 'so they paid my dowry to St Catherine's and put me here to rot.' She tossed her head and her braid shimmered with movement.

Nicholas was both captivated and amused. 'What did you do to make them want rid of you?'

She ran the wimple through her fingers. 'I spoke my mind. And when my stepfather beat me for doing so, I fought back tooth and nail.' Suddenly she almost smiled. 'I set the house on fire and caused such a scandal that half of Lincoln turned out to line the road the next morning when I left for this place.'

'An unruly shrew then,' he said and grinned.

'I am learning not to be unruly.' For a moment she answered his grin, making him think that it was a long time since he had seen a girl so attractive, but the expression was swiftly quenched. 'I hate it here,' she said. 'Mother Abbess thinks that one day I will come to accept it, but then she has the spur of my dowry to goad her hope. All I have is the knowledge that there is nothing else for me – and that is enough to drive me to despair.'

Nicholas shifted uncomfortably. 'Mayhap the Abbess is right. Mayhap as time progresses you will find it easier to fit in.' He knew that he was mouthing platitudes. Listening to the vehemence in her voice, looking at her, the long braid shining in the candle-light and her head held high, it was difficult to imagine her spending the rest of her life on her knees to God.

'If I do,' she said, 'it will be because the best part of my life has withered away.'

Without warning, the curtain across the small alcove was jerked aside and a nun even more enormous than Sister Margaret filled the entrance, her arms akimbo.

'Sister Miriel, what indecency is this?' Both expression and voice were incredulous and the flashing dark eyes held a glint of triumphant malice.

'Nothing, Sister Euphemia,' Miriel said swiftly. 'My wimple was loose. I took it off so that I could arrange it properly.'

'You must think I was born this morning!' The nun drew herself up, towering over the younger woman like an enormous black thundercloud. 'How dare you play the whore in God's house! Cover your hair immediately!'

'Sister Miriel has behaved with the utmost discretion in my presence,' Nicholas interrupted as he saw the panic flare in the girl's eyes. 'Indeed, it shocks me to hear you use such harsh words against one of your own.'

'Your opinion of discretion is scarcely the convent's,' snapped the nun. She bestowed a basilisk glare on him, then swivelled again to Miriel. 'It's straight to the Abbess for you, you hoyden.' Seizing Miriel by the arm, she began dragging her away.

Miriel cast a frantic glance over her shoulder at Nicholas. He threw the bedclothes aside and started to rise, but he was dizzy and weak from his illness. The breath he gathered to argue with the older nun was squandered in a bout of coughing. By the time he recovered from the spasm and eased himself up against the bolsters, he was alone and the curtain had been very firmly drawn across. Plainly Sister Euphemia would rather he choked to death than interfere with her purpose.

Swearing to himself, he reached for the clothes, but the effort of putting them on was too much for his weakened condition and, in mid-struggle, he fell asleep.

An hour later he woke with a start. The curtain was still drawn across, but now another nun stood at his bedside. In contrast to the quivering, furious bulk of Sister Euphemia, this one was small, composed and elegant. The cross on her breast, although starkly simple, was of intricately worked silver and her air was one of authority, not menace.

Nicholas realised that he was lying half-across the bed, wearing only his shirt and braies. Quickly he drew the sheet across his loins and reached for the tunic.

'I am the Abbess here,' the nun said without preamble, her tone clear and cold. 'I do not know what went forth in here before vespers this evening, but from what I have heard, I can make an educated guess.'

'And I do not know what you heard but—'

'Please.' The Abbess stopped him with a raised hand. Her skin had the slick, transparent sheen of old age and hard work. 'Sister Miriel is our concern, not yours. Perhaps it is only natural that you should wish to defend her, but you can best help her cause by leaving this place as soon as you are able.' Her blue eyes were as clear and cold as her voice. 'It is wise, I think, if you do not see Sister Miriel again.'

Nicholas met the wintry displeasure of her stare. 'Nothing happened between us,' he said with dignity.

'I believe you.' The nun inclined her head. 'If I did not, you would be on the road even now and fortunate to escape imprisonment. I need not tell you that the punishment for seducing a nun is severe.' She pursed her lips. 'It may seem to you that Sister Miriel has little vocation, but I have great hope for her in the future if she can only be brought to our ways. The very strength of her will is the life blood our house needs to survive. It is my duty to channel it, to ensure that it works for the good of all and is not wasted in folly.'

Nicholas bowed in deference to her years and authority, but he could not let her words go entirely unchallenged. 'But you may find that you have destroyed what you sought,' he said, remembering Miriel's bitter remark that if she ever yielded, it would be because the best part of her had withered away.

The Abbess sighed. 'It is a risk I must take. You must understand that there is no place for the girl outside of St Catherine's. Her family has entrusted her to us, and for various reasons there would be little hope of her making a respectable marriage if she returned to her own community. As far as I am concerned, today's incident was just another lesson she has learned the hard way.' The nun's expression grew stubborn. 'She will come into the fold; I will not let her stray.'

She bade him a frosty goodnight. Long after she had gone, Nicholas lay on his back, his arms pillowing his head, and thought about the day's happenings. They troubled him, but, like the Abbess, he had a pragmatic streak. It was a pity that the girl had been forced into the convent. He felt sorry for her, but she would not be the first young woman to suffer the fate, and it was the way of the world. Soon, as the Abbess said, he would be gone. He had his own way to make, a new life to forge. While grateful to the nuns for his life – to Sister Miriel in particular – they had no part in his future.

Closing his eyes, he turned on his side and dreamed of wealth, of salt spray in his face, and of the deck of a sleek, beautiful ship beneath his feet.

CHAPTER 6

Miriel was accustomed to enduring bread and water penances. Not a month had gone by without one since her arrival at St Catherine's. For two days she was confined to a solitary cell, bare of furniture save for a thin mattress on the floor of beaten earth and a crucifix on the limed wall. The wind whistled through the barred shutters and it was unbearably cold. She wrapped the scratchy woollen bed blanket around her shoulders like a cloak and paced back and forth across the tiny room in an effort to keep warm. At one point she contemplated tearing the mattress into shreds and setting fire to it with the tiny cresset lamp that was all she had for light. It remained no more than a notion. The bracken stuffing would only give off heat for a short while, and her punishment would be redoubled. She would endure; it was only two days.

Sister Adela brought her a loaf of coarse brown bread and jug of water each morning, but Sister Euphemia was on hand to oversee the proceedings and there was little opportunity for the girls to speak.

'Are you all right?' Adela managed to whisper on the second morning as she entered the cell. She looked pale and frightened. Perceived as the novice closest to Miriel, she was being made to witness her friend's humiliation and punishment as a warning of what happened to transgressors.

Miriel forced a smile and touched her head. 'I will survive,' she said. 'It will grow back in time.' Her wimple covered the shorn spikes of hair that were all that remained of her glorious tawny tresses. Since the charge raised against Miriel by Sister Euphemia was grave indeed, the Abbess had approached

St Catherine's priest concerning Miriel's punishment. Full of righteous disgust, Father Gundulf had quoted biblical verses about a woman's hair being a symbol of vanity and whoredom, and pronounced that Miriel's should be shorn to her scalp to remind her that she was God's servant.

It had not been easy. There were huge, hand-shaped bruises on her arms where Sister Euphemia had pinned her fast, although Euphemia herself walked with a limp where Miriel had put in several useful kicks. They had burned her hair on the fire, purifying by immolation that which was unholy.

'The man has moved into the guest house,' Adela added with a swift glance over her shoulder. The shuffle of Euphemia's footsteps was growing louder. 'He said to tell you that he's leaving on the morrow and he wishes you well.'

'Leaving!' Miriel cried in panic. 'But he can't, he's not well enough yet!'

'Hush, don't shout!' Adela flapped an agitated hand. 'Mother Hillary said he had to go as soon as possible. That's all I know.' She backed to the door just as Euphemia appeared.

Miriel gave the novice mistress a single frozen look and turned her back to kneel and pray at the crucifix high on the plain white wall. Euphemia eyed her narrowly before pulling Adela away from the door, banging it shut and sliding the bolt.

It was after midnight when Miriel was released from the cell to rejoin the other nuns in the first service of the day. She was so cold by now that she could not feel her hands or feet. The words of the priest passed over her head, but she managed to repeat the chants by rote. Her breath was a white vapour in the air, and by each exhalation she marked the time to the breaking of fast when there would at least be hot gruel and a hearth for warmth. And Nicholas would be gone, leaving her a prisoner in this bare, joyless world.

The thought ate at her through the interminable hours of the service. Her attention wandered and Sister Euphemia's willow switch lashed across her knuckles, but to little effect since her fingers were too numb with cold to feel the pain. She looked at the developing welt whilst she considered the punishments of shorn hair and isolation that had brought her to this moment, and arrived at the decision towards which she had been travelling for a long time.

Raising her head, she gave her responses in a voice of renewed firmness and clarity that earned her wondering looks from the other novices. Miriel paid them no heed, for her eyes and mind were fixed upon her inner vision.

The nocturnal services ended and the women filed out of the chapel to wash their hands and repair to the refectory. Miriel broke her fast and forced herself not to wolf down the bowl of grey barley gruel. She behaved with modesty and decorum, listening attentively to the sister who read out the lesson from the gospel of Matthew as the women ate. She knew that the others were speculating about her, wondering if she had finally been brought to her senses. From the glances she had received in chapel, she knew that there was a mingling of sympathy and righteous satisfaction at the severity of her punishment. Little did they know how much more speculation there would be by the day's end.

Following the meal, the nuns went about their various duties. Miriel was summoned to the Abbess's chamber and there given another lecture about applying her will to becoming a worthy nun instead of bringing disgrace and disrepute upon herself and the convent.

'I promise I will try,' Miriel said with what she hoped was convincing penitence and to this end kept her head bowed and her eyes lowered.

The Abbess gave her a dubious look. 'I hope you will. Perhaps Father Gundulf was unduly harsh in his punishment, but you had committed a grave breach of our rule.'

'Yes, mother, I know, and I am sorry.' Which was true. If Miriel had known what discomfort lay ahead, she would never have removed her wimple to show off her hair to Nicholas.

Mother Hillary's expression softened. 'I trust that you are. It distresses me to have to chastise any of my daughters.' She brought her palms down on the trestle to emphasise her next point. 'Our guest is leaving us this morning, so temptation will no longer be in your way, and that can only be to the good. I was young once, and I well understand the man's attraction to a girl not long of the noviciate.'

Miriel felt the heat of a blush crawl up her throat and across her face, although for more complex reasons than those imagined by the Abbess.

'You will not see him again, child. I have made as much plain to him and, to his credit, he was disposed to agree with me.'

'Yes, Mother Hillary,' Miriel said meekly without raising her eyes lest the look in them give her away.

'Good, I am glad you understand. You will spend the rest of today in the infirmary with Sister Margaret. She needs help with brewing syrup for winter coughs.'

Dismissed from the Abbess's parlour, Miriel walked swiftly – but not so swiftly that she was chastised for haste – through the cloister to the abbey kitchens. Here she purloined bread and cheese with the excuse that Sister Margaret needed them for the infirmary. A quick, furtive visit to the guest house revealed that Nicholas had left but, glancing up the path, she saw him talking to the porteress at the door. He now had a dark travelling cloak to go with the hood, and he was leaning on a stout quarterstaff.

Miriel darted back inside the guest house. She hastened to Nicholas's bed, grabbed the blanket he had left neatly folded and opened it out to use as a cloak. Off came the linen bolster case, and into it she stuffed the bread and cheese.

From the guest house, Miriel sped round the back of the necessarium to the abbey gardens. Ladders were propped against the orchard trees in readiness for harvesting the late season crop of apples and pears. She stooped to add several of the less bruised windfalls to her bolster case, then dragged one of the ladders over to the garden wall. She propped the ladder against the rough-cut stone and ensured that the feet were safely embedded in the soft ground. Her heart hammered and panic chivvied her to move ever faster. Someone was going to see her. Sister Euphemia was going to drag her down off the rungs and whip her senseless with the willow switch.

As Miriel scrambled up the steps, her foot caught in a fold

of her habit and almost sent her toppling. Cursing, she took a grip on her imagination and tugged the surplus fabric through her rope girdle. No one was going to catch her. She wouldn't let them.

Soon she was straddling the top of the wall. For the briefest instant she paused to view the stone and timber abbey buildings. Smoke rose from the louvres in the kitchen roof and she could hear the squeak of the windlass on the well-housing as someone drew a bucket of water. For almost six months Saint Catherine's had been her prison, but now she had sprung her own lock.

A swift glance in the opposite direction granted her the sight of open fields on the higher silt, changing gradually to reed fen on the horizon. Immediately below her, the abbey's two mules grazed the home meadow with a herd of goats. She also glimpsed Nicholas emerging from the gatehouse, his hood raised against the chill of autumn. She watched him wave to the porteress and set out on the path that would take him to the Lincoln road. Once out of the nun's sight, however, he doubled back, and took the track leading towards the coast. Miriel watched him with narrowed eyes. Something was afoot here, something curious and interesting that made the shorn hairs tingle on the nape of her neck.

Aware of her vulnerable position on the wall, she leaned down to the ladder and with a grunt of effort, hauled it up, over and down the other side. It was an awkward descent. She was dreadfully hampered by the bulk of her skirts and the precariousness of the ladder, but finally, gasping with fear and effort, she reached the ground.

She beat at her habit which was badly stained with moss and stone dust. The goats came to investigate, drawn by the appetising smells coming from the bolster bag. Miriel slapped them away and made shooing noises, but to little avail since the goats were accustomed to such human abuse and ignored it. The mules joined in, long ears pricked with curiosity and nostrils ruffling.

Miriel eyed the animals. Unfastening the rope girdle at her waist, she caught the nearest mule by its fuzzy mane and threw a makeshift halter around its neck. Docile with age, it ambled after her willingly. So too did the goats until they reached the bank of a ditch filled with soupy brown water. With a shudder, Miriel bunched her habit and undertunic on her free arm and waded across. The water was freezing and took her breath. The mule balked and had to be persuaded to follow her with much tugging and encouraging clicks of her tongue. At last it consented, and splashed across, soaking Miriel in dirty spray. The goats, to her relief, chose to remain in their pasture, and the other mule, although it set up a loud braying, did not follow its companion.

Wet, cold, but fired by determination, Miriel set off in pursuit of Nicholas. He was but a moving dot in the distance, but she did not seek to close with him. There was time enough for that. Just now she was vastly curious as to his intentions. Why was he going to the sea instead of taking the road inland? If he walked along the coast, he would come to some hamlets in a few miles, but they had nothing to offer unless he wanted to hire a fishing boat. He might be on his way to pay his respects to those who had died, but Miriel doubted it. They had been his companions in disaster but, by his own admission, his enemies too.

The late October sun made a white haze through the clouds. Except for the crying of gulls and the hiss of reeds in the brisk wind off the sea, there was silence. Occasionally Miriel glanced over her shoulder, expecting to see a host of irate nuns in pursuit, Sister Euphemia in the lead like a bloodhound, but of course there was nothing. Even when the women did discover her missing, they would look to the Spalding road first, and probably not even consider the marshes.

Near the mouth of the estuary, Nicholas stopped abruptly and turned in a half-circle as if taking his bearings. Miriel hastily crouched, so that if he looked round, all he would see in the distance was a grazing animal. He stood for a long time just staring. Then slowly, measuring each pace, he retraced his steps, veering a little to the right, where a bank of trees rose above the reeds and grasses.

Miriel thought that she was bound to be discovered, but

his angle of direction grew sharper so that even in his side vision he would not have been able to see her.

When she decided it was safe to move, Miriel rose from her crouch and continued to follow him.

At first Nicholas had a dread that he would be unable to find the place where he had concealed the chest. The memory lay on the other side of high fever and near-death. The fens had been swallowed in fog when he had hidden it, and he had been close to collapse.

As he walked, that initial fear subsided. He possessed an innate sense of direction that had been honed on numerous journeys across the seas between Flanders, Normandy and England. He would find the chest; it was a matter of trusting to instinct.

He curbed a desire to rush for he was still weak from his illness. Although he felt bright for the nonce, he knew he did not have the lasting stamina of full health. A mount would have been useful, but he could not have asked one of the nuns. They had already given him clothing, a day's food, and enough money to buy him lodgings for at least two nights. He was counting on the contents of the chest to provide him with the means to buy transport – to buy a new life, come to that. It was the least that the House of Anjou owed him.

Once he had the sensation of being followed and glanced round sharply. A shape in the distance proved to be a grazing animal and he let out the breath he had sucked in. The glance showed him what he had missed before and he turned to retrace his steps. Then he left the path and pushed through the tall, yellow grass towards a thicket of alder and willow trees growing on the edge of a small mere. The water was dark and peaty, its surface a mirror for the autumn leaves flickering from the trees like twists of shaved gold.

The hiding place was innocuous. Despite his extremity, he had concealed it well, and it looked so natural that he even began to wonder if he was standing on the right spot. He reached for the costrel bottle that the nuns had given him and, drawing the stopper, took a fortifying swallow of strong, sweet mead.

As it surged through his veins, he set to work, casting aside the dead branches and sheaves of grass and reaching inside the alcove to drag the chest from its hiding place. Sweating and trembling with excitement and effort, he rested a moment to let the strength flow back into his limbs. A breeze shimmered the dark surface of the mere and the tree reflections performed a dance of running gold, eerie and beautiful. A fitting backdrop. Feeling stronger, he gave his attention to the chest. It was heavily salt-stained and a little battered, but still intact, the red and blue enamels sharp enough to cut the eye.

'God, if you love me, show it now,' he entreated and, licking his lips, set the tip of his eating knife to the brass hasp.

Opening the chest was far more difficult than the finding. It took Nicholas several nicked fingers from slips of the knife and a mountain of struggling and swearing before the fastenings finally yielded and he was able to throw back the lid and gaze upon the contents.

Leather money pouches were packed two layers thick around a second box with exquisitely carved ivory panels and fastenings of wrought gold. With unsteady hands, Nicholas lifted out one of the pouches and loosened the tough drawstring cord. A shimmer of silver pennies poured out into his cupped palm, each one stamped with John's head one side, and a deeply scored cross on the other. Nicholas estimated that he was looking at about forty shillings in all. If each bag held the same, then the stuffing around the smaller chest was worth four hundred marks, sufficient to carve himself a fresh life twice over. As a footsoldier he would expect to earn five shillings a week if he was fortunate. Now he would be able to equip and accoutre himself properly and become the master, not the hireling. He smiled at the irony. From his grave, King John was paying back some of what he owed to the de Caen family.

With great care, he tipped the coins back into the pouch and, wiping his damp hands on his tunic, he turned to consider the second chest. As with the first, there was no key and he had to break the lock with the point of his knife. He pushed back the lid to reveal a sea-stained cloth of embroidered purple silk which was swathed around a large circular object. Drawing it forth, he gently unwrapped the protective layers of fabric.

Pleasure and dread flowed through him as he stared at the crown. It wasn't John's; it was too small and was wrought in an older style. This had been made for a woman and consisted of a wide golden band bordered with pearls and set with huge, square-cut gemstones. Two arches of enamelled gold curved over each other above the circlet, each one hemmed with more pearls and smaller beads of precious stone. Fine gold chains dangled beneath the crown at regular intervals and at the end of each chain was a golden trefoil, each leaf set with a pearl.

'God's eyes,' he muttered, knowing that there was no safe way to keep the object. Yet it would be sacrilege to melt it down and destroy such craftsmanship and beauty.

A sudden intuition, coupled with the enormity of what he had rescued from the sea, caused him to spin round. The nun ducked down among the grasses, but not quickly enough. The bay mule at her side did not even flinch at her sudden movement but stolidly munched a mouthful of yellowing grass.

'Come out,' Nicholas commanded, the crown still in his hands, for it was too late to conceal his prize. He too had not been quick enough.

Slowly Miriel stood up. Her face was flushed with chagrin, but there was a familiar thrust to her jaw that told him she was ready to fight.

'What are you doing?'

She shrugged. 'I followed you to see where you would go,' she said, as if the notion was perfectly reasonable. 'When you left St Catherine's, so did I.' She held up the bolster case in her right hand. 'Bread, cheese and fruit,' she said. 'It was all I had time to bring.'

Astonishment and fury made Nicholas brutal. 'You need not think you are travelling with me,' he snarled. 'I want neither you nor your company.'

Her face whitened but she stood up to him and took a deliberate pace closer to the box. 'I would say that you have no choice.'

Nicholas moved to bar her way so that they stood mere inches apart, the crown glittering between them. 'But I do,' he said, his voice breaking hoarsely in the aftermath of his illness. 'Do you think with this fortune in my hands that I would balk at killing you?'

She met his eyes without flinching, then dropped her gaze to the sheathed knife on his hip. 'Yes, I think you would,' she said calmly. 'Besides, you are newly risen from your sick-bed and I am easily a match for your strength. You would not succeed in disposing of me. Indeed,' she added with a half-smile, 'I might win.' She reached to touch one of the pearl trefoils swinging on the end of its chain. 'You owe your life to me; I am only claiming the debt.'

Nicholas snatched the crown away. 'I owe you nothing,' he snapped, knowing the opposite was true and feeling all the more enraged because of it. 'I gave you no encouragement. Go your own way, not mine.'

She shook her head. 'Believe me, I would, but it is impossible for a woman, even a nun, to journey without escort in these times.'

'You should have thought of that before.'

'I did.' She gestured impatiently at the crown. 'I wondered while you lay sick if you knew something about the treasures lost in the quicksand, but it was no more than a fancy born of something you said in your fever. I never thought in my heart that it was true. All I knew for certain was that I had to escape from St Catherine's, and you were my means.'

Nicholas raised a sceptical eyebrow.

'You owe me your life,' she repeated stubbornly. 'The least you can do is escort me to the nearest town where I can abandon these nun's weeds and find work.'

He snorted. 'That's a foolish notion.'

'No more foolish than the idea that I could ever become a nun.' Her brown eyes could have been stones. 'Surely it is not too much to ask.'

Nicholas glared at her. 'They will search for you. They will put out word that one of their novices has absconded at the same time as a departing guest. I cannot afford to be caught with a runaway nun.'

She eyed him with scorn. 'You can afford whatever you want,' she said coldly.

Nicholas considered bribing her with a bag of silver, but, even as the thought occurred, knew that it would not work. What she wanted, as she said, was a masculine escort to lend her protection and a degree of respectability. Whilst he could provide both, all she would be to him was a hindrance. He disliked the way she was looking at him – as if she could read his mind and thought him a worm that had just crawled from under a rock. 'Perhaps I do not want to pay your price.'

'Do you set so little worth on your honour?'

'My honour?' He gave a humourless laugh. 'If you knew anything about my family's honour, you would seal your lips rather than ask such a damning question.'

A look of bewilderment tinged with fear flickered across her face, but her chin stayed high. 'I do not give a fig for your family's honour, only for yours that you keep it.'

'Only for yourself,' he said.

'Then we are evenly matched.'

Nicholas felt the situation slipping rapidly from his grasp. Whatever he threw at her, she had an answer, and in truth she was right. Despite his intense anger and irritation, he had neither the physical strength nor the mental capacity to murder her. King John's treasure did not confer on him King John's nature.

'We are not,' he contradicted, giving her a vexed look. 'You have the measure of me and you know it. To the nearest town and no further.'

She nodded briskly like a merchant concluding a business arrangement. 'As long as it be not Lincoln. I am known there and it is the first place they would look. If I am discovered, my family will hand me straight back to the Church.' She clasped her hands together in a gesture of agitation rather than nun-like control.

Nicholas could well understand why her folk desired to keep her at arm's length, but there was something about her stance, a vulnerable core behind the stubborn façade that ignited a spark of sympathy. Almost despite himself, he found that he still liked her.

'You can escort me to Nottingham,' she said. 'I have been there with my grandfather several times and I know its streets tolerably well.'

He gave her a grudging nod. 'Fair enough.'

She rewarded him with a wary smile and, as if his agreement had given her sanction, once more reached to the crown. 'I have never seen anything so beautiful,' she said with a look of haunted longing in her eyes.

Nicholas resisted the urge to snatch it away. 'I think it must have belonged to John's grandmother, the Empress Mathilda. I once saw John's queen wearing her royal crown and it was a dainty circlet, nothing like this.'

'What will you do with it?'

'I have not thought.' Nicholas turned it in his hands and the soft October light gleamed silkily on the gold.

Her gaze sharpened. 'You will not melt it down?'

'That depends on circumstance.' He was unwilling to be drawn. 'Not for the moment at least.'

'May I look?' She gestured at the two boxes behind him.

Nicholas shrugged. 'I do not know why you bother to ask,' he said ungraciously, but stood aside.

She stepped forward and crouched. Her fingers, elegant and slim, stroked the exquisitely carved ivory box. With misgiving he saw her eyes linger on the money pouches and develop a feral gleam.

Then, with a sigh and a shake of her head, she rose. 'Is this what you meant at St Catherine's when you spoke of Pandora's box?'

'What?' He gazed at her blankly.

'In your fever you kept muttering about Pandora's box. We didn't know what you meant, although I wondered if you were speaking of the King's treasure.'

For the first time in their conversation, Nicholas's lips parted in a grin, albeit mirthless. 'Oh yes,' he said. 'What you see before you definitely belongs to Pandora.'

She frowned.

'Pandora was a woman in old legend who was warned expressly not to open a beautiful box; but, of course, she did. Unfortunately the box contained all the world's woes, and these were unleashed on mankind never to be recaptured.' He returned the crown to its stained silk wrapping. 'Only hope remained.'

She gave a little shiver. 'You could leave it here.'

He slanted her a glance from beneath his brows. 'Would you?'

She considered the boxes, but only for a brief moment. When she looked at him, the hue of her eyes mirrored the colour of the gold. 'No,' she said. 'Whatever the trouble, I would still have the hope.'

CHAPTER 7

Nicholas and Miriel spent the first night of their journey in a shepherd's hut belonging to the monks of Spalding Abbey. It was in a poor state of repair but, despite the leaking, mouldy thatch, there were hearth stones in the centre of the tiny room. A small supply of old kindling outside allowed them a meagre fire. They had bread, fruit and cheese between them, and wine to drink.

'So,' Nicholas said as he passed her the costrel and she set it to her lips, 'if I give you three pouches of silver for the hire of that mule and see you safe to a town of your choosing, we call it quits and each go our own way.'

The tart red liquid hit the back of Miriel's throat. 'Quits,' she said, lowering the costrel and wiping her mouth. She did not think that three pouches of silver was particularly generous, but she was tired and for the nonce it did not matter. There was time enough to do battle. Nicholas looked tired too. Deep shadows stained his eye sockets and his face was drawn. He should have been resting in the warmth of the guest house at St Catherine's. Had it not been for her rash nature and the nuns' intolerance, they would both still be there, he in his bed and she on her knees. Miriel smiled with irony at the thought. Now, because of the nuns, they were alone in a shepherd's hut, sharing wine and fire and temptation. She could imagine the horror on the good sisters' faces if they could witness this scene, and the smugness of Sister Euphemia at being proved right about Miriel's character.

'Where will you go with your vast wealth?' Of its own volition, her glance embraced the chest in the corner of the tiny hut, its enamels burnished by firelight. 'Back to the rebels?'

He shook his head. 'John is dead and his heir a child of nine. I have no grievance against the lad; my quarrel was with his hellspawn father. Nor do I harbour a grudge against the men who are to be young Henry's regents. William Marshal and Ranulf of Chester are both honourable men.' He leaned forward to poke the fire with a stick of kindling and stared into the surge of flame.

Miriel studied him across the blaze. The pallor of his skin was disguised by the hot colours of the fire, but the shadows threw his bones into sharp relief and emphasised how thin he was in the aftermath of serious illness. Even in repose there was a wariness about him, as if he had not slept safe in his bed for a long, long time. She was stirred by a pang of compassion, and, mingled with it, a deep curiosity.

'Your grievance,' she said softly. 'You told me a little about it at St Catherine's, but not the full tale. Why did King John persecute your family?'

He lifted the kindling stick and watched the flame lick at the end and then extinguish to a black char. She thought that he was not going to reply, but at last he drew a breath and let it out on a deep sigh.

'Knowledge of murder,' he said. 'God knows John has done enough of it in his time – generally of folk too weak to protest and mostly by proxy.' His eyes narrowed. 'But at least once he committed the deed by his own hand, and to his own flesh and blood.'

The fire crackled, and in his pause for breath the tension in the air crawled down Miriel's spine.

'My father was a minor knight from a coastal village between Caen and Rouen,' he said. 'We were vassals of Robert de Vieuxpoint, bailiff of Rouen, and we owned a fine, large nef in which we shipped wine and delicacies. For a month and ten days of each year it was our feudal duty to guard the Duke of Normandy's interests in the Narrow Sea. In truth, I almost grew up on the deck of that vessel.' As he gazed at the blackened end of the stick, the poignant smile on his lips slowly died and his eyes grew blank. 'It was a good life until the day we brought the *Péronnelle* up the Seine to the Tower of Rouen with a cargo of smoked English oysters for the royal table. I was eleven years old and I can still remember that journey, the splash of the water against the stones, the weed fanning out like mermaid hair, and a fair wind at our backs.' He swallowed and shook his head. 'God help us, we had no idea.'

This time the silence was longer than a breath and Miriel's fingers clenched in the coarse wool of her habit. 'What happened?' she asked, unable to bear the unspoken words lurking in the firelit shadows.

Nicholas set the point of the stick back into the flames and watched the tip become a translucent crimson. 'We were rolling the barrels along to the store room when John himself came staggering down the passage towards us. We could see that he was well marinated, but it was not Gascon wine that soaked his clothes, but blood, more than I have ever seen in my life. His hands, his face, his hair.' Nicholas shuddered and flicked the kindling into the fire. 'I could smell it too; it was like the stench of a Martinmas pig-sticking.'

Miriel watched with him as the twig burned, and pressed her hands to her mouth.

'When he saw us, he yelled that if we did not keep out of his way he would kill us too. He would have pulled his knife, but the sheath at his belt was empty.' Nicholas swallowed against the croak in his voice. 'My father hid me behind his back while John cursed at us like a drunk in the gutter. He struck my father across the face and a ring cut his cheek to the bone. My father could do nothing. To have retaliated would have meant his immediate death for the crime of *lèse-majesté*. I do not know what we would have done, had not Robert de Vieuxpoint and William de Briouze appeared and taken John in hand between them. They warned us to say nothing of what we had seen and bore the King away. He was still cursing. Even now I can hear him and it freezes me to the marrow.'

Nicholas rubbed the knuckles of his clenched fist against the open palm of his other hand. 'We made all haste to finish our task and be gone. I can still see my father's face, blood streaming down his cheek into his beard, and the look in his eyes. I was too young to realise it then, but he knew that we were dead.'

'Why?' Miriel asked through her fingers, her own marrow thoroughly chilled.

He looked at her, his gaze quenched and dark. 'As we were casting off, de Briouze and de Vieuxpoint emerged from the cellars and threw something in the water. By the lantern on our prow, we thought it was a body, but we could not be certain. A few days later we heard a rumour that Prince Arthur had been found in the River Seine, weighted with a stone and stabbed in the throat. He was John's nephew, but he was also a rival for John's throne and it was common knowledge that there was no love lost between them.'

'So John murdered him?'

Nicholas shrugged. 'The finger was pointed, but nothing was ever proven. Anyone who could have shed light on the truth was either bought or destroyed, including de Briouze and de Vieuxpoint. Our lands were taken from us and bestowed elsewhere. We were branded traitors and forced to flee.' His voice grew harsh and bitter. 'We lived from harbour to harbour and hand to mouth. My mother and sister died of the coughing sickness during a bad winter in Boulogne. When I was barely sixteen years old my father was "lost" at sea and I have been a rebel with a price on my head ever since.' He drew a deep, emotional breath and pinched the corners of his eyes between forefinger and thumb. 'I have never told anyone this story before, and God alone knows why I'm telling you.' With a sudden oath, he put his face in his hands, his body riven by tremors.

Miriel heartily wished that she had never asked about his dispute with John. It was as if she had opened Pandora's box herself and she was appalled at what he had told her. Her own difficulties were as nothing compared to the life that he had endured. 'I'm so sorry,' she whispered, hating the inadequacy of the words, but unable to think of better.

'Don't be. I have never sought anyone's sorrow or pity.' He raised his head and flashed her a fierce look from tear-glittered eyes.

'Neither have I.' She met his gaze. 'I too am not of that nature. I wanted to offer comfort, but I did not know what to say.'

'Nothing would be wise.' Turning from her, he rolled himself in his cloak, hunching the fabric around his ears, thereby ending their discussion.

Her mood pensive and uneasy, Miriel lay down too, but sleep did not come for a long time, and when finally she drifted off, it was to dream of being chased across quicksand by a faceless man with hands reaching out to throttle her. He never quite caught her, but by the same token, she never quite escaped because she was weighed down by manacles fashioned of jewel-studded gold.

In the morning, both Nicholas and Miriel were subdued and scarcely spoke to each other as they loaded the mule and continued along the banks of the Welland. In mid-afternoon, they arrived at the town of Stamford.

It was smaller than Nottingham or Lincoln, but it had thriving cloth and leather trades, several churches, a castle, and a Benedictine nunnery. Miriel felt as if all eyes were upon her as she and Nicholas walked up Highgate and approached the bridge into the town. She could not even hide her habit beneath her improvised cloak because it was being used to cover the chest on the mule's back. The wind sliced through her garments, but not as keenly as her fear of being discovered and incarcerated in St Michael's Priory until Mother Hillary arrived to take her back to St Catherine's.

'I need ordinary clothes,' she hissed to Nicholas, certain that a priest they had just passed had given her a strange look. Nuns were seldom seen outside their religious houses and, when they were, they were usually high-ranking women on important business, not novices. They were certainly never accompanied by single male civilians. 'Something quiet and respectable that no one will notice or remark upon.'

They approached the defensive gate in the town walls where a guard was collecting tolls from people entering. He had propped his spear against the stonework and his helmet lay on the ground beside it. He wasn't expecting trouble.

'Keep your eyes down, your hands clasped in front of you, and say nothing,' Nicholas replied. 'Then all folk will see is a pious nun. If you look round with wild eyes and fidget all the time, they will see a runaway for sure.'

'Easier to say than do,' Miriel said with a hint of panic as they drew closer to the guard.

'Just follow my lead,' Nicholas muttered impatiently. 'There are bound to be shops and stalls aplenty in the town where we can garb you more fittingly.'

Almost choking on the lump of fear in her throat, Miriel folded her hands and bowed her head to watch the flare of her skirts as she walked. Her heart thundered against her ribs as they drew abreast of the guard.

'Fine day for the end of the year,' Nicholas said pleasantly as he handed over the penny toll.

'Aye, 'tis that.' The guard looked him and Miriel over with cursory interest. 'You come from roundabouts?'

'Over Newark way,' Nicholas answered in the same, easy tone, and led the mule forwards. 'We are travelling to Sempringham Abbey.' He glanced briefly at Miriel.

It was enough to put the suggestion in the guard's head that Nicholas was an abbey servant and his business legitimate. The soldier nodded, his attention already on the next person in the queue.

'See,' said Nicholas as he and Miriel continued up St Mary's Hill and into the town, 'you can get away with anything if you show the right face to the world.'

Miriel's palms were damp with sweat. 'Mayhap,' she said shakily, 'but I will not feel safe until I am rid of these weeds. What if he had been suspicious? Supposing he had wanted to search us?'

'But he wasn't suspicious because we did not give him cause,' Nicholas said with exasperation. Then he looked at her and his expression softened. He drew her to the side of the road. 'There's a churchyard yonder. Go and pray by one of the graves and I'll find you some clothes in the market.'

Miriel was none too sanguine about entering any kind of religious precinct, but knew she had small choice. Her legs were still trembling from their encounter with the guard, and it would be unwise to wander around the booths and stalls with Nicholas. A nun showing interest in secular women's clothing was bound to be cause for speculation.

'I'll take care of the mule.' She grasped the scuffed, salt-stained bridle that had once belonged to the royal pack pony.

'No.' He clamped his hand over hers. They looked at each other. Miriel wished that she were half a foot taller so that she could meet him eye to eye.

'I will return, I promise,' he said.

Miriel clung stubbornly to the bridle. 'How do I know you'll keep your word?'

'You don't. You'll just have to take me on trust.'

Miriel stared at him, as if she could pierce his intentions just by concentrating on his face. But his sea-dark eyes gave nothing away.

'As I took you on trust when I told you about my family and King John,' he added.

Biting her lip, suddenly feeling small and mean, Miriel released the rein. 'Do not be too long,' she entreated.

Without reply, he turned the mule around and clicked his tongue. Miriel felt a surge of panic as she watched him leave the graveyard. Small and mean or not, her doubts persisted. This might indeed be the last view she ever had of him and the wealth that could change her life. She ought to run after him, grab his arm, and brave the crowds, but for the nonce she was just too tired and cold and frightened. The last two days had taken their toll on her courage and she had none left.

She knelt by one of the graves and clasped her hands, and then, because it seemed disrespectful not to do so, said a prayer for whomever was buried beneath the mound of turf. The cold seeped through her habit and linen undertunic, two damp, dark stains spreading at her knees. She was reminded of the bleak February day when they had buried her grandfather, and with him, sewn up in the shroud, all her hope and security.

Two women crossed the graveyard, taking a short cut from the market place to their homes. They paid her scant attention, a solitary nun, her hands steepled in prayer. Miriel darted a look at the women from beneath her lids and frantically murmured the words of an Ave until they had passed from sight. She wondered what to do if a priest emerged from the church and challenged her, then decided not to think about it. Fixing her gaze on the churchyard entrance, she concentrated with all her might on willing Nicholas to return.

The church bell struck the hour of noon, the heavy bronze clang resounding in her head. At St Catherine's the nuns would be resting over quiet tasks following the midday meal. Sister Euphemia would be standing guard in the cloisters with her switch, her eye cocked for unseemly behaviour among the novices. In the infirmary, Sister Margaret would be napping, her chin on her chest, while Godefe tiptoed around seeing to the patients.

Doubtless Mother Hillary had led them in prayers that their wayward sister would come swiftly to repentance. All that Miriel repented was letting the Abbess down again, but otherwise felt no remorse. Any guilt that might have existed had been cut away with her beautiful hair.

The gateway remained empty. With a hollow feeling in the pit of her stomach, Miriel began to wonder if her trust had been misplaced. What if he had abandoned her?

A sound from behind made her leap round with a stifled scream, expecting arrest by the incumbent priest. Instead she came face to face with a stocky brown cob. She looked beyond its liquid brown gaze to Nicholas who was holding a second horse too, and the mule. While she had been intent on the gateway, he had come round by the side path.

'Where have you been!' Miriel cried with the fury of relief. 'You said you wouldn't be long. I've been worried out of my wits!'

'I was only as long as it took.' His reasonable tone was in direct contrast to her agitation. 'The horse coper wanted a criminal sum for these two nags. It would have looked strange if I had not bartered him down. And then I had to find some suitable clothes at the rag stall, and that took some doing as well.' He tilted his head and studied her. 'You didn't truly think I would leave you?'

Miriel's eyes began to sting. 'No, of course not,' she snapped, 'but kneeling in the mud at some stranger's graveside is scarcely a pleasant way to mark time.' She knew from the sardonic curve of his lips that he could read her thoughts and it did nothing to improve her humour.

'No, I suppose it isn't,' he agreed and, in almost direct repetition of her act to him at St Catherine's, handed her a bundle of clothing. 'Not the best I could find, but I did not think you would want a laced dress of yellow silk in this weather, and besides, it might have attracted unwanted attention.'

Miriel nodded, thinking that a laced dress of yellow silk would be unfortunate in any weather since she could not wear the colour without looking as if she had a terminal disease.

She unfolded the clothes that Nicholas had brought and shook them out, determinedly putting to the back of her mind the thought that in all likelihood these were the garments of a dead person. The rag stalls relied on the relatives of the deceased to keep them supplied. She had frequently heard them touting for custom in Lincoln's streets: 'Highest prices paid!'

The dress was a shapeless affair cut from two rectangles of coarse woollen fabric with two more rectangles for sleeves. The colour was a dingy brownish-grey that the previous owner had sought to enliven by embroidering the throat, cuffs and hem with overlapping circles of bright green thread. Nicholas had added a plain leather belt, another rectangle of green fabric that Miriel assumed was a wimple, a hood with a sheepskin lining, and a mantle that, while not outworn, had obviously weathered a long career. Miriel pulled a face. The outfit was serviceable and nondescript, but it did nothing for her vanity. Although Nicholas had chosen wisely, she felt resentful. He might at least have included an attractive wimple band instead of the narrow strip of leather lying like a dried-up worm amongst the garments. She thought that on balance she would rather have had the yellow silk.

'What do you think?' he had the foolishness to ask.

Miriel shuddered. 'Horrible. They stink of smoke and

they've not seen a laundry tub in the God knows how many years since they were first stitched.'

He shrugged. 'Beggars cannot be choosers. Besides, it's not as if you have to wear them next to your skin. Your undergown will protect you and whatever else you've got underneath that.'

Miriel's cheeks grew hot. It was an innocent enough comment, but his reference to her undergarments made her feel vulnerable, not least because her linen loin cloth and coarsely woven hose were a close match except in cleanliness for the garments he was expecting her to don.

Tight-lipped and scowling, she reached to the hem of her habit and dragged it off over her head. For a moment her undergown threatened to depart with it and shame her already compromised modesty, but she managed with a contortion to pull it back down.

The bitter wind cut through the white wool undertunic which was all that now clothed her apart from hose and loin cloth. She did not wear a breast band for her body was well toned and her bosom too small to warrant binding. The slight curve of her breasts and the buds of her chilled nipples were plainly obvious beneath the fabric, and Nicholas stared with a gleam of pleasure.

She saw the direction of his gaze and, with a murderous glare, fought her way into the voluminous grey dress. Beneath the smoke was the sweaty smell of another woman and the lingering aroma of grease and soup from the numerous meals she must have cooked in this gown. Even if it was a good disguise, it was thoroughly disgusting. Donning the garment dislodged the already precarious position of her nun's wimple, and as she caught it in her hand, the cold air bit her naked ears and throat.

'Dear, sweet Christ,' Nicholas said huskily.

She looked up. He was still staring at her, his expression no longer of pleasure, but of horrified shock. 'Your hair! What happened to your lovely hair?'

Miriel raised her hand to touch her viciously shorn scalp. 'They cut it off,' she said, not having to specify which 'they' she meant. 'It was a cure for the sin of vanity, they said – a punishment for the harlotry of letting down my hair to tempt a man in God's house.' Her voice was tight and hard. At the back of her mind she heard the slicing crunch of the shears and felt again the bruising pressure on her upper arms as they held her down. 'Now you see why I could not stay.'

He cursed softly. She thought he muttered something about 'dried-up bitches' but the words were indistinct. Taking the new wimple, she wound it expertly round her head, adding a stylish little twist to one corner and securing the whole with the strip of leather. 'It will grow again,' she said like a general on the battlefield admitting that he has lost the skirmish but has every confidence of winning the war.

'I'm sorry.' There was genuine sympathy and regret in his eyes. 'I did not realise they had treated you so harshly.'

'They called it being cruel to be kind,' Miriel said neutrally as she donned the mantle and fastened it with the plain bone pin provided. Then she bundled up the habit and white wimple. 'These can burn on our fire tonight. From this day forth I am Miriel of Stamford, a respectable widow.' A poor, respectable widow, she thought with distaste as Nicholas cupped his hands to boost her into her mount's saddle.

But not poor for long if she had her way.

Chapter 8

The afternoon was late and wintry when Nicholas and Miriel arrived in Nottingham after two more days on the road. Although their cloaks had kept out the worst of the icy rain, they were chilled and tired, Nicholas in particular. His cough was harsh and his cheeks were flushed. For the last mile he had not spoken.

Miriel said nothing to him, but she was worried. They needed shelter and food in short order. There were several taverns near the castle, including a fine new one established at the time of King Richard's crusade. After a short consideration, Miriel discarded these, aware that they would be full of soldiers from the garrison. Instead, she headed for the old Saxon quarter of the town on the far side of the Corn Market. The streets were mired in the sludge of advancing autumn, not yet cold enough to freeze solidly underfoot. Smoke twisted from the holes in the house thatches and folk were preparing to retire to their hearths. Miriel vaguely remembered that there was a hostelry on a low hill near the town wall. Her grandfather had lodged there once when his preferred place near the castle had been full.

Nicholas coughed into his cloak. 'Do you know where you're going?' he demanded hoarsely. 'Seems to me you're directing us in circles.'

'Of course I do,' she snapped. 'It's just up here.' She ducked her head as a fresh gust of rain buffeted them. 'They have a main dormitory in the loft and sleeping space in the cellars too.' Crossing her fingers on the wet bridle, she hoped that it was where she remembered and that there was sleeping space.

The Bull was a hostelry serving the merchants and traders who entered Nottingham from the direction of Derby and Stafford. It had begun life at the time of the Conquest as a common alehouse displaying a green bush on a pole every time there was a fresh brewing. These days, the inn sign was a permanent painted shield, and the symbol of a bush had been replaced by the more fanciful device of a charging black bull.

Its proprietor was a red-faced Anglo-Norman called Baldwin, with a booming voice that seemed to come from somewhere deep within his enormous drum of a belly.

'Aye, we've room,' he declared stridently to Miriel and Nicholas's utter relief. 'Although if you'd come a fortnight ago, I'd have had to turn you away. Full to the lintels we was with folks visiting the great fair.' He had a lad take the horses away to the stables at the back of the premises and directed an older man to pick up the blanket-bound chest unstrapped from the mule.

'Staying long?' he asked as he kindled a lantern and led the way towards a set of steps cut in the rock at the back of the room.

'No,' Nicholas replied. Now he was out of the wind and cold he had rallied a little. 'My business lies in the South.'

Miriel said nothing. Let the landlord think that Nicholas spoke for both of them. The less explanation, the easier her new life would be. She lowered her eyes and clasped her hands in her sleeves, the image of modest womanhood. There had been plenty of opportunity to practise the pose at St Catherine's.

'I don't envy folk as has to travel on roads to make their living,' Baldwin said in the cheerful tones of one who knew better. 'Give me a roaring fire and home comforts any day.'

'Amen to that,' Nicholas coughed.

If not for the light shed by the lantern, their surroundings would have been pitch black. The temperature was chilly, and the smell of underground stone pervasive. The Bull, like most dwellings in Nottingham, had its own caves hewn from the sandstone on which the town was built.

'Here we are.' Baldwin guided them under an archway

and into a surprisingly spacious room. Cut from the rock face it was shaped like the rounded belly of a drinking cup. There was a hearth with kindling laid ready in one corner, and a smoke hole above. Starting at the curved wall half a dozen mattresses were arranged with an arm's length between each one.

'Stuffed with the best goose down,' Baldwin said proudly. 'No straw. My wife makes 'em to sell. Famous as far away as Doncaster, she is.'

Miriel nodded and gave him a preoccupied smile. The servant set the covered chest down beside one of the mattresses and left. Baldwin kindled another lantern that stood on a shelf chopped out of the gritty rock.

'I know it's not home, but you'll be comfortable, I promise.' Setting his hands on his hips, he looked round with a proprietorial air.

'Just now I could even sleep on a bed of nails,' Nicholas said.

'You travelled far then?' Baldwin enquired.

Nicholas shook his head. 'I've recently been ill.' He smiled bleakly. 'Neither I nor the good mistress would be making this journey unless it was entirely necessary.'

'What you need is a bowl of my wife's beef broth to warm your cockles. Best in four counties. I'll have some sent down.'

Baldwin's boastful pride in his wife was borne out. The mattresses offered seductive, cocooning support and the cheerful blankets covering them were reasonably fresh and not too coarse. A shy serving girl brought them steaming bowls of clear beef broth and a small basket of golden wastel loaves. Miriel wolfed hers in short order. After the bread and water privations of St Catherine's and cold food eaten by the wayside, this was manna indeed. Nicholas, however, had exhausted all his reserves. He ate about a quarter of his broth and one small loaf. Then, beneath Miriel's anxious gaze, he lay down on his pallet and closed his eyes.

Dusting the crumbs from her hands, she approached him and laid her palm across his brow. With relief she noted that it was cool; at least he wasn't feverish. His breathing was slow and deep, with just the slightest catch of chestiness at the end of each inhalation. Now and then his body gave a muscular twitch. Her palm still on his brow, Miriel studied him long and hard. At last she sighed and moved away to light the kindling in the firepit, occupying her hands while her mind pondered.

She had asked him to bring her to Nottingham, and now that he had, there was no reason for them to remain in each other's company. She knew that he wanted rid of her, that she was a burden he could do without. And he was probably right. They knew too much about each other and it was best that they came to a parting of the ways.

She struck a spark from the fire-steel and applied it gently to the kindling. One of the few useful things her mother had taught her was how to lay a fire and make it burn with a clear, bright light. She gave all her attention to the task, but once the flames were licking eagerly at the twigs and branches, her glance strayed to the shrouded chest standing beside Nicholas's pallet. He had more than enough to start afresh, but all she had were the clothes on her back and three pouches of silver if he was disposed to remember their bargain.

Biting on her underlip, Miriel crept to the chest and stealthily unfastened the ropes binding the blanket. She tugged the coarse wool aside and ran her fingers gently over the gorgeous but salt-damaged enamelling. Very softly, very slowly, she raised the lid by its knife-scored hasp. A furtive look over her shoulder reassured her that Nicholas still slept deeply and by the looks of him was unlikely to waken even for the trumpets of Judgement Day. She could do whatever she wanted – abscond with the entire chest if she had such a mind.

The thought warmed her for an instant, but at the same time made her feel soiled. Her conscience would not let her go so far and, besides, there was plenty for them both. How much to take was the question. Enough for her needs, but not so much that she would be plagued by guilt.

She cupped her hand around one of the satisfyingly heavy money bags and the feeling of warmth returned, sensual as a blanket drawn over her body by a lover's hand. Fetching the bolster that she had brought from St Catherine's, she fed it with a dozen pouches of the silver. It was sufficient to establish herself comfortably and still leave him enough for his own designs – whatever they might be.

The reflection of the flames danced on the ivory surface of the second chest, emphasising the carved lines and ornamental goldwork. The object's beauty called to her with a siren song she was unable to resist. She told herself that she would take one more look at the fabulous treasure within – the royal crown of an empress. But when she opened the chest and removed the silk wrappings, just looking was not enough. She held Mathilda's crown in her hand. The power of queenship rippled from the bejewelled gold into her veins. Symbol of authority, symbol that a woman's place was not just by the hearth. Mathilda had gone to war to defend her rights and had counted herself the equal of any man.

Acting on the feeling in the pit of her belly, ignoring the voice that told her what she was doing was dangerous and foolhardy, she shrouded the crown in its purple silk and added it to the pouches in her bolster.

It was well past dawn when Nicholas awoke, although it was impossible for him to tell the time by the darkness in the cave. The room was warmed by the embers in the firepit, which gave off a dull, red glow, just sufficient for him to kindle a flame on a spill of wood and light the lantern. Blearily, he rubbed his eyes and stretched. His mouth was dry and his stomach felt as hollow as an empty barrel. He plucked with distaste at his rumpled clothes and gazed around the womb-like cavern. There was no sign of Miriel except for a slight depression on the mattress nearest the door arch. Thinking no more of it, Nicholas went to find her, the time of day and something to eat.

The door of the hostelry's main room opened on to the street and revealed an overcast morning full of urban bustle: the clop of hooves; the creak of cart wheels; the ring of a farrier's hammer as he shod two oxen across the way. Nicholas sat at one of the oak trestles and rubbed his face.

Baldwin appeared with a jug of ale and more of the wastel loaves, their centres dug out and filled with a stuffing of chopped mushrooms and fried breadcrumbs. Of Miriel there was still no sign, but looking at the hour, Nicholas judged that she was probably out and about, reacquainting herself with the town.

'You feeling better this morn, sir?' enquired Baldwin.

Through a mouthful of bread and mushroom, Nicholas nodded that he was.

''Bout dead on your feet you was last night.' The landlord tucked his linen rag in his belt and watched Nicholas eat. 'The lady said we was to leave you to sleep and not go disturbing you.'

Nicholas took a drink of the yeasty, golden ale, cool from its storage in one of the caves. 'Where is she?'

Baldwin blinked in surprise. 'You don't know?' he said, as if he expected Nicholas to do so.

Nicholas shook his head and felt the first stirrings of unease. 'I have only just awoken, and we did not speak last night.'

Baldwin scratched his head. 'I cannot tell you her whereabouts, sir, only that she left almost before it was light. Paid me fair and square she did, and my wife gave her some of those stuffed loaves for her journey.'

'Her journey?' Nicholas set his cup down, his unease turning to downright misgiving.

'Oh, no.' The landlord tucked his hands into his armpits. Curiosity glinted in his eyes. 'She said this morn as she needed to be on her way, but that you wasn't up to the journey so she'd find another escort. Said it kindly, like. She wasn't complaining behind your back.'

'And she didn't say where she was bound?'

The man shook his head, beginning to look serious as he caught the scent of Nicholas's anxiety. 'No, sir, but I took it to be south like you said yester eve.' He unfolded his arms and placed them on his hips. 'Is there something amiss?'

Nicholas grabbed at his scattered wits. 'No,' he said quickly, 'she has taken me by surprise, that is all.' Which was certainly true.

'Hah, nothing would surprise me about the ways of the gentler sex,' Baldwin snorted. 'You take my wife for instance. When she . . .'

Nicholas jumped to his feet and, ignoring the landlord's attempts at empathy, strode back to the cellar chamber. He tripped over a step in the dark and scraped his knuckles on the walls as he clutched it for support. Cursing, sucking the peeled skin, he limped over to the chest and, snatching off the blanket, flung back the lid.

For a moment he was flooded with relief, but that rapidly turned to suspicion. Everything looked all right on the surface, but it wasn't. Some of the pouches were missing – a substantial minority in fact. And when he checked the ivory box, it was bare.

He sat back on his heels, his breathing ragged and rage cording the sinews of his throat. 'Bitch,' he said through his teeth. 'Conniving, thieving bitch!' The outrage cut like a sword. She had robbed him whilst he lay helpless. She had betrayed the trust that he had not given lightly. He slammed his fist against the side of the chest, further abusing his knuckles. He should have known from the moment she set her eyes and hands on that crown. It had been lust at first sight.

'Sir?' Baldwin said from the archway.

Nicholas threw the blanket over the coffer and spun round. 'Have your lad saddle my horse,' he commanded.

'If there's a dispute between you and the lady, she's got a long start over you.' Baldwin eyed him shrewdly. 'The best road south is out by St Mary's Gate and over the river at Briggford.'

Nicholas nodded stiffly. His heart still thundered in his throat but the full flood of his rage had reduced to a steady trickle of anger. He told himself that when he caught up with her he was going to wring her neck, but the image that filled his mind as he made swift preparations to leave was not of his hands at her throat, but around her waist, and all his energy was expended in kissing her lying, sultry mouth.

CHAPTER 9

Miriel left Nottingham by the south road and made sure that she spoke to the gate guard so that he would remember her. Then she rode around the town walls until she came to the entrance at Cow Lane. Dismounting, she persuaded a farmer heading into the town to take her on his cart, saying that her mount had strained a foreleg. Now her tracks were covered if Nicholas pursued her. The guard on St Mary's Gate had seen her leave. His counterpart at Cow Lane, if questioned, would not associate the woman riding on the cart, a horse tied behind, with the one who was sought.

The subterfuge gave Miriel a certain pleasure, mainly from the exercising of her wits, although her delight in her own cleverness was marred by an element of guilt. She knew that she was not being fair to Nicholas, but then life had never been fair to her. Her grandfather had been right when he said that to succeed you had to be ruthless.

Her next step was to find lodgings. Once the farmer had deposited her in the market place, she sold the horse to a hiring stables and began asking around. Her enquiries harvested three possibilities, two of which proved untenable, being in poorer parts of the town where families were renting sleeping place on their floors to eke out meagre incomes. The third option was close to a bridlesmith's shop on the high ground at the far end of Cow Lane. Although a modest dwelling, it was in good repair and well appointed.

'Belongs to Master Gerbert Woolman,' said the bridlesmith's wife as she unlocked the heavy oak door and showed Miriel the main room with its central hearth, shelves on the wall, and wooden bread cupboard. 'He's our neighbour and we keep the key. He'd likely show you round himself but he's away at a cloth fair. He lives up the hill near the Weekday market.' She gestured with her hand.

Miriel nodded and paced around the room, noting the burnished cauldron suspended over the hearth, and the kindling laid ready together with a hod of dry timber. There were candles in the holders and the walls of wattle and daub gleamed with new lime-wash, of which there was a strong aroma. The place was not as fine as her grandfather's dwelling in Lincoln, but it was better than she had hoped to find at such short notice.

'Belonged to Master Gerbert's brother,' Mistress Bridlesmith said. 'He died a childless widower at Michaelmas, God rest his soul.' She crossed herself.

Miriel respectfully signed her own breast. The house bore no essence of the former occupant's personality. There were no inexplicable cold spots in the room as there had been in the house at Lincoln after her grandfather had died.

'This will suit me admirably,' she said.

'Master Gerbert will talk to you about the rent himself, but I can tell you that he will expect three months' payment in advance.' The woman's tone was dubious as she looked Miriel up and down.

Miriel shrugged. 'I can pay.' She plucked disdainfully at the coarse grey weave of her skirt. 'I wear this simple garb to deter thieves. They do not think it worth their bother to rob a poor widow.'

Mistress Bridlesmith nodded approval of this sensible precaution, but still her expression was wary. 'Forgive me,' she said. 'Are you not a little young to be a widow?'

Miriel felt an uncomfortable jolt of anxiety. Once started on the slippery slope to falsehood, the lies gathered in number and momentum until it was impossible to stop. Perhaps inserting a grain of truth into the fabrication would slow the headlong rush and make her feel less guilty 'Indeed I am too young.' She dabbed at her eyes for effect. 'My husband was one of the soldiers who lost his life when King John's baggage train was drowned in the quicksand.' She sniffed and turned away, but not before she had seen the woman catch her breath and cup her palm to her mouth.

'I don't like to talk about it,' Miriel whispered. 'We had only been married a few weeks.' The thought of Nicholas lying on his pallet in vulnerable sleep did indeed bring a tear to her eye.

'Oh my dear, of course not. I am so sorry for your loss!'

Miriel shook her head as if accepting the comfort but lost for words. Inside, she was full of self-disgust at deceiving this good woman.

'Have you no family to succour you?'

'No,' Miriel said in a waterlogged voice. 'Leastways, none with whom I could live in amity, and my husband had no living kin.' She sat down on the bed bench at the side of the room and averted her head. 'I am very tired. Perhaps if I paid you the rent, I could stay here now?' She hoped that the woman would take the hint with the money and go.

Mistress Bridlesmith, however, had other ideas. Her gossipy, maternal heart was filled with compassion for Miriel's plight, and she insisted that Miriel should come home with her to a warm fire and hot food. Miriel could hardly refuse without seeming graceless, and she needed Mistress Bridlesmith's good opinion to secure her tenancy of the house. Putting on her bravest face, she followed the woman across the narrow street and into another abode similar but larger than the one she was intending to rent. The room was filled with the cosy, warm fug of smoke and human occupation. The bridlesmith and his eldest son were busy in his workshop at the back of the house, but Miriel met the other seven grown and half-grown children that the business supported.

With great pride and tenderness, Mistress Bridlesmith introduced her offspring to Miriel. Their names went in one ear and out of the other, but the children themselves left a lasting impression, not least that there were seven of them and an eighth elsewhere. Although women bore babies in prolific numbers, it was not often that they survived infancy, or their mother the frequent strain of childbirth. The youngest was a toddler still in tail clouts, the eldest an adolescent girl with silky black hair and bright, dark eyes. But what struck

Miriel the hardest was the noisy companionship, the sense of belonging and the value that each member of the family set upon the other. Even when her grandfather had been alive there had been no such atmosphere of comfort or security in their superior stone house in Lincoln. There had been cold pride and duty, dark looks and disapproval. Miriel did not have to pretend her teariness as she was furnished with a cup of mead and offered small, spicy pancakes off the griddle.

Fortunately she did not have to say much, for the Bridlesmith family did all the talking. It would have been beyond her for the nonce to flesh out the bones of her invented past life. Her silence, her game attempts to smile, were seen by Mistress Bridlesmith as evidence of Miriel's grief over losing her husband and, feeling sorry for the young woman, she plied her with more kindness than ever.

To Miriel it was unbearable. 'Forgive me,' she swallowed. 'I must seem very ungrateful, but I need to be alone for a little while.'

'Not at all,' said the woman sympathetically. 'We're a bit much when we're all crowded together, aren't we?' Standing up, she reached for her cloak. 'Come, I'll take you back over. Master Gerbert won't mind you moving in before he's seen you about the rent. I trust you and that's enough for him.' She preened her wimple in a small gesture of pride. 'He says I'm the best judge of character he's ever known; I can spot falsehood a mile away.' She touched Miriel's rigid arm. 'Visit us again when you're feeling better.'

Miriel nodded, thinking that she would never feel better. Simmering in her breast, tightening with pressure, was the urge to scream into their innocent faces that they were being deceived, that she was on the run from a convent with a bag full of twice stolen coin and part of the royal regalia. But she bit her tongue and dammed the scream inside her.

'I know it's hard,' Mistress Bridlesmith said as she unlocked the door of the house and presented Miriel with the key. 'My sister lost her first husband when she was young. You don't think it now but, mark me, you'll recover. You'll marry again and raise a brood like mine!' She gave Miriel an impulsive hug. 'You know where we are if you have need.' Finally and mercifully she left her alone in the neat, cold room, bereft of all warmth and atmosphere.

Miriel flung herself down on the bed bench and burst into tears, pounding the wood, drumming her heels as the pressure released itself in a violent storm, made all the more debilitating because it had been gathering ever since her grandfather's death. She swore, she threshed, she cursed, until nothing remained but a husk – hollow, drained, exhausted. Her face ravaged and tear-streaked, Miriel curled into a ball and fell asleep.

As she slept, Nicholas rode past the neat little house on his bay cob, the mule on a leading rein behind. The young man's face was grim, and it too wore the ravages of recent days.

Miriel woke in the mid-afternoon with a pounding head and dry mouth. She sat on the edge of the bed bench, knuckling the sleep from her sore eyes and taking stock in the aftermath of the storm. She had a strong urge to curl up again and turn her back on the world but she fought it off. Such an attitude made a mockery of all her striving to be free. Life was what she made it; the onus was on her to seize her opportunities and live it to the full.

Leaving the bed, she went outside to the generous back yard with its central focus of a stone well-housing. Three apple trees tossed threadbare branches in the wind, and there was a small vegetable garden still invested with the leeks and cabbages of its former occupant. She drew a bucket of water and splashed her face. The cold made her gasp with shock, but it was revitalising. It was also a reminder of her daily ablutions at St Catherine's and made her realise with a twinge of guilt how fortunate she was.

Having tidied her appearance, Miriel donned her mantle, took the bolster bag, and went from her lodging up the hill to the market place near St Mary's Church. The market had stood in the same place since Saxon times and, despite the building of a castle on the other side of town and the establishment of a larger market square down the hill, still bustled with activity. Now, with dusk due in an hour, the stallholders were packing up their wares. Many had already departed, making a good start before the city gates shut for the night.

Miriel walked among the remaining booths and managed to buy the necessities of bread and cheese for her next meal, and a small crock of honey for breaking her fast on the morrow. From an apothecary, she obtained a pot of stavesacre ointment to rid herself of the body lice which had accompanied the grey gown to its new owner.

The haberdasher had almost finished stowing his wares, but the flash of coin persuaded him to unpack his braids so that Miriel could select two belt lengths and a pair of silver strap ends. She also bought needles, thread and shears.

The rag stall, run by a wizened little stick of a woman, was still open for business and, after some hard bargaining, Miriel obtained a woollen working gown in a becoming shade of warm russet.

'Good dress that,' the hag said, sucking on her few remaining teeth. 'Belonged to an alabaster merchant's wife, God rest her soul.'

Miriel shuddered. Another dead woman's garment. She could not wait until she had fine clothes of her own again.

'This un's not bad either.' The old woman pulled a gown of expensive dark blue-grey from the bottom of the pile. 'Got a cinder burn on the front, but you could patch it,' she added.

The garment was in the fitted style with the flared skirts and hanging sleeves favoured by wealthy women who had servants to do all the fire-tending and cooking. Not practical, but good for making an impression.

'Is the previous owner dead too?' Miriel asked, pulling a face.

The woman snorted with amused contempt. 'Nay, mistress. If you're finicky about such matters, you can rest easy wi' this un. Belonged to the sheriff's wife, but she had no use for it once it got burned. Gave it to her maid but she had no use for it neither – you can't stir a cauldron wi' sleeves like that, so she sold it on to me.'

'How much do you want?'

The woman named an incredible sum. With the instinct

that her grandfather had laughed at and nurtured, Miriel settled down with pleasure to bargain.

A little later, flushed with victory, gowns both blue and russet over her arm, Miriel sought among the rapidly diminishing stalls for a draper. When she found one, he was almost ready to leave, but she smiled and fluttered her eyelashes, persuading him to unpack his linens so that she could buy enough for two undergowns, and finally a length of fine grey wool with a fir-green thread running through it for an overdress. Her eye lingered wistfully on a bolt of soft plum-red, a colour almost identical to her favourite gown in Lincoln, but she curtailed the impulse to buy. She was a widow, and for the nonce must make do with sombre robes and colours.

As the sky darkened and an evening chill stole up from the river, Miriel made her short way home. The smells of cooking fires and candle-light filled her nose. She was part of a steady stream of people turning hearthwards, and it gave her a warm feeling of sharing, of not being entirely alone.

Once inside the small house, she set about lighting the fire and tipping water into the cauldron. Humming to herself, she lit the candles in the iron holders. While waiting for the water to heat, she ate the cheese and half the bread and sorted through her purchases. The russet dress would do for everyday wear, the blue-grey for more formal occasions. Miriel was deft with a needle and the cinder burn could easily be darned. The linen undertunics would not take long to fashion and she could employ a sempstress to make her a handsome gown from the grey and green.

With a small sigh she looked round the bare little room, devoid of all the trappings that had once made it a home. There was not the slightest echo of the former occupant unless it lingered in the neatness and order that spoke of the bare bones of a bachelor existence without the clutter of a large family. She smiled bleakly at the thought. All that had changed were the gender and age of the tenant. Then she shook her head. On the morrow she would buy a mattress for the bed bench and a colourful blanket. She would put hangings on the walls and buy green-glazed pottery for the shelf and the house would be a home, not a monastic cell.

Now came the moment she had been savouring. Miriel drew the bolster case into her lap and with tender reverence took the crown from its purple shroud. The gold reflected the fire glow and the gemstones danced with dark light, offsetting the sea-shimmer of the pearls. Miriel was tempted to set the crown on her head, but a shiver of superstition prevented her. Only a queen had the right, and only then by the grace of God. But it was still a symbol of the power a woman had once wielded and it fascinated her.

The cloud of steam rising from the cauldron fetched her out of her reverie. With great care she replaced the crown in its silk shrouding, put it in the bolster, and concealed it beneath the two dresses. Then she set about her ablutions. The hated grey gown was tossed in a corner. For a moment she considered burning the thing, but decided to give it the benefit of the doubt first by pummelling it in scalding water laced with stavesacre ointment. At the worst, the dress would shrink, but since it hung on her like a bed curtain, that would be no bad result.

When she was naked, Miriel took her new shears, and cut a square from the length of linen she had bought. She shuddered to see the rash of louse bites all over her body, with roseate congregations in her armpits and groin. Dipping the cloth in the water which by now was almost too hot to bear, she began to scour herself.

Beneath the vigorous motion of her hand, her body turned from goose-flesh white to rosy pink. At the back of her mind dwelt the notion that she was shedding her old lives with her old skin and taking on a new identity where she would make the rules. She scrubbed the crevices of her groin, her fingers touching without thought or modesty the place that the nuns said was sinful, equated with the mouth of hell in the view of many priests. The place tingled and her belly tightened, but she did not linger to explore the sensation. Despite the fire, the room was still cold from weeks without occupation and she had yet to wash the stubble on her scalp that passed for hair.

Her head was deep in the well bucket and her ears were full of the sound of her own breathing and the rasp of her fingers against her soapy scalp, so she did not hear the soft tap on the door, nor a moment later a key turning in the oiled lock.

An elderly man took one step over the threshold, then stopped and stared, his eyes almost bulging from their sockets and the veins swelling in his throat at the sight of the young woman's slender, naked body, her breasts wobbling as she massaged her scalp. Runnels of water streaked towards her erect pink nipples and dripped off the end. Against his thigh, his manhood stirred in a response that he had almost forgotten. 'Jesu,' he said hoarsely, not knowing whether to advance or retreat.

Alerted by the sudden gust of cold air on her body, Miriel raised her head to peer through stinging, half-closed eyes, and leaped to her feet, screaming.

'No, mistress, no!' Hastily he closed the door and fanned his hands in a gesture of negation. 'Pray do not fear. I am Master Gerbert Woolman, your landlord. Mistress Bridlesmith told me about you, and I did but stop by to introduce myself. I did not think that you would be . . . would be . . .' He gestured and swallowed, his complexion a dusky crab-red.

Gulping with shock, teeth chattering, Miriel snatched up the length of linen and wrapped it around her nakedness. 'Why didn't you knock?' she demanded in a voice half strangled with fear and fury. She cast about for a weapon and with her free hand grasped and brandished the candlestand. The flame streamed back at her in a soot-edged ribbon of heat.

'I did, mistress, I swear I did. You must have heard me.' He was breathing as swiftly as Miriel, his white beard shuddering with the hard pulse that beat in his throat. She judged him to be about sixty years old with the complacent paunch of good living girding his belt and filling out a tunic of very expensive bright blue wool. 'I pray you, put that candlestand down. I mean you no harm.'

Miriel kept a firm grip on the wrought iron. Terror had given way to outrage, but the word 'landlord' prevented her from attacking him with it. 'Do you want your rent now?' she enquired with icy civility, her fist clenching in the folds of material across her breasts.

He swallowed and, shaking his head, backed towards the door. 'No, no, the morrow will suffice. Indeed, I am deeply sorry to have disturbed you thus, mistress.'

Miriel said nothing, maintaining her rigid pose until he closed the door behind him and turned the key in the lock. Only then, shivering with cold and shock, did she return the candlestand to its niche and collapse on the bed bench. He was the owner of this house and it was obvious that he would have a second key, but until now she had not considered the fact. He could come and go at his will and that violated her sense of security. He might be old, but that did not mean he was harmless. Slowly, hands trembling, Miriel dried herself and resolved that on the morrow she would have a bar fitted across the door so that he would not surprise her again.

Arriving home, Gerbert Woolman closed his own door and leaned against it panting, while his heart ran wild and threatened to leap out of his body. He shouldn't have walked so briskly up the rest of the hill, he shouldn't have let his thoughts shake him so much; it wasn't good for a man of his years. But his mind's eye would not relinquish the image of the woman's slim, naked form, the water streaming down her breasts, nor the vision of her facing him in outrage, draped like a pagan goddess, her features sculpted and pure.

Gerbert pressed his hand to his pattering chest and lurched across to the oak sideboard where his servant Samuel had left out a pitcher of wine and a gilt goblet. With trembling hand, Gerbert poured himself a measure and gulped it down without time to savour the bouquet and rich, red taste.

When Eva Bridlesmith had told him that there was a new tenant in his brother's house, a young widow, he had not been prepared for how young, how nubile. Her flesh was as taut as a virgin's; she had never borne or suckled a child, he would wager on that. His wife, dead these past five years, had been a buxom armful at their marriage, but as the years of child-bearing took their toll, her body had become as slack and shapeless as a sack of cabbages. He had not loved her in the sense that the troubadour's sang of love, but it had been a lifetime bond of companionship and toil, and he missed her. He missed the feminine presence in his household, the little touches that went overlooked by Samuel, no matter how diligent and well meaning the servant was.

The wine coursed through his veins, warming and soothing. Gerbert began to feel a little better and eased himself down in the carved chair beside his hearth. Rubbing his aching knees, he wondered why her hair had been shorn – perhaps a sign of grief at her husband's passing. He had known women do that before. Whatever the reason, it had given her an air of gamine vulnerability that had touched his heart and quickened his loins.

He did not have to touch his crotch to know that he was flaccid now, but still a spark of potential remained, waiting to be kindled anew. He wanted to know more about 'Mistress Miriel'. Where had she come from? How was she going to support herself now that her soldier husband was dead? As her landlord, he had a right to know and every opportunity to find out. Gerbert flicked his finger against the side of the goblet and listened to the satisfying ring of the metal. On the morrow he would take her a gift of wine and an apology. That much decided to his satisfaction, he relaxed in his chair and his head began to nod.

CHAPTER 10

Gradually Miriel settled into her new life in Nottingham. She bought her wall hangings and green-glazed pottery, her mattress and a blanket striped in red and green napped wool. She had a carpenter fit a stout draw-bar on the inside of her door so that never again would she be surprised in the manner of that first evening. When she was sure of her privacy, she dug a hole in the corner of the main room, and in a plain, wooden casket, buried six bags of the silver and Mathilda's crown. Then she stamped down the earth, covered the place with floor straw, and stood her new clothing coffer on top.

The autumn season advanced and darkened into winter. It was a time to embrace the hearth, to hibernate and wait out the twilit days and miserable weather. Despite the chill, the heavy rain and the noisome torrents running down the streets to make a stinking quagmire at the foot of St Peter's Gate, Miriel felt blessed. At least here she had the comfort of her own fire, a varied hot diet, and decent, warm garments. No one dragged her out of bed in the middle of the night. No one made her perch on a hard wooden bench in a freezing chapel to pray for hours on end. No one slashed her knuckles for tardiness. She could live as she pleased.

Although the memories of St Catherine's remained vivid, each day of freedom made them seem less real and more like a nightmare from which she had awoken. The idea of the experience being a nightmare was increased by occasional troubling dreams of Sister Euphemia chasing her across the marshland, the willow switch threatening in her fist. The chase went on for ever, and although Miriel was never caught, she had to run as fast as she could just to keep the distance between them. Sometimes Nicholas would surge up from a hole in the ground, his arms outspread to trap her. She would awaken with a scream of terror, her body streaming with sweat and her heart thundering as if she had indeed been running for her life.

During the day she seldom thought of St Catherine's, but she did wonder about Nicholas and how he would react if they ever came face to face again. She imagined the conversation, trying out different scenes and emotions, from killing rage to forgiveness and admiration. The former was the more likely she suspected, and therefore did not dwell on it very often. It was more pleasant to linger over imaginary but unlikely words of conciliation and praise.

Admiration was certainly not lacking from other quarters. Several bachelors in the neighbourhood had already paid their respects to the new young widow. Miriel kept them at bay with cool indifference and the declaration that she could not possibly consider entertaining male company with her reputation to consider and her beloved husband so recently in his grave.

'You are very wise, my dear,' said Gerbert when he came on one of his regular visits, not so much to collect rent as to enjoy the company denied to his younger peers. 'They pursue you out of lust for your possessions and your body.' His skin flushed darkly as he pronounced the opinion.

Miriel was amused if a little irritated by his concern for her welfare. She sensed that his indignation on her behalf would have been considerably less had she been longer in the tooth.

'They will just have to lust, for I have no intention to remarry,' she said lightly as she delved in the basket of evergreen bought in the market that morning. Christmas was on the threshold. In her grandfather's house they had always celebrated the season with holly, ivy and fir, a huge yule log garnishing the hearth.

'Hold this.' She gave Gerbert a swath of ivy. Taking a small hammer and a hobnail, she pinned the foliage to the wall. The wool merchant reminded her in a way of her grandfather, being of a similar age, with the same soft white beard and rotund girth. He saw the world through an old man's eyes as her grandfather had done, was finicky and pedantic, and given to liking his own way. But Gerbert was less cynical than her grandfather, and his character had an eager, child-like quality that Miriel found endearing.

Following the embarrassment of their first meeting, their relationship had progressed on a steadier footing. Gerbert had presented her with a flagon of wine and an apology. Miriel had accepted graciously, agreeing that they would start afresh. Now Gerbert visited her at least once a fortnight to ensure that everything was in order, and usually he would bring a small gift – some wine, a box of spice, wax candles.

Miriel was not blind to his motives. The trick was to keep him friendly but at arm's length. It was a delicate juggling act that took all the skills she had developed over the years with her grandfather.

He stood back to view the effect of the evergreen. 'But surely you are too young to remain a widow the rest of your life?'

Miriel shrugged. 'Why should I not?' She made a few small tweaks of adjustment to the decoration. 'What is there to be gained from marrying again except a big belly and a husband who will dispose of my wealth in one gulp and make me his chattel?'

Gerbert's stare was so comical that Miriel had to suppress a giggle. She knew that her forthrightness unsettled him. He often told her that he could not understand how someone so young and gently bred could talk as plainly as a soldier in a tavern. But it didn't stop him coming back for more.

'You must have a very sour view of marriage to speak thus,' he said gruffly. 'Do I assume that you were unhappy with your husband?'

Now it was Miriel's turn to stare while she sifted through things she had told him on previous occasions and hoped that she would not contradict herself. 'That is my business,' she said primly.

'Very well then.' Gerbert rumpled his hair and shuffled his feet. He cleared his throat and looked at her under his brows like a dog begging a morsel. 'If you have no other plans, mayhap you would care to spend the Christmas feast in my household instead of dining alone.'

Miriel shook her head. 'That would not be—'

Gerbert raised his hand. 'L-lest you think I am being f-forward, we will not b-be alone,' he said, stumbling over his words in his haste to assure her of his honest intentions. 'It is to be a gathering of friends and acquaintances – other m-merchants and their wives. My god-daughter and her husband will be there too.'

Despite herself, Miriel's lips twitched at the earnestness of his expression. 'No hungry bachelors then?'

'Heaven forfend!' He scowled, not in the least amused.

The twitch of Miriel's lips became a full smile. 'Then, on that condition, I accept.'

The day of the Christmas feast arrived and Miriel dressed with care in the blue-grey gown that had once belonged to the sheriff's wife. She had concealed the cinder burn with a scrollwork of embroidery and had stitched a new trim of silvery silk on the sleeves and hem, thereby making the dress individually her own.

She covered her head with a wimple of sombre grey linen, secured by a band of twisted silver wire. Miriel had never explained her shorn hair to Gerbert, only hinted that it was a deeply private matter. She knew that he must be curious, but he had never stepped over the line to ask and she certainly was not going to encourage him. The sooner her cropped locks grew back into a full, shining braid, the better.

Donning her winter cloak with its cosy sheepskin lining, she secured the circular pin and set off up the hill towards St Mary's Gate. Gerbert's house stood on the brow of the hill close to the church. It was a fine, large dwelling built in the time of the second Henry, with a wood shingle roof and storage barn facing inwards to a small courtyard and a stable cut out of the rock.

The oak door with its ornate wrought-iron work and griffin's head knocker was opened to Miriel by Gerbert's servant, Samuel. Bowing, he ushered her into the spacious main room and took her cloak. A long trestle table covered in a cloth of shimmering red damask stood at one side of the hearth. The limed walls were brightened with colourful embroideries and from the rafters hung brass lamps, their soft light smudging the room with warm gold. Astringent scents of pine and juniper mingled pleasantly with the domestic aromas of fire, smoke and mouth-watering wafts of roasting meat.

The other guests were already seated at the trestle, talking and laughing like old friends. As Miriel hesitated, Gerbert rose from his place at the head of the table and, exclaiming in welcome, beckoned her to an empty chair at his right-hand side.

Not without a little misgiving, Miriel advanced upon the gathering. Gerbert kissed her cheek and bade her be seated, pleasure shining in his eyes as he introduced her proudly to his guests. Murmuring polite responses, smiling fixedly, Miriel wondered if they were all assessing her, marking Gerbert for a fool and herself a mercenary bitch with an eye to his wealth.

There was a wine merchant and his plump wife whose every finger was adorned in heavy gold rings, proclaiming her husband's wealth. Beside them, accompanied by both wife and mother-in-law, was a stone carver whose alabaster effigies were sought after throughout England. On his other side sat a florid-faced draper who dealt in Flemish cloth, and a thin, sharp-eyed woman called Alice Leen who was a weaver's widow and could have been any age between fifty and four score. Her spine was as rigid as an ash pole, and her mouth as tight as a new drawstring purse.

The final guest at the table was a handsome man of middle years. His wiry blond hair had the merest salting of white at temple and nape and his greenish eyes were seamed with attractive creases at the corners. Gerbert introduced him to Miriel as 'Robert Willoughby. My god-daughter's husband and heir to my trade.'

Robert Willoughby smiled at the introduction and inclined his head to Miriel. 'But not its inheritor for many years yet, I hope,' he said gracefully.

Gerbert snorted. 'Watch him, lass. His smooth tongue's his finest asset.' He spoke in jest but there was an edge to his words.

Willoughby shot the older man an amused glance. 'The finest of many assets,' he answered lightly.

'Modesty not being one of them.' Gerbert looked slightly irritated. 'It is a great pity your wife could not attend the feast today. I haven't seen her since Michaelmas.'

The humour left Robert's gaze. 'But for an ague, Juetta would be here. You know how much she loves your Christmas gathering.' He bowed to Miriel. 'I know she would have enjoyed meeting you, Mistress Stamford.'

'And I her,' Miriel said politely. 'Perhaps another time.'

'I am sure that could be arranged.' Robert's smile dazzled out, causing Gerbert to frown.

Over roasted squabs in green herb sauce accompanied by spiced frumenty and apples stuffed with dates and breadcrumbs, Gerbert silently fumed while Robert Willoughby talked of the wool trade upon which he and Gerbert had built their prosperity. 'We contract for fleeces from manors and abbeys, and sell them on, some to Flemish merchants, some to town weavers like Alice here to make homespun yarn and cloth.' The wry humour flashed again. 'We go wool-gathering, so to speak.'

Mellowed by the excellent wine, Miriel's caution slipped. 'I know the wool trade well,' she said. 'I come from a family of master weavers, and my grandfather used to select and buy our own fleeces.'

'Indeed?' Robert leaned on his elbows and gave her his full attention. 'So which, in your opinion, are the best sheep to use?'

'Well, that would depend on whether you are intending to full your cloth or not. If you are, then you need a short wool sheep, and fleeces from ewes rather than rams. If not, then Lincolnshire sheep are the best.'

Robert listened and nodded. So did Alice Leen, her dour expression brightening with curiosity and challenge. 'I buy Leicester fleeces myself,' she said.

'That too is good wool,' Miriel replied diplomatically. But

it was not of the superlative quality that her grandfather had insisted upon.

Alice asked her some hard and pertinent questions about the weaving process. Feeling as if she was on trial, and a little resentful, Miriel answered with opinion and spirit. Respect grew in Alice's eyes and the drawstring line of her mouth relaxed somewhat. 'You still have a deal to learn, young woman,' she said sternly. 'Some things can only be gained by experience.'

'Of which I hope to gain more,' Miriel replied with a tactful smile.

'You did not mention to me that you had connections with the wool trade,' Gerbert muttered in a disgruntled tone. He had invited her to this feast because he wanted to show her off to his colleagues and friends, to introduce her into their society so that she would become a part of it. He had not expected matters to develop so quickly, particularly her rapport with his handsome partner.

Miriel raised her brows at his tone. 'You never asked me, and it never cropped up in our conversations.'

Gerbert tried to smile, but the result was weak. 'I wonder what other gems of experience you're keeping to surprise me.' The remark was supposed to be light, but a weight of possessiveness dragged it down and caused a moment's awkward silence.

Miriel looked at him. She could feel a blush rising to heat her face. 'Think how dull life would be without surprises.'

'Mayhap, but there is also comfort in routine, and much to be said for it.'

'It depends upon the routine,' Miriel murmured, thinking of the daily grind at St Catherine's.

Gerbert compressed his lips and retreated, but Miriel could still feel the weight of his disapproval. Soon after that, the guests began to depart. Alice Leen invited Miriel to visit her workshop below the castle rock, and Miriel was surprised to find herself accepting with alacrity. Robert Willoughby took his own leave by kissing Miriel's hand after the manner of a courtier.

'I meant what I said. You must come and meet Juetta.'

'I will look forward to it,' Miriel answered warmly.

When it was her turn to go, Gerbert caught her sleeve as she was thanking him for his hospitality.

'Have a care where Master Willoughby is concerned,' he muttered. 'I am not sure that his intentions towards you are entirely honourable.'

Miriel laughed. 'Master Willoughby might be handsome and eloquent of speech, but I am no foolish maiden to let such things bedazzle me.'

Gerbert gave a wriggle of embarrassment. 'It is just that I would not see him take advantage of you. It shames me that you should have been pursued when I promised you a haven at my table.'

'He took no advantage,' Miriel said, a little impatient now. 'I enjoyed our conversation and now he has gone home to his wife.' She stepped firmly over the threshold into the biting air. Behind her the draper and his family were waiting to bid their farewells. Gerbert could not continue to remonstrate without seeming to make a fuss.

'Aye, well, take heed of my advice, mistress,' he said as he bowed her on her way.

Miriel responded with a curtsey and a smile but no undertaking that she would do so.

A bitter winter progressed by slow stages into a late, rain-washed spring, and then blossomed into a glorious early summer. Miriel's hair reached her jawline and when she combed it at night, she could see in her silver-backed hand mirror that it was long enough to shimmer if she tossed her head.

Life was good and improving, almost as if the length of her hair was the yardstick by which she measured her fortunes. She used some of King John's silver to buy thirty Lincolnshire ewes and a fine Lindsey ram, individually choosing each sheep for the quality of its fleece. They grazed on rich meadow pasture across the Trent which she rented from the Lord of Briggford, and she employed a shepherd to tend them. Gerbert offered to buy their wool come shearing time, but Miriel put him off. Flanders was crying out for good English fleeces. She knew that she could turn a tidy profit if she sold them on but her intention was to make her own cloth.

Visits to Alice Leen's weaving sheds filled her with nostalgia. Walking between the tall, upright looms, her fingers twitched with the need to handle a shuttle, to feel again the prickly yarn as she wove it between the warp threads and beat it down with a comb. To see the pattern emerge, diamond twill, striped tabby, three-shed twill. When asked, Alice grudgingly gave Miriel permission to weave a row. Although the old woman had merely grunted and folded her arms at Miriel's effort, a steady respect, if not friendship, had sprung from that moment. Recently Alice had offered Miriel the use of a loom in her workshop and Miriel had accepted with delight. It didn't matter that it was Alice's oldest upright piece and not a patch on the magnificent Flemish broadloom to which Miriel was accustomed in Lincoln. It was a start and she intended to make it worth while. Now all she needed was the wool from her sheep.

Gerbert continued to visit Miriel regularly. She was polite but distant with him, making it clear that while she appreciated him as her landlord and a man of standing in the community, she would not brook his interference in her life. She declined further invitations to dine with him, hoping that eventually he would take the hint, but if anything his persistence increased, especially when his god-daughter died of a congestion of the lungs on the eve of St Benedict. Gerbert seemed to think that Miriel was going to throw herself incontinently into Robert Willoughby's arms while the poor woman was still warm in her grave.

'And that is ridiculous,' Miriel said with exasperation to Eva Bridlesmith as the two women walked among the stalls of the Weekday market, baskets on their arms. 'I feel sorry for Master Willoughby, nothing more.'

'Aye, poor man.' Eva shook her head. 'It's the second time he's had to bury a wife. I well mind his first one. Died o' the sweating sickness in the year that King John came to the crown. I remember because it was the year I wed my Martin.'

Miriel made a sympathetic sound. After the Christmas

feast she had paid a visit to Robert Willoughby and his wife Juetta. The woman had been a pale skeleton, wasted, frail and suffering. It was too late to discover if they had anything in common, if they would have liked each other, but Miriel had felt great pity and discomfort for Juetta Willoughby waiting to die and for Robert watching her . . . as he must have watched his first wife too.

'Master Gerbert is only concerned for your welfare, you know,' Eva remarked with a sidelong glance. 'He has ever been one to bluster and worry. Besides,' she added with a mischievous smile, 'he's quite smitten by you.'

Miriel pulled a face. 'I know.' She nudged Eva Bridlesmith crossly. 'And it is no cause for laughter. I respect his years and his honesty as my landlord, but I cannot bear the way that he watches my every move and then lectures me as if I was five years old.' Her voice took on an exasperated note. 'Any woman with eyes in her head can see that Robert Willoughby is handsome. I like him and I feel sorry for him, but that does not mean I am lovesick.'

Eva lifted a large iron frying pan from a stall of similar implements and studied it with a keen eye. 'I would be,' she said. 'Do you think this is big enough?' She turned the pan this way and that.

'Pigswill!' Miriel snapped. 'You and Martin are thicker than two peas in a pottage. Anyway,' she sniffed, 'I'm not you.'

Eva made a non-committal sound. She tapped the base of the pan with her fingertips. Then she said, 'There are many women who would give their eye teeth to be in your position. Gerbert's wealthy. You could marry into a fortune.'

'I don't want a fortune,' Miriel snapped.

'Oh, you have one of your own then?' Eva tucked the frying pan under her arm and prepared to haggle a price with the stallholder.

'I have enough for my needs without yielding my freedom to a man three times my age,' Miriel said through compressed lips. 'I have no need of a man – whatever his age – to make me complete.'

Eva shrugged and shook her head. 'I cannot help thinking that you would make a good abbess,' she jested.

Colour blazed in Miriel's cheeks. She did not know whether to lose her temper or laugh. 'The Church is not for me either,' she replied in a rather choked voice.

'Then what do you want?' There was genuine bafflement in Eva's eyes, for her own idea of fulfilment was keeping the hearth for her husband and their robust brood of children.

'Nothing,' Miriel said tersely, 'except to live as I choose without being pestered to change my ways.'

Eva glanced heavenwards to show that she thought Miriel impossible, but abandoned the subject and settled down with enjoyment to bargain.

Returning home, Miriel decided that in the afternoon she would ride out to visit her small flock. She needed to clear her head of Eva's half-serious teasing and focus on her own plans, which involved Gerbert not one whit. She could make her way in the world without a husband – no matter how rich.

Unbidden, the image of Nicholas de Caen entered her mind: the sea-glint eyes, the dark hair with its hidden burnish of gold, the slanting grin. Her body responded to the image with a treacherous melting, while her emotions drifted from guilt, through longing, to self-irritation. She had made her bed, she would lie in it, and in the end it was better by far to lie with Nicholas's ghost than with Nicholas himself. All the same, she wondered how he was faring and what he was doing with his new wealth. Did he think of her with other than contempt or hatred? She turned from the thought with a shiver. It was a Pandora's box best left well alone.

CHAPTER 11

SPRING 1217

She rode at anchor, the grey waves of Southampton Water lapping her strakes and a warm spring wind ruffling the canvas of her furled sail. Her high freeboard and stocky build set her apart from the lighter nefs surrounding her. Although she was not as sleek or elegant as her sea-wolf companions, Nicholas was besotted with her.

'What do you think?' asked Rohan de Voss, the master ship-builder who had sailed the cog from her birth place on the banks of the Schelde to her new English home.

Nicholas shook his head, lost for words.

'She sails well – very stable, good, deep draught.' Pride enriched de Voss's heavy Flemish accent. 'We had a squall the first night out and she rode it like a dancer. I have built many fine vessels in my time, but she is the best so far.'

'I can believe that,' Nicholas said huskily and trod up the gangplank and on to her deck. Unlike the lighter nefs with their Scandinavian dragon prows, their sleek, shallow lines and their side rudders, the *Pandora* was a cog of substantial size, designed to transport cargo in speed and safety. Her hull was short, her sides high, and her rudder centre-lined at the stern. The best vessels and the most experienced boat-builders were found in Holland, Flanders and the Baltic where the cog was extensively used. In England, the cog's popularity was growing by the year, but the *Pandora* was still enough of a novelty to draw curious merchants and ship-owners to her mooring.

Nicholas prowled the entire length, breadth and depth of his new ship. His father's vessel, the *Péronnelle*, had been a large nef with an open deck and a keel that cut through the water like a knife. The *Pandora* would slice the sea with the power of a heavy sword.

'She'll take about a hundred tons in her hold,' Rohan said as Nicholas leaped down into the dark cavity beneath the deck boards. 'Wool, you said you were hoping to carry.'

Nicholas shrugged. 'Wool, wine, whatever pays well for her passage.'

Rohan stroked his beard. 'Sometimes it takes a while for a new ship's master to build custom.'

'Especially one young and untried,' Nicholas said with a smile and a sidelong glance. 'That is what you were going to say?'

Rohan spread his hands, displaying fleshy, work-callused palms. 'You are only right in the young. I know that, as the son of Alain de Caen, you are anything but untried.'

Nicholas turned away to inspect a nailed timber.

Rohan studied him shrewdly. 'My father built the *Péronnelle* for him. I was sorry to hear that he had died.' He hesitated. 'Even the most seaworthy ship and skilled captain can fall victim to a rogue wave.' He spoke on a slightly rising note as if asking a question.

Nicholas snorted. 'My father fell victim to other men, not the sea,' he said without looking round.

'Pirates, you mean?' Rohan nodded. 'I thought it strange at the time.'

'You could call them that.' Nicholas pushed his way past Rohan and went back up on deck. He breathed deeply of the brackish, grey air and watched a gull settle on top of the mast. The weather had been glass-calm when the *Péronnelle* had supposedly foundered. No trace of cargo or crew had ever been found; no word or hint had broken a single bubble on the surface.

'Come,' he said abruptly to Rohan, 'let's drink to the *Pandora*'s success.' He headed toward the gangplank. 'Time enough on the morrow to assemble a crew and sail her out.'

Rohan followed him with the rolling gait of a seaman. 'Why *Pandora*?'

'It's from Greek legend,' Nicholas answered with a sudden

narrowing of his eyes. The ship that haunted his dreams still bore the name of *Miriel* but he had no intention of commemorating such folly in solid wood. After what had happened in Nottingham, he was doing his best to forget the lying vixen. A search had proved fruitless. It was as if she had vanished off the face of the earth – which she could well afford to do with all the wealth at her disposal. His anger and bitterness had made it difficult, but eventually Nicholas had dismissed her as one of life's lessons learned the hard way.

He was well known in the wharf tavern and he and Rohan were quickly shown to a clean trestle and furnished with a pitcher of Gascon wine. An ageing merchant with whom he was on nodding terms acknowledged him from a neighbouring trestle with a raised cup and a smile. His luscious companion, most definitely not his wife, gave Nicholas a bold stare then looked modestly down. Nicholas briefly admired the tilt of her nose, the ripe curve of her lips and the magnificent swell of her bosom. Then he ruthlessly dismissed her from his mind. Ships were far less trouble than women.

'To *Pandora*.' Rohan raised the toast.

'The *Pandora*,' Nicholas echoed.

Rohan cupped his hands around his drink and looked at Nicholas. 'Are you not afraid that she too will fall victim to sea-raiders? Since your father died, the problem has increased apace. With this war between Louis of France and your young King's regents, the northern seas are infested with thieves and profiteers. That I arrived in Southampton whole owes much to the roll of fortune's dice.'

'I know there is danger,' Nicholas said soberly. 'She will not sail from harbour unarmed. I intend to man her with a full complement of footsoldiers and archers.'

'You will need to carry a rich cargo to offset your costs,' Rohan said with a hint of scepticism.

Nicholas knew that the shipwright was vastly curious as to the source of his wealth. The de Caen family, even at the height of their fortunes, had only been moderately prosperous, certainly not rich enough to afford a cog like the *Pandora*. He lifted his cup. 'Don't worry; I'll make my way in the world.' He fished a coin from his pouch to pay for the wine. A stylised portrait of King John's head was stamped into the silver. 'I only wish my family was here to see me do it,' he said grimly.

That night he slept aboard, rolled in his cloak on the crenellated platform above the stern rudder. The gentle creak of her timbers as she rocked on the water was soothing. The stars were white gemstones in the night sky. Nicholas counted them off in a sleepy murmur: Orion with his belt of crystal studs; the Plough; the Great Bear; all as familiar to him as the breath in his body. They were friends to be sought on a midnight ocean.

When he slept, it was deeply, and he did not dream.

A handful of costly gold rings shone on the coffer. Neatly folded beside them was a gown of blue linen, an exquisitely embroidered chemise and a pair of yellow silk hose with matching garters. Kneeling naked on the bed, red hair tucked behind her ears, Magdalene kneaded the old man's crêpy flesh with her strong, white fingers until he groaned with pleasure. She had been his mistress for three years and she knew what he liked.

'Edwin, who were those two men in the tavern?' she asked as she worked on his knotted shoulders.

'Which two?'

'You know, you raised your cup to them.'

Edwin turned his head on his pillowed arms. 'I assume you're interested in the younger one?' he said in an amused voice.

'Don't tease.' The tips of her manicured nails dug into his flesh, and he gave a luxurious wriggle.

'Sweetheart, you'll make me hard doing that.'

Magdalene compressed her lips on the retort that it would be a miracle. Edwin needed his illusions and she was all part of the pretence. It was their bargain, and her livelihood. Rather this than gutting fish any day.

At fourteen she had been a fisherman's daughter dwelling in poverty when the lord of the manor had chanced by on an inspection with his bailiff. An hour later she was no longer a virgin, but richer by the fortune of three silver pennies. The next day Lord Engram had returned for her and she became his permanent mistress. She never wearied of the post. Indeed, she set out to keep it for she knew the alternative. Having worn beautiful clothes and fine jewellery, having eaten white bread off a silver platter, she would rather have died than return to her former life. When Engram had a fatal fall from his horse four years later, she immediately sought and found a replacement in Edwin. He wasn't a baron, but he was wealthy, she liked him and the only demands he made were for the benefit of public show and private reassurance. 'It was no more than curiosity,' she said with a shrug.

'I'm sure it was. Lower, girl, ah, that's it.' He made slow, thrusting motions with his buttocks.

Magdalene arched her brows. He was certainly labouring the virility tonight.

'He's from Normandy,' Edwin said through the pillow of his crossed arms. 'Goes by the name of Nicholas de Caen, and he's just bought a cog that's the envy of every ship-owner in the port. That is all that anyone knows of him.'

Magdalene massaged the small of Edwin's back, and thought of the young man, the firm skin and taut muscles, the fierce, interesting features.

'Oh, and he's not one for the women,' Edwin added drily, then chuckled. 'That's stopped your chicks from hatching, hasn't it?'

Magdalene's disappointment was balanced by a surge of relief. Wary of jeopardising her security, she had thus far resisted the temptation offered by younger men, but she liked the look of Nicholas de Caen, and he must be rich to afford a ship like a cog. 'He likes men, you mean?' She wondered if his companion in the tavern was his lover.

Edwin rolled over. His paunch curved like a whale's back, complete with blow hole. In its shadow his genitals cowered on his thigh. 'I mean he doesn't have time for either, and it would take more than you to convince him, sweetheart.' Grasping her hand, he placed it on his flaccid penis. 'You could always convince me instead. I might not rise to the occasion like some of them, but even an old dog needs a stroke sometimes.'

Sighing inwardly, a smile on her lips, Magdalene applied herself to his demand.

Chapter 12

Robert Willoughby's hazel eyes crinkled with astonishment and laughter. 'You have done what? Bought Alice Leen's weaving trade?' He draped his arm across the back of Miriel's wall bench and crossed his legs. He was in Nottingham to conduct business with Gerbert, but had detoured to call upon Miriel to see how she was faring and discuss the price of wool. 'That's very . . . er . . . enterprising.'

Miriel glowered at him until his face straightened. 'If I was a man you wouldn't sit there chuckling,' she snapped. 'Alice would never have sold to me unless she thought I could continue her success.'

'Of course not,' Robert said quickly and smoothed his moustache. 'It is just that you looked so fierce when you told me – as if you were waiting for my objection so that you could pounce.'

Miriel coloured. There was more than an element of truth in the statement. She was so used to fighting for what she wanted that it was now ingrained. 'Well, why did you laugh?'

The humour returned to his eyes and deepened the attractive creases in his cheeks. Miriel felt a stirring of warmth. If Gerbert was like her grandfather, then Robert was the father she had never known.

'Because you took me by surprise,' he said. 'I know from what Alice has said that you are probably competent to run a business, but you still seem so young.' He raised and wagged his forefinger as she drew breath. 'Before you rail at me again, let me add that I am also full of admiration and pride.'

Miriel bit her lip. Compliments were almost harder to accept than disapproval. She was unaccustomed to receiving praise. To distract herself, she rose to replenish his goblet. 'She's retiring to Lenton Priory. Says that another winter would prove too difficult for her old bones and she cannot give the weaving the attention it needs to flourish.'

'So she has sold you everything?'

Miriel nodded. 'As it stands.'

'You must have quite a store of wealth at your disposal then.' The last word ended on a rising note of question as he took the cup.

'Enough,' Miriel fenced. She met his gaze steadily, revealing nothing.

'And your past would seem to be a blank slate,' he mused. 'The few times we have met, you have been at pains to avoid the subject.'

'Because it is my own business,' she said stiffly.

He swirled the wine in his cup, then took a drink. 'That is true, but your very secrecy makes me curious.'

'Then curious you must remain.' Miriel's heart pounded in response to the potential danger. 'I thought you came to talk of wool prices, not to satisfy your desire for gossip.'

'Oh, I have several desires to satisfy where you are concerned,' Robert murmured in a voice so soft that Miriel was not sure she had heard aright. She stared at him, her breath quickening with anger, with fear, and with an emotion she was unable to identify.

'I think it best if you leave,' she said stiffly.

Robert extended his hand in a gesture of contrition. 'I meant no offence, Mistress Stamford. I did but tease, and out of turn, I can see.'

Miriel studied him warily. The tone of his voice when he spoke of satisfying desires had sent a jolt of not unpleasant warmth through her loins and she found herself wondering what it would be like to kiss him. It was a notion that she swiftly dismissed. She needed no such complication in her life. 'You would not have teased had I been a male acquaintance,' she said frostily.

'That is true, but it is a response you will find time and

again in your dealings.' Finishing the wine, he set his cup on the coffer. 'Men will react to you in that way because you are a rich and attractive young widow. They will think your life lacking without that which they can provide – if you take my meaning.' He raised and lowered his brows.

Miriel's face grew hot for she did take his meaning and it ran on a parallel course to her wayward thoughts of a moment since. 'I understand what you are saying,' she said with a curt nod. 'It might be useful to employ an agent to negotiate for me.' She looked down at her hands, which were tightly clasped in her lap, then back at him, through the guard of her lashes. 'But I also know that I am the best negotiator of my business interests. Men might view me as weak because I am a woman, but they have their own weaknesses to be exploited too . . . do they not?'

The humour returned to Robert Willoughby's gaze. 'I see that you are going to be a formidable opponent.'

'Business partner,' Miriel contradicted with a smile and put her own cup down. 'Now, we were talking of the price of wool, and I want to know how much per sarple you were charging Alice.'

Two days later, at her new weaving shed below the castle rock, Miriel took delivery of the sacks of wool she had bought from Robert Willoughby. Old Alice was on hand to inspect the fleeces as Miriel distributed them to the local good wives for carding and spinning.

'They'll do,' Alice said grudgingly as she fingered the oily, yellowish wool. Miriel took the remark as a compliment. It would be a relief when the old lady moved to her new home at the priory next week.

'What did you pay for 'em?' Alice gave her a narrow look.

'I got a good price,' Miriel said, refusing to be drawn. Rubbing her hands, which were sticky with oil from the fleeces, she went to watch Thomas the senior weaver at work on a light brown serge woven with a red stripe. A loud clatter came from the loom as Thomas worked the foot treadles to raise the shed between the threads and pass the loaded shuttle through the gap. Beside him, one of the apprentices was winding a hank of yarn on to a ball ready for use on the loom. Thomas's wife was busy at a smaller loom, making braid from odd ends of wool that would otherwise go to waste.

Miriel had to admit that Alice ran a clean and thrifty business. It was much smaller than her grandfather's, but he had been one of the most important weavers in Lincoln, his cloth of Lincoln greyne famous throughout England. Miriel intended setting up a couple of looms to make Lincoln weave as soon as she had familiarised herself with her new business.

Alice sighed as she watched Thomas passing his loaded shuttle under and over. 'I shall miss all this,' she said. 'It has been my life since my Herbert died. We started from nothing in the time of old King Henry and we became the best weavers on the banks of the Leen.'

Miriel had heard the sentiment twenty times over, but she mustered her patience. In forty years it might be her standing in Alice's place telling the same story to another young woman. The thought made her shiver. 'And it shall continue to be the best, I promise you.' She found a smile and gave Alice's stick-thin arm a squeeze.

'Aye, well, I'll visit often.'

'You will be most welcome,' Miriel murmured, being sparse with the truth. She furnished Alice with a seat in the corner and a cup of good wine. Then she flattered the old lady by asking her opinion on a number of matters. While Alice might be irritating, she had a lifetime of knowledge and Miriel had no intention of cutting off her nose to spite her face by being too proud to ask. What she did not want was a watchdog peering over her shoulder all the time.

Alice's weaving shed had its own private dwelling at the side, composing of a ground floor hall and an upstairs sleeping chamber reached by way of a wooden outer stair. Miriel had already decided that when Gerbert came home from his wool-gathering, she would give him notice and move into her new accommodation.

That evening when she returned from a long day overseeing

the bustle of the weaving shed, her head was ringing with the remembered clatter of the looms, her eyes were heavy with fatigue, but the tiredness was pleasurable and it was with satisfaction that she sat down in her box chair and gently rubbed her aching feet. Elfwen, the eldest Bridlesmith daughter, earned herself a wage by doing small tasks for Miriel. This evening she had prepared a supper of eggs, bacon and wheat waffles, which Miriel attacked with hungry gratitude. 'I swear food has never tasted so good,' she praised. 'You're the best cook along the whole of Cow Lane.'

Elfwen blushed with pleasure. 'I like cooking,' she said. 'I like keeping house.'

'Each to their own. I'm glad that you do,' said Miriel who was not particularly fond of either. She sent the girl home with a silver quarter penny and the promise of a wimple length of cloth from her first batch of weaving. Then she slotted the bar across the door and leaned against it, smiling contentedly.

The hot food had restored her energy. A cup of sweet honey mead was a further boost and she decided to make a start upon packing her belongings for the move to the weaving house. She barred the shutters upon the soft summer twilight and the chatter of folk lingering outside their homes to talk. The walls closed around her, but their solidity was like the comfort of a womb. Fire- and candle-light filled the room with a golden smokiness that she savoured for a moment before fetching a spade from the rock-cut store room. Dragging her clothing coffer away from the wall, she started to dig.

A fist banged on the door. 'Miriel, open up. You can't be abed this early!' yelled Gerbert in a peremptory voice.

She whirled with a gasp and her heart began to pound as if it would break from her body. 'Yes I am. I have a megrim,' she improvised. With shaking hands she threw the spade in her coffer.

'This is important; I have to speak with you.'

'Can it not wait until morning?' Miriel stooped to throw floor straw across the revealing hole and dragged her coffer back into place. She swished her hands in the tepid water of the cauldron and patted her face.

'No, it can't. Open up!' Gerbert's voice had a hard edge

that Miriel had never heard before. She wondered if he had discovered her intention to quit the tenancy and wanted to talk her out of it. If so, she could think of nothing more tiresome to end the day. He did not sound as if he was prepared to be side-tracked or placated.

'Very well, but not for long, I've told you, I have a megrim.' She went to open the door.

He strode over the threshold and Miriel could tell at a glance that he was deeply upset. His clothes were rumpled and travel-stained, his white beard bristled like the fur of an angry cat and his complexion was the dusky colour of a man on the verge of apoplexy. She began to wish that she had kept the bar on the door.

'What's wrong?'

He gave her a furious look. 'You might well ask, Mistress Stamford.' The title emerged as a sneer.

Miriel's stomach gave a queasy leap. 'Would you like some mead?'

She watched him strive to control himself, opening and closing his fists, his jaw working. Finally he succeeded, and with a stiff nod and precise movements, seated himself on her coffer.

Miriel turned away to the flagon. It had a handsome finish of green glaze and the spout was fashioned in the shape of a horse's head. She comforted herself with the feel of its cool, polished surface. He was upset because he had found out she was leaving this house, and he had formed an attachment for her. That was what was wrong. She poured the mead and gave him his cup. 'Now then,' she said in a soothing voice. 'What have I done that you should give me such black looks?'

'You have deceived me,' Gerbert growled and took a deep drink.

Miriel raised her brows. 'Deceived you?'

He rested the cup on his knee. A slight tremor in his wrist made the mead shiver and ripple. 'Need I say more to you than St Catherine's?'

Miriel took an involuntary back-step and her knuckles whitened on the flagon handle.

'You do not deny it then?' His face sagged with an incongruous mingling of triumph and disappointment.

Miriel felt sick. How much did he know and how had he found out? 'Deny what?' she challenged, as always fighting back from a position at bay. 'I have done nothing of which I am ashamed.' Which was not entirely true, but that was a private matter between herself and Nicholas.

'Then you are a brazen whore.' The veins swelled alarmingly in his throat and his complexion grew plum-dark.

Miriel almost dashed the remains of her mead in his face. Only the very real dread that he might have a seizure prevented her. 'Those who cast stones are not spotless themselves,' she said contemptuously. 'The past is finished and I am doing my best to make a decent life for myself.'

'Built on a foundation of lies.' His voice thickened and choked. 'I trusted you. I thought . . . I thought you were an honest and innocent widow in need of protection.'

'I am honest.' Miriel offered a silent prayer to God for a small amount of leeway. 'And I am innocent. I do not know what you have heard of me and from whom, but there are always two sides to a tale.' It was the overturning of his trust which had distressed him, she thought, the realisation that his initial judgement had been wrong.

Gerbert savagely gulped at his mead and glared at her. 'At St John's fair in Boston I negotiated a contract to buy the wool from St Catherine's Abbey. There had been a rift with their former buyer and they were in search of an agent.' His eyes nailed her. 'A rift concerned with a young nun absconding over their wall with a guest. The nun was Miriel Weaver, granddaughter of the renowned Edward Weaver of Lincoln, and the guest, an itinerant mercenary who went by the name of Nicholas de Caen.'

Miriel gnawed her lip. 'It is not what you think,' she said.

'How do you know what I think?' He plundered his cup a final time and banged it down on the coffer.

'It is there for me to read in your face.'

His beard jutted. 'What you read is anger at the way you have lied and deceived.'

'What harm have I caused?' Miriel made a throwing gesture. 'Have I not kept this house in good order and paid my rent on time? Have I not contributed to the livelihood of the people around me and shown my determination to settle here as a responsible townswoman?' She stamped her foot. 'Have I ever conducted myself in a manner to bring down scandal on your good name as my landlord?'

'What harm have you caused?' Gerbert's voice was a bellow of pain. 'Jesu, girl, you can hardly begin to know.' He looked at his cup. Miriel did not offer him more mead. Her stepfather's temper had always grown a stage more ugly with each measure he drank.

'What happened to your lover, this Nicholas de Caen?' Gerbert demanded.

'He wasn't my lover,' Miriel snapped. 'He came to St Catherine's sick with fever. I nursed him back to health and he was grateful enough to repay the debt by seeing me safe to Nottingham. Our bodies never once touched in lust and I still have my virginity to prove it!'

'A virginity you surely owed to Christ.'

Miriel bared her teeth at him, thoroughly furious and past caring. 'I owe nothing to Christ because I never took my vows. My beloved family forced me into that nunnery because they didn't want me and those sweet and saintly nuns cropped my hair as a punishment for defying their rule. They locked me up in a cell with bread and water and expected me to repent. When the opportunity arose, of course I ran away!' She drew herself up, tears of rage brimming in her eyes. 'I owe them nothing,' she spat. 'My life is my own, to make of it what I will, and neither you nor anyone else will tell me how to live it!'

The choking fury melted from Gerbert's face, leaving remorse in its wake. He rose, hands outstretched. 'Don't weep,' he implored. 'I cannot bear to see a woman's tears.'

'Then why drive me to the edge?' Miriel scrubbed her cuff across her eyes and jerked aside from his supplication.

'You lied to me; I was angry, I thought you had a lover. Don't, sweeting, please don't.' He put a clumsy arm around her shoulders and kissed her cheek.

She felt the heat of his breath, the bristle of his beard and with a gasp pushed out of his embrace. 'I think you should go,' she said, mustering her dignity. 'And you might as well know that I intend to dwell in Alice's house at the weavery. I was going to leave next week, but now I will make it the morrow.'

He looked at her in dismay. 'There is no need for that.'

'After the things you have said, there is every need,' Miriel contradicted grimly.

Gerbert swore beneath his breath and rubbed his thick, spatulate hands over his face. Then he gathered himself, his pugnacious chin jutting. 'I will leave when I have had my full say,' he announced with the pomposity of a village elder at a meeting. Going to the flagon, he poured a fresh measure into his cup and took a deep swallow.

Miriel eyed him warily, wondering what he was going to throw at her next.

Gerbert squared his shoulders. 'I came to face you with what I had found out. Indeed, I was in half a mind to report you to the sheriff and the Church, but I decided against it.'

'That is kind of you,' Miriel said with sarcasm.

'No, it is selfish.' He faced her, his legs planted apart, his chest and stomach puffed out in a single portly curve. 'I do not wish to see you whipped out of town or put in the stocks for what has happened in the past, but I will if I must.'

'If you must?' Miriel's sense of unease increased.

Gerbert drank his mead, his other hand wrapped tightly around his belt. He cleared his throat. 'I want you to marry me,' he said. 'I am weary of being a widower and my household is a dolorous place with only Samuel for company. It needs new blood, new life.'

'Marry you?' Miriel almost choked on the words. His interest had been present ever since that first night, but in her folly she had thought she could keep him at bay. Now he had a dangerous lever to use against her. 'Do not be a fool,' she said brusquely. 'You will keep me from one scandal only to throw us both headlong into another. When a woman weds a man three times her age, tongues grow busy and very sharp.'

'Let them wag,' he said stubbornly. 'The wonder will soon die down. I'm respected in the town for my sound judgement. What better than my wool trade should unite with that of the best cloth-weaving house in Nottingham?'

If Miriel could have moved, she would have grabbed her frying pan and chased him from the house without heed for the consequences. 'I will not yield up my business to you,' she said through her teeth.

Gerbert shrugged. 'I would not expect you to. By all accounts you know the weaving trade. I would leave it entirely in your hands.'

'And pigs might fly and roost in trees!' she spat. 'Virgin I may be, but I know all about the dishonest ways of men!'

'My word is my honour, which is more than can be said for yours,' he choked.

Miriel's cheeks flamed as though he had struck them with the flat of his palm. 'Then why do you want to marry me, if not to further your own interests?'

'Damn you, wench, of course I want to further my own interests, I'm not a saint!' he roared. 'I do not deny that my trade and yours fit neatly sword in sheath, but there is more to it than that. Jesu, I could have courted Alice Leen long ago if all I desired was the business!'

Miriel nodded viciously. 'But it's changed now, hasn't it? Instead of Alice Leen, there is me. You desire the feel of my body beneath the sheets; you desire to have me on your arm and show me off to your friends whose own wives are old and dowdy.'

She thought that he was going to strike her. In a way she hoped that he would, for it would make her decision simple. But he found the control and his hands remained around his cup and his belt.

'I do desire you,' he said in a voice that shook with the effort of remaining calm. 'What man in his right mind would not? And indeed I would be proud to have you at my side.' Now his hand left his belt and stretched beseechingly towards her. 'I want to cherish you, I want to protect you.'

Miriel narrowed her eyes. She was beginning to understand now. 'From men like Robert Willoughby, you mean?' Whose own interests were inextricably bound up with Gerbert's and the weaving trade.

He made a brief gesture. 'That is part of it, but not the whole.'

'And you think me incapable of defending myself?' The frying pan was within easy reach. All she had to do was grab it and let fly. 'Are you not taking advantage of me in your own way?'

'For your own good,' he said righteously.

'It was for "my own good" that I was sent to St Catherine's.'

Gerbert sighed and shook his head as if at the grizzling of a tiresome infant. 'I will not argue with you further. You can have until dawn to think the matter through. On the morrow you will give me your reply and I will act upon it. I promise that if you say yes, you will not lose by it. If you refuse' – he glowered beneath his brows – 'you know the consequences.' He went to the door and, on the threshold, paused to look over his shoulder. 'I do not mean to be harsh, Miriel. I swear to be the most tender and loving of husbands.'

She clenched her fists in her gown. 'Then why come wooing with a club?' she demanded.

He flinched as if she had struck him and left without another word. Miriel seized the frying pan off its hook and hurled it with all her might at the door he had just closed. It bounced off with a resounding clang, leaving a dint in the wood. The strength drained out of Miriel's legs and she collapsed on the bed bench.

She could pack her belongings and move on to the next town, Newark perhaps, but if Gerbert alerted the authorities, as he had threatened, her past was as likely to catch up with her there as it had now. She could gamble that he was bluffing, but if she was wrong, she would be ostracised, perhaps as he said put in the stocks or turned over to the ecclesiastical courts for punishment.

Or she could marry him. Give him a husband's rights over her person and property. Miriel buried her head in the darkness created by her arms and the bright blanket. He was old, past three score at least. The thought of sharing a bed with him made her recoil. The more pragmatic part of her mind told her that such marital duty was bound to be infrequent. Indeed, given Gerbert's years and the way he was prone to puffing up like a frog when agitated, she might be single again before long, and twice as rich with a very lucrative wool-gathering business to boot.

Face or flee. Slowly Miriel sat up and gazed into the fire, a frown of concentration on her face. She had been able to wind her grandfather round her little finger, why not Gerbert? Let him bind her in marriage, she thought grimly. She would tie him in a knot of his own making and still have her way.

When she fell asleep, she dreamed that it was her wedding night, but her lover's body was young and hard, and her loins ached with unbearable sweetness as he kissed and fondled her, his hips rocking on hers.

She woke sweating and gasping, a twist of sheet rucked between her thighs, and the dawn chorus clamouring at the shutters.

Chapter 13

Miriel was married to Gerbert Woolman on an August morning at St Mary's Church. Although attended by many members of the merchant fraternity, the ceremony was a simple affair. Miriel and Gerbert exchanged vows before witnesses in the church's stone porch. Since Miriel had no family to witness for her, Master Bridlesmith stepped into the role with earnest enthusiasm. 'Practising for when our Elfwen ties the knot,' he said with a grin.

Once the seal ring of heavy gold had been placed on Miriel's finger, the couple entered the church itself to kneel before the altar for the rites of the wedding mass.

Gerbert, having got what he wanted, beamed with unalloyed delight. Miriel's smile was strained. She knew that folk were looking at them, speculating as to who had married whom – the attractive young widow seizing on the old man for his wealth in the knowledge that his years were numbered, or the wily old man gaining a toothsome bedmate and a very fine weaving business as an extension to his wool trade.

Feeling Gerbert's hot damp hand on hers, Miriel suppressed a shudder. The thought of the night to come made her feel sick, made her even wish in a corner of her mind that she was still a nun at St Catherine's.

'Congratulations, Mistress Woolman,' said Robert Willoughby, finding her briefly alone whilst Gerbert spoke with other guests. The greenish eyes held their customary glint of humour. 'If I had known the old fox was going to be so swift about his wooing, I'd not have tarried myself.' Leaning forward, he kissed her cheek, and she was enveloped in the powerful masculine aromas of spikenard and cedar.

'If I had known it, my feet might have run faster,' Miriel admitted ruefully.

'He forced you?' Willoughby's glance shot to Gerbert who was hastily disengaging himself from his guests to rescue his bride.

Miriel smiled and shook her head. 'Not in the way you mean. Besides, some would say that I had the better part of the bargain.'

'Then they are blind.'

Miriel blushed. There was more in his expression than mere courtesy, although it was swiftly veiled as Gerbert arrived to seize her arm possessively.

'You're a fortunate man, Godfather,' Robert said.

'Yes I am.' Gerbert tightened his grip on Miriel's sleeve, his beard bristling.

'I wish you both joy and prosperity of your marriage.' With a graceful bow, Robert moved off to mingle with the other guests.

Gerbert watched him narrowly for a moment until Miriel pinched him. 'I am not a bone to be fought over,' she said. 'He did but pause to offer congratulations. If you are going to suspect every man who speaks to me, then what hope does that wish for joy have?'

Taking her other hand, Gerbert turned her to face him. 'Yes, I know,' he sighed. 'I am pleased that others admire you, but I cannot help be a little jealous. Robert has a way with women.'

Miriel sighed too, already wondering if she had made the right decision.

In contrast to the simplicity of the ceremony, the wedding feast was a lavish affair. Gerbert had spared no expense to fête his bride and had hired an army of cooks, servants and entertainers for the occasion. The summer's end had provided a glut of foods for the table. Aside from the usual sucking pigs and roasted squabs, there were plump chicken breasts in a piquant sauce. The meat from the rest of the carcasses had been chopped and baked with onions and spices in succulent little pies. There were sides of pickled salmon and salvers piled high with oysters. Gerbert ate greedily of these, prising open the shells with dextrous twists of his knife and sucking out the contents to much innuendo and bawdy laughter.

Miriel, who usually adored oysters, could scarcely open her throat to allow even one to slide down. She was terrified of the next stage of the wedding rite. She knew the rudiments of the mating act, knew that the organ between a man's legs was designed to fit in the secret sheath between a woman's thighs where the monthly blood flowed and babies emerged nine months after the seed was planted, but otherwise she was ignorant. Men enjoyed the deed to judge by their boasts. She had heard her stepfather and mother in bed sometimes. The moans and groans, puffing and panting, made the act of procreation sound about as much effort and pleasure as pushing a massive boulder uphill.

The feast progressed through its various courses and the wine flowed with abandon. Miriel partook sparingly. If she drank herself into a stupor she would not be aware of what was being done to her. While not keen to acquire the knowledge, she needed to know.

As the guests became rowdy under the influence of wine, Miriel modestly begged leave to retire. Her departure was greeted with cheers and whistles. Gerbert was slapped on the back and teased mercilessly. Another platter of oysters was shoved under his nose.

In the quiet of the bedchamber, Miriel removed her wimple and sat down on the coverlet of embroidered Flemish wool. The bed had been made up with crisp new sheets to honour the occasion, and strewn with sweet-smelling herbs to promote fertility. Against one wall stood Miriel's coffer, and inside it, at the bottom, the smaller wooden chest containing the remaining pouches of silver and Mathilda's crown. Both coffer and chest were locked and Miriel kept the keys about her person, but still she was nervous. It was not a safe hiding place. As soon as there was a convenient moment, she intended finding somewhere more secure.

Her moment of solitude was brief. Before she had collected her thoughts, Eva Bridlesmith and young Elfwen appeared in the doorway, eager to act as her attendants. Chattering with pleasure, they helped her to remove her outer dress of slate-blue linen, and her pale green undertunic. Elfwen tidied the clothes while her mother drew a bone comb through Miriel's hair until it hung in a honey curtain to her collarbone.

'At least you'll know what to expect,' Eva said as she cleaned the comb of stray hairs before going to turn down the bed covers. A wine-glow had flushed her cheeks and put a sparkle in her eye.

Miriel's nod was far from convincing. As she climbed into bed, she could not prevent her teeth from chattering.

'I know that this match is a business arrangement between the two of you, but still, I'm sure you'll be content together. There's much to be said for the steady ways of older men.' Eva squeezed Miriel's hand. 'Why, you're colder than an icicle!' She gestured briskly to her daughter. 'Bring that flagon over here.'

A cup of spiced wine later, Miriel felt little better. Although the drink had warmed her veins, it had also made her feel light-headed.

'You'll be all right,' Eva soothed. 'Gerbert might not be much to look at, but he's experienced in the ways of the world. Young husbands have fine bodies, but they've more notion how to please themselves than their wives.'

'Does that mean I should marry an old man?' Elfwen asked saucily.

Her mother batted her hand at her daughter's jesting. 'It means you should choose wisely.'

The noise of laughter and heavy footfalls on the outer stairs alerted the women to the arrival of the bridegroom and his party for the bedding ceremony. Feeling sick, Miriel clung to Eva's words about a business arrangement. This was just part of the bargain that had to be fulfilled, she told herself.

Gerbert was slightly unsteady on his feet and, against the white fluff of his beard, his complexion was wine-red. His less than sober companions divested him of tunic, chausses and shirt, but left him the dignity of his braies. Although past three score years, Gerbert still retained his height and flesh.

His freckled stomach bulged above the drawstring waistband of the braies. His chest was wide, the pectorals sagging and the nipples edged with curly silver hair. Stocky thighs tapered into rounded calves and broad feet with horny yellow skin on the big toes.

After one horrified glance, Miriel avoided looking at him. The covers were thrown back, and he was pushed into bed beside her.

'Let's have a good night's sowing and weaving!' a merchant punned.

'Aye, run your shuttle through the loom, warp and weft!'

'Give us a shout if you need help wi' the threading!'

'Go on, be off with you!' Gerbert swatted at his companions in amused irritation. 'Leave my wife and me in peace, or the cloth won't be finished ere daybreak! And no listening outside the door, you buggers!'

With much laughter and yet more teasing and innuendo, the guests eventually took their leave and went downstairs to finish off the wine and what remained of the food.

Gerbert looked at Miriel. 'Well, wife,' he said with forced jocularity, 'alone for the first time today.'

'Yes.' Miriel managed the barest stretching of her lips in response, realising at the same time that Gerbert was nervous and uneasy too. The rapid beating of her heart was only a mirror of the pulse hammering in his throat beneath the combed white beard. He had been chewing aniseed to freshen his breath and the scent of the herb engulfed the bed. More than ever he reminded her of her grandfather. Lying with him would seem like incest. Blessed Mary, how was she going to cope?

'Do you want some wine?' He indicated the flagon near the coffer.

Miriel shook her head. 'I have drunk enough already.'

'I just thought it might ease you.' Gerbert poured some for himself and gulped it down like a soldier bound for a battle. His hand shook and a red rivulet dribbled down his wrist. 'Ah God,' he laughed, 'I'm like a green boy with his first woman, so eager and afraid that I fear I will shame myself.'

Miriel clenched her fists in her chemise. 'I'm afraid too,' she said in a small, forlorn voice.

With a wavering hand, Gerbert plonked the cup on the trestle. 'Don't say that, sweeting, you've nothing to fear from me. You know I'd not harm you.' His voice was gruff with tenderness, and he gathered her resisting form against his breast. 'Will it help if I snuff the candles?'

Now that the moment was at hand, Miriel lost her nerve. She had intended remaining sober and all-seeing, but suddenly the darkness was a refuge too welcome to resist and she gave a wordless little nod.

Lumbering from the bed, Gerbert extinguished the thick wax night candle on its wrought-iron stand and blew out the smaller cresset lamp on the coffer, thereby plunging the room into complete darkness. Miriel felt his weight settle back on the bed, heard the rapid saw of his breathing, and imagined that she was in the lair of a wild beast.

He turned to her and, as his hands circled her waist and he pressed his body to hers, she realised that he had taken the opportunity of extinguishing the lights to remove his braies.

Holy Mary, Mother of God, I pray to you now in my moment of need. Miriel closed her eyes and clenched her jaw, her entire body rigid with rejection. Gerbert's lips quested at her throat; his beard rubbed her tender skin. Thick fingers plucked at the laces of her chemise, pulled wide, then delved inside to fondle her breasts. Gerbert groaned in the same fashion that she had heard her stepfather groan behind the bed curtain with her mother. He pinched her nipples, rolling them between forefinger and thumb, but Miriel was too revolted and frightened to become aroused.

His hand left her breasts and groped at the hem of her chemise, tugging it free of her legs, bunching the fabric above her thighs to her waist. Gerbert's touch wandered greedily over her body and he began to puff and gasp as if he had just run a mile in lead boots.

'Take it off, sweeting, there's a good lass,' he panted, yanking at the chemise.

When Miriel did not move, he sat her up like a child's rag moppet and pulled the garment over her head himself. Then he grabbed a pillow, placed it beneath her hips and climbed upon her naked body.

'Sweet,' he muttered, sucking at her breasts, rubbing himself upon her. 'Very sweet, ah Jesu, ah Jesu!'

A hard, hot swelling nudged at the juncture of her thighs. Gerbert probed at her pubic triangle, snagging the hairs, making her arch with pain. 'Open your legs for me, lass, let me in.'

It was the last thing Miriel wanted to do, but to save herself from the scrabbling of his fingers, the sharpness of a rough fingernail, she parted her thighs.

'That's it, that's it!' he panted and, cupping her buttocks, raised her to meet the thick rod of his erection. 'It'll hurt only but a moment.'

He stabbed and jabbed at her softness while Miriel clenched her teeth and fought not to scream.

Suddenly Gerbert stiffened above her and his breathing stopped. Then he let out a strangled sob and his hips jerked in spasm. Warm wetness spattered Miriel's belly and Gerbert collapsed on top of her.

Thoroughly frightened and revolted, Miriel fought her way out from beneath his corpulent bulk. The sound of his harsh breathing echoed inside her skull.

'Sorry,' Gerbert gasped without opening his eyes or turning his head. 'Spent myself too soon. Too eager, haven't had a woman in five years. Be better next time, I promise.'

Miriel struggled off the bed and grabbed the towel that Eva had thoughtfully left beside a ewer of water. Almost retching with disgust, she wiped her belly and thighs and changed her chemise. Unable to bear the thought of returning to lie with Gerbert, she swung her cloak around her shoulders and sat in the chair near the empty brazier, tucking her knees up to her chin in a defensive gesture. Then she buried her face against the wool of her cloak and burst into tears.

Oblivious to the small sounds she made, Gerbert turned on his back and began to snore. Miriel wondered bleakly why she was muffling her distress. She wanted him to hear her pain. She wanted him to rise and put his arm around her shoulders in paternal benevolence and comfort her. But Gerbert was nine fathoms deep in a stupor of wine and sated lust. In her heart she knew that even if she wailed like a banshee she would go unheeded.

At last the storm of tears ran its course. Miriel blew her nose, dried her eyes, and tried to think calmly about the situation. Vague though she was about the details of copulation, she knew that she was still a virgin, that Gerbert had not succeeded in penetrating her body. The discharge on her belly contained his seed, and if it had gone inside her, it might have taken root in her womb and grown into a child. But it hadn't and, unpleasant though the experience had been, she had learned a great deal from it. Gerbert said that it would be better next time. She was certain that it wouldn't, but he would expect her to lie with him as her marital duty. She could not bear the thought of him invading her, of being made dependent on him by a burgeoning belly, of expending her efforts and energy on a child when she wanted to give her all to her weaving business.

Tonight, however, all unwittingly, Gerbert had shown her a way to maintain the balance. She chewed her fingernail thoughtfully.

Education was what she needed, and quickly.

CHAPTER 14

'You can't have her, my lord.' Nicholas glared furiously at Hubert de Burgh, Royal Justiciar, Earl of Kent and Governor of Dover Castle. 'I'm due at Boston in two days' time.'

Behind the two men, the great stone keep towered over the harbour. Scarred but undefeated by months of siege during the war with King Louis of France, repairs and improvements were being carried out apace. The clink of masonry chisels carried on the wind, and the powdery smell of stone dust. Scaffolding enclosed the north gateway and men scurried along its walkways with plumb lines and buckets of mortar.

'It is my right,' answered Hubert de Burgh implacably but without raising his voice. He had the red face and the bulk of a man who liked his food but he was also as active as a mastiff. 'I may commandeer any vessel in this port providing I pay you and your men a standard wage for each day of service, and compensation should your cog be damaged. But deny me your vessel and you will be guilty of treason.'

'Treason!' Nicholas choked on the word. It was his good fortune, for it rendered him speechless, whatever his congested expression might say. He had sailed into Dover to offload his cargo of wine and mend a torn sail. Both had been accomplished, but instead of setting out for Boston on the morrow, Hubert de Burgh was demanding he yield up the *Pandora* and her crew to fight French pirates in the Channel.

De Burgh looked at Nicholas and stroked his beard. He had been one of John's most senior and powerful barons. Now, as one of the lords entrusted to administer the realm during young Henry's minority, that power had increased five fold. Earlier in his career he had been the custodian of the Donjon of Falaise where Prince Arthur had been held in captivity before his transferral to Rouen. There were rumours that de Burgh had had a hand in Arthur's disappearance, rumours that de Burgh, tough and honest, had grimly denied.

'Nicholas de Caen,' he murmured. The great seal ring of his office flashed as he thumbed his chin. 'I seem to remember seeing a despatch somewhere about a dangerous rebel of that name.'

Nicholas flushed. The soldiers of de Burgh's escort tightened rank a little. Mail flexed and threatened. Nicholas drew a deep, steadying breath. 'Like many, my grudge was against King John. I bear his son no ill-will, nor do I give a bean for the claims of Louis of France to this country. I am a merchant now, and I have a living to make.'

'Which you will not do while the French control the Narrow Sea, and Eustace the Monk raids from the ports of the Channel Islands.'

'There are other seas, other ports,' Nicholas said, but knew that the battle had been lost from the beginning. Hubert de Burgh would take the *Pandora* because he needed her and there was nothing he could do.

De Burgh had never been in any doubt of the outcome. 'Make her ready,' he said brusquely. 'Whether you care a bean for Louis or not, the word is that his wife is sending him seventy ships laden with supplies. If he receives them, then his threat to our young King becomes potent again. If we can stop him in the water, then it is likely he will give up the fight and go home.' He laid a meaty paw on Nicholas's shoulder. 'You will not go unrewarded, I promise. You'll find valuable contracts put your way by grateful men like myself.'

Fortunately the hand lifted before Nicholas could cause insult by shrugging it off, but his expression showed his distaste.

De Burgh's features tightened with controlled irritation. 'There is a meeting for all captains in the great hall yonder an hour from now. Be there.' He swung on his heel, his spur scraping the stone.

Clenching and unclenching his fists, Nicholas watched the Justiciar walk away. 'You whoreson,' he said through his teeth with quiet venom. Turning to regard the *Pandora,* he half contemplated casting off and sailing for Boston on the instant. The knowledge that that was all it would take to turn pirate stayed his hand.

'Sir?' said Martin Wudecoc, his first mate, who had heard most of the conversation. He was a tall man, whipcord-lean with lugubrious features and an air of quiet confidence.

'You heard his lordship; we're to prepare her for war.' Nicholas glanced sidelong at the sailor. 'If you want to abandon ship, go now and as fast as you can. If they don't have enough willing crewmen, they'll press whoever they can find into service by means of club and sword.'

Martin sucked his teeth and contemplated. 'Seventy ships, Lord Hubert said.'

'Carrying supplies to King Louis, although there are bound to be soldiers aboard, and such a large convoy is sure to have an escort of fighting ships.' As he spoke, Nicholas felt a treacherous glimmer of interest, a sense of challenge welling within him. He wondered how the *Pandora* would perform in a battle. Her height in the water and the wooden lookout 'castles' built fore and aft would give her a tremendous advantage over the sleeker but lower-slung nefs.

Martin looked thoughtful. 'What about Eustace the Monk?'

'What about him?' The second mention of the name in five minutes caused Nicholas's stomach to leap. Eustace the Monk was a notorious pirate with respect for neither God nor man, but a tremendous talent for reading the seas. At one time he had served King John and reaped great rewards. Following an acrimonious quarrel with his erstwhile employer he had changed sides. Now he worked for Louis and terrorised all shipping in the waters of the Narrow Sea – apart from the French.

As a child, Nicholas had encountered Eustace once or twice, fortunately on dry land where he posed less of a threat. His father had been on nodding terms with the pirate, but tried to avoid him. 'A man who has already sold his soul will not balk at removing anyone else's,' he told Nicholas grimly. 'Eustace is the kind to smile in your face whilst plunging a knife in your back.'

'Will he be with the French?' There was a note of apprehension in Martin's voice. Such was Eustace's reputation that ordinary sailors had imbued him with demonic powers rather than the good fortune and expert seamanship that were the truth.

'God knows. He changes sides more often than a whore lifts her skirts for business.' Nicholas shrugged at his anxious mate. 'Which would you rather? Put to sea, or face a prison cell and the chance that you might be hanged?'

Martin scowled. 'Not much of a choice, is it?'

'No,' said Nicholas. 'It isn't, but it is all we have.'

By the following dawn, the *Pandora* had been laden with weapons. The floorboards of her fore and aft castles were edged with stones of varying sizes, some that would fit neatly into a hand-held sling, others which would have to be heaved two-handed. Large clay containers of pulverised lime were stored ready in the dry hold together with sheaf upon sheaf of arrows for the archers who were pouring steadily on board. Spears and grapnels were added to the arsenal, and a pile of old-fashioned round shields and smaller bucklers.

Nicholas looked at his merchant cog, now bristling with a host of weapons and warriors, and hid his misgivings behind a stony countenance. Martin crossed himself, a mingling of pride and unease on his face. 'God be with us,' he said, 'because the Devil is likely with the French.'

Nicholas grunted but said nothing. At the captains' meeting yester eve, Hubert de Burgh had told them he had intelligence that Eustace the Monk was leading the French force. Such was the man's reputation that several of the captains had refused to put to sea until de Burgh had offered to cut off their heads and declare their vessels forfeit to the crown. 'You think it dreadful to face Eustace the Monk!' he roared, the veins bulging in his neck like blue worms. 'How much more dreadful will you think Louis of France if those supply ships land to reinforce his army? How much innocent blood will you have on your hands then?'

Through sheer force of character and the loudest voice, Hubert de Burgh had won, but it had been a close-run thing.

'We have a task to perform,' Nicholas said to his mate, 'one that I relish no better than you, but if we are to emerge unscathed, we have to put our hearts into the effort. Show a yellow tail to "the Devil" and like as not he will bite it off.' He slapped Wudecoc's bony shoulder. 'If we do well and de Burgh rewards us as promised, I will buy another ship and she will need a good captain. Think on that.'

Martin cleared his throat. 'You need not resort to bribery with me, sir. I'll stand by my duty.'

'It wasn't a bribe and I know you will.'

The wind was blowing southerly as they unreefed the single huge sail and tacked out the safety of Dover harbour. The water was blue and choppy under the keel and a deeper reflection of the breezy sky. Hubert de Burgh's fleet emerged on to the open sea like a herd of frisky horses, banners snapping from masts and castles. There were sixteen large ships, a mixture of cogs and nefs, all armed to the top strake, and twenty smaller vessels, well manned but of less calibre. Thirty-six, facing a convoy of seventy supply ships and ten escorting sea-wolves, armed to ram and destroy any who dared challenge them or the carriers.

The English sighted their French quarry off the Kentish north Foreland, heading in formation for the mouth of the Thames.

Nicholas narrowed his eyes and through the bluster of wind counted the number of sails, finding that it tallied with the intelligence report. His heart began to pound like a drum and his palms were damp as he checked that his sword was properly fastened at his hip.

The French spotted them and, distantly, Nicholas heard jeering laughter. With Eustace the Monk leading them in and the English beaten at every turn in the Narrow Sea, the French were not unduly bothered by the motley collection of vessels standing off to windward. They clewed their sails ready for battle, but without urgency or alarm.

The jeering increased when Hubert de Burgh commanded

his flagship to veer away from contact. On the nearest French ships, figures could be scene capering and making obscene gestures with fists and forearms.

'That will soon change,' Nicholas murmured. His belly churned but with a surge of aggression rather than nausea. 'Martin, bring her round.'

'Aye, sir.' Martin cupped his hands and began yelling orders.

'Ready with arrows and lime, Master Sorale?' Nicholas asked the commander of the soldiers occupying the raised decks of the *Pandora*'s two castles.

Sorale adjusted the strap on his helm and wiped his forefinger beneath his nose. Already pink runnels of sweat were striping his cheeks. 'Aye, we're ready, but I cannot see why you ask when we're running in the opposite direction.'

'We're not.' As he spoke, the *Pandora* kicked and began to wear ship in a cream of spray. The wind bellied into her sail and suddenly she was surging like a wild horse towards the French ships.

'See, we've taken their wind.' Nicholas grinned wolfishly. 'There's nothing they can do except be run down.'

Sorale took to his heels, bellowing orders to his men. Shading his eyes, Nicholas stood at the *Pandora*'s prow. The stiff breeze whipped his garments against his body and buffeted him so that he had to grasp a rope to steady himself.

Ahead of the *Pandora,* the ship under the command of Philip d'Albini came within range of the first French vessels and attacked. A swarm of arrows whined through the air and plummeted into wood and rigging, sails and flesh. The jeers became screams of agony and panic. Second and third volleys increased the destruction of the first and the French unclewed their sails and tried to run.

A large nef bearing the fleur-de-lis banner on the wooden platform over her rudder hissed through the water towards the English lines. Spume netted her bows and jewels of water dripped from the fangs of the dragon head on her prow. The French soldiers on board returned the arrow fire as she heeled in close to the smaller nef of Richard FitzJohn, just ahead of the *Pandora.*

'Christ, she's going to ram!' Nicholas paused by the mast and stared in horror. There was a choked scream as one of their own soldiers took a French arrow through the arm. 'Hold her steady!' Nicholas bellowed.

The French ship ploughed into the smaller nef in a crunch of timbers. The sea lashed in white tongues between the two vessels. Grapnels were thrown and sword steel flashed in the summer blue. Cries for King Henry, cries for Louis, were ripped by the wind amid less articulate battle howls as soldiers and sailors from both sides clashed. There was nowhere to run. It was either kill, be killed, or drown.

The *Pandora* hove in fast across the Frenchman's bows, and Captain Sorale's men began bombarding the enemy with the stones and the pots of pulverised lime. The clay containers smashed upon the wash strake and open deck, enveloping the French crew and soldiers in stinging clouds of white powder. Blinded, choking, they could neither defend themselves, nor flee. Their sail was clewed up ready for battle and they were burdened with a cargo of horses and a huge, stone-throwing trebuchet, dismantled in pieces across the open hold.

Soon the French flagship was surrounded by four English vessels, all plying grapnels. Choking on lime, Eustace's men were helpless to defend their ship.

Nicholas leaped across the tight-lashed grapnel rope and on to the Frenchman's deck. Trapped on all sides, the nef lurched and sawed in the water. Drawing his sword Nicholas attacked not men, but the rigging that bound up the great sail. Martin Wudecoc ran to his aid with a Dane axe. Between them they hacked through all the vital halyards then leaped aside, exchanging broad grins. With a sound like a massive roll of thunder, the sail collapsed in a great smothering blanket of canvas, engulfing all beneath it.

The end came swiftly after that. The French surrendered and the fleur-de-lis banner flying from the stern of the flagship was ripped down and brandished to a massive English cheer. On seeing their flagship taken, the rest of the French fleet scattered in disarray, many to be captured by the jubilant English.

Nicholas's eyes were pouring with tears from the effects

of the powdered lime. Blinking hard, trying not to rub them, he was about to reboard the *Pandora*, when another triumphant shout made him turn. Captain Sorale emerged from the hold with the master of the fourth English ship, a man named Stephen Trabe. Between them, they escorted a squat, powerfully built sailor with a weather-browned pate, bordered at the base of the skull by a horseshoe of corn-white hair. His face was pocked and scarred, and his protuberant blue eyes were red and streaming.

'Here he is!' boomed Stephen Trabe, his lip curling in a sneer. 'The greatest mariner and pirate in northern waters, and the scum of the world. Look well, every one of you. Look well on the face of Eustace the Monk. Not so fearsome now, is he?'

Eustace shrugged within his captors' grip and stared insolently around the circle of witnesses. 'I care not a fig for your opinions,' he sneered. 'For if I am scum, none of you is worth more than a pot of leper's piss. Were my ship not so laden, I would still have defeated you with my hands tied.' Twisting his head, he spat in Trabe's face. 'You're a pirate yourself, Trabe, a filthy mackerel feeding off better men's leavings.'

Trabe turned as red as his hair, then white. Jerking Eustace out of Sorale's grip, he slammed the prisoner down on his knees and drew his sword. 'You have a choice,' he choked. 'Either I slice your head from your neck across the main beam of that trebuchet, or I use the ship's rail. Which is it to be, you whoreson traitor?'

'Your choices are about as imaginative as the size of your mind,' Eustace sneered. 'What will Hubert de Burgh say when he discovers that you had slaughtered me rather than accept a pledge of ten thousand marks for my life and the promise of fealty to King Henry.'

There was a stunned silence. Everyone knew that Eustace had changed sides more often than a dinner table in a busy great hall, but this was unbelievable. So was the sum of ten thousand marks.

Trabe snorted down his nose. 'Hubert de Burgh will say that I chose well.' Before anyone could move to prevent him, he raised his sword, bringing it round and down in a single razored swipe. Head and body hit the deck simultaneously but apart and men leaped away in horror to avoid the spray of blood. Nicholas's gorge rose and he had to swallow hard. He had seen and encountered hard battle more than once in his life, had killed in the heat of it to save his skin, but he would never grow accustomed, or develop a relish for it as some men did. There was exhilaration in outwitting an enemy and emerging alive from the fray, but not in slaughter.

Trabe lifted Eustace's body, and without heed for the blood, shoved it over the ship's side. There was a flat smack as it hit the water, and then a green wave closed over the corpse and took it down. With a grunt of approval, Trabe turned away. Taking a spear from one of the soldiers, he rammed Eustace's head on to the iron point and set it at the prow like a figurehead. It dripped in the sea-wind, an obscene grin on its face.

Sickened, almost retching, Nicholas made for the haven of the *Pandora*.

CHAPTER 15

In Dover there was great celebration at the English victory. Most of the larger French ships had escaped intact to Calais, but many of the smaller ones had been captured with their supplies, thus depriving Louis of his provisions and his hopes of winning England for himself.

Besides some fine horses and the trebuchet, Eustace's vessel had yielded several chests of coin and bolts of silk intended for Louis's royal household. Hubert de Burgh divided the spoils, and Nicholas found himself the recipient of a pouch of gold bezants and a length of flame-coloured silk. He distributed half the money to his crew. The silk could be sold for a profit in Boston; he had no intention of keeping it, magnificent though it was. The associations were too dark.

The head of Eustace the Monk was paraded on the walls of Dover keep. It seemed to Nicholas as if the entire population of the port came out to see the grisly token and cheer. Eustace had been hated in the town for the suffering he had caused to English shipping and to English sailors, many of them Dover men. The air was festive, the taverns full to overflowing with celebrants.

As captain of one of the vessels that had captured Eustace, Nicholas was fêted at the castle and plied with wine and mead until his head spun. He made a determined effort to shake off the memory of Stephen Trabe hewing Eustace's head from his body and ramming it on that pike. It was difficult when Trabe himself was accounted the hero of the day for his deed with toast upon toast raised in his honour.

Wearying of the feast, Nicholas made his excuses and wove

somewhat unsteadily from the hall in search of a garderobe to ease his bladder. There were several communal ones on the first floor, built into the thickness of the wall. The pungent stink of urine and faeces was intensified by the waste channel of damp stone. Holding both penis and breath, Nicholas finished as quickly as he could, and hastened away from the place, but not back to the hall. He could not stomach any more celebration. Instead, he wandered the labyrinthine keep, investigating nooks and stairways, peering out through thin arrowslits on a darkness that was filled with the roar and surge of the sea.

He came eventually to the lower floor chapel. This was not the grand one for the King's use, but a smaller, less ostentatious affair for the members of the garrison. Nicholas hesitated. The light of votive candles flickered in cressets and the soft, golden darkness beckoned to him. Although a priest had shriven him that morning before putting to sea, he still felt that he had business with God – to thank Him for surviving, to pray for the souls who had not.

Entering the darkness he crossed himself and paused to light his own votive taper with a hand made unsteady by drink. Then he bent his knee to the altar cross and genuflected. Raising his bowed head, he realised that he was not alone. A woman was already kneeling on the chapel floor, her hands clasped in prayer. She looked round at him and he saw the pale oval of her face and the coppery gleam of her braid showing below her wimple. Tears glinted on her cheeks and he could hear the shaking of her breath as she strove to control her weeping. He thought he recognised her, but wasn't sure.

'Forgive me for intruding,' he said, his voice a little slurred.

She shook her head. 'You are not intruding. I was about to leave.' She rose to her feet in a single fluid motion that made him acutely aware of her height and the lush curves of her body.

'Not on my account, I hope.'

'No. I have said my prayers.' She wiped her face on the back of her hand and as she looked at him, Nicholas remembered her. Edwin le Grun's statuesque mistress. Edwin's ship, the *St Jerome*, had taken part in the battle, but Nicholas could not recall seeing its small, portly master in the hall tonight.

'Edwin's dead,' she said as if reading his mind, and sniffed into a linen kerchief she pulled from her sleeve.

'Dead?' Nicholas frowned. As far as he was aware, the only serious fighting had been in his section. Otherwise the French had run like chickens with salted tails. 'How?'

'A seizure on board as he went to the attack.' She blew her nose. 'The crew say that he just dropped like a stone.'

'I am sorry to hear that. I saw him yester eve before the battle and he appeared hale and hearty then.'

'He was.' Fresh tears brimmed in her eyes, accompanied by a tremulous smile. 'More so than in a long time.'

Lost for words, Nicholas could only gaze at her in sympathy and speculation.

'They are taking him home to his wife.' Her voice wobbled. 'People think I stayed with him for his wealth, but there was more to our bargain than money alone.'

'I'm sure there was,' Nicholas murmured uncomfortably.

She shot down his platitude with a single look. 'You find it hard to believe in a whore with a heart,' she said contemptuously. 'Well, perhaps you are right. Perhaps I should go and bury mine deep where no one will ever find and probe its soft parts again. I have a living to earn, after all.'

In a swish of skirts and a waft of musky perfume she hurried from the chapel. Nicholas jumped up and stumbled after her, catching her clumsily by the arm and turning her to face him. 'What I find hard are the words to say, especially when two quarts of Gascon wine are hampering my tongue,' he said ruefully. 'What was between you and Edwin le Grun is your concern. I was not judging you. I am sorry he is dead and I can see that you grieve for him.'

The stiffness of fury left her body and her face crumpled. 'I am sorry too, for being so swift to anger.' She swayed against him and he tightened his hold, thinking that she was going to faint and hoping that she would not because his own balance was precarious.

A group of revellers straggled past in search of a garderobe and lewd shouts of encouragement were tossed at Nicholas, together with several lucrative offers to his companion.

'You see,' she said with a weary gesture, 'there is no shortage of takers.'

Nicholas furrowed his brow. The image of her being used by those drunkards was distasteful, but he was aware of being a drunkard himself, his thoughts blurred and slow. 'Do you need a safe haven to spend the night?'

She looked up at him. 'Are you offering?'

'Just a place to sleep,' he said quickly, 'nothing more . . . I mean it,' he added swiftly. 'No ties.'

She chewed her lower lip and studied him, considering. Even slowed by drink, his body began to react to the pressure of hers. Heat pulsed into his groin. He shifted so that her weight was taken on his hip, for he did not want her to think that he was saying one thing and intending another.

'No ties,' she repeated with a slight narrowing of her eyelids, and then with a determined sniff drew herself upright. 'Where did you have in mind?'

By the time they reached the *Pandora,* the drink had taken full hold of Nicholas's senses. It was all he could do to walk up the gangplank without falling into the water. He gestured to the timber castle built over the stern rudder and told his companion to bed down there.

'Blankets in the hold,' he said carefully, waving a hand vaguely midships.

She smiled. 'I'll find them.'

He nodded and started towards the other castle at the cog's prow, but suddenly stopped and turned, almost overbalancing. 'I don't even know your name,' he said.

Her smile deepened, causing two dimples to appear either side of her luscious mouth. 'I doubt that you'll remember in the morning, but it's Magdalene.'

'Magdalene,' he repeated, capturing the syllables before they could vanish into the wine haze. 'Magdalene.'

He slept heavily. During the night he was visited by a shockingly vivid erotic dream. Strong fingers stroked his body, smoothing over his ribs and abdomen, rubbing his thighs, gently kneading his penis until he writhed and groaned. Then the fingers were replaced by a clinging sheath that sucked and squeezed until there was nothing but pure, fierce sensation. His hands were taken in other hands and guided to large, firm breasts, the skin like cool silk. The night breeze had stiffened the nipples into firm buds.

'Jesu God!' he gasped and opened his eyes.

Fingertips pressed gently against his lips. 'Lie still,' Magdalene murmured. 'This is my gift to you.'

'I don't—'

'You do,' she interrupted, rising and falling smoothly upon him, until the pleasure was too much and he arched like a taut bow, and then loosed himself, hurtling through ecstasy and into oblivion.

In the morning he woke to a splitting head, a dry mouth and the general malaise that came from a quart too much of Gascon wine. Gingerly he sat up and squinted at the sun which was well above the horizon. A huge herring gull sat on the *Pandora*'s mast and fixed him with a cold, yellow stare. There was something he had to remember. He rubbed his aching forehead and groaned.

Then he saw her crossing the deck towards him, a cup in her hand. She was fully dressed, her wimple neatly pinned.

'It is only water,' she said, 'but I have heard it is as good a remedy as any for a thick head.'

He took it from her with a bleary word of thanks.

'Well,' she said with a faint smile, 'do you know my name?'

He drank deeply, replenishing his body, then looked at her across the cup. She had given him the prompt and from somewhere he delivered the answer. 'Magdalene,' he said wryly, 'which is a heroic feat, since I am not sure that I know my own.'

She laughed, but not unkindly. 'You were well gilded last night.'

He nodded agreement and finished the water. 'Indeed I was, and I have the head to prove it this morning.' He squinted at her through light-sensitive eyes. 'Your name does not appear to be the only thing I remember from last night,' he said slowly. 'Was I dreaming that you came to me, or was it real?'

A delicate flush spread from her throat and mantled her face. 'It was whatever you wanted it to be,' she said.

Nicholas gazed down into the empty cup, his eyes tracing the spots of water on the glazed inner surface. He tried to think beyond the miasma in his skull. With Edwin dead, she was in need of a new protector and he could see himself being fitted for the role. Last night he had been given a taste of the goods on offer.

He looked up to find her watching him. 'I hope that it was real,' he said carefully. 'I seem to recall you saying something about a gift, so I will not insult you by offering payment.'

'You would have it flung back in your face if you did.'

He did not know what else to say, how to refuse without rejecting her outright, or seeming churlish. 'I am glad that you stayed,' he said at last, 'and I would enjoy your company again, but I am not Edwin, and I have no intention of offering you his kind of bargain.'

Her hands went to her hips. 'Have I asked it?'

'It is best to know the ground on which we stand.'

'You want me, but you don't. Fair enough.' She turned away.

'Oh, for Christ's sake, Magdalene.' His raised voice made his head pound with sickening force.

She looked at him over her shoulder, but instead of the petulance he expected, he was met by a wry smile and a coquettish shrug of one shoulder. 'Why shout? I said fair enough; I meant fair enough. Thank you for my night's lodging. Should you want me – for any reason' – here she raised a delicate eyebrow – 'I will be at The Red Boar – although next time it won't be a gift.'

And with that, she left. Nicholas curbed the impulse to go after her. She was right. He wanted her and he didn't. This way he maintained the balance without making a commitment and she was free to seek elsewhere.

Footsteps sounded on the deck and he looked up to see Stephen Trabe approaching.

'I just met with your guest,' Trabe said with a gesture towards the gangplank, a smile in his eyes which were remarkably bright given the amount of carousing the previous night. 'Small wonder you left the celebrations early. I would have done too.'

Carefully, Nicholas eased to his feet. He could feel the hair rising on his nape. 'What can I do for you, Master Trabe?'

The sailor's teeth flashed in a piratical grin. 'Nothing for the moment. I was on my way to my own ship and I came to thank you for your part in Eustace's capture.'

Nicholas turned away to don his tunic. 'There is no need,' he said flatly and then, because it was festering within him and could not be contained, added, 'If I had known that you were going to execute him without justice, I would never have cast my grapnel ropes.'

'He got justice,' Trabe said. 'Short, brutal, and what he deserved.' He drew breath as if to say something more, a speculative expression in his eyes, but then thought the better of it and turned away. 'Every ship's master on England's seaboard will sleep easier now. It had to be done, and I for one was glad to do it.'

As his footsteps retreated, Nicholas let out his breath on a shudder. As far as he could tell, there was small difference between Eustace the Monk and Stephen Trabe. Both were pirates with morals on the wrong side of damnation. The King was dead, long live the King.

The education that Miriel sought following her wedding night came from a quite unexpected quarter.

Seated on a bench outside the weaving shed, Alice Leen rested her stick against the wall and allowed the warm morning sun to seep into her old bones. Miriel brought her wine and politely enquired if she was settling into life at the priory.

'Too quiet,' Alice snapped. 'And too many monks.'

Miriel took the response in her stride. If Alice had not grumbled, she would have thought the woman seriously ill.

She wondered rather grimly how long this particular visit was going to last.

'And you, my girl, how is marriage suiting you?'

'Well enough,' Miriel replied warily.

Alice made a rude sound and drank her wine with the speed and expertise of a common soldier rather than a frail old lady. 'Just you wait until you've got a brat at your feet and another in your belly. It'll not suit you so well then.'

Miriel struggled with the urge to slap her tormentor. Shrewd as ever, the hag had hit the target with precision. She drank her own wine and remained on her feet, hoping that Alice would take the hint and leave.

Alice did no such thing. 'I know what it's like, my girl. Wouldn't wish it on anyone.' She looked pointedly at the flagon and, when Miriel pretended ignorance, eased to her feet and hobbled to refill her own cup.

'How would you know?' Miriel demanded. 'You don't have any children.'

Alice sucked her teeth. 'Not now, but I bore 'em when I was a young un like you. Four, one after the other, less than a year atween each. Nigh on killed me.' She limped back to the bench and carefully let herself down, her dark eyes moist and fierce. 'Before you ask, they all died. One at birth, two o' the spotted fever and one of a splinter that festered.'

'I'm sorry.' Miriel suddenly felt small and mean for her brusqueness towards Alice.

'What's to be sorry for? It's my grief, not yourn.' She swallowed her second cup of wine and a pink tinge began to lift her sallow complexion. 'You never get over it, losing them,' she said. 'You bear them in pain and that pain increases like a knife in your heart as they grow. And when they die untimely, the knife stays in and you bleed forever.' There was anger in her voice, burning and bitter.

A lump tightened in Miriel's throat. She would have put her arms around Alice's thin shoulders but knew that she would be immediately shrugged off.

'I'll not have you pitying me,' Alice snapped. 'Couldn't stand it then, and I won't stand it now.'

'I wasn't pitying you,' Miriel lied in a choked voice. 'I . . . I was hoping that it never happens to me.'

'Oh, it'll happen,' Alice said savagely. 'Likely you're with child even now.'

Despite the knowledge that it was impossible, Miriel pressed her hand to her flat belly in panic. 'I'm not,' she said, 'and I know I am not. My flux came two days ago.'

'You might escape once or twice, but you always catch in the end – unless you're barren, or you can keep your husband's seed from your womb.'

Miriel looked sharply at Alice. 'Do you know the method?' Her tone was eager with hope. She had not relished the thought of seeking contraceptive advice from the town whores or a wise woman of dubious repute, and it was hardly something that she could ask the likes of Eva Bridlesmith.

Bleak amusement sparkled in Alice's eyes. 'I know several. Decided after bearing and burying four that the candle wasn't worth the game.' She held out her cup. 'Might as well fill it up, wench. I'll be here a while yet and I can see you're not so keen to be rid o' me now.'

Chapter 16

Autumn 1218

In Lincoln Annet Fuller stirred the gently simmering mutton ragout, tasted it, and added more wine from the nearby jug. Nigel was dealing with a valuable customer who might be staying to dine and she was justly proud of this particular dish. It might look like an ordinary stew, but its taste was fit for a king – or a wealthy Italian merchant in England to buy woollen twills and worsteds.

Guido of Florence usually sent his agents, but this year he had come in person. He was travelling to the great autumn fair in Nottingham, but visiting other towns on his way.

Annet left the stew to bubble and whisked around the room, giving it an unnecessary tidy. Everything was immaculate, not even a floor rush out of place. The hearth was swept, the napery so white that it gleamed, and the delicate scent of rose pot-pourri was not quite overpowered by the delicious aroma of the ragout.

Whenever Annet was nervous she took to household duties with a vengeance. They needed Master Guido's order. Of late business had been dwindling. Many of her father's former customers had gone elsewhere when he died, and after the scandal of Miriel and St Catherine's, that particular supply of first-grade wool had dried up and Nigel had experienced difficulties replacing it. Damn the girl. Why couldn't she have been a good and dutiful daughter? *Just like you*, said a voice inside Annet's head, causing her to dust a coffer top with renewed vigour.

'Yes, just like me,' she said aloud, her voice full of bitterness. What would have happened, she wondered, if she had eloped with the troubadour instead of staying at home? Probably she would have died in a ditch, cold and hungry, but was it any worse than the way she lived now? Miriel had taken her chance, had run away with her soldier of fortune. Annet realised with a sudden flash of clarity that she was angry with her daughter because she was envious. And that was stupid, completely and utterly.

She returned to the stew, her grey eyes filling with tears of frustration. The door banged open and with a guilty leap she spun to face her husband. He was alone and his expression was thunderous.

'Where's Master Guido?' she asked. 'Is he not staying to dine?'

Nigel strode into the room. 'No, he says he has other weavers to see.' He spoke through his teeth.

Annet's stomach lurched. 'Has he committed himself to buying any of our cloth?'

'What do you think?' Nigel snarled. 'Oh, the oily bastard was diplomatic about it, said that he could not come to a decision until he had looked at other workshops, but I know when I'm being given the elbow. If we had stood any chance, he'd have been with me now.'

Annet swallowed. She knew how much hope Nigel had been pinning on Guido's contract.

He strode past her, launching a kick at the cauldron. Annet had to jump to avoid being splashed by the scalding mutton stew.

'But why? He's always bought from us before.'

'Wrong,' Nigel growled. 'His agent has always bought from us before.' Reaching the wall he flung round and paced back across the room. 'You should have seen him. Poking into every corner, examining the raw wool, counting the number of threads to the inch on the cloth with some sort of glass disc.' He spat into the rushes.

Annet winced. 'No one makes better cloth in Lincoln than you. He'll just look at the others and come back to us.'

Nigel grunted and bit on his thumb nail. 'He's going to look in Nottingham too, at the great fair.'

'Well, there's never been anyone to rival you there, either.'

'There is now. Take a look at this.' He pulled a square of wool from his pouch and tossed it at her. 'One of the pack-pony men bought an ell of it from a booth on Leenside. It's a match for our best greyne.'

Annet looked at the red cloth in her hands. It was more than a match for theirs, the weave finer and the wool of a better quality. It was like the cloth they had produced when her father was alive, but she dared not say so to Nigel. 'Then offer him a price he cannot refuse.'

'No,' Nigel snapped. 'I'll not be driven into a corner.'

But he would walk into one of his own accord. Annet sighed inwardly, suddenly feeling very tired. 'Then what will you do?'

He shrugged. 'I'll think of something.'

Her father would have made a decision immediately and driven forward. But Nigel was not her father, his grip was less sure. 'Do you want some ragout?'

He shook his head and, snatching the scrap of cloth from her hands, went to the door. 'I have no appetite.'

She shuddered and closed her eyes as he slammed out. Not for the first time she wished that she had entered St Catherine's and left Miriel in her place. It would probably have suited everyone better. She hooked the cooking pot off the flames and lifted her cloak from the peg in the wall. Usually she would have sent one of the servants out to the market, but the room was poisoned with Nigel's anger and her own anxiety. She needed space to breathe. Calling to one of the women to mind the fire, she collected her willow basket and went out.

The market place was busy. Annet wandered among the booths and stalls like a ghost. She had no idea what provisions they needed because she had not checked. Her only concern had been to escape.

Acquaintances greeted her and she answered them with smiles and the right words, but her eyes were distant, her mind a blank. She didn't want to think because thinking made her realise how trapped she was and induced a choking sensation of panic. As long as she played the role of efficient and well-to-do housewife and believed in it, she was cushioned. When the belief wavered and threatened to dissolve, so did she.

Saffron, they needed more saffron. She paused at a spice-seller's booth to buy some of the dark yellow strands. And some cinnamon sticks too, for simmering with the garden pears. She had no enthusiasm for haggling, but forced herself to do so. It was all part of the role, and besides, if Guido of Florence did not buy, they would need to trim the fat much closer to the lean.

Across from the booth, on the road that climbed towards castle and minster, she became aware of the jangle of tambours and the groan of bagpipes.

'Looks like the sheriff's got himself some entertainment for the night,' remarked the spicer, setting his hands on his hips and grinning.

Slowly Annet turned and her hand shook as she placed the saffron and cinnamon in her basket. A troupe of players was dancing up the road, their costumes a gaudy blend of reds, yellows and blues. Four men, four women and two youngsters. One of the women juggled with batons as she walked. The other swirled brightly coloured ribbons on a stick whilst a child danced around her with the tambour. Annet stared while her hard-built world fragmented around her. The man who led them stepped out with the casual grace of a cat. He was tall and slender. The sleek amber-blond hair had receded and there were deep lines like pen strokes carved into his tanned features. But Annet knew that if he looked her way, his eyes would echo the carefree joy of the music and she would be fourteen years old again.

'Mistress Fuller?'

She did not hear the spicer's voice, nor a moment later his cry of alarm as he reached to grab her and missed. She did not see the cart rumbling towards her as she stepped out into the road. All she saw was a man with sunlight in his eyes and her own dancing feet.

Miriel watched the Italian merchant from the corner of her eye while she poured him wine. Guido of Florence was in

Nottingham to sell red silk cloth dyed in the workshops of Florence, and to buy English twills, worsteds and serges.

Miriel had given the Italian trader a tour of her weaving sheds on Leenside, showing him with justifiable pride the first of their bales of Lincoln cloth, spun from the finest diamond ewe's wool and dyed soft green and rich greyne-red.

'You tempt me sorely, Mistress Woolman,' Guido said, accepting the wine she gave him. There was a twinkle in his black eyes, but he sobered quickly as he caught Gerbert's scowl. 'It is very fine cloth that you have for sale. Indeed, it is as good as any I could buy in Lincoln itself. Of late my supplier there has not been offering me the quality I demand, and your price is competitive.'

'Then what stops you from yielding to your temptation? Eustace the Monk is dead, and your ships can sail without being robbed of their cargo.' Miriel's voice was a trifle breathless, but not owing to his flirting. She was well accustomed to that particular hazard in her business dealings. What did give her a queasy jolt was the fact that Lincoln's main producer of the famous red and green cloth was the house of Edwin Weaver, now in her stepfather's mediocre, if not incompetent, hands.

Guido shrugged expressively. 'I am a businessman. I have to decide whether it is worth my while.'

Miriel pursed her lips and nodded. 'You must do as you see fit for your livelihood, Master Guido, but so must I. I need to know by the morrow's noon if you intend to purchase my cloth, for I do have other buyers waiting.'

She presented Gerbert with his cup of wine and, as she touched his shoulder, gave him a sweet, placatory smile. Essentially she dealt with him as she had dealt with her grandfather. She delighted him with her energy and her youth, she kept him amused with her whims, listened patiently to his ramblings, soothed his aching feet in hot salt water, let him show her off, made him proud.

Her nocturnal duty, for which she had no experience to fall back upon, was not particularly pleasant, but she had her ruses. Oiled by her third cup of wine, Alice Leen had become most informative and eloquent. Accordingly Miriel was able to keep Gerbert at hand's if not arm's length in bed, and as they had grown more familiar with each other, his old man's ardour had dwindled to a pale flame seldom kindled.

Guido drank his wine and made a sound of appreciation for its quality. 'Madonna, I let you know in the morning, before the hour of prime,' he announced, setting his cup on the oak sideboard.

Miriel nodded. 'Would it be asking too much to know the name of your weaver in Lincoln?'

Looking amused, he told her, and Miriel let out a little breath, her colour high.

'I see by your face that you are acquainted with him, madonna?'

'I know of his household, yes.'

'It is so sad about his wife, no?'

Miriel's spine turned to ice. She had to lock her knees to stay on her feet. 'His wife?' she said hollowly.

'She walk out in front of a loaded cart and she die in the street,' said the Italian with an expressive gesture. 'No reason. He very upset.'

Miriel clenched her hands in her gown, her fingernails biting half-moons in her palm while she struggled to keep the expression of a sympathetic stranger on her face.

'That is sad news indeed,' Gerbert rescued her, heaving his bulk from the chair. 'We will pray for him and the repose of his dear wife's soul when next we attend mass. And now you must excuse us. My health has not been good recently and I am swift to tire.'

'But of course.' Guido of Florence rose smoothly to his feet, and if he was surprised by the abruptness of the end to the meeting, he was too good a diplomat to show it. 'I will return in the morning, madonna.' He bowed to Miriel, and then to Gerbert.

Miriel saw him to the door and his servant summoned. Her lips stretched in a smile and she murmured courtesies that she was not later to recall. And when he was gone, she turned back into the room and eased herself down on the bench against the wall like an old woman.

'My mother,' she said, and pressed her hand against her lips.

Gerbert poured fresh wine into his cup and brought it to her. 'I'm sorry, lass.' Clumsily he patted her rigid shoulder. 'It must be doubly hard to bear such news when it comes in casual gossip from the lips of a stranger.'

Miriel lowered her hand to her lap and clasped it inside her other one, making a tight double fist that matched the knot of misery in her abdomen. 'I thought I hated her,' she said in a small voice, 'and now that she's dead, it's too late to discover that I don't.'

Gerbert plumped down beside her, his weight creaking the bench, and reached out his arm to pull her into his bulk. 'You have a good cry if you want,' he said, his hand patting her back like a mother with a baby. 'Better out than in.'

'But I don't want,' she said, blinking fiercely. 'What will it avail me?' She jumped to her feet, freeing herself from his grip, seeking self-containment like a cat. 'All the tears in the world will not bring her back to life, nor make amends.'

'Nay, but they may give you ease,' Gerbert said with gentle sadness. 'When my Sybil died, I wept fit to fill a bucket, and felt the better for it. Light candles, say prayers, God will hear.'

Miriel made a small sound and shook her head. She had prayed for God to visit a murrain on her stepfather, and so he had, but at a price whose payment had returned to haunt her. 'God hears only too well,' she said.

Guido of Florence bought all the cloth that Miriel's looms could produce and sent his agents back for more. Throwing herself into her trade with a vengeance, Miriel toiled from before dawn until after dusk, substituting hard work for grief, regret and guilt. She had the excuse of Nottingham's October fair to keep her busy. Traders came from all parts of the country to the gathering and if Miriel had been busy before, now she was frantic with the effort of producing enough cloth to sell at her booth. All the Bridlesmith children who were competent were employed in spinning yarn. Old Alice emerged from her retirement to help and Miriel worked until long after candle-light. Night after night, Gerbert came down to the sheds and fetched her home to supper where she would almost fall asleep over her dish. Clucking to himself, shaking his head, Gerbert would help her up to bed and tuck her in tenderly like a child. He understood what drove her, but after the fair, it would have to stop. He wanted a wife and a companion, not this haunted creature goaded by her past to prove herself when nothing needed proving.

On the eve of the fair, Miriel was in the candle-lit workshop, conducting a final inspection before Gerbert arrived to take her home. She paused beside each loom to examine the work in progress, and moved on to the bales of finished fabric awaiting transportation to the morrow's fair. She touched the soft cloth, fingering the luxury of the nap that she herself had cropped with the shears. From being a contender in the market place, she was fast becoming a power, and that feeling went some way to comforting the small, lost child cowering behind the façade of industry and confidence.

Humouring that child, Miriel left the looms and the bales of fabric. She took a candle lantern off the shelf and descended the rock-cut steps into the store rooms at the back of the shed. By the leaping gold of the flame, she gazed round at bales of wool and dyed yarn, at the spare Flemish loom and the shuttles piled beside it. The smells of stone and wool hung in the air, blending with the aroma of candle wax.

Miriel crossed to a large oak chest at the back of the store room. The piece was crudely carved and of small value, the sort most women kept in their houses to hold spare pots or clothing. This particular one contained a motley collection of drop spindles and different-sized weights of stone, clay and bone. No one would have given it a second glance, or paused for one moment to notice that it had a greater exterior depth than its internal dimensions suggested.

Miriel knelt beside the chest and put her lantern on the floor. She ran her hand beneath the furniture until she touched a small wooden peg. Swivelling it, she released a hinged flap, giving access to a small, hidden compartment. Tenderly, Miriel lifted Empress Mathilda's crown from its hiding place and unfolded the silk wrappings. It had been a long time since she had possessed an opportunity to look on the object and her sense of awe was heightened by the surrounding darkness of the cave, lit only by her lantern flame. It was almost like worshipping at a shrine.

She found herself talking to the crown as if the object had a life of its own. She whispered her regrets, her fears, her needs and ambitions, how far she had progressed, how far she still had to go in her search for security. She told it about her mother, her sorrow, her grieving for what might have been and never was. The jewels gleamed at her like dragon's eyes, the pearls shone like the finest white silk, and the gold flickered with the red of fire.

Bedazzled, it took her a moment to realise that the flicker was a reflection, and not of her lantern. Miriel whirled and saw tongues of flame leaping from a yarn basket in the main room. She heard the crackle of fire and inhaled the stench of burning wool. With a cry, she thrust the crown into its wrappings, stuffed it back into its hiding place and ran upstairs to the weaving shed. Choking on smoke, her eyes stinging and streaming, she grabbed the wooden water pail from beside the door and deluged the flames. Retching and coughing, she seized a besom and beat at the stray tendrils of fire.

A man's shape loomed in the doorway, blocking what little light remained in the dusk. 'Don't just stand there,' Miriel snapped, thinking it a neighbour, 'come and help, or go and summon others.'

He entered the room, positioning himself to confront her with clenched fists. Miriel stared into the handsome, petulant features of her former stepfather and shock struck her like a physical blow. 'Nigel!' she coughed. 'This is your doing, you whoreson!'

He stared back at her and, through the look of loathing and rage on his face, she saw astonishment too. 'You hell-spawned bitch!' he snarled. 'I might have known that you'd set out to ruin me, you vindictive slut. It's not enough that you have disgraced your family, but now you must destroy the trade that supported it too.'

'You're not my family!' Miriel spat. 'And it is through

your own incompetence that your trade has failed. Yours.' She jabbed the broom handle at him, tears of rage and grief blurring her eyes. 'You couldn't even keep my mother!'

He leaped nimbly aside. 'Her death was God's will,' he said hoarsely. 'Christ Jesu, you're not part of my Annet, you're a changeling. They should have let you die at the hour of your birth!' He hefted a bale of fabric from the table and advanced on her.

She braced the besom like a quarterstaff and circled the smouldering basket, attempting to keep it between them. And she tried to scream for help, but her throat was too roughened by smoke and she could only cough. Surely someone would have seen the fire. Surely someone would come.

Nigel leaped, knocking the broom from her hand and bearing her to the ground. His weight flattened her and he pressed the end of the bolt of cloth over her nose and mouth, stretching it tight, sealing off air. Miriel clenched her fist and punched it as hard as she could into the centre of his throat.

He recoiled, crowing for breath, and Miriel grabbed the loosened cloth in her own hands and surged to her feet.

'Bitch, I'll kill you!' he choked, and lunged again.

They grappled in the dark. Miriel bit and scratched, fighting like a wild cat to be free, but Nigel held on grimly. One hand found her throat and squeezed.

'Mother of Christ!' exclaimed Gerbert from the doorway, the horn lantern in his hand illuminating the scene. He bellowed the alarm and waded into the room, snatching a pair of nap shears from a hook on the wall.

Nigel flung Miriel aside and turned to face the new threat. She crashed against one of the looms, hit her head on a wooden yarn rack, and dropped like a poled ox.

'Robbers, murderers!' Gerbert yelled and stabbed the shears at the dark shape in front of him. The blades passed through tunic and shirt, grazing Nigel's flank, but inflicting no mortal wound. Nigel jerked his knee into Gerbert's paunch and, as the wool merchant doubled over, wheezing, made his escape through the doorway into the heavy dusk.

Inside the shed, Miriel crawled to her hands and knees.

There was a swelling bruise the size of a goose egg on the back of her head and she felt sick. She could hear Gerbert groaning. Then he made a strange, gargling sound. Light tore at her eyes and a strong arm curved around her shoulders. She screamed and tried to fight it off, but her limbs were as useless as tangled yarn.

'It's all right, it's all right, help is at hand. No one is going to hurt you,' soothed Robert Willoughby's strong voice. 'What happened?'

Miriel shook her head and felt it buzz as though it contained a swarm of bees. 'He tried to set fire to the shed, and to kill me,' she answered, her voice distant and slow. It was an effort to speak. Robert's face swam in and out of focus and her belly churned.

'Who did, who tried to kill you?'

A cold rim was set against her lips and a fiery, sharp-scented liquid trickled down her raw throat. She choked and coughed. 'My stepfather. He has a grudge against me.'

'Your stepfather?'

Miriel compressed her lips. 'Personal,' she said, and closed her lids, feeling a great weariness overlaying the nausea. 'Too long a tale.'

Robert Willoughby gave her a thoughtful look out of slightly narrowed eyes. 'But perhaps it will bear telling,' he murmured.

His words came as if from a great distance, blurred and faint. She did not want to hear them and sought the darkness, covering herself in its deepening layers. When he tapped her face to waken her, she moaned at him and flopped in his arms.

'Bear them both home,' Robert said to the master weaver who stood to one side, rubbing his beard in agitation. 'Mistress Woolman may be able to tell us what happened when she recovers, but for now, there is nothing we can do but make sure this place is secure and alert the Watch.'

'Yes, sir,' the craftsman said with obvious relief at having someone there to take control. 'I'll move a mattress in here and bed down with the looms myself lest the rogue returns.'

'Is the mistress going to be all right?' asked the weaver's wife, her face pale within its frame of hastily donned wimple.

Robert looked down at Miriel cradled in his arms – the fine-grained skin blotched with developing bruises, the lantern light making silky shadows of her lashes. 'Yes, I think so,' he said softly, and in his voice there was tenderness and possession.

Miriel opened her eyes to the sound of the wind roaring down the chimney and rattling at the shutters. A cold draught fluttered the wall hangings and threatened to extinguish the flame of the night candle.

She sat up and a nauseous pain shot through the back of her head. Swallowing, she pressed her hand gingerly against the bruise and explored the size of the lump. Her throat felt as if she had been drinking fire, and her limbs as if someone had torn them off and then cobbled them back together in the same brutal fashion. She was wearing her undertunic, but no wimple. Her overgown had been hung neatly on her clothing pole, and her shoes placed side by side beneath it.

Hazy memories darted through her mind like fish in a murky stream – swift silver flashes interspersed with nothing. She had been at the weaving shed. She had seen fire reflected in gold, then Nigel had appeared out of nowhere and . . .

'Holy Mother,' she gasped and dived for the piss bucket. She hung over it, dry-retching, her vision throbbing with little blobs of light. The fish had become an entire shoal and she could see everything.

There came the sound of rapid footsteps. 'I told you not to leave her alone!' Robert Willoughby said grimly.

'I'm sorry, sir,' came Elfwen's frightened voice. 'I did but go to fetch fresh candles.'

Once again, Robert's arm curved around Miriel's shoulders. 'Steady now, steady,' he soothed.

Miriel gulped. The spasms subsided, leaving her shivering and tired to death. He led her back to the bed and gave her sweet mead to sip.

Miriel looked at him, at the weary pouches beneath his eyes

and the deep lines graven from nostril to mouth corner. The significance of his presence in her bedchamber hit her like a stone. 'Where's Gerbert?' she asked unsteadily.

Robert gazed down at the coverlet for a moment, then drew a deep breath and took her hands in his. 'I am sorry, Miriel, but he is dead. He suffered a seizure on the weaving-shed floor. We bore him home with you, but he died ere he was over the threshold. There was nothing we could do. He has been taken to St Mary's and lies before the altar.' He squeezed her fingers, his hazel eyes pensive and sorrowful.

'Gerbert, dead?' Miriel whispered. Her mind filled with a vision of him standing among his wool sacks, hands resting on his large belly, his air one of pleasure and complacence. Then she thought of the small, concerned frown knitting his brows as he told her that driving herself would do nothing to banish her troubles, for where she moved, they went too. 'It can't be true,' she whispered.

'I'm sorry,' Robert said again.

Miriel took her hands from beneath his and struggled from the bed. The world pitched and swayed, but she tottered gamely to her clothing pole and took down her overdress.

'What are you doing?' Robert demanded, his eyes full of astonishment.

'I am going to kneel at Gerbert's bier,' she said in a thin, determined voice.

'But you are in no fit state. You should still be abed!'

'Nevertheless, I must go. It is my duty.'

Robert opened his mouth to protest and she faced him, her eyes cloudy with concussion, but her jaw as tight as a vice. 'It is my grief and my right,' she added grimly. 'Will you deny me that?'

He sighed and, with a shake of his head, stood up. 'Nay, mistress, I will not deny you, even if I think it ill advised. But let me escort you there at least. From the looks of you, you need an arm to lean upon.'

She nodded brusquely, still very much on her dignity, but had to yield when she could not stoop to put on her shoes and had to ask Robert and Elfwen to help her. She did indeed welcome the support of Robert's strong arm as he led her the short distance to St Mary's Church.

'The sheriff has launched a search for the thief who set fire to your shed and attacked you both,' he murmured as he pushed into the vigorous autumn wind, his free hand clapping his hat to his head. 'It's a matter of murder now.'

The cold wind scoured through Miriel's skull, blowing away the fog to leave an echoing cavern.

'He'll want to talk to you, but I told him that you were in no condition.' Robert stooped round to look into her face. 'I did not tell him what you said about your stepfather. I thought I would ask you first.'

Mercifully they arrived at the church door and Miriel was spared the difficulty of making an immediate reply. Her thoughts flew in the hollow chamber of her mind. What had she said about her stepfather? How far had she exposed herself and how far could she trust Robert Willoughby?

Lamp- and candle-light filled the church, flickering in every corner and crevice, illuminating the blue cloak draping the alabaster statue of St Mary, dancing off the painted sandstone columns with their vigorous scrollwork coils. The church had been sacked during the uprising of old King Henry's sons thirty years ago, and this was a new building, standing on the ashes of the several that had gone before.

Gerbert's body lay on a bier before the altar, surrounded by yet more candles. His hands were folded on his breast and clasped a wooden cross. He was wearing the green gown in which he had died, and his scuffed old boots. A linen bandage bound up his jaw and his hair and beard had been combed.

For an instant, Miriel was back at her grandfather's wake, kneeling in the cathedral nave at Lincoln. Her belly heaved and she compressed her lips and swallowed.

'I should not have let you come,' Robert murmured in her ear.

'The decision was mine to make, not yours.' Miriel lit a candle with shaking hands and then knelt beside the bier to pray.

Robert crossed himself and knelt with her. 'He had his faults, but he was a good man and my friend,' he said.

'He deserved to die in his bed, not in so vile a fashion.'

Miriel bowed her head over her steepled fingers. Beside her she could feel Robert Willoughby's presence like the touch of a heavy hand. 'My wits are scattered to the four winds. What did I say to you about my stepfather? I remember not a word.'

'That he was responsible for the attack and that it was a long story.'

She bit her lip.

'Are you not going to speak?'

Miriel looked at him sidelong, at the forceful, craggy features, the strong carved lines and hard stare of a man accustomed to obtaining his way. And just now she was in no case to resist him. 'Do I have your word that you will not go to the sheriff?'

'No, you do not.' His voice barely carried through the space between them, but it was full of indignation and anger. 'My kin by marriage, a senior townsman, lies murdered. You could be dead too, and yet you ask me not to speak out?'

'Then I will say nothing. I will say that I do not remember.'

He made a sound in his throat, got up, walked away.

Miriel tried to pray. The candle shadow rippled like waves over Gerbert's waxen features. It was her fault he was dead, but all the remorse and guilt in the world would not bring him back.

'Very well, I swear that whatever you say will not go beyond these walls.' Robert Willoughby returned to her side. His brows were drawn into a deep frown and he was obviously unhappy with the decision.

Miriel hesitated, trying to assess him, but neither eyes nor mind would focus. She gave a deep sigh and a small gesture of capitulation. 'My stepfather is Nigel of Lincoln, a weaver and fuller, although not a master one as my grandfather Edward was. We hated each other; we argued all the time and he used to beat me. As a young girl my mother bore me out of wedlock to a travelling player and Nigel thought me tainted. So I . . .' She paused, and looked down. There was no need to tell him everything. 'So I ran away, and Gerbert took me in.' A fold of Gerbert's tunic was hanging over the edge of the bier and she rubbed it between her fingers, taking comfort in the feel of the prickly green wool. 'The rest you know, Master Willoughby. Gerbert was a good husband and he knew my past. There was never any question of me duping a foolish old man. Indeed, his eyes were more open than mine.' Miriel shook her head. 'I did not set out to ruin Nigel's business, but I will not deny that there was pleasure in doing so . . . until now.'

'So your stepfather, Nigel of Lincoln, is the man responsible for this,' Robert said, his eyes narrowing.

Miriel fought a new surge of nausea. 'His intention was to put an end to a business that was taking customers from him. He did not realise until he saw me that I was the one responsible, and then he was overcome with a madness of rage – it was ever in his nature.'

There was silence for a while, broken only by the soft voice of the chanting priest before the altar as the bells rang out the hour of prime and daylight gathered at the windows.

'And if the sheriff comes to hear these things, you will be dragged down with your stepfather,' Robert said, eyeing her shrewdly. 'Folk will hear how Gerbert's wife is in truth a runaway daughter with a poor reputation.'

Miriel bowed her head. 'I would not want that to happen for my sake, or for Gerbert's memory. People would pity him for a duped old fool, and disdain me for a self-seeking hussy, and both are far from the truth.'

'And what is truth, since it changes according to each individual's perception?'

She did not know whether the arch of his brows was genuine or sarcastic, nor did she really care. 'Then make of it what you will,' she said wearily. 'I have no more strength for explanations.'

'One question.' He balanced his chin on his steepled palms. 'How came you by the means to play the wealthy widow if you were a runaway?'

She looked at him. 'I took money.'

Robert returned her look, his eyebrows remaining aloft.

Miriel coloured. 'It was owing to me. Every woman has

a dowry.' Let him assume that she had robbed her family's coffers. It was an obvious move to have made, and it kept the rest of her past hidden.

His mouth corners twitched. He folded his smile within his praying hands and bowed his head. In short order, the humour creases departed eyes and lips, leaving his countenance intent and still, like a predator considering its prey.

CHAPTER 17

SUMMER 1219

The *Empress* was a large nef with a dragonhead prow and the sleek lines of her Viking ancestors. She rode at anchor on Boston's river quay with the *Pandora* and a small cog, the *Grâce-Dieu,* newly returned from Flanders. English wool had been the cog's outward export; finished cloth her homeward cargo together with a chest of rare spices and a set of exquisite silver-gilt goblets for Nicholas's client.

Since the sea battle off Sandwich and the execution of Eustace the Monk, Hubert de Burgh had been as good as his word. Lucrative business had come Nicholas's way – so lucrative that he had been able to furnish himself with two more ships. The large nef with her speed and elegance was frequently commissioned by de Burgh as a courier vessel. Nicholas had navigated her up the Scottish coast bearing emissaries, had crossed to Scandinavia and down to the Low Countries. With the proceeds he had commissioned Rohan to begin a fourth cog of the same dimensions as the *Pandora.*

Now, Nicholas stood on the quayside watching the crew unload the *Grâce-Dieu.*

'Sea was rough for June, but it troubled her not one whit,' said Martin Wudecoc who had captained her. 'We put in at Antwerp ahead of time.' He smiled, his teeth dazzling white against his sea-burnished skin. 'Home early too.' Inside his tunic, something bulged and wriggled. Grimacing, the sailor delved inside his neckline and out popped the fluffy head of a tiny black and white puppy. 'And all the cargo intact,' he said before his voice suddenly rose and squawked: 'Hell's bollocks, the little bugger's pissed on me!'

Nicholas laughed heartily. Then he shook his head. 'I've never understood why women like to keep such animals.'

'Hah, I've never understood women!' Martin answered, wiping his hand on his tunic. 'And here's Alyson to prove it!' He waved at a woman who was hurrying along the quayside, a basket over her arm.

Grinning, Nicholas watched Martin Wudecoc run to his wife, sweep her round on his arm, and kiss her soundly. That was what a homecoming should be, he thought. There was no one to greet him. Magdalene was in Dover, and of his own volition, he held slightly aloof. He was too busy building a reputation and fortune to go courting. The only time he gave it consideration was on occasions such as this when he paused for breath and saw other men fulfilled.

Hubert de Burgh had dropped hints about finding him a rich and titled wife, someone who would give him a claim on land as well as sea. Nicholas pretended to be deaf. Rich, aristocratic women usually possessed rich, aristocratic ways and a passel of difficult relatives. His ships were his mistresses, his lovers, his wives. And when he did have need of feminine company there was Magdalene.

His brief reflection was curtailed by the appearance of a bold, masculine figure, decked out in a tunic of expensive blue cloth. A fur-lined cloak flew from his shoulders, and the sun caught gleams in his thick fair hair.

Nicholas faced him and bowed courteously, but without deference. They were men of equal standing in their own professions. 'Master Willoughby,' he said. 'You are timely arrived.'

The wool merchant smiled, revealing strong, square teeth. 'And so is your vessel, Master de Caen.' He cast a pleased eye over the bustle on the small cog's deck. 'Did you obtain the items I requested?'

Nicholas gestured at a chest that had already been unloaded on to the harbour side. 'The goblets and the spices are in there. The bolts of fabric you requested are being attended to.'

Willoughby nodded. 'I'll look in a moment,' he said and stroked his beard. 'What about the other matter?'

Nicholas cupped his hands and shouted over to his captain. Martin left his wife and came over, the pup cradled in his large seaman's hands.

Willoughby's eyes lit up, but narrowed slightly when Nicholas told him the price. 'For a dog!' he exclaimed. 'Jesu, pound for pound, these little beasts are more expensive than pepper!'

Nicholas shrugged. 'Dogs like these are in such great demand that they're hard to come by. Every woman wants one to tuck in her sleeve. There were four other buyers waiting for this one alone if I had not met the asking price. If you are not content . . .'

'Nay, nay, I'll take the thing and pay,' Willoughby said with a terse gesture. 'It's a gift for a lady, and if it advances my cause with her, then I'll be well repaid.'

Nicholas started to grin, but quickly wiped it off behind his hand as the merchant glared.

'Not that sort of a gift for that kind of service,' he said icily. 'I hope to make the lady my wife in due course.' He took the dog from Martin Wudecoc and bundled it up in a fold of his cloak.

Nicholas inclined his head. 'I hope she will be delighted.'

Willoughby nodded stiffly to show that he had taken no lasting offence. 'You sail with the next cargo when?'

'Day after tomorrow, as soon as her hold's laden and the tide's in. We'll have your wool on the looms of Bruges by the end of the week.'

'That's why I use you,' Willoughby said. 'There are other captains I could hire at less cost, but none that I have found to be as swift and reliable.'

'It is a good partnership,' Nicholas agreed and shook the merchant's proffered hand.

Thoughtfully, he watched Robert Willoughby walk away, and began to breathe a little more easily.

'I'm glad we're not his enemies,' muttered Martin.

'You felt it too?' Nicholas glanced at his captain.

'Aye, sir. A man of appetites that one, and not given to having them refused.'

'I hope his intended wife knows that,' Nicholas said wryly.

* * *

The effigy that lay upon Gerbert's tomb in St Mary's was fashioned of the finest alabaster from the quarries of Chellaston. Gerbert's hands were clasped in prayer on his breast and his feet rested on a stone carved in the shape of a wool sack. His face was altogether more lean and handsome than it had been in life, with a fashionable hairstyle, the ends flicked out, and a neatly trimmed beard.

Still, Miriel was pleased with the result. Even in death, he had dignity and standing in the community, and the quality of the effigy showed that his widow respected and honoured his memory.

Laying the bunch of freshly picked blue irises on the tomb, Miriel left the church and entered the sun-streaked graveyard. All around her a new summer was blossoming. The sunshine was still clear without the dust haze and somnolence of the later months, and it quickened in her blood.

The weaving business continued to prosper. She had taken on two new apprentices, and each day several women from the town came to spin wool on their drop spindles to provide yarn for the weavers.

Having inherited Gerbert's part of the trade, Robert Willoughby now managed all the wool-gathering. Although his business was mostly with Flanders, he reserved the best fleeces for Miriel and made sure that her looms never stood idle. Indeed, she thought with a mingling of gratitude and unease, he had been very good to her since Gerbert's death – always there if she was in need, but never intrusive. It would be so easy to drop her defences and depend on him.

As she left the church and turned homewards, he was waiting for her, a smile on his face, his beard and hair freshly groomed, and his garments immaculate as always. Miriel greeted him with a smile of her own, albeit a cautious one.

'You are back early,' she said. 'I thought you would still be in Boston.'

He took her hands in his and squeezed them. 'My business was quickly concluded there. I've found an excellent ship's master to carry my wool. Meticulous vessels, never late, and always in profit.' He kissed her cheek. 'You're looking lovely today.'

Miriel thanked him, pleased that he had noticed her appearance. While she might have to wear the plain colours of a widow to respect Gerbert's memory, they were of the finest fabrics and stylishly cut. Today she wore a gown of dark green twill trimmed with green and cream braid and a plain wimple of bleached linen.

'You will stay to dine?' she asked. The question was a formality. Robert had always taken food with Gerbert when in Nottingham and it was a foregone conclusion that he would eat with Gerbert's widow.

Once home, she set Samuel and Elfwen to preparing the meal, and poured wine for herself and Robert. He took his cup outside into the garth with its herb patch and cherry orchard, the fruits now setting on the trees. There was much evidence of new planting and industrious weeding.

'Gerbert never bothered much with the garden after his first wife died,' Miriel said, joining him. 'And I had only just begun to replant when Gerbert was taken. I thought this would be a good way to hold the life in his memory, and I have always liked tending plants.'

For a while they discussed the layout of the flowerbeds, what was to go where, the colours, the perfumes.

Robert gave her a possessive glance that she did not see. 'You were fond of him, weren't you?'

Miriel gazed at a tumble of cream and gold honeysuckle. 'I was,' she murmured, and felt a sudden sting of tears behind her eyes. 'But not as fond as he would have liked. He wanted to be a husband, but I always thought of him in the same way that I thought of my grandfather.'

Robert nodded. 'That is understandable, he was much older than you,' he said gruffly, 'but you were still a good wife to him.'

Miriel shook her head. 'He died because of me.'

'Oh, that is foolish,' Robert said firmly. 'He died because of circumstance, because of another man's wickedness and greed.'

Miriel said nothing, just looked out at the burgeoning garden. The guilt was harder to bear than the sorrow.

'Besides, Nigel of Lincoln has paid for his sins,' Robert added with a shrug and drained his cup.

'What do you mean?'

'He's dead. Robbed on the road by outlaws.' He spoke coldly, without inflection.

Miriel felt the hairs at her nape prickle upright. 'What do you mean "dead". How do you know?'

Robert shrugged. 'I heard it in Boston. News of merchants murdered while about their business always travels fast to others who have to brave the same routes. He was attacked on the Sleaford Road, his purse robbed and his throat cut. Men are travelling together for safety now lest the same should happen to them. Call me pitiless if you wish, but I say it is divine judgement on the man.'

Miriel suddenly felt cold and sick. She staggered to a small arbour bench surrounded by the fragrance of pale pink dog roses and sat down. Nigel had never been her family, indeed she had hated him, but he had been a connection. Now there was nothing. No one to love or hate her, just a yawning void.

'At least you need worry no longer about your past being discovered.' Robert sat down beside her and took her hands in his. 'Jesu, how cold you are. I'm sorry, I did not think you would take it so badly. I thought you would be pleased.'

'Shocked,' Miriel said. 'And it is one thing to wish someone dead, another to have it happen. God's mercy, I cannot believe it is true.'

'Your heart is too tender.' He kissed her brow, put his arm around her shoulders and drew her in close.

Miriel leaned against him as she had done before on the night of Gerbert's death. She felt his solid strength, the steady beat of his heart and drew comfort from him.

Robert was a shrewd and patient man. Even though he could have risked pressing his advantage, he did not. The time, he judged, was ripe, but not quite at hand. And so he waited until she had command of herself again, and then he took his leave, saying he had a small matter of business to attend to and promising to return later to eat with her.

Miriel opened the door to him herself. Outwardly she was composed, but the façade of her immaculate appearance concealed a vulnerable desolation. She had cursed her family and her family was dead. She had fought them and now there was no one to fight except herself.

A fixed smile on her face, she stepped aside so that Robert could enter. He inhaled the aroma of pork simmering in the cauldron with appreciation and nodded pleasantly to Elfwen and Samuel.

'That sea-captain I mentioned earlier,' Robert said, 'I asked him to obtain a sleeve dog for me while he was in Flanders.'

'A what?'

'One of these – to keep in your sleeve.' From the depths of his cloak he produced the puppy and placed it in Miriel's startled arms. 'It was the "matter" I had to attend.'

She gasped and almost dropped the little creature in her surprise. It was all ears and tail, the latter of which wagged frantically as it strained toward her, licking the tip of her chin with a furious pink tongue. Laughing in delight, still in shock, Miriel fell in love.

Robert watched her with pleasure. 'His naming is yours. For the past week he has just answered to "pup", and worse when he has fouled in the wrong places.'

'He's beautiful! I don't know what to say!' Standing on tiptoe, she kissed Robert in gratitude, all wariness flown and all darker emotions temporarily forgotten.

'I knew you would like him.' He put his arm around her briefly, squeezed her waist, then tactfully released her and handed his cloak to an expressionless Samuel.

Miriel and Robert dined outside in the garth at a trestle table set up in the shade of the largest apple tree. The sun was hot but benign, and now and again its concentration was broken by a shield of small white clouds. The wine was smooth and potent, the pork stew tender and full flavoured. She fed the puppy slivers of meat from her hand until his little stomach was as tight as a drum and he curled up beneath the bench and went to sleep.

'I shall call him Will,' she announced, glancing from the little animal to the man who had given him to her. 'Short for Willoughby.'

Robert snorted with amusement. 'It is not every man who can claim a dog as his namesake.'

'You will be even more insulted if I say that it was meant to be a compliment,' Miriel teased.

'I am not a man easily insulted, although I warn you, I take strict measures against those who do.'

'Oh dear.' Miriel put her finger to her lips and regarded him with widening eyes. The wine had gone to her head, as had the delight of his gift and the pleasure of the meal, following as they did the disturbing news of her stepfather's violent death. They were props to help her forget.

Robert returned her look, his own index finger slowly circling the rim of his goblet. 'I don't want to take any measures against you,' he said huskily, 'but I do desire very much to tread one – that of the marriage dance.'

'Oh dear,' said Miriel again.

'That is what I thought myself. She is only nine months widowed, I said; she will refuse you. You were Gerbert's godson by marriage and his partner. How could you be thinking of such a thing so soon?' Rising from his side of the trestle, he came round to hers and sat beside her, close now so that she could feel the heat emanating from his body. 'I pride myself that I am a man of reason, but no amount of reasoning or considered thought can put the notion from my head. I want you to wife, Miriel.'

She shook her head, but that only served to increase the wine-lightness. 'Please, say no more,' she implored. 'I am not ready to listen. It is too soon.'

Robert ignored her and took her hands in his. 'Truly it is not as foolish as it seems,' he said persuasively. 'We would each fill the void in the other's life, and our trade would be even stronger for our union. We have too much in common, too much need of each other to let it pass by.' He released her hands, but only to take her by the shoulders. 'I swear I will cherish you for ever; you will not lack for anything, and no one will harm you ever again. Only say yes, Miriel.'

His mouth swooped on hers in a demanding kiss that tasted of wine. Strange sensations played through her body, sucking her in, making her loins molten and tender. When he withdrew, gasping like a man who had run a mile, she followed blindly for a moment, and then drew back herself and looked at him with the eyes of a doe run to ground.

'Say yes,' he repeated through the harshness of his breathing. 'If you have any shred of pity, Miriel, say yes.'

She swallowed, fighting the heady seduction of lust and wine. Wiry golden hair glinted at the throat of his tunic. She could sense and scent the power of his maleness and it reached out to her like a sheet of fire.

Despite the intensity of his persuasion, she might have stood her ground, but there were subtle undercurrents at work and he had probed her vulnerability with skill. He had offered her companionship in her loneliness; he had brought her the gift of faith in the little dog curled up against the bench and, with the skill of a consummate tactician, he had chosen his moment.

Now he left the bench and bent on one knee. 'I am no knight,' he said, 'but you are my lady and always will be, whatever answer you give.'

It was the stuff of dreams. It was what a troubadour would have said as he knelt at the feet of a queen in the hall of courtly love. Perhaps in the distant past, a minstrel had knelt at the feet of Edwin Weaver's virgin daughter and declared the selfsame thing. Whatever its ancestors, the speech, accompanied by the rustle of sun-warmed leaves, reached out and unfastened the last knot of Miriel's resistance.

She reached up to touch Robert's mane of gold and silver hair. 'Then what answer dare I give but yes?' she whispered.

Chapter 18

Miriel's second wedding was an echo of the first, but with subtle differences. Since she was scarcely out of mourning and Robert himself was a widower, the marriage celebration was grand, but not boisterous. There was little talk of impropriety. Most folk had regarded Miriel as a good if overly young wife to Gerbert. It was only natural that she should wed again, and Robert Willoughby was an obvious choice. It was true that he was older than Miriel by more than twenty years, but it was much less than the forty that had separated her from Gerbert. Only Alice Leen introduced a sour note to the proceedings by muttering that only a wench who was an utter fool leaped out of the frying pan directly into the fire.

Miriel was not sure that Gerbert would have looked on her remarriage with a kindly eye either. While alive, he had made no secret of the fact that he viewed his partner as a rival for her affections, and Miriel had been scrupulous in her avoidance lest Gerbert's suspicions prove their ground. Now they had. She was Mistress Willoughby, and still not quite sure how it had come about. However, done was done. She had reservations but no regrets.

This time there was no noisy, joyful bedding ceremony. She and Robert departed the wedding feast for Robert's home across the Trent at Briggford. Miriel wore a warm cloak for the evenings were beginning to draw in and there was a nip in the air. She sat pillion on the bay cob, facing sideways to Robert's forward. The strange notion came to her that although they were travelling to the same place, they were facing in different directions, and she shivered.

Once free of the city, they took the path across the broad cow meadows and over the bridge that spanned the river at Briggford. Behind them on its sandstone mount, the castle shone like copper in the last gleams of sunset. Below it, the town was a smudge of thatched and shingled roofs, hazed in the blue smoke of cooking fires. Miriel was tempted to leap from the horse and run back towards the comfort and familiarity. What in God's name was she doing here?

As if attuned to her mood, Robert swivelled in the saddle and covered her hands with one of his. 'You are quiet, sweetheart.'

She forced a smile. 'I'm unaccustomed to riding pillion,' she said lamely.

He searched her face. 'It isn't far now,' he said gently, and his broad fingers squeezed hers. 'Soon be home.'

Miriel swallowed and nodded. His reassurance fell on stony ground. The closer they came to their destination, the more nervous she was growing.

Robert withdrew his hand and clicked the cob onwards. Within quarter of a mile he entered a courtyard behind a large cruck-frame house and drew rein. A servant ran out to take the horse. Robert lifted Miriel down from the saddle as if she weighed no more than a feather and planted a cold kiss on her lips. Grasping her hand, he led her towards the main dwelling, much as the groom had led the cob to its stall.

The door was open, shedding a path of torchlight through the gloaming. Robert swept her up in his arms and carried her across the threshold. 'Mine, now,' he said triumphantly as he kicked the door shut. 'All mine.'

Miriel felt a qualm at the possessive note underlying the pleasure in his voice. The inevitable duty of the bedchamber loomed and she felt sick.

Food and wine had been left out for them – a dainty supper of cold spiced chicken served with an onion frumenty and beans tossed in oil and vinegar. There was a honey curd tart and a dish of fig and apple compote. In a bucket of cold well water stood a stone costrel filled with wine. Miriel looked at the delectable fare, at the care which had been taken, and knew that she would be unable to do justice to either.

'I'm afraid I'm not hungry,' she said with an apologetic little smile.

'But you must be. You hardly ate a morsel at the other table before we left.' Robert picked up a sliver of the spiced chicken, bit off half and popped the rest in her mouth. 'It's delicious,' he said.

Miriel thought she would choke. The delicate aroma bounced off her palate and filled her mouth and nose. Swallowing was going to be impossible when it was all she could do not to retch.

Robert drew the costrel from the bucket and filled two goblets. 'To us,' he toasted her, taking a robust swallow.

She watched the powerful ripples of his throat as he drank, and filling her mouth, somehow managed to gulp down both wine and chicken.

Lowering his cup, he looked at her. 'What's wrong?'

'Nothing.' She tried to smile, but her body was slowly freezing with fear.

'That's a lie.' He put his wine on the table and took her in his arms. 'You're trembling like a leaf, sweetheart. Surely you are not afraid.'

She looked up into the eyes of a lion. Strong, vital, ferocious. It was too late now. By her own words and actions she had walked into his den, pretending to be a lioness when she was no more than a terrified ewe.

'I am virgin still,' she whispered, her throat so tight that it was almost impossible to talk. 'Gerbert never took his full marital rites.'

His eyes narrowed, but not with displeasure. A sensual smile curved his lips. He looked her slowly up and down. 'You are innocent then.'

Miriel raised her chin. 'I know what to expect of my duty,' she said with defensive hauteur, but that only made him smile the more.

He stroked her cheek. 'Oh,' he said softly. 'I do not think that you do.'

Miriel winced and tried without success to ease her position in the saddle. It was the second day of their journey, and she and Robert had been on the road since dawn, hoping to arrive in Lincoln before nightfall.

The movement of the horse and the bump of the saddle caused an almost unbearable friction against the tender space between her legs. There was a dull ache in her lower back, and cramping pains in the muscles of her upper thighs. Her new husband was a large and vigorous man in every sense of the word and took his pleasure at a full, determined and prolonged gallop – once at night and once on waking.

She glanced at him sidelong. He rode easily beside her, the sun sparkling on his wiry golden hair and beard, a good-natured smile curving his mouth. He had said that she would grow accustomed to the act in time, that it wasn't a matter of duty, but of love and respect, and that despite what the Church said, it was there to be enjoyed.

Miriel had never taken much notice of what the Church said anyway, but from her own experience and observation had come to the conclusion that the deed was more necessary and pleasurable to men, and that women received by far the worst of the bargain. The promised pleasure was elusive. There was the fear of pregnancy, of childbirth, and once an infant was born, the burden of caring for it, of having a being dependent on you, and being dependent yourself. Miriel bit her lip and frowned. If Robert continued to lie with her so frequently, it would not be long before she found herself in that situation. He was not going to be satisfied with the means that had contented Gerbert – or only as a small part of his sexual diet. Robert needed to possess and, to him, possession meant penetration.

During their frank discussion over a year ago, Alice had advised Miriel that placing a wad of sheep's wool soaked in vinegar high in the birth passage would help to prevent conception, but Miriel did not think she could bear a substance as caustic as vinegar anywhere near her tender membranes just now.

Yet she was fond of Robert. He was affable and generous; he gave her love and support. When he kissed her and held her close she felt safe and cherished. He liked his own way as much as she, but even in disagreement he was good-humoured. She could not imagine him ever striking her as Nigel had done. She had a good bargain; she should be grateful.

He caught her looking at him, and raised his brows in a smiling question. Miriel shook her head. 'I was just counting my blessings,' she said, with a touch of irony detectable to herself because of her thoughts, but Robert took it at face value.

'As many as my own, I hope.' He reached across the space between their mounts to touch her hands. From his perch on her horse's withers, Will growled and bared his teeth.

'I see I brought home a rival,' Robert said jovially, although the crinkle to his eye corners was slightly contrived. Miriel received the distinct impression that while the gift of the dog had been a good idea at the time, it had been a means to an end and was rapidly outliving its usefulness. Robert preferred big dogs with big teeth that reflected his masculinity. Little snappy ones were game to be kicked. But of course he couldn't kick this one.

'Indeed you did,' Miriel laughed and ruffled the pup's absurdly enormous black ears. 'You'll have to think more carefully about what you bring me in the future, won't you?'

'Hah, so you still expect gifts?'

'But of course.' She looked at him through her lashes. Flirting with Robert was fun because it gained her his attention and made him receptive. The trick was to do it in the open and in public where there was no immediate recourse to a bed.

'What would you like?'

She looked at the sky as if in deep thought. 'A blue dress, a gold collar,' she reeled off. 'A set of drinking cups in green chalcedony, an embroidered pilgrim bag, some Flemish wall hangings, a gold ring for every finger, a—'

'Stop, stop, I yield!' Laughing, Robert threw up his hands.

Miriel grinned at him, sharing in the moment of humour, but then she sobered. 'But what I really want is to be content,' she said on a more wistful note.

'You mean you are not content at the moment?' Robert

ceased laughing and his expression grew sharp with concern.

Mentally, Miriel cast a deep sigh. She should have seen the pit yawning at her feet. Robert might be affable and generous, but he expected praise and gratitude in return. 'I would not have you think that I am discontented with you,' she said quickly. 'I have never been happier in my life,' which was almost true, and not difficult given her past circumstances. 'I just meant that contentment seems so hard to come by that it is worth more than worldly goods. Sometimes it would be pleasant to sit and be still and want nothing more.'

He grunted and relaxed in the saddle, appearing mollified. 'You'd soon grow bored, lass. We are of the same kind, you and I. The day we want nothing more is the day we die.'

Miriel said nothing. It would be too difficult to explain to him the pleasure of retreating from tumult. He would not understand, and she did not believe that she could make him. They might be of the same kind, but not born from the same mould.

It was strange returning to the house of her birth, to the weaving sheds and wool store that had been her grandfather's pride and joy. Stranger still to find the place in dusty, demoralised disarray with only one weaver and a four-year apprentice remaining. Stocks of yarn were almost nil, and four of the six looms stood empty.

'The sheriff's escheators found you then, Mistress Miriel,' said Ham, the senior weaver. He had been in his prime during her grandfather's day. Now there was a milky growth covering one eye, which suggested one of the reasons for the decline in quality that the Italian merchant had complained about.

'Found me?' At the mention of the word 'sheriff', Miriel's heart began to thump. The image of Mathilda's crown and the bags of silver was so clear in her mind's eye that she had an irrational fear that others would see it too. What if Nicholas had been caught? What if he had told them everything and they were on her trail?

'You being the heir to the house and the weaving sheds,' he said. 'If you were not found within a year and a day, it was all to go to the Earl of Lincoln.' He wiped his grizzled upper lip. 'There's been naught but grief since old Master Edward died, and that's the truth, God rest his soul.'

Miriel felt weak with relief. She was being hunted but to her own advantage and her secret was safe. 'I came because I heard that both my mother and stepfather had died,' she said with a swift glance at Robert, who was standing behind her and a little to one side, studying the shed with a thoughtful eye. 'God rest their souls too,' she added dutifully, and crossed herself.

Ham muttered the same and echoed her gesture. 'Are you here to stay then, mistress?' Hope filled his eyes until he reminded her of Will, pleading at the table for scraps of chicken.

'Not for the moment,' she said. 'We are bound for Boston to take ship for Flanders.' As his face fell, she felt a pang of compassion and added, 'But there is more demand for my cloth than I can supply. These looms will soon be busy again, I promise.'

The old weaver nodded but continued to look sombre. 'St Catherine's won't supply us with wool any more,' he said. 'They sell it all to some merchant in Nottingham.'

'Don't you worry about supplies of wool and yarn, Ham,' she said briskly, avoiding her husband's eye. The merchant had been Gerbert and when he died the contract had fallen into Robert's hands, but Robert was unaware of her connection with the nunnery. 'Obtaining good wool is not a problem. I can have these looms working again within the month.'

Ham wiped his mouth again. 'We ain't received a wage since Master Nigel was murdered,' he said.

Miriel tightened her lips. Behind her she could feel Robert's irritation. 'Come and see me on the morrow before we leave. The lad too.' She gestured at the apprentice.

'Thank you, mistress. I knew if you were found, you'd do right by us.'

'I value fairness,' she answered with a half-smile. 'Since it was never meted out to me, I am careful that others should receive it.'

Robert gave an impatient grunt and, leaving the shed, marched across the cobbled yard towards the house.

Ham bowed to Miriel as she turned to follow him. 'Me 'n' Walter never believed them stories spread about you, Mistress Miriel. We all knew that you and Master Nigel never saw eye to eye.'

'What stories?' It was perhaps better not to know, but Miriel was still drawn by a dreadful fascination to ask.

Ham shuffled his feet and cleared his throat. 'That you ran just as wild at that convent as you did here.' His weathered cheeks darkened and he fixed his eyes on the floor just beyond his scuffed shoes. 'That you fornicated with a guest under their roof and then eloped with him—'

'That is a vile lie!' Miriel's face flamed and she drew herself up. 'I did no such thing!'

'We said to ourselves that you didn't,' Ham said, still gazing at the floor. 'But then St Catherine's stopped sending us their wool and Master Nigel called you some terrible names.'

Miriel compressed her lips. 'What did my mother say?' Probably '*Yes, Nigel*', she thought bitterly.

'Nothing, mistress.' Then Ham pinched the end of his nose and risked a glance at her. 'Well, no, that ain't true. Master Nigel drank too much and said in front of us all in the workshop that it was like mother like daughter, and Mistress Annet spoke up, saying that you weren't like her at all, because you had had the courage to run with your desire.'

'My mother said that?'

'Aye, mistress.'

Miriel swallowed and turned away, tears suddenly tightening in her throat. How little they had known of each other, how little they had understood, and now it was all too late.

In the house, Elfwen had built a fire and set a cauldron to simmer. The stones still gave off a musty smell and dust motes hung in the air, but at least a fire in the hearth had started the home's heart beating again.

Will circled the room, snuffling in the corners, investigating all the strange smells. Miriel's head was throbbing. All she wanted to do was lie down in a dark corner with a cold lavender compress across her brow.

Robert, however, had other ideas and, ignoring Elfwen as if she were an inanimate piece of furniture, took Miriel in his arms. 'I had no idea your family was wealthy enough to afford a house built of stone,' he teased.

Miriel shrugged indifferently. Just now she did not want to talk about her family or evaluate the potential of her inheritance. There were too many treacherous cross-currents to negotiate.

When she did not answer, Robert nuzzled her wimple aside to kiss her throat and lowered his hands to her hips, pulling her against his crotch. 'I wonder if the bedchamber's comfortable,' he muttered.

Miriel clenched her eyes at the thought of enduring another bout of his vigorous lovemaking. 'I am a little sore,' she said.

His breath was hot in her ear. 'Aye, it's to be expected, but you'll soon grow accustomed.' He cupped her breasts. 'A bit of goose grease will ease the way. Don't refuse me, sweetheart, I've been hard all day just thinking of you.'

Miriel forced a smile. 'Could we not at least eat and refresh ourselves first, Rob?' She used the abbreviation of his name and stroked his beard, holding back by leading him on. 'I'm so hungry and travel-tired.'

He kneaded her buttocks for a moment longer, then released her with a reluctant sigh. 'If that's what you want, sweetheart. And in truth, I could eat a horse myself.'

Miriel was swept by a wave of relief, followed by anxiety. She had only put off the moment, not avoided it.

They sat down to a simple meal of bacon, eggs and bread, washed down with cider, although there was nothing simple about the pewter dishes and silver-gilt cups off which they ate and drank.

'You'll not be keeping that old man at the loom once you've found skilled weavers in Flanders,' said Robert as he mopped the last traces of salty grease and egg-yolk from his platter with a hunk of bread.

'Why not?' Miriel raised her head in surprise. 'Ham's worked here since before I was born.'

'Precisely. He's well past his prime. Small wonder that your stepfather's business was in decline. The man's half-blind, and what use is a weaver who cannot see?' He crammed the bread into his mouth and chewed vigorously.

'He has knowledge and skills to pass on, and he can still work on pieces that do not need great attention to detail.'

Robert shook his head. Swallowing, he wiped his mouth on a napkin, and then his hands. 'You need to clear out and begin afresh. Your Flemings won't want to work with him, and he'll only cause trouble. He'll think that he has the right to be cock of the dunghill because he's been here the longest.'

'Ham's not like that,' Miriel protested, her face beginning to flush.

'Allow me to know better, sweetheart. I've been a merchant for five and twenty years – longer than you've been born. It is one thing to be fair in your dealings, quite another to let your heart take over. I am sure your grandfather would agree with me if he were here.'

Miriel pushed the congealed remains of her food to the side of the platter. She was filled with anger and not a little dismay. That he was probably right did not make his words any easier to swallow. 'He is here, in me,' she replied. 'And I do not believe that he would have Ham thrown out on the street. If I allow you to know better, then you must allow me to use my instinct.'

Robert leaned back in his chair and half closed his lids. 'In truth, I do not have to allow you anything,' he said. 'In law you are my wife, and whatever is yours is mine also. I can, if I choose, ride roughshod over every decision you make. I can confine you to the hearth and the bedchamber and appoint my own man to oversee the weaving.'

Miriel blenched. 'You would not!' she gasped. The force of her shock and rage made her dizzy. 'I would kill you first!'

'Don't be a goose.' He gave a good-natured wave of his hand as if dismissing the tantrum of a loved but unruly child. 'I did but make a point, and a valid one at that. Many a husband would not hand you so free a rein.'

'I begin to wonder if I should have remained a widow.' Miriel tossed her napkin down and rose from the trestle.

'Oh, come now, sweetheart.' Robert pushed to his feet and advanced on her. 'I spoke in jest to see how you would respond, and now I wish I had not opened my mouth. By all means keep the weaver on if he means so much to you.'

'I intend to,' Miriel said stiffly, her back turned. The indulgent note in his voice was almost more than she could stand.

Robert set his hands on her shoulders and rubbed them gently. His lips sought her throat, nipping and nuzzling, and her tender skin was prickled by the wiriness of his beard and moustache.

'Be not wroth, Miriel, be sweet,' he muttered.

Sweet was the last thing that Miriel felt like being, but she was too tired to continue the argument. Robert had exposed disturbing facets of his personality and she did not want to see them emerge in any more depth.

And so she let him lift her in his arms and bear her above stairs to the sleeping loft, and place her in the bed where her grandfather had died and her mother had slept with Nigel.

She was so tight with resentment that, even with the liberal use of goose grease, he struggled to enter her, grunting and groaning as he forced his way inside. Miriel bit her lip and gazed over his shoulder at the rafters, tensing afresh at each forceful surge, willing him to finish, and praying desperately not to conceive.

Miriel had crossed the sea on a couple of occasions with her grandfather. She remembered the events as great adventures and had loved every moment. The weather had been excellent and she had stood for hours near the prow, inhaling the salt tang of the spray and watching the sun sparkle on the wave crests.

Now, even though it was raining and a summer squall had turned the sea to a churning, sulky grey, Miriel boarded the vessel with alacrity. Will ran about the deck, snuffling in corners and wagging his tail in a frenzy of excitement.

Robert watched them both with a superior smile. 'Wait until we're out of the harbour. You'll not be so eager then,' he said.

Miriel shrugged. She had not told him that she had sailed before, nor did she intend to. Let it take the wind from his sails when she showed him that she had better sea legs than he.

She mounted the ladder to the small castle built above the cog's rudder housing. The crenellations had been gaily painted with bands of red and yellow, and a banner fluttered from a socket in one corner, bearing the rather incongruous device of a chest with the lid thrown back. Probably it had to do with the fact that she was a merchant vessel. On the quay, two labourers worked the windlass on a wooden crane lowering a hooked sarple of wool into her hold.

'What's her name?' Miriel asked as Robert joined her on the castle, his eyes narrowed against the slant of the rain.

'*Pandora's Daughter,*' he said. 'I'm told it's from Greek mythology. Something about a foolish woman opening a box she was supposed to leave well alone.'

A jolt went through Miriel at mention of the name. That explained the open chest on the banner. 'Yes, I know the story of Pandora,' she murmured.

He set one heavy arm across her shoulders, his hand dangling relaxed, his body pressed front to spine against hers. 'You never cease to surprise me. Most women barely know anything beyond neighbourhood gossip, but you have a mind that would match many a man.'

Miriel gritted her teeth and smiled sweetly. She could not decide whether Robert was complimenting or belittling her. Either way she was irritated. Reminded of Nicholas by the vessel's name, she wondered what he had done with his life. She had a strong and not irrational fear that he might even be the master of this ship. He had told her that he came from a family of seafarers, and the cog's name was unusual. Most merchant vessels bore the names of saints who could be invoked in times of difficulty, and those that did not had warlike titles, inherited from their Viking ancestors, names like *Serpent, Wolf,* or *Dragon.*

Robert suddenly pointed. 'Here comes the master now.'

A tall, lugubrious man in his early thirties walked up the gangplank and on to the deck. His cropped brown hair stood straight up from his brow line and he had a wide, serious mouth, which broke into a smile as he saw the dog. Miriel felt a rush of relief and disappointment. What would she have done if the ship's captain had proved to be Nicholas de Caen? More to the point, what would Nicholas have done when he saw her? Perhaps it was just as well.

The man scooped up the dog in his long arms and bore him aloft to the castle, where Robert introduced him to Miriel as Master Martin Wudecoc.

'You like the little fellow then,' he said as he handed Will into her arms.

'I adore him.' Miriel gave the dog a hug and it wagged its tail and swiped a small pink tongue across her cheek. 'The best gift I've ever been given.' She twisted to bestow a soft look on her husband. Amongst her doubts and irritations, there still shone reasons like Will for her to have faith in him.

Robert smiled tenderly. 'Worth every penny,' he said.

'Me, or the dog?'

'Both of course.' He kissed her and ruffled the dog's coat the wrong way. Will showed his sharp little teeth and his chest rumbled. Robert prudently removed his hand. The smile stayed on his face, but his jaw muscles tensed with the effort of holding it there.

Bowing, Martin Wudecoc excused himself to his duties. Within the hour as the grey tide filled the Wash, *Pandora's Daughter* sailed out of Boston harbour, bound with her cargo of fleeces for the Flemish port of Antwerp.

With the promise of work for the looms and continuing wages to keep the wolf from the door, Ham Weaver had immersed himself in ale and celebration at Dame Gilda's alehouse in Grope Alley. The surroundings were not of the most salubrious, but the ale was the best to be had for miles around and a fresh brewing always attracted customers in their droves.

Ham gave a satisfied belch and reviewed the world through a golden haze induced by drink and failing eyesight.

'Mind, I've still got a few years left in me yet,' he told Walter the apprentice who had matched him drink for drink and now could barely hold his head off the trestle.

'Coursh you have.' The younger man tipped the rim of his cup to his lips.

'Made a good job of teaching you, haven't I?'

'None better.'

'I know Mistress Miriel. She won't throw me out . . . and her husband seems a decent sort.'

'Aye, decent short,' the lad repeated obligingly before laying his head on the trestle and closing his eyes.

Ham rose unsteadily and lurched his way out of the alehouse into the evening drizzle.

Sporadic torchlight flickered from the houses either side of Gilda's establishment, illuminating muddy puddles and soft, rutted surfaces, all a blur to Ham's vision. But he had lived in Lincoln all his life, had trodden the path to and from Gilda's alehouse twice a week for the past forty-five years. Irrespective of his failing sight, his legs bore him homeward, and he began to sing.

D . . . dronken –
Dronken, dronken, dronken,
. . . dronken is Ham atte wyne
Hay . . . suster, Walter, Peter,
Ye dronke al depe
And Ichulle . . .

The song never finished. As Ham lurched over a deep wheel rut at the juncture of an alley, soft footfalls stole up behind him. The first he knew of the danger was the moment that a muscular arm wrapped around his throat, choking off his voice and then his air.

His legs gave way and he went down into the mud. His assailant fell with him, but the pressure never let up. Instead of a squeeze, it became a steady, relentless push. Mud and water filled Ham's mouth and nostrils, then blotted the final flicker of vision from his staring eyes.

In the dawn, no one looked twice at the gong farmer's cart as it creaked out of the city gates laden with its noisome load of ordure and straw from Lincoln's gutters, privies and dung heaps. No one considered for one moment delving beneath the layers of excrement, the dead dogs and old floor rushes to look for the corpse of Ham the weaver, missing since last night – or if they did, quickly thought the better of it. The gong farmer himself left it to his temporary assistant to unload the cart's contents into a rubbish pit. What the eye did not see was no grief to the conscience, and two shillings in silver pennies was a sum to turn any man's head in the other direction.

When the unloading was finished, the gong farmer returned to town, whistling, and his assistant unobtrusively slipped away, leaving the corpse of Ham Weaver to rot in its unquiet grave.

Chapter 19

Autumn 1219

Miriel stood in her Lincoln weaving shed and watched the three Flemings at work. Jan and Willelm were brothers. Gerda was Jan's wife, a heavy-boned woman with blonde plaits and a laugh not unlike the screech of a magpie. All three were excellent weavers and eager to please. In their native Antwerp, competition was fierce and there was never enough wool for the looms. At home their trade was dependent on imported fleeces and yarn from England and Spain. Here, their supply was on the doorstep and starvation a distant, unlikely prospect.

The sound of cheerful voices calling to each other in Flemish rose above the hubbub of the clacking loom shuttles where broadcloths in blue, red and green stripe were being produced at a rate that Miriel could scarcely believe.

Walter, the apprentice, was occupied in warping up another loom with yarn ready for weaving. His expression was morose, and he made no attempt to join in with the Flemings' banter.

'No news of Ham, Walter?' Miriel asked sympathetically. She came to stand at his side.

His fingers grew clumsy beneath her scrutiny. 'No, mistress. They say that like as not he fell in the Witham, and because it had been raining the river was in spate. Poor old sod didn't stand a chance.' He bared his teeth. 'I should ha' walked home with him that night. Stupid bugger couldn't see the nose in front of his face, and he was well gilded too.'

Miriel laid her hand gently on the youth's narrow shoulder. 'It is no one's fault,' she said firmly. 'I have arranged to have masses said for the safety of his soul wherever it might be.' She had also sent a pouch of silver to Ham's wife and would continue to do so at regular intervals, but that was between the woman and herself. Prudence made her circumspect. After the fuss that Robert had raised about keeping Ham on at the weaving shed, she had decided that for the sake of domestic harmony, a little reticence on the matter would not go amiss. Despite Robert's generosity towards herself, the trait did not extend as far as his business dealings, where his fist was tightly gripped around the neck of his purse and he was utterly ruthless.

'But you think he is dead, mistress, don't you?'

'I think it likely, but there is no use in brooding. Look, we are growing short of green yarn. Leave the loom and go over to the dyehouse to see if Master Jack's got any.'

'Yes, mistress.' Walter rose with alacrity and almost ran out of the door – as if he were trying to outrun his thoughts. Miriel sighed, and with a shake of her head took his place to finish the task. She could imagine how he had sat here brooding, his hands busy but his mind free to wander.

It was pointless to speculate about Ham's disappearance. The old fool had drunk one too many cups of ale and paid with his life. She did not doubt that he was dead. He was too well known in the community not to be discovered, and too lacking in eyesight to get very far. He had doted on his wife and would not have left her worrying and wondering.

Robert had been taciturn on the subject, but generous enough not to remark that it was for the best, and Miriel had been glad at his restraint. On the few occasions that they had quarrelled, Miriel had found herself struggling, faced by a player of great skill and subtlety. Robert neither blustered nor raged; indeed, he seldom raised his voice. He got his way by a mingling of fact-twisting, bullying, cajolery and what seemed at the time like plain reasoning. Somehow he always made the cause of the argument her fault, and even if she did gain her way, it was still as if he had won.

Eyes narrowed in concentration, she brought the russet-coloured thread round and up, securing it through the notches in the heddle, then round and up again. Her back ached and she felt a flooding sensation in her loins. This morning, as she rose from bed, her flux had started, and she had gone in search of linen pads with a feeling of relief. For all Robert's industry beneath the sheets and between her legs, she was not yet with child. Robert had shrugged at the news. 'What God wills will be,' he had said, and patted her shoulder. It was an unusual statement for her husband to make, since his philosophy was God helped those who helped themselves.

At least she wouldn't have to deal with his demands while her flux ran its course. Although her body had grown a little more accustomed to the vigour of his lovemaking, it was still a discomfort that she endured as a marital duty. The other side of the coin were his kisses, hugs and cuddles, which she actively enjoyed. It was comfortable to sit with him before the fire, her head on his shoulder, while he stroked her like a cat and they talked of the day's doings.

She finished warping the loom and Walter returned bearing a pannier full of green yarn. Robert followed him into the shed, a new cap of Lincoln weave set aslant on his tawny mane, a peacock feather waving jauntily at the autumn day. He was stocky, carrying just a little too much weight about the jowls and midriff, but in motion he had the graceful tread of a man much lighter.

The Flemings ceased their chatter to rise and bow. Smiling, he waved them back to work, and came to greet Miriel.

'Sweetheart.' He kissed her cheeks and then her lips. 'We've a guest tonight. I've promised him a fine supper and excellent conversation.'

'A guest?' Miriel looked at him, not entirely delighted. The ache in her back was fierce and she knew from experience that it would grow worse. And some of Robert's merchant friends and clients could be tiresome.

'The ship's master,' Robert announced. 'He'd been escorting a cargo of spices upriver by barge, and I met him in the market place.'

Miriel relaxed slightly and smiled. She liked Martin Wudecoc, and it would not be so much of a chore to provide for him. 'I had best go to the market place myself then,' she said and, in a deft movement, unhooked Robert's purse from his belt.

His eyes widened and he puffed out his chest, before releasing his breath on a reluctant laugh. 'It's your cloth he carried to Flanders as well,' he pointed out.

'But you invited him, and I'm the one who has to see to this "fine supper",' Miriel retorted smartly, and swept out of the door.

Nicholas sat on the feather mattress in The Angel's loft room. A full pouch of silver had ensured that he had to share neither room nor bed with occupants other than of his choice.

'What is he like, this merchant who has asked you to dine?' enquired Magdalene, tucking the fresh linen sheet around her ample, freckled breasts. She had departed her regular employment at The Red Boar in Dover in favour of a journey to Lincoln with Nicholas.

'He's an important wool merchant. I'm contracted to carry his fleeces on *Pandora's Daughter*, so most of his dealings have been with Martin, but we meet now and again to negotiate and discuss business.' He left the bed where they had recently spent a pleasant hour's dalliance, and took a fresh linen shirt from his baggage.

Magdalene eyed the lean contours of his body with appreciation and tucked a silky strand of red hair behind her ear. 'Is he rich?'

Nicholas donned the shirt and regarded her with amusement. 'Very, and never late to settle his account.' He reached for his tunic. 'Unfortunately, his invitation did not run to a companion.'

Magdalene pouted. 'You just don't want me to meet someone who might take an interest.'

'Oh come now!' he laughed. 'You know my kind, and I know yours!'

She scowled at him for a moment, her frown almost too large for her brow, and then her lips twitched. She grabbed one of the bolsters and threw it at him.

Nicholas gave an exaggerated duck and wagged his finger at her. 'Hurling the bedclothes at me won't change matters, and besides, Robert Willoughby is a soundly married man.'

'Most of them are,' Magdalene retorted drily. 'You, my love, are an exception to my usual kind of customer.'

He snorted and latched his belt. 'I'll take that as a compliment. What I meant was that Willoughby is but recently married, and to a lass at least half his age, according to Martin. A woman of means, brains and beauty. The merchant is besotted by her. You could walk into the room clad in naught but your hair, and he would not notice.'

Magdalene considered this and sucked her index finger. 'Then you had best behave yourself,' she murmured. 'I would hate you to return to me a gelding for the sin of eyeing up someone else's property.'

'Small chance of that,' Nicholas replied confidently. 'I'm not one to fall for female charms, no matter how temptingly wrapped. Business arrangements are by far the best.'

Magdalene arched her brow as he leaned over the bed to kiss her lips. 'I do try to please,' she said, with a hint of sarcasm that he chose to ignore.

Most people rich enough to possess napery liked their table cloths to be of tightly woven white linen with embroidered borders. Miriel, however, had chosen Egyptian cotton. This too was tightly woven with an Arabic damask pattern, and instead of being white, it was dyed a soft apple-green. Draping the trestle in the main room it was a perfect foil for the silver-gilt goblets and platters, and a newly acquired aquamanile in the shape of a snarling lion. Brass lamps suspended from the rafters cast a soft glow over the table, and their light was augmented by more silver gilt in the form of a candelabra standing on the thick stone sill.

Miriel placed a bowl of ground spices on the table and stood back to admire the finished effect. Perfect. Although there had not been time to arrange numerous courses, she had done her best, and from what she knew of Martin Wudecoc, he did not stand on ceremony and his tastes were simple. A pottage of cauliflower and cheese served with wastel bread, a pork stew simmered with honey, mustard and cider, and a raisin curd tart should satisfy the heartiest appetite and still keep the palate stimulated.

Satisfied, Miriel went to change from her working gown into a sleek affair of forest-green silk, the sleeves tight to the wrist. Robert would have liked to see her in extravagant hanging sleeves as worn by the women of the nobility, but Miriel found them so impractical as to be useless. It had been bad enough wearing the wide sleeves of a nun's habit, let alone dealing with swaths of fabric that trailed on the floor.

The drag in her loins felt like someone sharpening a dull knife on her pelvic bones and there was a solid ache at the back of her eyes. She drank feverfew in wine to blunt the pain and changed her soiled linens, adding an extra layer of padding. Elfwen arranged a simple veil of cream silk over Miriel's tawny braids, and secured it with a circlet of hammered gold.

Miriel studied the result in her hand mirror. The dark circles beneath her eyes made them look sultry, as if she had just risen from the bed of a lover. There was nothing she could do about that; resorting to cosmetics would only compound the impression. She pinched her cheeks and compressed her lips to give them a little more colour, then put aside the mirror and went below to await Robert and their guest.

They arrived together a little before dusk, having met by chance outside the great cathedral near the top of the hill. Will barked loudly at the door, and Miriel looked up from the weaving accounts and tallys she had been studying. The sound of masculine voices raised in good-humoured conversation filled the entrance. She stuffed the tally sticks back into their calfskin bag and hastened to greet the men.

Robert strode forward, a jovial grin parting his beard. 'Smells good,' he said, planting two hearty kisses on her cheeks. Then he stepped to one side and indicated his guest. 'Wife, I want you to meet Nicholas de Caen, owner of *Pandora's Daughter*.'

Miriel felt as if she had swallowed a gallon of ice. She stared at their visitor and swayed where she stood. He carried more weight than had the gaunt-boned youth at St

Catherine's, and his skin was an outdoor tan-gold, seamed with a sailor's creases, but none the less, it was him, and there was nowhere to run.

He returned her look, shock widening his eyes too. And then they narrowed, and his lips developed a sardonic curve.

'Mistress Willoughby.' He inclined his head in irony that was obvious only to Miriel.

She swallowed and raised her fingertips to the tight lump in her throat. 'I thought . . . I was expecting Master Wudecoc,' she croaked.

'He is one of my captains,' Nicholas said pleasantly, 'currently at sea with a cargo of alabaster for France. I'm afraid I will have to suffice.'

'Come, Miriel,' Robert chided, 'we don't want to stand in the passage all night, and I'm as hungry as a bear.'

Lowering her eyes and forcing her legs to move, although they felt as if they had been turned to wood, Miriel led them to the trestle she had earlier decorated with such satisfaction. She knew that she would be unable to eat a single morsel of the meal prepared.

Nicholas was gazing around the room, taking in every aspect, from the expensive stone chimney to the brightly painted shutters closing out the dusk. She could see his mind calculating and arriving at entirely the wrong conclusion. 'You have a very fine dwelling,' he said softly.

'It is my former family home,' Miriel answered, her cheeks blazing. 'I grew up here.'

'Indeed?' Nicholas raised the eyebrows of a vastly interested guest. 'And have you always lived here, Mistress Willoughby?'

'No,' Robert answered for her, waving an expansive hand. 'She was wedded to a good friend of mine in Nottingham, but after he died, we came to courtship and then marriage – and love her dearly I do.' He smiled benevolently at Miriel. 'Her kin that dwelt here died and, as sole heir, she inherited last year. We divide our time between here and Nottingham, don't we, my dear?'

Miriel smiled wanly. 'Yes, Robert.' Jesu, she thought, I sound like my mother. Her legs were shaking so badly with shock that it was a relief to sit down at the trestle and let Samuel pour wine into the silver-gilt cups.

'How many ships do you have, Master Nicholas?' she asked with a bright and brittle smile.

'Four for the nonce.' He rubbed the side of his jaw with his thumb. 'A fifth is due to join them soon, and I have a fleet of barges running from Boston up the Welland and Witham, carrying supplies inland.'

'You have made your fortune then.' She took a nervous gulp from her goblet and was shocked to find it down to the dregs already. Robert was giving her strange looks. Steady, she told herself, steady.

Nicholas's blue-green eyes were accusing. 'Against all the odds, yes,' he replied. 'I would have been in this position sooner, but some of my capital was stolen by a thief in the night.'

Miriel watched Samuel refill her goblet, and resisted the temptation to grab and down the Gascon wine in one gulp. 'How terrible,' she murmured.

He shrugged. 'I'll get even someday.'

Miriel clasped her hands and looked down at her empty platter, soon to be filled with cauliflower pottage. Please God let me wake up from this nightmare, she prayed. Not that she had any hope of God listening after the way she had treated him at St Catherine's.

Robert looked at Nicholas, respect in his eyes for a man after his own heart. 'Aye, so would I from anyone who trod on my toes,' he said. 'But at least it has not set you back too far.' A note of amiable envy entered his voice. 'I wish I had been as successful at your age.'

Nicholas smiled. 'I suppose that hardship breeds determination. I've been fending for myself a long time.'

Samuel served the cauliflower pottage and the white wastel rolls. Somehow, Miriel forced her will beyond the fact that her stomach was sticking to her spine, and managed to swallow a passable amount whilst making polite conversation. Her worst nightmare had come true: Nicholas had found her. The only consolation was that the prospect of him doing so no longer hung over her like the sword of Damocles, and she could prepare to do battle. In a way, it was almost a relief.

'Are you married, Master Nicholas?' she enquired as the pottage was cleared away and the pork stew served.

Nicholas, who had shown no sign of nerves and scraped his dish clean, turned to her with a glint of sardonic amusement in his eyes. 'In truth I have no time for a wife,' he replied. 'The sea and my ships are all the women I need. It might have been different once, but the wench in question proved not to be all that she seemed.'

Heat burned Miriel's face. 'None of us are,' she retorted, and again caught Robert's questioning stare.

The ghastly evening dragged on. Will disgraced himself by taking an instant liking to Nicholas, begging at his feet and finally ending up in his lap, an expression of doggy delight on his little pointed face. Miriel could have kicked him.

Robert grimaced. 'The nearest he gets to affection for me is pissing in my boots.'

'I've known women similar,' Nicholas commented, making his host chuckle. 'The wrong sort, of course,' he added, and then inclined his head to Miriel who was scarlet with rage and mortification, her lips pursed in fair imitation of Sister Euphemia. 'I apologise if I am embarrassing you, mistress. When a man spends so much time at sea, in the company of other men, he tends to forget his manners in a gentler presence.'

'I am no tender flower to take offence so easily,' Miriel answered, but her tone was far from gracious. 'I could not run my weaving business successfully if I was offended by every snippet of foolish banter.'

Nicholas grinned, conceding her the point. 'I am glad you see matters in that light,' he said, and smoothly changed the conversation, asking Robert about his wool quotas.

Finally, as the candles burned low, Nicholas rose to take his leave, dusting white dog hairs from his dark woollen tunic. 'My thanks for the best meal I've eaten all year,' he said to Miriel at the door, 'and for an entertaining evening. I hope that we may share company again soon.'

Miriel forced a smile, her own hope precisely the opposite,

and nodded her head as if agreeing with him. She left Robert shaking Nicholas's hand and wishing him well, and returned to the main room where Samuel and Elfwen were clearing the trestle. The pale green cloth was stained with gravy drips and crumbs. The candles on the sill were guttering. What had been perfect was destroyed. She had no doubt that he would seek retribution.

Robert came back into the room, rubbing his hands in the manner he used when pleased with life and himself.

'Well then,' he said as he tilted wine into a goblet, 'what did you think of our sea-captain?'

Miriel poured wine of her own and shrugged. It was safe to drink now, and she needed the oblivion.

'You have no opinion? That is unusual for you, my dear.'

'What is there to say?' Panic fluttered in her belly. What indeed? She imagined telling Robert the truth, and immediately cancelled the vision. Generous he might be, loving he might be, but understanding he was not.

Robert tilted his head to one side. 'I thought I detected a hint of hostility towards him earlier, and you're certainly on edge at the moment.' His voice ended on a questioning note.

Miriel cast hastily round for an answer. 'If I am, it is nothing to do with him,' she lied. 'I began my flux today and I'm out of sorts.'

'Ah yes,' he nodded, and scratched the side of his face in a covert sign of masculine embarrassment. A glint of disappointment filled his eyes too at the knowledge that for a week he would be unable to lie with her. 'But you still have no opinion?' he asked.

Miriel could have sown seeds of doubt in Robert's mind; she could have turned him against Nicholas and made sure that their door was barred to him in the future, but she found herself unable to pile a second treachery on top of the first. 'I think you have chosen a good man for the task,' she said.

'Yes. I thought at first he was too young, but he has scuppered my doubts.' He grinned at his own weak jest.

Miriel responded with a dutiful smile. 'Forgive me if I

retire,' she said. 'I'm weary.' It was not a lie; she felt utterly exhausted.

Robert made an open-handed gesture of dismissal, and sat down before the fire with the remains of the flagon.

Miriel climbed the stair and fell on to the bed. Her back was aching ferociously and she had a blinding headache. She craved the oblivion of sleep and knew with hopeless certainty that it would not come.

It was very late when Nicholas returned to The Angel. The cathedral bells had tolled the hour of matins and the city was dark and silent, all fires covered for the night, all the shutters barred. The landlord let him in with a heavy frown that was only lightened when Nicholas pressed a coin into his palm. By the sputtering light of a single rush dip, Nicholas skirted the trestles and made his way to the loft.

In the bed, Magdalene turned over and sat up. She had left a candle burning and in its glow her red hair shone like new copper.

'I thought you had abandoned me.' Her voice held a querulous note. 'I have been lying here listening to that damned bell ringing the hour and wondering where you were.'

Nicholas repressed the urge to snap at her. Tonight's happenings were none of her fault, and although their arrangement was one of business, still there was an undercurrent of care and concern. 'My client wanted to discuss shipping matters,' he said, extinguishing the rush dip and setting the holder on the coffer. 'I could hardly get up and walk away just for the lateness of the hour.' The lie and the slightly exasperated tone came easily. It was no concern of hers that he had been walking the streets of Lincoln for the past two hours, his mind a quicksand of conflicting thoughts and emotions.

Magdalene pouted at him, but more as an end to the protest than a continuing sulk, for she was essentially good-natured and solidly pragmatic. She flapped back the covers invitingly. 'Fortunately, I have been keeping the bed warm,' she purred.

The smell of her fragrance flowed out towards him in sensuous waves. The curves and hollows of her body beckoned, offering comfort, offering joyous, uncomplicated lust.

Tearing off his clothes in haste, Nicholas leaped into bed, pulled the covers over, and buried himself in her welcoming embrace.

When they had finished, and she curled up against him, murmuring sleepily, Nicholas lay awake, staring at the rafters. His body was sated, but his mind was far from a state of peace. Nor had he really expected the act of physical release to perform any alchemy. The spell was too deep for that.

He had found her, something he had dreamed of doing but never expected to happen. Gone was the nun with the haunted eyes, gone the drab 'widow' in that awful dress he had chosen for her. In their place was an elegant young woman, if not poised, then certainly accomplished and making as much of a success of her life as he had done of his. She had not looked ruthless, sitting there at the trestle struggling with her composure, but he had no doubt that she was. Robert Willoughby had said that she was the widow of a good friend. She must have wasted no time in finding a 'suitable' husband for protection the moment she had run from that alehouse in Nottingham. And on his death she had married one of the most influential wool merchants in the Middle Counties.

Jesu, she must be sweating now, Nicholas thought grimly. He could make things more than awkward for her if he so chose. And why not? She had stolen his money and the Empress's crown. But if he exposed her, then she would just as surely expose him and instead of being welcomed in the keeps and royal palaces of the realm, he would be hunted from boundary to boundary, coast to coast. In the end they would both hang.

He fell into a restless doze and half dreamed, half imagined that he and Miriel were prisoners, bound face to face on a muddy shore with ropes of gold. Out in the distance, beyond hearing, but trembling through their bodies was the muted thunder of the returning tide.

CHAPTER 20

At dawn, Robert left Lincoln for the monasteries at Nocton and Thornholme in search of more wool contracts. Miriel was relieved to see him go. He would be spending at least two nights away, giving her the time she needed to restore her balance. She would have found it impossible to act the role of cheerful, smiling wife so soon after last night's happening.

Usually she would have faced the business of the day with relish, but all she felt was dread as she forced down a crust with a cup of buttermilk. Bare of all napery, the trestle was just a plain board of scrubbed oak. A deep notch scarred the edge. She could remember cutting it with her grandfather's knife as a mischievous five-year-old. The deed had been whim and curiosity, rebellion and daring. Whether it had been worth the whipping she received was debatable.

Impatiently, Miriel pushed aside the loaf, donned her cloak and picked up the bag of tallies she had been sorting the previous day.

'You be going to the workshop, mistress?' enquired Elfwen as she removed Miriel's cup and the uneaten bread from the trestle.

'Presently,' Miriel nodded stiffly. 'First I have some other business in the town.'

'I'll fetch my cloak.'

Miriel grimaced. The girl had taken to heart the general rule that a woman of means should have a maid to accompany her wherever she went. 'No, that won't be necessary.'

'But it won't take me a—'

'I said, it won't be necessary,' Miriel snapped, colour

branding her cheeks. 'Give me leave to know when I do and do not need your attendance.'

Elfwen reddened too. The stiff curtsey she made had more than a hint of a flounce.

Miriel cast her eyes heavenwards. She had neither the patience to argue nor the slightest intention of yielding for the sake of Elfwen's notions of propriety. 'If I am sought, I will be in the workshops before the ringing of the prime bell,' she said haughtily and swept out. The dignity of her exit was somewhat marred by Will, who insisted on worrying at the hem of her cloak with ferocious growls until she was forced to pick him up and tuck him in the crook of her arm.

The landlord at The Angel knew Miriel. He had bought fabric from her family's workshop since the days of her grandfather's rule. Today he was wearing a handsome tunic of her famous Lincoln weave. 'Mistress,' he greeted her, 'what can I do for you?'

Miriel licked her lips and glanced around. It was never too early in the morning for customers at The Angel, and already two carters and an off-duty gate guard sat in conversation at one of the trestles.

'I understand that you have a sea-captain staying here, a Nicholas de Caen?'

The landlord's small eyes brightened in amusement. 'You would be understanding aright, Mistress Willoughby.' He leaned one forearm on a wine barrel; the other clutched a cloth at his hip.

'He dined at our house last night,' Miriel said with cold authority, although inside she was quivering like a marrow jelly. 'I have a message for him from my husband. Unfortunately he has business elsewhere this morn and cannot deliver it himself. I need to catch Master de Caen before he leaves.'

'Of course, mistress.' Not by so much as the flicker of an eyelid did he reveal whether he believed her or not. Miriel knew that the presence of a maid would have given her story more credibility, but she could hardly say what she wanted to Nicholas with Elfwen in tow.

The amusement deepened in the man's eyes. 'You will be pleased to know he has not yet departed. He rented the upper chamber for the duration of his stay. You go out the back and up the stairs on the right.' He nodded pleasantly toward the passageway.

Miriel swallowed the urge to stutter out further justification and excuses. 'Thank you,' she said curtly, and walked from the landlord's sight with a brisk confidence she was far from feeling. On the stairs to the sleeping chamber, her nerve failed and she hesitated. Why had she come? What was she going to say? How would Nicholas react? Jesu, this was folly. She tried to turn around, but her feet would not obey her will.

In her arms, Will whined and tried to lick her chin. She put him down, hoping that he would scamper down the stairs and give her the impetus to chase him. Instead, he ran up them, leaping mightily at each step until he stood outside the closed bedchamber door. Standing on his little hind legs, he scrabbled at the heavy wood.

Miriel swallowed, drew a deep breath and followed him. Clenching her knuckles, she rapped on the door and sealed her fate.

A woman's voice called to her to enter. *A woman?* With tremendous misgiving, Miriel set her hand to the latch and clicked open the door.

There were several beds in the room, but only the one near the shutters was occupied. A woman with creamy skin and sleep-tousled red hair leaned against a pile of bolsters, the sheets drawn up to her breasts.

Will darted past Miriel and leaped on to the bed, his tail wagging furiously. The red-haired occupant laughed with surprise and fussed his silky ears. Mortified, Miriel hastened after her wayward dog.

'I'm sorry to disturb your slumber,' she said. 'I was looking for another guest and the landlord directed me here.' She made a grab for Will, but he jumped off the bed and ran round, exploring the room.

The woman fixed Miriel with smiling eyes of woodsmoke-blue. 'No harm done, I was preparing to rise anyway.' Her voice had a husky undertone quite in keeping with the languorous aspect of her body. 'My employer has twice called me a slug-abed already.' Completely without modesty, she threw back the sheets and went to a pile of clothes draped across a coffer. Her curves were ripe, with a slight roll of flesh on her belly, offset by perfect, slender legs and good height. She donned an undershift that Miriel's experienced eye appreciated as expensive cotton, threaded with green silk ribbon. 'I adore little dogs like that.' Her gaze followed Will as he snuffled round the other beds. 'I've been promised one as a gift myself.' She eased a comb through the tangles in her thick, silky hair. 'Whom were you seeking?'

Miriel cleared her throat. It had been a mistake to come here; she knew it for certain now. 'A ship's master, Nicholas de Caen. He had business with my husband last night.'

'Ah.' The woodsmoke eyes tensed slightly and the good humour was suddenly overlaid by caution.

'You know him?'

The woman's hair crackled with life, rising from her scalp in sparkling coppery filaments. 'He is my employer,' she said, and although her tone was casual, it still managed to convey a note of challenge.

Miriel stared. It did not take a half-wit to fit the pieces together. The word 'whore' came first to mind, and with it a sting of anger. But a less reactionary part of Miriel's mind asked who was she to judge, and what business was it of hers? The woman had done her no harm. Now she knew why the landlord had been smiling as he directed her upstairs. 'Then do you know where I can find him?'

'He went down to the stables, but he should be back at any moment to see if I'm ready for the road.' She donned a gown of fine green linen, and topped it with an overdress of tabby-woven amber silk, becoming the image of a prosperous, respectable noble lady.

'Do you travel with him everywhere?' Miriel was driven to enquire despite herself.

'I keep him company when he asks.' The woman gave her a feline smile, sleepy and knowing. 'Men who sail the seas are a law unto themselves. Sometimes I do not see him for months on end, but that makes the reunions even sweeter.'

Miriel reddened. She could not bear thinking about a reunion with Robert after months on end. Jesu, his lust would be the death of her. 'In the stables, you said?' Miriel turned towards the door. She did not want to encounter Nicholas beneath the curious, knowing eyes of his casual mistress.

The redhead gestured. 'He will not be long if you want to wait, or you can leave a message with me.'

'Neither,' Miriel said with an inward grimace at such a thought. 'I'll go and find him myself.'

'As you wish.' With a shrug, the woman began braiding her hair into a thick, shining plait. Miriel had always been vain of her own honey-gold tresses, but they were no match for this whore's glorious mane. Disturbed and a trifle piqued, she grabbed Will and departed, leaving, had she but known it, very similar emotions simmering in Magdalene's breast.

It was a small mercy that Miriel did not have to walk back through the tap room and face the landlord's broad grin. The stables lay behind the inn within a stockade of various outbuildings and a small byre. Two horses and a pack pony were tethered outside the stalls, and a groom was busy with harness and tack. Nicholas was leaning against the daub and wattle wall, his arms folded as he talked to the man. Yet again, Miriel had to fight the urge to turn and flee. It was too late, she told herself, the wheels were turning too fast to be halted.

Nicholas raised his head and, glancing across the yard, caught her approach. The expression of casual ease departed his face to leave it taut as a wooden mask. He unfolded his arms and pushed himself off the wall. With a murmur to the groom, he walked to meet her.

'You are abroad early, Mistress Willoughby,' he said with a polite bow, made cutting to Miriel by the fact that she knew it was sarcastic. 'You have some urgent business perchance?'

'You know my business full well,' Miriel snapped. 'This matter between us has to be resolved.'

In her arms, Will wriggled and yapped excitedly. Nicholas fondled his silky ears and looked at Miriel with a gaze as cold as the North Sea. 'That is easily done,' he said softly. 'Give to me what is mine.'

Miriel's chin jerked. 'It isn't yours.'

'I damned near died to get it.'

'And if you are standing here now in your fine clothes with merchant ships to your name and a whore you can afford to clothe in silk for your company, then it is because I saved your life!' she hissed.

His complexion darkened. Will growled and bared his teeth. Nicholas looked down at the little dog and carefully removed his hand. He sucked a deep breath into his lungs and let it out slowly. His colour improved. 'When you argue,' he said, 'you go straight for the throat without seeking alternatives. Have you ever apologised to anyone in your life?'

'When apology is due.' Miriel stood her ground, her spine as rigid as an iron rod. She was not going to let him belittle or patronise her. She kicked her toe in the dust. 'I came to find common ground, not a battlefield. If that is going "straight for the throat" then you have some strange notions.'

He shook his head. 'Perhaps I have a different idea of what is common ground and what is a battlefield.'

'Nick!' A woman's voice floated across the courtyard. 'I'm ready, Nick.'

Miriel turned and saw the whore advancing on them, her head decently covered now in a wimple of cream silk, but her braids snaking to her waist and cross-gartered with green silk ribbons like the one adorning her shift. The cut of the silk overgown flattered her curves, and male heads swivelled at stockade and byre as she walked past.

'I see you found him,' she addressed Miriel warmly as she arrived. A possessive arm linked through Nicholas's, the fingers long, slim and finished with manicured half-moon talons.

'Thank you, yes,' Miriel replied tersely.

Nicholas's eyelids tightened. Excusing himself, he drew the woman to one side and murmured in her ear. Miriel saw him fish in his pouch and heard the musical clink of silver pennies. The woman shook her head at first, but then, with an exaggerated shrug of her shoulders and a heavy pout to her lower lip, took the coins. He kissed her cheek. 'I'll meet you back here at the prime bell,' he said.

'You hope.' She gave him a look through her lashes, deliberately ran her hand over his crotch for Miriel's benefit, and strolled away in the direction of the main thoroughfare.

Miriel drew breath, but Nicholas pre-empted her with a hand raised in warning. 'I will not hear a word said against Magdalene. She has never done another soul harm in her life, and while she likes the colour of money, her heart is as deep as her purse. I asked her to come with me to Lincoln, not the other way around.'

'What she is to you is your own concern,' Miriel answered frostily. She was a little irritated at having the jibe she had been about to make silenced. And his words had made her feel mean-spirited too.

'Then on that at least we have an understanding. Come,' he added, with a glance over his shoulder at the groom who was going diligently about his tasks with his ears obviously as wide as trumpets. 'I'll take you to see my new barges. That way, it will seem as if we are discussing the shipping business and there will be no cause for eyebrows to be raised any higher.'

Miriel could see the sense in this. Besides, if they were walking along, there was small chance of anyone hearing enough of a conversation to make matters awkward.

Side by side, but a decorous distance apart, they set off.

'Where is your husband?' Nicholas asked as they descended the hill and headed towards the river. 'Out of the way, I assume, or you would not have come seeking me quite so boldly.'

'Robert is out negotiating wool contracts, but he does not expect me to stay by the hearth minding my distaff in his absence. I would not have married him if that were the case.'

'So why did you?'

Miriel glanced at him and saw that he was as much curious as hostile. 'We had much in common,' she replied with a shrug. She was not going to admit that she had been vulnerable, that the strength of Robert's personality, his solid, mercantile bulk, had been somewhere to hide while she licked her wounds and prepared afresh for battle. That his vigour was both compelling and comforting . . . and sometimes filled her with fear.

'So he lets you have your way.'

Miriel gave an irritated cluck. 'As much as I let him have his,' she said crossly. 'I am his equal, his partner in trade.' She saw the sceptical set of his brows and had a powerful urge to kick him in the shins. 'Whatever you might think,' she added.

'I know your capabilities,' he said ambiguously.

They crossed the main thoroughfares and headed towards the river on the south side of the city. Clouds scudded across the sky, herded by a brisk wind with a sharpening of cold.

'Does he know anything of your past?'

Miriel peeled her billowing wimple off her face to look at Nicholas. 'Is that a threat?'

His eyebrows knotted in a scowl. 'Why must you take my every word as a threat or put-down?' he demanded. 'We have an opportunity to talk, and all you are doing is wasting it.'

Miriel flushed. He was right, but she was not going to admit it. If she was being awkward, it was out of guilt and defensiveness. Nicholas had not been far off the mark with his observation that she had never apologised to anyone in her life.

'He knows that I quarrelled with my family and that I ran away,' she said grudgingly, 'but not that I was shut away in a convent, and obviously he does not know about you.'

'Or the treasure.'

'No, of course not. No one knows about that.' She nodded a greeting to an acquaintance. A tilt of the head, a smile, gave the illusion that everything was as it should be.

'If I had caught you on the day you ran off with it, I would have killed you,' he murmured, inclining his head too for the sake of courtesy. 'You at least owe me a reason for what you did. I would have given you a fair share.'

'Including the Empress's crown?'

The speed of his step increased, the force of heel and toe

on the footpath thrusting him forward. 'Your fair share, I said.'

'Well, there you have one of your reasons. My notion of fair and yours are not the same.' Miriel lengthened her stride to keep up with him.

'Jesu,' he grimaced, 'I would hate to be one of your customers.'

'What makes you think I'd sell cloth to you in the first place?'

'Your eye for a profit.'

Miriel ground her teeth. 'Now who is wasting the opportunity to talk?'

'Then tell me why you did it,' he said vehemently. 'Why you had to leave in such an underhand manner? Fair or not – and we both see differently on the matter – you knew that it would leave a taint. Surely you must have lived in dread of ever meeting up with me again.'

'I thought the risk worth taking,' Miriel said bleakly. She ducked her head so that all she could see was the kick of her gown as she walked and nothing of his fierce expression. 'I will tell you now for the one and only time that you are right: I have felt guilt about what I did, and I hoped that a moment like this would never come about.'

He made a sound in his throat, whether of contempt or acceptance she could not tell. For a while they walked in taut silence, and then he said, 'You still have not told me why you did it.'

The smells of the river bank came strongly on the breeze as they approached the water: the eye-watering whiff of the tannery pits, and the woad vats at the dyers' establishments, where plants and urine decayed in a blend of evil stench to produce the deep blue dye for the cloth that came from the fulling mills upstream.

Miriel held her breath and put her sleeve to her face until they had passed the area. Beside her, she was aware of Nicholas choking and cursing under his breath.

'Small wonder that they banish these trades to the outside of towns,' he said in a strangled voice.

'But folk want their soft and supple leather, they want their richly coloured cloth,' Miriel replied with a shrug. 'This is the price they pay for luxury.' She tugged at the woad-blue tunic he was wearing to emphasise her point.

Nicholas grimaced. 'Give me the smell of the open sea and a plain linen shirt any day,' he said, then nailed her with a firm stare. 'An explanation,' he prompted.

Miriel gnawed her underlip and flicked him a glance from beneath her lashes. 'I had never seen anything so beautiful in my life, or so powerful. It called out to me, and I could not bear to think that you might tear out the jewels and melt it down.'

'I would not have done that!' he said sharply.

'On the marshland, when you recovered it, you were not so sure. You gave me no firm answer when I asked you, and I feared that it was because you intended to destroy it.'

He shook his head. 'If it crossed my mind, the notion never went further. It would have been sacrilege.'

'I was not to know how you thought,' Miriel said defensively, and when he did not reply, made an exasperated gesture. 'Do not ask what came over me; I cannot explain it even to myself. All I knew then was that I had to have that crown to look upon, to touch.'

He nodded as if in confirmation of a truth he had already suspected. 'So, where is it now?'

'Safe,' she said shortly. 'No one knows of the place except me, and that is the way it shall remain until I decide otherwise.'

He looked at her, his gaze steady and assessing, increasing her discomfort until she was forced to speak again.

'I cannot give you its value in coin, for it is beyond price, but I can return to you the marks of silver that I took.'

'Generous of you,' he said drily. 'And supposing I want more?'

Miriel halted. They had arrived at the quayside and numerous barges and punts bobbed at their moorings. Two men were operating a wooden crane, unloading bales of supplies from a nef with a red sail. 'Are you asking because you do, or just to watch me twist and turn?' she demanded.

He rubbed his jaw. 'A little of both, I think. Perhaps

allowing you to pay back the silver is letting you off too lightly for what you did, but then I remind myself that you saved my life, and that too is beyond price.'

'Then throw away the tally; call it quits. Each of us is capable of damning the other, and that must surely be a kind of balance.'

He shook his head and gave a reluctant laugh. 'Aye, the balance of a knife edge.'

'But what is the alternative?'

Three barges were moored in a row like a family of ducks. A new smell clung to their clinker-built strakes, the wooden bones and sinews of the vessels clean and sharp, without fuzzing of weed or barnacle. Nicholas leaped down into one of the boats, and it set up a small shuddering along its length as it absorbed the force of his landing.

'There isn't one.' He held out his hand, inviting her on board, inviting her to trust his grip. Somewhat gingerly, Miriel placed her fingers in his and stepped on to the deck, ducking her head to avoid the hemp stays securing the mast. His touch was warm and dry, his skin tough across the palms in contrast to the fine clothes he wore.

'Then we live with it.' She removed her hand from his for the contact disturbed her. Unbidden, an image of him stroking the whore's long red hair filled her eyes.

'And die.' He gave her a long, measured look. 'I will not quit the tally,' he said, 'but I will agree to a truce. Master Willoughby brings a deal of custom my way, and there will be times when you and I will have to share each other's company – my words last night were more practical truth than threat. I would rather it was in a bond of friendship than enmity – agreed?'

'Agreed,' Miriel nodded stiffly. It was the reason she had come to see him, to take the thunder out of the storm somehow. But she had the suspicion that although she had succeeded, she was only storing up trouble for later.

He stepped over the sail of reefed canvas and walked to the stern. 'She'll be loaded with bales of cloth for an Italian merchant and sailed to Boston. Then her burden will be transferred to the *Pandora* and taken across the North Sea and up the Rhine with a cargo of alabaster.' He flashed her a smile. 'You should come one day.'

Miriel gazed downriver to the bustle on the bridge. 'Perhaps one day I will,' she murmured.

'I know it is none of my business,' Magdalene said, 'but is it wise to have an affair with the wife of one of your best customers?' At the market booths she had bought herself a ring of twisted gold and silver wire and she was admiring it on her hand as she rode pillion behind Nicholas on the road to Boston.

Nicholas's eyelids tensed with irritation and amusement. How quickly scenes were assimilated, misconstrued, and the wrong conclusions made. 'I'm not having an affair with her.' For a start, Miriel wouldn't lower her guard so much as an inch.

'Then why the secrecy? Why dismiss me with a pat on the head and a bag of coins if you had nothing to hide?'

'You like your ring, don't you?'

'Yes, I do, but that is not what I asked.' She tilted her pert nose in the air. 'I know men and women, it's my trade, so do not tell me that there is not something between you and her.'

Nicholas repressed the urge to turn round and tell her either to mind her own business or walk the rest of the way home. He could not deny the sharpness of Magdalene's perception. She was barking up the right tree, except at the wrong branch. 'I tell you, I am not having an affair with Miriel Willoughby,' he replied with laboured patience and a pang at the mention of her name. 'As you say, it would be unwise given the status of her husband, although, in truth, I do not need his custom to survive. It was business that we had to discuss – a delicate matter concerning a cargo from some years ago.'

Magdalene was silent for a time, chewing this over. 'Her husband doesn't know about it, does he, or she would not have waited until he was out of the way?'

'What she tells her husband is her concern.' Sensing his tension, the horse jibbed and sidled, so that Magdalene had to make a grab for the crupper strap. 'You are making a great ocean out of a little puddle.'

Magdalene shrugged. 'The way she looked at me in your bed at The Angel, I could be forgiven for thinking that something was afoot between the two of you. If looks could kill, I would have been dead. I know jealousy when I see it.'

That was interesting. Perhaps the attraction was another reason why they fought each other with words, keeping at bay what would be more complicated to accept than reject. 'It wasn't the jealousy of a mistress, I promise you,' he said. 'And if I was going to have a liaison with her, I would not have brought you all the way to Lincoln for companionship, would I?'

Magdalene thought about that while she continued to admire the ring on her finger, and then with a sudden change of mood, flung her arms around his waist and pressed her cheek into the soft wool of his cloak. 'No, you are right,' she said. 'If there was any jealousy, it was mine.'

Feeling unworthy, Nicholas made a silent promise that he would make it up to Magdalene and buy her a brooch to match the ring.

CHAPTER 21

SPRING 1220

It was market day in Lincoln and mild spring weather following on the heels of blustery squalls had brought folk out in their droves.

Miriel stood at her drapery booth and gorged herself on the colour and bustle of her surroundings. She had always loved market days. Missing them had not been the least of her trials at St Catherine's. Here she was in her element. So was Walter the apprentice weaver. He was proving surprisingly adept at selling the cloth, and she was beginning to think that his future might lie in that direction rather than in the weaving itself. He was never going to attain the calibre of her Flemings at the looms, but he surely had the gift of tongues.

They watched a troupe of jongleurs entertaining the crowds with a display of music and acrobatics. Such folk always made Miriel uneasy. Her father had been one of them and she worried that someday she might see a man with honey-brown eyes tumbling for a living or throwing knives, his face gaunt with hunger and raddled by years of living from hand to mouth.

Today, however, she could bear to watch. None of the three was more than thirty years old, and the folk in the crowd were cheerfully disposed to reward them with a bounty of loose change.

'I wouldn't want to live like that.' Walter screwed up his freckled face. 'Give me a roof over my head and a steady wage any day.'

Miriel smiled and ruffled his hair. 'There but for the grace of God go we all,' she murmured. As she spoke, her gaze travelled beyond the three performers, caught by the familiar figure of her husband. He was talking rapidly to another merchant and it was obvious from the abrupt gesticulations and the jut of his golden beard that he was far from happy.

Moments later, he detached himself from the conversation and stalked across the road to Miriel's booth, his cloak flying and his expression grim. Without pause for consideration, he swept straight through the jongleurs' performance, scattering the wooden juggling batons from the hands of the woman performer. Neither by apology nor snarl did he acknowledge that he was even aware of having caused a disruption.

Walter, always clumsy and unsure in the presence of the master, wiped nervous hands down his tunic and busied himself with a customer who was tentatively fingering a bolt of green serge.

Miriel braced herself to face her husband. 'Whatever's the matter?' His complexion was dusky red and his eyes glassy with temper.

'That son of a whore Maurice de la Pole is snatching my business from under my nose – promising higher prices per sarple and taking less commission. This is my territory; he has no right.'

Miriel turned to the back of the booth and poured wine from a flask into a horn cup. 'Drink,' she said, 'and in the name of God calm yourself.'

Robert's nostrils closed and flared like those of a captured wild horse. He glared at the cup in her hand as if he might dash it to the ground. Then he snatched it from her and gulped deeply. 'He's stealing my customers too – offering them bribes and telling them that I make too much profit.' He drew his fist across the red droplets glistening in his beard.

'How many has he persuaded?' Miriel refilled the cup.

'Two at least. Edwin of Cotmore and Thomas Bowlegs.'

'But they're only recent clients,' Miriel said reasonably. 'And they came to you from someone else. It seems to me that they won't be satisfied anywhere.' She chose her words tactfully. Robert, she knew, was as forceful in his business dealings as in all aspects of his life and certainly not above pilfering weaker men's clients if the opportunity arose. Now that the same was happening to him, his indignation knew no bounds.

Robert took the refilled cup and drank more slowly, his complexion a lighter pink now and his breathing steadier. 'Like as not, but I still won't have that rogue spreading his poison and unsettling the others.'

'So, what will you do?'

He gave her a swift glance in which she saw calculation and the battle light of a man thinking on his feet. 'Talk to my clients, persuade them that I'm still the best man to sell their wool and make them a profit.' He took a last swallow from the cup and tipped the dregs on the ground. 'If I must, then I will offer them a better bargain than de la Pole.'

Miriel could see that the thought hurt him. The other merchant's action not only threatened his profit, it threatened his manhood too. 'You must do what you see fit,' she said by way of sympathy and support. 'De la Pole would not want your clients unless he knew they were the best.'

Robert nodded grimly, but found a smile for her. Briefly he cupped her face in his hands and gave her a hard kiss on the lips. 'I choose the best in everything,' he said.

Miriel sighed and watched him stride off. She was content in her marriage to Robert because the advantages to her business outweighed the disadvantages of living with him. He obtained the best wool for her looms and shipped her cloth with his fleeces, thus lessening the cost for both of them. She was grateful for his unflagging strength and admiring of his drive, but sometimes those very traits became too much. Like a bull-baiting dog, Robert would not relax his jaws for a single moment. Even at home he was planning and plotting how to grab a larger share. That was why he had displayed such affront at de la Pole's attempt to do the same. Competition was to be expected, but competition that came too close was an affront.

The beat of a tabor floated across the fairground from the jongleurs who were ending their act with an acrobatic dance. Among the crowd, a familiar figure applauded and cast his own handful of small coin into the dust for the tumblers to pick up. Miriel's breath caught and her heart skipped against her ribs.

In the six months since their conversation by the barges, she had seen Nicholas only once, and then in passing on a visit to Boston. An inner voice told her that contact was dangerous, that if she had any sense she would run and hide. But the only thing that Miriel had ever run from was a convent, and with this man for company.

As the dance ended, he strolled over to the booth and nodded pleasantly to Walter and his customer. Then he smiled at Miriel, the gesture putting attractive creases in his cheeks. 'Mistress Willoughby, it is good to see you again. I trust I find you in good health?' Courteous and smooth, playing out the role for Walter and the client.

Miriel's stomach plummeted. She had encountered men far more handsome in the perfect physical sense of the word, but none as attractive, nor with such knowledge of her past. 'I am well, thank you,' she responded, forcing a smile of her own. 'And yourself and Mistress Magdalene?'

His eye-corners creased with amusement. 'Mistress Magdalene is in fine fettle, although she has not accompanied me on this occasion. She has more than one fish on her hook.' He smoothed his hand over a bolt of the Florentine damask.

'So you don't want a few ells of this for a gift then?' Miriel held up her measuring stick.

He shook his head and smiled. 'Contrary to what some believe, I am not made of money.'

Miriel pulled a face at the remark, innocent on the surface, but laden with meaning to those who had reason to see beyond. He was never going to let her forget. 'Then how can I help you? If it's Robert you are seeking, he is occupied with business matters, although he may want to talk with you in the course of them.'

Nicholas began to shake his head, but then a gleam entered his eyes and she saw him change his mind. 'Well, yes, I did want to see him on certain matters, and I was hoping to beg an invitation to dine since the food and company of your household were so excellent last time. It would be combining business with pleasure.'

Against her better judgement, Miriel found herself agreeing and then wondered at her own propensity for self-inflicted wounds. The verbal sparring would continue; the game on a knife edge would continue. Did she want to keep him in her sight from distrust for what he might be doing out of it? Or was it just for the painful pleasure of looking at him? She feared that there was too much of the second in her reasoning, but it was too late to withdraw. Like the jongleurs, she would have to take the risk of juggling with fire.

They waited far into the dusk for Robert's return and, finally, Miriel gave instructions for her husband's portion to be set aside and the food served before it spoiled.

'I know Rob had business, but I did not think he would be this late,' she said with nervous irritation.

Nicholas shrugged. 'A springtide market day is always busy for merchants – as you must know yourself.'

Miriel pushed at the broiled trout on her trencher. She had little appetite, her stomach was all clenched up in knots. 'I know, but I'm worried about him.'

Nicholas started to rise. 'Do you want me to go and find him?'

'No.' She waved him to be reseated. 'I'll send Samuel. He knows the places Robert's likely to be.' She summoned the servant and within moments the man had swept on his cloak and hurried out on his errand.

Miriel continued to pick at her food and told Nicholas why she was worried about her husband. 'Supposing there is war between him and Maurice de la Pole. I have seen such things before. When I was a little girl, my grandfather fell out with another weaver over wool supplies and it came to blows in the street. The other man even tried to burn down our warehouse. For a time it was very ugly, and none of us dared venture out unless we had an armed escort. More recently there was trouble with my former stepfather when he lost some of his trade to my weavers.'

Nicholas pursed his lips. 'From what I have seen of your husband, he is strong enough to hold his own.'

'So was my grandfather.' She made an irritated sound. 'I

know that Robert is strong, but I don't want any repercussions flying back to my roost.'

'You mean that de la Pole might use you to get at your husband?'

She nodded, and then she gave a bleak laugh. 'Are you not disgusted with me? My husband in possible danger, and all I can think about is the effect on myself?'

'Neither disgusted, nor surprised,' he said wryly, and pointed his eating knife at her trencher. 'Eat something. You'll feel better.'

'I won't; I'll feel sick.' But even so, she went through the motions of flaking off a piece of flesh and putting it in her mouth.

The door opened and Samuel returned on a bustle of rain-laden wind. 'I've found him, mistress,' he announced with the triumph of a task accomplished. 'He's at The Green Bush tavern. Sends his apologies and says that he's still got business to finish that might keep him late. He'll see Master Nicholas on the morrow.'

Miriel thanked Samuel and dismissed him. Then she leaned back, weak with relief but still not hungry. 'I have been worrying needlessly,' she murmured, 'but you see what scars the past leaves on us?'

He raised his brows questioningly.

Miriel shook her head. 'My father seduced my mother, got her with child and went on his way uncaring. When my grandfather died, he left me at the mercy of my stepfather who cast me into St Catherine's. And then there was Gerbert, God rest his soul.' She made the sign of the Cross on her breast.

Nicholas turned the goblet in his hand, swirling the surface of the wine. 'You are saying that you have always been abandoned by those who should have cared for you,' he said thoughtfully.

Miriel pursed her lips in consideration. 'In truth, yes. Either that or they have mistreated me because of my sex.'

'And fending for yourself has forced you to become a she-wolf?'

'Is that how you see me?'

'I have a few scars to prove it,' he said drily. 'I know you will fight tooth and claw to protect every inch and more of what you consider yours.'

He was astute, and it amused Miriel that he did not say 'what is yours' but rather 'what you consider yours'. The matter of Empress Mathilda's crown still loomed between them and, despite the truce, it was obvious he had no intention of letting the matter lie.

So be it. Lifting the candle from the centre of the trestle with sudden decision, she rose to her feet. 'Come,' she said, 'I want to show you something.'

Draining his cup, he rose too. 'Is it what I think?'

Miriel shrugged. 'Since I do not know what you are thinking, I cannot say,' she answered demurely, and swept ahead of him out of the room and into the passage. His shadow clambered with hers in the gilded darkness as she opened the door which Samuel had left unbolted against the return of the master.

'Don't tell me you keep it in a stable?'

'Why not? Our Lord was born in one,' she retorted and led him outside into a clinging, cold drizzle. The candle hissed and sputtered, and she had to shade it with her hand. The heavy smell of smoking wax filled the air. Puddles winked in and out, sparkling with black light, and the shapes of other buildings loomed as deeper areas of darkness. The pack ponies shifted position and snorted in their stalls, but it was not to them that she led him, but to the door of the wool shed. Giving him the candle, she took a large iron key from the hoop at her waist and set it in the door.

'On the eve before I left for St Catherine's they bolted me in here,' she told him. 'I had fought with my stepfather and almost burned the house down around his ears.' She set the key in the iron grate and twisted, bracing her wrist against the heaviness of the lock until it gave with a sudden lurch. 'When you are seized by the hair and beaten, you are not supposed to fight back.'

'But you did.'

She took a sidelong glance at his face, uplit by the candle. His expression was thoughtful, but there was no inkling of what those thoughts might be. 'Wouldn't you?' she said, and set her hip to the sturdy wooden doors, opening them upon the vast cavern of the wool storehouse. As usual the pungency of unwashed fleeces and the mustiness of stone hit like a slap, then softened to a welcoming caress. Beside her, she felt Nicholas draw a sharp breath.

'You become used to the smell,' she said and, taking the candle, went to light a lantern standing on a small wooden shelf.

He nodded and gazed up at the thick roof timbers. 'Like the sea,' he said. 'First it seizes your breath, then it gives it back, and even when you're far away and doing other things it only takes the echo of its scent to fill you to the brim.'

'Yes, that's exactly how it is,' Miriel said with a pang of delight that he understood. Robert had no inclination to discuss matters beyond the practical and although it had been easy to adapt her manner to his, there were times when her thoughts went begging for a kindred spirit to share them.

She watched Nicholas walk around the warehouse, poking and inspecting. There was not much to see that was different from any other apart from the washing pits for the fleeces. She carried the lantern over to him and touched his arm. 'You will not find it,' she said, smiling. 'Even if it was under your nose, you would still be hard pressed.'

'So, are you going to show me, or do I have to guess like a twelfth night mummer?' He glanced down at her fingers on his sleeve and then into her face. They stood as close as lovers and suddenly Miriel's mouth was dry and her legs weak.

'Both,' she said hoarsely and, lifting her hand, led him to another door beyond the wash pits. It swung open on a small counting house with a table and curved box chair, shelves, and crude wooden coffer.

'It's in there?' he pointed to the coffer.

Miriel gestured. 'Look and see.' She leaned against the door, welcoming the cold, solid wood at her back.

He studied her as if trying to decide if she was teasing him, then stooped to the lid of the chest. 'It's locked.'

Miriel searched amongst the collection of keys at her waist, her fingers clumsy and hampered by the almost darkness. She found the one she wanted, but couldn't free it from the ring.

She cursed and struggled, the jingling of the keys magnified by her discomposure into a clamour as loud as church bells. Nicholas returned to help her. He was more dextrous than her, but still it took a few moments, and in that time they stood so close that their clothing clung and touched and, behind it, the pliable heat of their bodies.

At last Nicholas freed the key. For a moment neither of them moved, then he drew a shuddering breath and turned back to the chest. Miriel closed her eyes and swallowed. Jesu, Jesu. If this was lust then it was delicious and she was utterly unprepared for what it was doing to her bones and body, melting them, drugging her reason. The attraction she had felt for Robert paled to insignificance when compared with this. She was not just playing with fire. She was well and truly in it and burning up.

Nicholas removed rolls of parchment from the chest. He took out ink and quills, a bradawl and trimming knife. Bags of tallies and a squared counting cloth. He peeled back a lining of felted fleece to reveal the chiselled oak base, made from two planks so securely pegged together that they seemed like one whole. Around the outside, they were secured by firm iron bands crowned by a fleur-de-lis design. Despite its outward appearance everything fitted flush and perfectly, without warping or fault of design.

'I had it made when I married Gerbert,' she said, seeking to dilute the gathering sensations with words.

'But not for your linens, I'll warrant.' Nicholas sat back on his heels to consider the chest and all its dimensions. There was nothing about the internal structure to suggest a hidden compartment, and yet he was positive that she had brought him here with the intention of showing him the regalia. So, where was it? Behind him he was more than conscious of her rapid breathing. For two pins he would have abandoned the coffer and dragged her into his arms there and then. But the game had to be played out to his conclusion. He forced himself to concentrate.

'Well?' she said, and he heard a note of triumph in her voice. 'Do you yield?'

Nicholas snorted. 'Either you know me better than that

and the remark is no more than a goad,' he said, 'or you do not know me at all.' He stared at the chest, willing the damned thing to give up its secret, knowing that so much more depended on the moment than the discovery of the crown. If not inside or on top, then what about beneath? He slipped his hand under the chest and felt along the smooth wooden surface. Nothing. Miriel's breathing stopped. Nicholas felt further, and suddenly his fingers encountered an upright wooden peg. He twisted it to the horizontal and a compartment door fell open, giving access to a shelf running the length of the chest. And there was an object on that shelf.

'Well?' he demanded, twisting to grin at her over his shoulder. 'Which was it – a goad, or ignorance?' Delicately he withdrew Mathilda's crown in its silk wrappings.

'Neither.' She clenched her fists in her gown, obviously longing to snatch the object out of his hands, but holding herself in check.

'Then what?'

'A test, to see what you would do.'

'For your amusement?'

'No. To discover how much of my knowledge of you was quicksand, and how much solid fact.' Her voice emerged as a hoarse whisper.

Nicholas unwrapped the crown from its silks and gazed upon the soft gleam of gold and jewels, whose beguilement had almost cost his life. 'And your conclusion?'

She drew a trembling breath. 'That you are a rock, and I am the one drowning in quicksand.'

There was no mistaking what he heard in her voice. Gently he set the gold down upon the chest and turned round. 'Then we are drowning together,' he said, and this time he did pull her into his arms.

There was the tiniest moment of resistance, like a swimmer fighting against an inexorable tide, and then she yielded, her body melting against his. She was slender and supple, pliant in his arms, but not submissive. As his mouth descended on hers, she curled her fingers in his hair, drawing him down closer. The kiss seemed to go on forever, until his jaw ached and his head was whirling from lack of breath. There was a tender pressure in his groin, and he pulled her haunches against his, enhancing the sensation, until it was so exquisite that he groaned aloud, and had to tear his lips from hers to gasp for air.

She was gasping too, and her eyes were aglow. She rubbed against him, and any intention Nicholas had possessed of stopping, any last flicker of conscience, was subdued by a welter of lust and need, and a desire that had lain so long at the back of his mind that its surfacing was a tidal wave against which all reason was helpless.

In the dim light of the candle lantern and the gleaming presence of the royal crown of an empress, he laid his cloak upon the ground and drew Miriel down with him on to its soft fur lining.

With shaking hands, he unpinned her wimple and pulled it from the sheen of her silky hair, now regrown below her shoulders. She was another man's wife, but he did not associate what they were doing with committing adultery. He had been hers since the day she found him on the marsh, and she had been his since the moment she took off with the crown that now presided over this rite of possession.

'This is madness,' she whispered, but did not relinquish her grip on him. Almost feverishly, her fingers sought beneath his tunic and shirt for his naked skin. He sensed an urgency stronger than his own, bordering on desperation. It was as if that now she had made up her mind, she was determined to arrive at the core of the act without pause for dalliance and sweet words along the way. Dazzled, eager himself, Nicholas took his pace from hers. It was the work of a moment to push up her gown and free himself from his braies, to cover her and thrust into her body.

He felt her tense around him, gripping tight, and heard her gasp through clenched teeth. Her nails gored him, and he knew it was not with the force of urgent passion.

Hips pressed flat, unmoving, he raised himself to look at her. 'I'm hurting you,' he said. 'I thought you were ready.'

Her eyes, which had been squeezed shut, opened and she gave him a puzzled stare. 'I am ready.' She reached up to stroke his face with her fingertips. 'I want to give you pleasure.'

'And so you are, but I want to give you joy in return.'

Her look of puzzlement increased and he realised with a jolt that she did not understand, that despite her marital duty to Robert Willoughby, she was still innocent, and had probably never known pleasure beyond the first stirrings, like a fire that had been improperly set and never kindled beyond a weak flame.

'Like this,' he said, and dipped his head gently to nibble her throat, her earlobes, the exquisite line of her jaw. Taking his weight on one arm, he used his other hand to stroke and fondle, laying the foundations of a blaze that would burn hot and true.

In the moist fug of The Green Bush, Robert was securing the future of his wool trade with bags of silver and whispered instructions to the scarred, powerfully muscled man seated opposite on the trestle. 'An accident, you understand, it must look like an accident.'

Serlo Redbeard, former common mercenary in King John's army, and now retired to occasional but better paid employment, closed his fist around the pouch of coins and nodded. 'You can trust me,' he said, exposing a handful of yellow stumps, worn almost down to the gum. The magnificent copper-coloured beard from which he took his name bushed around his face like a scarf. 'No one's ever traced the old weaver's disappearance to your door, have they?'

'No,' Robert said, looking dubious as he made wet ring marks on the trestle with his cup. Going out on a limb to obtain what he wanted had its dangers. While he was prepared to accept them, his confidence had been shaken by the arrogance of de la Pole who had treated him as being of less significance than a fly. Nigel Fuller and the old weaver had been easy meat. Maurice de la Pole was somewhat larger prey and the risks correspondingly greater.

'Of course, if you don't trust me, you can always commission someone else to do the task for you.' Serlo Redbeard offered the purse back to him.

'I never trust anyone further than my eyes can follow them,' Robert growled. 'You know as well as I do that if I went elsewhere, I would be increasing the danger to myself.'

Redbeard smirked, but the expression was swiftly wiped from his face as Robert continued, 'And to mitigate that, I would have to pay my new source double to be rid of you as well. Do not overestimate your worth, Master Redbeard. As long as you do your job and keep your place you are useful to me and your fee reflects the price I set on your abilities and your discretion. I hope we have an understanding.' He leaned forward, staring hard, until the other man nodded and looked away.

'Aye, master, we have an understanding.'

'Good. Come to me when it is done, and you will receive the other half of your wages.' He raised a warning forefinger as Redbeard stuffed the bag of silver into the pouch tied to his belt. 'Remember, I don't want it doing in the town.'

'Leave it to me, master. You'll have no cause for complaint, I swear.' Redbeard drained his cup and swaggered out.

Robert huddled over his cup and ordered a new flagon. He did not want to go home just yet. A vigorous tumble in bed with Miriel might ease his need, but he was in too much of a tumult to bear the thought of waiting until their guest departed.

Plotting murder was distasteful even if it was necessary and done by proxy. He looked at his hands, and for a moment was filled with the vision of his right one clamped over Gerbert's nose and mouth. That too had been necessary, a kindness in disguise. The old man had been on death's threshold. Better to help him on his way than let him linger in suffering within his seizure-paralysed body.

He shook his head like a man irritated at a cloud of summer midges and glanced round the alehouse until he caught the waiting eye of one of its whores, a full-breasted freckled blonde who went by the improbable name of Corisande. Still, the fact that she was capable of thinking up such a courtly name for herself meant that she was a class above the other Hildas and Aggies offering their wares in the establishment. Returning her stare, Robert held up a coin, rolling it between his fingers in a practised trick. Hands on hips, she sauntered over, and helped herself to the wine in his jug.

'Ah Jesu, ah God!' Miriel's voice was a breathless sob. She twisted and threshed beneath the coaxing of Nicholas's fingers and lips, the gentle flicking of his tongue. She had possessed no inkling that this was the blaze of which the kindling was truly capable, and she was being immolated, running with liquid gold, stabbed with gemstones of sharper sensation on the points of a crown. It was unbearable, she was dying. And still within her, Nicholas had not moved, except to accommodate her twists and struggles.

She arched her hips in a dual attempt to escape and yet retain the pleasure that was killing her. He murmured love words against her throat and began to move, slowly, languorously. Miriel clutched the fur lining of the cloak, and then she clutched him, muffling her cries against his shoulder, digging her nails into his spine. His pushes grew stronger and faster, but still restrained and measured. Miriel raised her thighs and clasped him. She heard herself gasping at him to make an end, that she could bear no more, and suddenly all the gemstones gathered in the small pleasure core of her loins and splintered into thousands of tiny gleaming shards.

For a long, long time there was nothing but the wild gasping of her breath, the thundering of her heart against her ribs, the dying ripples of sensation. Awareness returned in fragments. The cool fur of his cloak, the draught from the door on her tear-wet face, the gleam of the crown in the lantern light. It was an enormous risk they had taken, and yet she had no urge to make haste and clear the evidence from sight. Lassitude and contentment flowed into her on the aftermath of the pleasure. For the first time in her life, she was not sore, but soaring. She looked at Nicholas. At some point he had withdrawn from her, and now lay on his stomach, elbows propped, and a concerned and tender expression on his face.

She felt suddenly shy beneath his scrutiny, not at the intimacy of what they had done, but at having been so vulnerable before him, of having yielded all control into his keeping. And she was piqued to discover how remarkably composed he was. Conning over her own small but significant store of knowledge, she frowned.

'You gave me a gift beyond price, and yet you did not take your own pleasure,' she said.

He looked surprised for a moment, as if he had not expected her to be capable of such perception. Then he leaned over and gently fingered a stray tendril of hair from her face. 'Because, as you say, it was a gift, and without a price. I did not want to get you with child. God knows, we have taken risks enough as it is.'

She shook her head. 'You would not have got me with child. I know that I am barren. I have been wedded to Robert for almost a year and he claims his marital right twice a day on all the days that the Church permits. If I was going to quicken with a babe, it would have happened long ago.' She pulled a face. 'Sometimes I think it is God's punishment because I ran away from St Catherine's, but in truth it bothers me little and Robert says it is of no consequence to him. I have the independence to pursue my trade and no ties to bind me to the hearth. Nor do I have to face the danger of childbirth.' Turning her head, she nuzzled against Nicholas's warmth. 'But still, it was chivalrous of you. I doubt many men would have been so concerned.' She drew his head down and kissed him, tenderly at first, then with growing enthusiasm. Her hand slipped down his body, palm curving across his hip until she brushed the tip of his erection and heard him hiss. She was on familiar ground now, and the balance of control altered in her favour. She toyed with him as he had earlier toyed with her, varying speed and degree of caress until the muscles strained in his neck and he was as hard and tight as a wound crossbow in the hollow of her fist.

She was wild with renewed excitement for now she knew what the reward could be, and the sight of Nicholas's tortured face as he fought for control was an added fillip. With great daring, she removed her hand and straddled him, her inner thighs smoothing against the outside of his as she took him into her body.

Now it was his turn to clutch and cry out, his hands

kneading her spine and his face buried in her shoulder as he shuddered within her.

Miriel sobbed and clenched herself fiercely around him as for a second time her loins were wrung by overpowering sensations. Oh God, one could die from this, she thought hazily as the ripples faded. She wanted to cling to the feelings for ever, but they dissipated as swiftly as steam from a cauldron.

With reluctance, she lifted herself from him and tugged the bunched fabric of her gown down over her legs. Still gasping, he adjusted his own clothing, and then he turned on his side and looked at her in the guttering lantern light. 'It shouldn't have been like this,' he said. 'If only you had stayed that night in Nottingham.'

She stiffened. 'As I remember, you wanted no truck with a runaway nun who might jeopardise your road to freedom. I had to fight tooth and claw to make you escort me. If you had a change of heart or mind, you never said.'

'You gave me no opportunity!'

'So the fault is all mine.' She started to pull away, but he caught her back, drawing her into his arms and holding her there.

'The fault lies with both of us,' he said, 'and there is no use apportioning blame. What I meant to say is that I wish it had been different.' He stroked her cheek.

She swallowed against the tightness in her throat. 'So do I.'

He pressed his face into her throat. 'You could leave with me now,' he murmured.

Miriel closed her eyes, squeezing back the weight of tears. 'I cannot.' Her voice quavered with the effort of maintaining control. 'The time when we could have been together has come and gone.' She wove her fingers through his hair, her emotions a razor of pain and joy that cut deep with each stroke of her heart. 'Tonight must be enough.'

'It will never be enough,' he muttered into her skin. 'For the rest of my life, I will remember this moment and starve.'

'No, you won't. You will find other outlets for your hunger, as you did before.' She let the gleaming strands slip through her grasp and forced herself to let him go, to push out of his arms and rise to her feet. 'Convince yourself it never happened. It is the only way.' She tried to wrap the crown in its silks, but her hands were shaking so badly that the task was almost impossible.

'I cannot do that any more than you,' he said bitterly. 'It is like giving a blind man the gift of sight and then shutting him up in a darkened room.'

'You had best leave,' she said in a choked voice, gazing upon her fumbling hands rather than at Nicholas's stricken face. 'Robert must return soon, and I do not want to face him like this.'

'Then how will you face him?'

'As his wife.' Miriel drew a deep breath and stiffened her spine. 'He's a good man. I would not have him suffer for what is none of his doing.' And he would suffer if he found out, she thought. He would want to know every detail, would spare neither her nor himself.

Nicholas rose and beating floor dust from his cloak swept it around his shoulders. 'So let the guilty suffer instead?'

'He is my duty, my obligation.' She gave him a pleading look, willing him to understand.

For a moment she thought that he was going to walk out on her, stalk away like an adolescent in a fury of hurt pride, but he took no more than two strides, and these brought him level with her. 'You know where to find me if you change your mind,' he said and, taking her shoulders, pulled her against him in a kiss that crushed the breath from her body. 'Or if you have need.'

Then he was gone and the lantern guttered out, leaving Miriel in bitter-cold darkness, the smell of burning wax in her nostrils, and the sharp feel of Mathilda's crown in her hands.

It was very late when Robert came to bed, lacking only a few hours until dawn. Miriel felt his weight settle on the mattress and inhaled the sour smell of wine and a scent that reminded her of stale attar of roses. She curled on her side, feigning sleep, expecting him to give her a nudge and make her turn over so that he could pay his dues, but he drew up the covers and, with a heavy sigh and a punch of the bolster, kept to his own side and began to snore.

Feeling relieved, Miriel relaxed. She had not been looking forward to performing her marital duty, fearing that Robert would notice a change in her attitude. It was her own guilt that made her think he would be able to tell she had given herself to another man, but she could not banish the thought. Nor did she relish the prospect of Robert's vigorous assault on her body. Not when she had been shown the difference. She was consumed by a bitter-sweet ache. To think of lovemaking with Nicholas and compare it with Robert's notion of the same was unbearable, and yet it had to be borne. She could not run from her responsibilities and duties as she had done at St Catherine's. Those had been created for the convenience of others; the ones that bound her today were of her own making and she was inordinately proud of them. She ought to have realised that pride always came before a fall. *Caveat emptor.*

Chapter 22

Nicholas's barges were laden with sarples of wool and bales of cloth from the Lincoln Fair, purchased by Guido of Florence and destined for the market places and dye shops of his native city. The dapper little Italian himself had ridden on to Stamford in search of more cloth, but had entrusted Nicholas to take his existing cargo upriver to his warehouses at the main port.

The flat fenland landscape stretched to the horizon, broken only by the occasional tower or steeple of a religious house, built to make the most of the rich soil and fine grazing reclaimed from the marsh. Built too in the right place to exploit the river for its eels, fish and human traffic. Hearing steeple bells ring out across the water, Nicholas thought of St Catherine's, of lying in the infirmary, weak as a new-born kitten, and setting eyes on Miriel for the first time. Just a nun, he had thought, a young nun. And even in those early moments, how wrong he had been.

Usually he enjoyed the leisurely journey up the Witham to Boston, but now it stifled him. There was too much time to examine his thoughts, to probe at them like a man examining an aching tooth. The more he poked and examined, the worse it became, and yet he was unable to leave it alone. He desired what he could not have. Robert Willoughby stood in his way, and he was a vigorous man, likely to live a long time yet. In the darkest part of his mind, Nicholas envisaged the merchant meeting with an accident, and then recoiled from the thought. Thus had his father been removed by King John. Even to contemplate doing the same to another man made Nicholas feel sick to the stomach.

But he did not regret lying with Miriel. Nor could he prevent himself from wishing it to happen again, even if it was against God's commandment. Her vulnerability, the way she had cried out in surprise and pleasure, and then, beyond her innocence, taken him in her hand with all the artistry and finesse of the most accomplished street woman. Each facet delighted him, filled him with wonder. Made him want more than he could ever have.

He knew that putting to sea would take the edge off the frustration seething in his blood. A salt wind in his face, the kick of a true ship beneath his feet instead of the lowly meander of a transport barge, would appease his hunger. And there was Magdalene to comfort and assuage him should he choose to seek her out. Unbeknown to himself, he grimaced.

The barges moored and their cargo safely stored, he repaired to The Ship on the edge of the market place to seek hospitality for the night. He knew from past acquaintance that the mattresses had feather stuffing, the wine was good and the food reasonable.

Among the other visitors gathered around the trestle in the main room was the merchant Maurice de la Pole, whose dealings in Lincoln had caused Robert Willoughby such anxiety. He was of an indeterminate age that could have been anywhere between fifty and seventy, slender and sallow of visage with eyes so dark that they appeared black. Although he smiled and made good conversation, his expression remained cold and watchful. Not someone to cross, Nicholas thought, and remembered Miriel's worry that she might become embroiled in the conflict between de la Pole and her husband. He ate his coney stew and entertained a vision of the two merchants killing each other. Then, because that too was against God's law, he tried not to think at all.

Following the meal, Maurice de la Pole brought out a merels board inlaid with flint and seashell and set it up on a low coffer.

'Do you play?' he asked Nicholas.

'Occasionally,' Nicholas answered. He had no inclination

to game with the merchant who he knew would want to wager money on the outcome, but could not see a gracious way of abstaining.

De la Pole gestured to the seat at the other end of the bench. 'Then will you consider humouring an old man?'

'I scarce believe you are in your dotage, sir.' Nicholas sat down, wondering how soon he could make his escape.

The merchant gave him a wintry smile. 'Time creeps up on us all. It seems not a season since I was as young as you, with a lifetime to conquer the world.' With quick, dextrous movements, he arranged the counters on the board. 'Now that lifetime is drawing to a close and I have hardly even begun. The man should rule the dream, not the dream the man, eh?' The smile developed a wry twist.

Nicholas shrugged. 'I am sure that is true, sir.'

'You know it is true.' De la Pole wagged a forefinger. 'From what I have heard, you are the youngest merchant sea-captain in northern Christendom, not only commanding ships, but owning them. A man of your age does not arrive at such a position unless he is filled with ruthless ambition.'

With a prickle of defensiveness, Nicholas opened his mouth to deny the statement, but found that he could not, because the merchant was almost right. He was indeed filled with ruthless ambition, but it was directed at proving himself rather than destroying his rivals. He was not, however, going to say as much to de la Pole. Instead, he gestured to the assembled merels board. 'Your move.'

De la Pole gave him a shrewd look. 'Aye,' he said, 'never let your opponent see what you are thinking.' He used his forefinger to push one of the counters from its position on the middle line of the outer of the three squares incised on the board.

They played several games and won an equal number each. De la Pole hated losing. Despite his dictum that it was unwise to reveal thoughts, his own were plain in the pursing of his lips and the tightening of the lines around his eyes.

'Call us evenly matched,' Nicholas said after six games, the last of which he had won, and rose from the bench.

'One more to decide,' de la Pole said, 'or do you walk away from the final challenge?'

Nicholas smiled and spread his hands. 'You said something earlier about ruling and being ruled. Tonight, I choose the first. I have no wish to sit at another game for the sake of pride – mine or yours.'

De la Pole eyed him thoughtfully. 'You have had enough then?'

'For the nonce.' Nicholas succeeded in keeping his tone polite and inclined his head, impatient to be gone.

But the merchant was not finished. As he began to gather up the pieces and return them to their leather pouch he said, 'I notice that you do much trade with Master Robert Willoughby.'

The name sounded a warning note in Nicholas's mind. 'Indeed I do,' he said warily. 'What of it?'

'Are you content with the terms you have negotiated?'

Nicholas felt uncomfortably like a fly being lured on to the sticky strands of a web. 'They are fair to both sides; I have no complaint. Why do you ask?'

De la Pole tightened the drawstring on the little pouch of counters. 'What if I were to offer you more advantageous terms than his?'

'Is that your intention?'

'It might be.'

'It would depend on your terms,' Nicholas fenced. He did not particularly want to offend the man, but he had no desire to deal with him. 'I would not give preference to a new customer if it meant slighting an established one.'

'A man of principle then.' The wintry smile returned.

Nicholas reddened. De la Pole could not know how much that remark stung. 'I try to be,' he said stiffly and, with a terse nod to conclude the conversation, went outside to relieve himself before the merchant could worm his way any further beneath his skin.

Outside, the spring air was sharp with the last echo of winter. Stars glittered between scudding clouds like tufts of scrap wool. Hugging his cloak, Nicholas breathed deeply and tried to shake off a feeling of aversion so strong that it was almost a bad taste in his mouth.

He knew that de la Pole was testing him, feeling his way

to see if he could damage Robert Willoughby's business by taking away his means of transport. Even though he had refused, he still felt sullied, not least because of what had happened between himself and Miriel. While it did not put him in the same skin as Maurice de la Pole, it certainly made them rub shoulders. It was just a matter of degree, of how deep the stain.

Frowning, Nicholas stopped at the midden pits near the stables, raised his tunic and parted his loin cloth to relieve himself. Behind him the noise from the tavern was a raucous testament to the power of Gascon wine. Torchlight flickered over the courtyard immediately outside the hostel, painting the white daub and wattle walls with a yellow gloam between the ragged banks of flame-shadow. A figure was briefly outlined in the doorway. Nicholas pulled a face as it stumbled away from the threshold and into the illumination of the torch flare, then began heading down the path towards the midden. He had stomached all he could of Maurice de la Pole for one night.

He looked down to shake the last drops from his penis and readjust his clothing in the hopes of making a swift escape. When he raised his head, it was to see a piece of shadow break from the fluttering darkness, seize Maurice de la Pole round the neck, and make a vigorous plunging motion. De la Pole fell from the light with a single, startled cry, the sound abruptly cut off as his attacker stabbed down again.

Shouting the alarm, Nicholas sprinted from the midden towards the scene and the killer took to his heels, but not before Nicholas had glimpsed the man's full red beard and battered, aquiline features.

Maurice de la Pole was beyond mortal help, Nicholas could tell that just from the lake of blood, shining black in the torchlight. Shouting again for help, Nicholas ran in pursuit of the assassin, but the man was fleet of foot and had a good head start, and the dark, twisting alleyways of the tavern's neighbourhood were a labyrinth. Nicholas caught a single glimpse of what might have been a fleeing figure and pursued its elusiveness to the wharves and the dark barrier of the river. There was nothing. Black as de la Pole's blood, the water shone in the light of a watchman's fire, and the flames cast deep shadows in which a hundred men could have hidden with knives. The watchman himself had seen nothing.

'Save for a fisherman in a rowboat,' he said to Nicholas's enquiry. 'Or at least that was what he seemed to me.'

Giving up the chase, Nicholas returned to The Ship. Maurice de la Pole had been brought inside and laid on a bench. The two stab wounds had bled him white. His money pouch was missing, slashed from his belt by the same blade that had taken his life. Nicholas shuddered, thinking how nearly it might have been himself lying there. De la Pole had stood no chance against the suddenness and ferocity of the attack. Usually cut-purses were more circumspect; it was the money they wanted, not the notoriety that came with murder – unless murder had been the intent all along. Nicholas shivered, the cold he felt not of the flesh, but of the spirit. When death of this ilk breathed on him, it evoked memories of his father, of the accident that was no accident, of grief and loss and injustice.

'He's dead as you ordered,' Serlo Redbeard reported to his employer with the satisfaction of a job well done.

Robert Willoughby stared out over the tenting ground by the fulling mill. Bolts of newly washed and thickened cloth were being stretched on frames to dry before the process of napping and shearing. It was a good day for the task, blustery and bright. He withdrew a pouch of silver from beneath his cloak and weighed it in his hand. 'How did you do it?'

Eyes on the pouch, Serlo licked his lips and told him. 'Two thrusts of the dagger to make sure, and I stole his purse. The authorities think that the deed was done by a common thief.'

Robert nodded. A surge of triumph tingled through him, but even so his eyes narrowed. 'You have fulfilled the task I set you,' he said, 'but it was a foolish place to carry it out. You might easily have been caught.'

Redbeard shrugged. 'But I wasn't,' he said with an impatient scowl. 'I knew what I was about.'

Robert arched his brow and handed over the coins, which

disappeared into Redbeard's tunic faster than a weasel into a coney burrow. That was the difficulty with employing a man like Redbeard. While he would not balk at whatever had to be done, he was not always reliable in the detail, and that led to risk.

Dismissing the man, Robert went home to wait for the news to break in town.

'I did not like the man,' he told Miriel that evening when a barge-master from Sleaford had made the tale public. 'I could be uncharitable enough to say that he got what he deserved, but in truth, it is disgraceful that such a thing should happen. It goes to show that you can never trust anyone.'

'No,' Miriel said with downcast eyes.

She had been quiet these past few days and Robert wondered if she had somehow found out about himself and the whore from The Green Bush.

'There is to be a mass said for his soul at St Botolf's. I said we would both attend. It would be churlish of us not to do so.'

'As you wish.' She gave him a sidelong look. 'Although I suspect that you will not be so much praying for the soul of Maurice de la Pole as thanking God for removing him from your path.'

Robert cleared his throat and smiled sheepishly. 'I am not a saint,' he said, and decided to commission a jewel-covered Psalter for her to carry when she went with him to worship. She deserved the best, and it would assuage his guilt over the tavern whore.

Besides, with his rival removed, his profits this year would be large enough to allow several little luxuries. At the mass for de la Pole he could talk to clients who had changed their allegiance and persuade them to return to him. After that he could visit the wool producers who had relied on de la Pole to sell their annual crop of fleeces and offer them his services. Life could not be better.

CHAPTER 23

Bound in calf hide and gold leaf, the Psalter gleamed from a cedarwood box inlaid with mother of pearl. The front of the book bore an ivory centre panel, exquisitely carved in a representation of the Virgin and Child. Miriel gasped at the sight, hardly daring to take the object from her husband's extended hands.

'It's beautiful!' she said with awe. 'Rob, it must have cost a fortune!'

'I count it worth every penny if you like it.' His expression was warm with pleasure. 'You do, don't you?'

'Oh, yes, but I'm overwhelmed!'

He laughed and kissed her mouth. 'That wasn't my intention. You know it delights me to give you presents. Besides, I wanted you to have a reminder of me while we're apart.' He lifted the Psalter gently out of the box and unfastened the ornate silver clasp. 'See, there's a dedication to you on the first page.' He pointed to her name, inscribed in Latin, and turned the vellum pages to reveal lovingly executed illuminations in jewel-rich colours.

Miriel shook her head, lost for words, swimming in a sea of guilt. 'I don't deserve this,' she said in a choked voice.

'I know of no one more deserving – except perhaps myself.' He chuckled and kissed her again, this time with more purpose, squeezing her haunches to his.

It was mid-morning and through the open shutters of the hostelry, the clamour of Boston's busy dockside surged into the room. 'There isn't time,' she protested. 'It'll be high tide soon, and I need to be on board before then.'

'Time enough,' Robert muttered thickly, his hands already gathering her skirts in folds around her hips. 'I won't see you for at least a month.'

'No, but I—'

He covered her mouth with his and bore her back on to the hostelry's truckle bed. She heard the frame groan in protest as it took their weight. His hands cupped her buttocks, raising them, drawing her on to his hugeness. Miriel bit her lip and stifled a scream. It would soon be over, she told herself. Robert was always as vigorous as a ram in rut, but he was as fast as one too. A mixed blessing because, as he said, there was always time enough and, true to his word, within moments he was gasping his pleasure as he collapsed on her.

Half smothered, Miriel listened to the thunder of his heart battering against her body, the roar of his breath in her ear, the solid rock of his manhood impaling her. She felt as if she had just been devoured by a wild beast. At last he softened and withdrew. Rising on one elbow, he gazed down into her face and stroked her cheek. 'I will miss you,' he said softly.

'And I you.' Miriel forced a smile, wishing him gone, wishing the time her own. And then, feeling guilty at such thoughts, she stroked his face in return. He captured her fingers in his and kissed them.

'You are my heart's treasure. I would come with you if I could.'

'I know.' And because there was no chance of that happening, she was able to fill her voice with generosity and reassurance.

Robert left soon after that, murmuring regrets which were genuine, but with his eye already on the horizon. He had escorted her to Boston because he was fishing for new clients in the territory so recently vacated by the demise of Maurice de la Pole. He had catches to land before anyone else hooked them.

Miriel herself was bound for the great cloth fair of St John at Troyes. It was not an event that she visited every year, but it did no harm to be seen now and again and besides, she had a longing to wander this year. There was a restlessness in her spirit, as if she were an autumn swallow preparing to take wing.

Bidding Robert farewell in the hostel courtyard, Miriel returned to the room above to secure her travelling chest. With a small grimace, she picked up the Psalter. It was a costly personal gift, beautifully crafted. As a symbol of the store that Robert set by her it weighed like a shackle because she knew herself unworthy.

It was so hard pretending that she was unchanged when a single evening had altered the balance for ever. She had tried to shut the memory of that night away, concentrate on her business, be a good wife to Robert. Outwardly she had succeeded. Only she knew of the chaos within. Jesu, if only Nicholas knew the craving he had awakened – or perhaps he did. Perhaps he too was craving. She told herself that in time the sharpness of that need would dull. Layers of work and domesticity would blunt the pain – but they could hardly bring her to her senses when it was Nicholas who had shown her what senses were.

Walter and Samuel carried her travelling chest to the dockside and she boarded *Pandora's Daughter*, joining the cargo of wool sarples and bales of cloth. Nicholas's ship, she thought with a frisson as she trod the deck and ascended to the aft castle. Even though it was not captained by him, but by his senior master, Martin Wudecoc, she could feel his presence in the creak of the timbers and the bold scarlet flag snapping from one of the wooden turrets.

Martin Wudecoc came to greet her, a smile on his long, pleasant face. He stooped to make a fuss of Will and the little dog wagged around his feet, yapping ecstatically.

'Aye, you still remember me then, lad,' he said with a grin and looked at Miriel. 'I bought my wife one o' these little creatures on my last voyage. She was so taken with this little chap when she saw him that she nagged me day and night for one of her own. Mind you,' he added, 'I prefer a bigger dog myself, something more than a mouthful.'

'He suits me well, Master Wudecoc,' Miriel defended Will. 'And he makes up in courage what he lacks in size.'

'Oh, no doubt, I would not missay the little thing, but his

sort are bred for the lap and the bower, not to run for miles at a man's side.'

'Women's dogs,' she said with a smile, and then asked nonchalantly how Nicholas was faring.

'Well enough last I saw him, mistress. He commissioned another ship some time ago, and he's in Antwerp to fetch her.'

'Another ship?'

The sailor smiled at her raised eyebrows. 'Master Nicholas has no home on land, no family ties to make demands on his profits. What he earns he puts back into his trade.'

'And he has no need of other company?'

Martin tugged at his beard. 'Of an occasion, he sups with me and my wife when we're in port,' he said. 'And there are customers such as yourself and your husband who provide the kinder comforts of life.'

Miriel blushed at that one. If only he knew the sort of kinder comforts. A spark of devilry prompted her to add, 'I saw him with a red-haired woman once, and I thought that perhaps he had taken a wife.'

Martin cleared his throat and looked at his boots. It was plain that he knew all about Magdalene, but was not prepared to discuss her with Nicholas's clients. 'No, mistress. If he is wedded, it is to his ships.' And with that remark, he escaped to prepare the vessel for embarkation.

With a restless sigh, Miriel went to inspect her bales of cloth in the hold, Will scampering at her side. She had to put Nicholas from her mind; there was no future in thinking about him or the different path she could once have taken. Asking about him and his leman was just self-torture. Staring at the bales sewn up in parcels of rough sacking for the journey, she acknowledged that there was comfort in that torture, in thinking his name and summoning his image to her mind's eye: melancholy pleasure, a feeling of hollowness beneath her heart and an ache in her loins that had no connection whatsoever with Robert's rough attentions. Even a prisoner in the deepest dungeon could dream and make life more bearable.

* * *

The cloth fairs in Champagne were huge gatherings compared to those of Stamford, Lincoln and Boston. Miriel was able to walk all day amongst the booths and stalls, and still not see every one. Fifty different tongues proclaimed the language of profit. There were silk merchants from Venice and Florence with bolts of cloth that rippled in the light like liquid gold. Men of Lombardy and Genoa had brought cargoes of alum and spices to barter for fabric. Blond traders from Novgorod clad in the fashion of old Norse sea-raiders rubbed shoulders with slender, dark-eyed sellers of glass and cotton from the lands of the Nile.

Miriel traded some of her cloth for coin, but exchanged most of it for silk and cotton fabrics that would show a high profit on the drapery side of her business. Oriental and Mediterranean expertise shimmered through the cloth, delighting the eye and entrancing the hand with its cool, luxurious feel. Miriel was acquainted with several worthy burgesses in Lincoln and Nottingham who would be unable to resist the lure – herself included. She had already chosen a gown length of red-gold damask and a bolt of Italian-spun creamy silk to make an undertunic.

Most of the other traders were men, but Miriel was accustomed to dealing with them. Indeed, her femininity was a definite advantage to her business. As well as being able to barter the hind leg off a donkey and meet her masculine counterparts on their own ground, she had the weapon of flirtation to call upon. It was astonishing what admiring eyes and a coquettish giggle could accomplish when all else had failed.

A week later, greatly satisfied, she set out for home, her sumptuous purchases a guarantee of the vast profits waiting to be made in Lincoln.

She was expecting to board *Pandora's Daughter* in Rouen, but the vessel was not moored at the wharf and there was no sign of Martin Wudecoc. Instead, a magnificent cog glittered in the autumn sunset, her paint fresh and bold, her timbers clean as a boy's chin and no sign of sea-weathering to mar a single aspect of her pristine appearance.

'What do you think of her then?' Nicholas asked from behind.

Miriel spun with a gasp. 'What are you doing here?' Her heart lurched and then began to pound.

'Preparing to sail for Boston on the morrow's tide.' His shrug was casual, his smile easy, but beyond that was the look in his eyes, and it turned her knees to water. 'Or perhaps,' he said softly so that the words carried no further than the space between them, 'I should make her safe and sail her out on to the open ocean with no thought of making landfall for at least a year and a day.'

Miriel swallowed. 'I thought . . . I . . . Where's Martin?'

'Heading for Bristol with a cargo of Rhenish wine, I hope,' Nicholas said. He gestured at the cog. 'As far as others are concerned, she's named the *St Maria*, but to me she is the *Miriel*.'

Miriel gazed, drinking him in. She longed to step inside the space that separated them, to place her fingers on his sleeve in the light possession of a lover and lock her eyes and smile with his. So great was that longing that she deliberately leaned away from him and folded her arms beneath her breasts to resist temptation. 'You did this apurpose. It is not happen-chance that you are here.'

He rubbed his jaw. 'Well, not entirely,' he conceded. 'I thought you might be attending the fair, but it is completely in the hands of fortune that you do not have your husband's company.'

'And if I did, what then?'

'Then we would not be engaged in this conversation, would we?'

Miriel drew a shaky breath. 'There can be no future in this,' she said bleakly.

He looked down for a moment, then half turned to study the large cog dancing at anchor. Finally, he fixed his gaze on her again. 'I know. You gave me your reasons before.' His voice was filled with regret and resignation, but not defeat. 'But for a few days at least, can we not suspend that future, pretend that it does not exist?'

Her glance followed the wake of his to the ship. The suggestion clenched her stomach with a volatile mingling of hope and despair. Would the snatched happiness be worth the guilt? Would the pleasure compensate for the pain of parting? Common sense told her that she should refuse, but the words stuck in her throat. Since escaping St Catherine's, her life had been one long façade, but with Nicholas, there was no need to pretend – except that they had a future. He knew her better than she knew herself, or else why would he be here?

'I do not know,' she answered, meeting his eyes, the only contact there could be for decency's sake on the bustling dockside, but the look that passed between them burned away all notion of propriety. 'But we can try.'

Miriel lay upon Nicholas on the cramped pallet, and listened to the shrieking of the gulls. Daylight seeped through the canvas deck shelter, warning her that their stolen time together was almost at an end. Nor had that time run to days. It was more a matter of hours, of circumspect minutes that could be snatched and not noticed as odd by the members of Miriel's household. Exquisite torture, as much pain as pleasure, and yet neither Miriel nor Nicholas would have denied them.

'I should be going,' he said, kissing her face and throat, still hectic with the flush of lovemaking. 'I have been here too long already, and your maid will be wondering what kind of respects I have been paying you.'

Miriel tightened her grip around him for a moment, savouring his salty masculine aroma and the wiry tautness of his muscles, so different to Robert's well-fleshed bulk. She did not speak, for there was nothing to say that had not already been said. The only way they could be together was for her to leave her husband and become Nicholas's mistress. Simple to say, and on the surface simple to do. But like casting a stone in a pool, the repercussions would be far greater than the original deed. She and Nicholas would be ostracised by the English mercantile community and their livelihoods threatened, if not destroyed. There was no telling what it would do to Robert, her lawfully wedded husband to whom she had given her promise of fidelity. She had seen his tenacity and anger when he felt threatened. He was too possessive to let her go with equanimity.

'I do not know if this is better or worse than nothing,' Nicholas groaned, as he struggled into his clothing in the cramped confines of the deck shelter.

Miriel ran her hand beneath his shirt to the smooth skin on his back. 'Just accept it,' she said.

'And if I can't?'

'You have to.' Her voice was fierce. 'This is all we have. I don't want the memory tarnished by bitterness and argument.'

'Even accepting will not stop me from wishing you were mine,' he said grimly. 'Every second of every hour of every day.'

'Oh Nicholas, don't.' She laid her fingers against his lips, tears gathering in her eyes.

He groaned and pulled her into his arms. They kissed frantically, almost savagely, snatching at the last few moments and desperately aware that the sand in the hourglass had run beyond its limit. With one final kiss, hard enough to bruise, he broke away. His breath was shaking; so were his hands as they fumbled to latch his belt. 'Keep me in your heart,' he said, then he was gone, leaving behind a tang of cold salt air as he stepped on to the deck and dropped the shelter flap behind him.

Miriel wiped the back of her hand across her eyes and gulped back a wave of grief and frustration. She forced herself to practical matters by securing her wimple and smoothing her clothes, becoming the outward model of a respectable married woman. She was not sorry for the time that she and Nicholas had snatched together, but she wished it had never happened. She had tried to pretend and failed. There was a price to be paid and she had a nagging premonition that it would beggar them in the end.

As she lifted her cloak from the coffer, she uncovered the Psalter that Robert had given her. It lay upon her spare gown and chemise, accusing her with its intricate, biblical beauty. With a gasp Miriel grabbed a fold of chemise and threw it over the book, then slammed down the lid.

The *St Maria/Miriel* sailed into Boston, her hold full of plunder from the Champagne fairs: expensive cloth of

Italian manufacture, silk damask, samite, and fine-spun cotton.

Standing at the prow, Miriel was aware of Nicholas in every fibre of her being. The length of the deck separated them, but it meant nothing. She could feel the tug of the connection as if they were pressed side by side. All his concentration was given to steering the cog as she entered the estuary, but she knew his senses were attuned to hers.

'I love you,' she whispered, tears glistening in her eyes. As the anchor broke the brown water and the mooring rope snaked out to a bollard, she took a last drenching look at him. Then, biting her lip, fighting for composure, she turned to view the bustle of the port.

Waiting for her on the jetty was Robert.

CHAPTER 24

Robert wrapped Miriel in his huge embrace and kissed her heartily. 'Sweetheart, sweetheart, I've missed you,' he said huskily. 'Have you fared well?'

Miriel fought her horror at seeing him, the smothering wave of fear and shock. 'The hold is full of fine cloth,' she heard herself say in a voice that was almost normal. 'And you?' She could not bring herself to return his kiss with the taste of Nicholas still in her mouth.

'Excellently.' He flexed his hands on her arms in a grasping motion. 'I've regained the customers I lost to de la Pole, and added a few of his former ones to my tally.' He smiled broadly. 'That means I now have time on my hands to lavish attention on my beautiful wife.' He gave her another hug, then let her go, retaining only her hand in his powerful grip. 'I've taken a room at The Ship and we can be comfortable there tonight.'

Miriel shivered at the implication of that remark.

'Cold?' Robert removed his hand from hers and draped his arm solicitously across her shoulders.

She shook her head. How could she be cold on a day that would have been sweltering except for a slight freshening of sea breeze? 'A little queasy from the journey,' she said.

His eyes gleamed and he nuzzled his beard against her jaw. 'I'll take you to lie down awhile then.' He turned her on his arm, then paused to stare up at the overlapping oak strakes and the boldly painted colours. 'I had not realised that his ambition stretched this far,' he murmured.

Miriel said nothing, not trusting herself to speak. It was as if she were being torn in two. The feelings of dread and guilt she had experienced at the sight of Robert waiting for her on the jetty were too great a burden to bear. For her peace of conscience, she had to give Nicholas up, but the pain of the notion was almost as bad as the guilt of adultery.

Nicholas slowly descended the wooden walkway on to the jetty. She saw him hesitate for a moment, gathering himself, then stride firmly forward, his expression set and blank. It would have looked strange if he had not paused to greet a regular customer.

'A fine ship,' Robert said with a friendly smile.

Nicholas inclined his head, his lips curving in the semblance of a response. 'Indeed she is.'

'Does she sail as well as she looks?'

'I think so, but the weathering of autumn storms will prove it.'

'I only wondered,' Robert said pleasantly. 'My wife tells me that she feels a trifle queasy, and she is not one to suffer the sailing sickness.'

Nicholas met Miriel's eyes briefly, then looked away. 'I am sorry to hear it,' he said.

'It is only the stepping from sea to shore,' Miriel said quickly. 'The voyage itself was as smooth as glass.'

'Then I will try her myself next time I have occasion to journey abroad.' Robert extended his hand to Nicholas. 'I must thank you for bringing my most precious cargo home safely.'

Bile burned in Miriel's throat. This was more dreadful than she could ever have imagined. She watched Nicholas with anguished eyes.

'It is my duty,' he answered politely and, without hesitation, shook Robert's hand. She saw that her lover had mastered himself, that, as at Stamford when he had walked jauntily through the town gates, he was playing a role to save both their lives, and playing it well. Miriel stiffened her spine. She would not fail him. When he inclined his head to her and then excused himself, she returned his nod and gave her attention to Robert as if her heart was not breaking inside her.

* * *

Robert ate heartily of the mutton ragout and herb griddle cakes that The Ship's landlord set before him and Miriel. The food was delicious, and Robert was cautiously pleased with the world at large.

'Not hungry?' He nodded at the barely touched stew on Miriel's trencher. 'I don't know when I've tasted better.' Reaching over, he speared a chunk of her abandoned mutton on the point of his knife and conveyed it to his mouth.

Miriel looked at the grease shining on his lips and felt nauseated.

Robert continued with his meal, clearly relishing every tender mouthful. 'You have excelled yourself at the Troyes fair,' he said. 'I have never seen such fine cloth, and you managed to sell all of ours.'

Miriel gave him a strained smile and agreed that she was pleased with it. For the moment the art of conversation was beyond her, even in the matter of business upon which she could usually hold forth with vehemence.

Robert sucked on a sliver of bone and fiddled it out of his mouth. 'You have not had a difference of opinion with Nicholas de Caen, have you?' he asked suddenly.

White-hot panic shot through Miriel. Dear God, did Robert suspect something? 'No, of course not. What makes you say that?' Her voice was swift and breathless.

'It was just an idle thought.' He flicked the thin shard on to the floor. 'I sensed that you were not at ease with each other on the wharf; there was a constraint as if you had quarrelled.'

Miriel shook her head and gazed at the food congealing on her trencher. The hammering of her heart was so loud in her ears that she was positive Robert would hear it. 'Not at all,' she murmured.

Robert dipped a sop of bread in his gravy and pushed it into his mouth, then sucked his finger and thumb. 'Indeed, when I think on the matter, it seems to me that you have never been at ease with him.'

Miriel swallowed. Although she had scarcely eaten, it was as if a huge morsel of stew were constricting her throat. 'No one can be at ease with everyone,' she said in a tight voice. 'I admire his seamanship, but . . .'

'But what?' Robert leaned forward, his cup in his hands.

She licked her lips, fighting the nausea. 'But we are too much alike.'

'I wouldn't say that!' Robert snorted.

'I mean that our ambitions have risen out of nothing. We have strong opinions and ideas.'

'I don't see that has any bearing on the matter.'

'We grate together like two stones in a fast-running stream.'

'Well, I have strong opinions and ideas, and they don't grate on you – or perhaps they do?'

Miriel almost shuddered. 'We are the same stone,' she lied.

Robert grunted. 'I suppose I see what you mean,' he said dubiously, as if he was not quite sure but did not want to admit it. 'Best if you sail with Master Wudecoc in future then. I hate to see you in such a downcast humour.'

'Yes, best,' Miriel murmured, feeling utterly trapped and dejected.

He took her to bed and she was pliant beneath his demands. But when he was done and had withdrawn, he heard the shakiness of her breath through the roar of his own, and realised that she was weeping.

'Sweetheart?' Concerned, he touched her shoulder and then her wet face.

She drew another breath, deeper than the others, striving to control herself. 'It is nothing; I'm tired and out of sorts.' Her voice was choked. 'Men do not suffer the same.'

By which he deduced that her monthly bleed was imminent, which would explain many facets of her behaviour. But although he had known her snappish, she had never wept before, and that perturbed him.

'Truly, nothing ails me but a woman's malaise. Go to sleep,' she said, turning on her side away from him.

Frowning, Robert lay on his back and gazed at the hostel's rafters. Something had happened to Miriel of late, something that was beyond his understanding, but only because he did not have sufficient knowledge about what was bothering her. He hated being shut out; he hated the lack of control. Turning his head on the pillow, he gazed at her huddled outline and promised himself that he would find out.

'Aren't you pleased to see me?' Magdalene stood on the deck of the *St Maria*, her hands on her hips, her head tilted to show the alluring curve of her white throat.

Nicholas scowled at her. The answer was no. 'What are you doing here?' he growled.

'Visiting an old friend.' She came towards him and the heavy scent of rose attar wafted on the air. 'They told me at The Ship that you were in port with your fine new cog. I thought you would take supper and a room, but since it is past twilight and the cauldrons scoured out, I realised I was waiting in vain.' She tilted her head to study him. 'So I came to find you instead.'

'Did it occur to you that I might not desire company?' he said shortly.

'Oh, yes.' There was a wry smile on her lips as she reached his side. In the light swinging from the mast, her long braid shone like a copper rope and her eyes glistened. 'And I know why.'

He sighed. 'Because I'm tired, because The Ship is always full of fat merchants and drinkers and . . .'

'And whores?' she finished for him with a raised eyebrow.

Nicholas swore beneath his breath. 'Magdalene, leave me alone.'

She clicked her tongue in exasperation. 'I came here because I knew you would need me.' Leaving his side, she wandered around the ship, touching this and that with a languid hand. 'Your pride and joy, Nick,' she said, and turned to face him. 'But you don't look very joyful. I have seen condemned men look happier.'

'Perhaps if you were to go away, my mood might lighten,' he said through his teeth.

'I doubt it.' She pointed to the flask of wine in his hand.

'If I were to go away, I think you would drink yourself into a stupor.'

The fact that she was right did not make her presence any more palatable. Nicholas had retired to lick his wounds in private and he wanted no witnesses to his grieving.

Magdalene pursed her lips. Turning on her circuit of the deck, she approached the canvas deck shelter with its cramped sleeping quarters. 'You are not at The Ship because she is,' she said. 'And with her husband. Do not deny it, I am no fool.'

Nicholas took a long drink from the flask and went to lean against the ship's side. It would soon be curfew, the time when all open hearths were banked and covered to prevent outbreaks of fire, but for now, the deepening dusk was beaded with their glow. The church of St Botolf rang out the hour of compline, the sound sweet and melancholy. 'It is no business of yours,' he said tersely.

She returned to his side. 'But it is my business because I care about you,' she contradicted, laying her long white hand upon his. The gold ring that he had given her caught a gleam of lantern-light as she removed the flask from his grasp and took a drink herself.

While his back had been turned she had removed her wimple and circlet. Now her thick copper braids hung unfettered to her waist and made her look as young and fresh as a girl. He thought of Miriel baring her hair at the convent, one moment a nun, the next a startlingly attractive young woman. Then he remembered it shaven from her skull for what the nuns saw as her transgressions. It was too much. The recollection made him thrust away from the side and stride across the deck with the agitation of a trapped animal.

Magdalene watched him with troubled eyes and took another drink of wine for courage. 'You still have me,' she said softly. 'I may not be what you want, I may be a poor second best, but are not a few crumbs of comfort better than nothing to the starving?'

He swung round from his pacing, his fists clenched at his sides. 'I am not that hungry,' he said brutally out of his own pain. He felt a stab of satisfaction followed by acute self-disgust as Magdalene flinched.

'No,' she whispered with brimming eyes, 'but I am, and I see that I am a greater fool than you.' Casting the flask to the deck, she gathered her skirts and ran.

Nicholas stared at the wine, puddling and glimmering in the lantern-light, spilling towards him like blood from the neck of the flask. 'Christ Jesu,' he groaned and, from utter stillness, broke into a run. 'Magdalene, no, come back!'

She had been hampered by the fullness of her skirts and he caught her at the foot of the gangplank. Sobbing with fury and humiliation, she fought him, but although she bit and scratched and kicked, it was without the full wildness that might have won her escape. 'You whoreson, let me go!'

'I didn't mean what I said, I just lashed out in anger!' Nicholas panted.

'You did mean it, every word. And why shouldn't you, when I'm nothing but a convenience to be had for payment and then forgotten?' Her tone scalded him.

'Magdalene, that's not true.' Bloody and bruised for his pains, heaving with exertion, he finally succeeded in pinning her within his arms. 'You're a damned inconvenience, and how I can forget you when you dog my every footstep is beyond me.'

She glared up at him, and began to struggle again, but his mouth covered hers and they kissed, with heat, with rage, with need and despair.

'If we are to be fools, then we might as well be fools together,' Nicholas gasped as they broke apart. 'I am sorry for what I said, and you are right, I do need you. Stay with me tonight. Be my talisman against the world.' Taking Magdalene's hand in his own scratched one, he kissed her palm.

She made a sound that was half-laugh, half-sob and, unresisting, followed him back aboard the *St Maria/Miriel*.

In the night Nicholas awoke and for a moment imagined that he was at sea and his pallet was occupied by Miriel's sweet naked warmth. As he came to his senses, he realised that the gentle rocking was only the cog at her moorings, and the heavy warmth numbing his arm, the cool spill of hair on his shoulder, belonged to Magdalene. His imagination had built a dream out of the flawed reality. But then it was only flawed if he allowed it to be so. Gently, with great sadness, he stroked Magdalene's silky hair and tried not to think of Miriel.

In the morning, the barges were loaded with their cargo of cloth for transport to Lincoln. Robert stood in close scrutiny, conducting operations, and Miriel stood with him, her face puffy and wan from lack of sleep. Robert had told her that he was summoning a physician the moment they returned to Lincoln. He was sure that her humours were unbalanced and he did not want her to end up suffering from an excess of yellow bile like his second wife and die of a wasting melancholy.

Exhausted though she was, Miriel could not wait to be on her way home. With Nicholas in port, the temptation to look upon him for one last moment ate at her vitals. Her eyes flickered across the water to the jetty in mid-river, hoping and dreading to see his lean figure at the gunwale.

'Ready, wife?' Robert took her arm in a solicitous grip as if she needed holding up.

She found a smile and a nod. Across the water, a figure moved on the deck of the *St Maria/Miriel.* Narrowing her eyes, Miriel stared, unable to help herself. So did Robert. And then he spluttered with amusement.

'The randy dog!' he chuckled.

Leaning over the rail, studying the bustle on the main wharfside, was a woman, her waist-length red hair lifting like a banner in the breeze. A bedsheet was wrapped around her otherwise naked body. Clutching the linen to her cleavage, she raised the other hand to sweep that glorious hair out of her eyes in a gesture both confident and sensual.

Miriel's stomach heaved with an excess of the bile about which Robert was so concerned. Nicholas had not even allowed their love-bed to cool before he took another woman into that narrow, intimate space. A vast surge of grief and rage assaulted Miriel. How could he do this? How could she have been so blind?

Behind the vision that Magdalene made now, Miriel saw an older one of the whore sitting sleep-tousled among the rumpled sheets at The Angel in Lincoln. She remembered how the woman had brushed her hand possessively over Nicholas's crotch and given him a look of intimate amusement. Perhaps Magdalene was the true owner of Nicholas's heart, and herself a pale usurper. Perhaps Nicholas had seduced her in revenge for the stealing of Empress Mathilda's regalia. Yet surely no man could look and act as he had on that voyage in a spirit of deceit?

Staring across the water as Magdalene turned from the cog's side and disappeared, Miriel grimaced to herself. Had not her own father deceived her mother with sweetness and promises, then abandoned her to face the world and the consequences of trusting too deeply?

'Love, what is wrong? You are as pale as winding sheet!' Robert's voice was full of tender concern.

Miriel was glad of the support of his arm and leaned upon him for a moment. Then she rallied and, with a shake of her head, stood tall. 'Nothing,' she said, forcing a smile. 'The sun was in my eyes for a moment, that is all.' She tugged on his arm. 'We have a journey to travel and no time to tarry – however salacious the sights.' Her eyes were dry and burning and her heart would have broken except that she refused to allow herself to feel. Shut it away; pretend it had never happened. Easy enough when it seemed that it had all been pretence from the start. The hollowness she felt inside was the reality.

Robert grinned. 'You can't blame a man for looking, sweetheart.'

'Not for looking, no,' she answered dully, and walked downriver towards the leading barge. She did not turn round again.

Chapter 25

It was sweltering harvest weather. August toiled towards September, growing more swollen with heat as each day built upon the next, heavy, sticky, shimmering. Mopping sun-scorched brows in the relentless blue, the reapers suffered, yet refused to pray for rain until the corn was cut and stacked, the fields gleaned, and the sheep sent in to graze the remains and manure the soil.

In the weaving shed, the heat was stultifying, even with the door propped open on a stone and the shutters thrown wide. There was not a hint of breeze, only the scorching beat of the sun and the overpowering stink of raw wool. Puddled in sweat, the weavers sat at their looms wearing only their braies as they created heavy woollen fabric for a winter season they could hardly imagine.

Miriel could not bear to go near the weaving sheds. She had begun to suffer from a malaise of the stomach that made her sick in the mornings and queasy throughout the rest of the day. If she visited the sheds in the relative cool before the hour of prime, she was still fighting her gorge and by the time the sun had feasted on the wooden roof shingles for a couple of hours, the heat and the smell turned her settling stomach upside down again.

The most she could do was sit in the shade of the apple garth with the women who spun the raw wool into yarn, and wind the thread off the distaff ready to be woven. Although she said nothing to anyone, Miriel was terrified that God had punished her adultery by visiting on her a mortal sickness. She could not eat; she was nauseous all the time, and so tired that it was only her stubborn will that dragged her out of bed every morning to go through the motions of running her business.

The physician whom Robert had brought to see her almost two months ago on their return from Boston had said she was suffering from an excess of melancholic humours and had prescribed daily doses of parsley leaves and grated ginger steeped in hot wine to restore her balance. The ginger did indeed settle her stomach for a time, but the symptoms always returned, and the lethargy had worsened as August burgeoned until it seemed that the days would split asunder like seeds bursting from an overripe pod.

Robert had been absent almost the entire month, wool-gathering, sweetening his clients, building his business. She was glad that he was away. The bed was hers alone. She could push her limbs into the corners and draw the coolness from the crisp linen, and when it was gone, she could lie naked on the counterpane and know that her body was not in danger of assault from the grunting forge heat of her husband's. She had time to indulge in mourning, to wallow in self-pity over her affair with Nicholas and wonder how she could have been such a fool. Her thoughts became a part of her physical condition, adding to the weight of her misery until she felt as if she were carrying a lead weight in her belly.

In the convent of St Catherine's-in-the-Marsh, Robert sat in the Abbess's private rooms. The fine hangings on the walls and the quality of the wine in his silver goblet surprised him not one whit. The abbey had prospered on the backs of its large herd of longwool sheep whose fleeces were avidly sought by weavers from Lincoln to Florence. St Catherine's had begun selling its clip to Gerbert in the year he had married Miriel. Following his death the abbey had traded with Robert, but last year the Abbess had changed allegiance and contracted to sell her fleeces to Maurice de la Pole.

'He offered me eighteen marks a sack,' said Mother Hillary defensively. 'You were only giving me fifteen. I have to look to the prosperity of the abbey.'

'Of course you do.' Robert took a drink of his wine. 'And

three marks per sack is no sum to overlook, even in the interests of loyalty to your usual buyer.' He waved his hand to show that he was not censuring her. 'It is quite understandable, Reverend Mother. In your situation I would have done the same.'

She gave him a severe look. 'May I remind you that Master Woolman's contract to buy was transferred to you on his death, but only for that one year. That does not make you my usual buyer or convey an obligation of loyalty.' She reached out to stroke the fur of a moth-eaten grey cat that was curled in dribbly sleep on the table between them. 'Even so,' she added, 'I am not indisposed to deal with you now, depending, of course, on how much you are prepared to offer.'

The old nun might look as ancient as her cat, but her wits were still intact. Robert folded his arms and mustered his argument. 'Maurice de la Pole offered you eighteen marks because he wanted to take away my clients. He was paying you a greater price than your fleeces were worth.'

'No,' she said firmly. 'They were worth eighteen marks to him. Are you saying that they are worth only fifteen to you? If that is the case, then I shall have to find another buyer. I am sure that there are others like Maurice de la Pole who would enjoy the opportunity to make me an offer.'

Briefly Robert wondered how easy it would be for Serlo Redbeard to wring the nun's scrawny neck, but decided that the villain would be far too conspicuous anywhere within twenty miles of the nunnery. 'You need not put yourself to the trouble of searching further afield, Reverend Mother,' he said smoothly. 'I am willing to look at your flock and reassess the value of their wool. And perhaps we could discuss a payment for your continued loyalty on top of whatever I offer you for your fleeces.'

The old nun considered and gave a cautious nod. 'Perhaps.'

Robert finished his wine and they continued to negotiate until they arrived at a settlement, hard-driven on both sides but satisfactory to each. He felt a grudging respect for the old nun, even if she did look as if she had been summoned from her crypt to do business with him.

'I must be the only wool merchant cutting off my nose to spite my face,' he said with a wry grin. 'God alone knows what Miriel will say when I tell her how much I have agreed for these fleeces.'

The nun gave a startled blink. 'Miriel?'

'My wife,' he said. 'She has weaving sheds in Lincoln and Nottingham.'

'Your wife.'

Robert hoped the Abbess hadn't suddenly become senile. She was staring at him in a strange way. 'Yes, my wife,' he said in a loud, deliberate voice. 'She comes from a family of Lincoln weavers.'

The Abbess gave a little shudder as if shrugging off an unwanted touch.

'Is there something wrong?' asked Robert.

'Would your wife's stepfather happen to have been Nigel Fuller?'

Now it was Robert's turn to stare, that same shudder running down his own spine. The Abbess's expression told him that there was going to be no joy in the association. 'Yes, it would. Why?'

The nun's hand went to her breast and grasped the silver crucifix hanging there. 'I wondered what had happened to her,' she murmured distractedly. 'We all worried for her and prayed that God would keep her safe despite her folly.'

Robert flexed his fingers and fought the urge to strangle the old nun. 'What folly?' he demanded. 'What are you talking about?'

She looked at him. 'You do not know, do you?'

'Know what? Are you telling me that my wife is a nun?' His voice carried a rising note of incredulity and dismay.

Mother Hillary raised her palm. 'Calm yourself, Master Willoughby. Your wife was indeed a novice here, but she never took the vows.'

Robert eased back into the chair and unbidden by the Abbess poured himself another cup of wine. He hated to be at a disadvantage in any situation. 'She came to you of her own will?' he asked and drank deeply.

'Her family felt that she was unsuited to marriage, and it

would be best if she was fitted for a life in the Church,' Mother Hillary said. 'I agreed to take her for I saw that she had intelligence and ability, albeit that she was headstrong and deeply resentful of being placed in our care.' She shook her head and sighed.

'Then what happened? How did she come to leave?'

'There was trouble with some of the other sisters – not all of Miriel's making, I will say in her defence . . . and then with a young man at the time when King John's baggage train was lost.' She had hesitated over the last part as if not sure that she should speak, and her eyes were troubled.

'Indeed?' Robert clung to composure but, despite the wine burning in his belly, felt winter-frozen.

Mother Hillary was silent for a time and Robert was filled with the anxiety that she might not continue, but finally she steepled her fingers beneath her chin and spoke.

'The young man was very sick. At one point we thought he would die. She formed an attachment to him while nursing him back to health and, when he was well enough to leave, she went with him. There was some suspicion that they were lovers. What happened after that I know not. She took my mule, but he turned up in his old field three months later with no explanation as to how he came to be there.'

Robert had always known that there was more to Miriel than met the eye; it was part of the reason he had desired her to wife. But a young lover? He thought of the men of her acquaintance in Nottingham when she was wed to Gerbert, but no single one stood out as a candidate for the role. All the merchants and artisans who paid their respects were long-established dwellers in the city or came from well-known families. He would have noticed any strangers, any rivals for her attention and there had been not the slightest whisper of scandal attached to Miriel's behaviour.

There could not have been anyone since her marriage to him; he kept her too busy for that, asserted his rights as often as he could. Yet even as he reassured himself, he remembered her recent downcast moods, the way that she wept when he claimed his rights on her body.

'Do you know his name?'

Mother Hillary thought, but shook her head. 'It was several years ago and I have had more important matters to fill my mind since then. It was Norman I think; he was not English born. Clearly, if she is wedded to you, she has parted company with him.'

Robert nodded. 'Clearly,' he said in a wooden voice.

'I am as shocked as you,' said the nun, 'but I am glad too to hear that she has made a life for herself and found a good husband. My fear was that she would end her life in a ditch.'

Robert smiled without warmth. 'Whatever happened in the past is finished. I could not ask for a better helpmate and I love her dearly,' he replied, wondering just how dearly.

A tap on the door announced the arrival of the steward to show Robert the abbey's flocks. He rose with alacrity, eager to be gone from the room's enclosing walls and the Abbess's all too probing stare.

After he left, Mother Hillary poured herself another half-cup of wine, which was sinful and foolish given that she had already taken a full cup on an empty belly, but she needed something more than prayer to steady her shaking hands. Once she had relished greeting guests, negotiating with merchants, dancing attendance on the bishop when he visited, but she was becoming too old for this kind of fencing and it drained her to the marrow. She swallowed the wine; her chin nodded on her chest and she started to snore. When she woke with a jerk half an hour later, the bells were ringing out for the nones service and her memory was as sharp as crystal.

The steward led Robert past an area of cleared ground where labourers and masons were busy at work. The Abbess had swiftly taken advantage of Maurice de la Pole's extra three marks per sack, Robert thought, and asked his companion what the new building was going to be.

'Houses of retirement for wealthy widows and the like. Women who wish to renounce the world without taking vows.' The man waved his hand. 'In return for money or property rents, they'll dwell here and be looked after in both body and spirit until their dying day.'

'I see.' Robert studied the building work with a thoughtful eye. The other matter nudged at him but he refused to acknowledge its existence. 'Profitable?'

'Yes, but more trouble than sheep,' the steward said drily. 'We've got four lodgers at the moment, housed in those buildings by the wall.' He pointed to a row of neat dwellings far to the right. 'Sometimes the women choose to retire of their own will, but often the choice is made for them by their families who want a safe haven for them.'

'Interesting,' Robert said, knowing full well that 'wanting a safe haven' was a polite term for 'wanting rid'. Doubtless St Catherine's would make a rich profit. His respect for the Abbess increased tenfold.

When he returned from inspecting the flocks on the marshland, dry now in the basking summer heat, she was waiting for him like a little black bird of ill-omen.

'That young man,' she said. 'He was called Nicholas de Caen.'

On the tenth day of September, the heaviness was more oppressive than ever. Miriel was wearing her lightest cotton chemise and silk gown, her thinnest wimple, and still she felt as if she were wilting. The hue of the sky had progressed through the day from high dawn blue, through shades of flax and hyssop, and was now turning the colour of the best woad-dyed cloth, a suggestion of purple at its edges. There was absolute, utter stillness, not the single flutter of a wilting leaf or waft of cloth from linen sheets hung on a line to dry in the yard.

'Going to be a frightener of a storm,' said Hildith, one of the spinners, her eye cocked on the darkening heavens as her fingers teased the wool from distaff to spindle with a dexterity too swift to follow. 'If the harvest's not in, it won't be after this.'

'But it must burst,' Miriel said, her own actions much slower. 'The sky cannot hold any more.' She looked at Will where he lay at her feet, his pink tongue lolling and his little sides heaving like bellows. There had been a storm at sea on that last voyage with Nicholas. She could remember the pattern of the lightning against her eyelids, the slam of the rain as their bodies met and parted, the growl of the thunder covering the sounds they made as they tried not to cry out. Glorious self-destruction. At the time it had been worth the price, but hindsight showed that she had been paying for dross.

Hildith tucked her distaff in her belt and went to retrieve the sheets from the line. Miriel rose and wandered restlessly back to the weaving house. The looms clacked as the weavers changed sheds and wove their shuttles through. Young Walter struggled, his tongue protruding between his teeth in concentration and beads of perspiration clinging to the downy moustache on his upper lip.

Outside she heard the sound of hoof on baked earth and, going to the door, saw Robert ride into the yard and dismount. His garments were travel dusty and his fair complexion the same colour as a length of her best cloth. Sweat was trickling in rivulets down his face. As a pillar of the community it would have been unseemly for him to ride through town clad only in shirt and braies and so he was wearing his tunic and heavy chausses.

Miriel's heart sank. The last thing she wanted to do was kiss him, but she forced herself to go forward and offer him a dutiful welcome on his wet cheek and parched lips. Close up the smell of him leaped through the disguise of spikenard and ambergris and almost made her retch. Through her garments she felt the pressure of his hot, damp hands at her waist.

'You must be dying of thirst,' she said, breaking away. 'Go and sit in the orchard and I'll bring you fresh pressed apple juice. Walter, leave that and attend the horse.'

The youth laid down his shuttle with a look of relief and went to do her bidding. Pulling off his tunic, Robert entered the garth and sat down heavily on the bench beneath the apple tree.

Miriel had promised herself that she would be the perfect wife to Robert, attentive to his every whim in atonement for what she had done behind his back. But the promise in her head was not as easy to fulfil in practice. If their partnership had been one of business, steady, practical and cold, she could have borne the burden easily. It was his physical demands on her that she found hard to bear. She did not melt at the sight of him and she was coming to hate his pawing assaults on her body.

With a heavy heart she carried two goblets of cloudy pressed apple juice into the orchard.

Robert was staring at the darkening sky, emperor purple now over the outline of the cathedral, but as she approached, he turned his eyes on her with a look that was sharp and thoughtful.

'Has your business gone well?' Miriel seated herself beside him, careful to keep a small distance. Even had she enjoyed the physical contact it was too hot for skin to press on skin.

'As to that, I do not know. I have more knowledge, but whether it be for good or ill, I cannot say.'

Miriel arched her brows in question, but he shook his head and gulped down the apple juice. 'Perhaps later,' he said. 'For now I just want to sit here and rest my eyes on you.'

'That's very flattering.' Since Robert was never one to sit still, Miriel was surprised at his admission. Perhaps his years were catching up with him, or the heat of the day had become too oppressive even for his restlessness.

'But the truth. You're a sight to refresh even the most jaded traveller.'

Miriel looked down. Her hands were folded around the base of the goblet in a grip that showed the whiteness of bone through her skin. Accepting compliments had never come easily to her, and when Robert gave them, she wanted to scream with guilt and anger and unworthiness.

He asked after her health. Miriel sipped the apple juice, which at least she could tolerate better than wine. 'Middling,' she said. 'I am still sick to the stomach, especially in the mornings, and if there were more hours in the day, I would sleep through all of them. Perchance I will feel better when this storm has broken.'

The sharp look had returned to Robert's eyes as she spoke and his lips tightened. 'If you do not,' he said, 'then I will dismiss that physician and send for someone with a better knowledge of such maladies.'

The storm shattered over the land an hour later, creating a premature dusk from the dark intensity of the sky. Unclosed shutters jerked at their fastenings or slammed against house walls. Roads became brown torrents and wooden roof shingles streamed like the scales on a sea-serpent. People ran for cover, drawing cloaks over bowed heads, and those animals not penned in shelters turned their rumps to the rain and huddled together for comfort and protection.

Within the house, bathed and refreshed, Robert sat casting his accounts by the light of a candelabrum, the light flickering as the wind hurled against the shutters and found gaps through which to squeeze. The wall hangings fluttered and the smoke from the hearth fire sporadically blew back upon itself instead of making its orderly way up the chimney.

Miriel sat in her favourite curule chair, Will in her lap. She had some sewing to hand, but had scarcely touched it, preferring to gaze trance-like at one of the embroideries on the wall, a biblical scene of Noah preparing to set sail in an ark that very much resembled a large cog. Robert paused from counting the notches on the tally stick in his hand and studied her with a tension almost akin to the heaviness of the storm. She had scarcely eaten a mouthful of supper this evening. There were deep circles beneath her eyes and gaunt hollows in her cheeks. Always slender, she was now close to naught but skin and bone. Pining for de Caen? Mayhap, but if so, there had been several years when she had not pined. Or perhaps they had been lovers throughout that time, but now he had a new woman. That would explain much. All he had to do was ask her. Simple. Except that he knew he would be unable to bear her reply if it was the wrong one.

The tally stick snapped between his fingers. He gazed at the broken ends and very gently set them down on the trestle. He would not lose control – of himself or others. Like the clients whose wool provided his livelihood, Miriel was his property and he would brook no trespass. He had liked and trusted Nicholas de Caen, and was not going to find better vessels to take his wool to Flanders. But the young man had committed treason. Again he looked at Miriel. So had she. A vast pain of love and grief welled up inside him, but, unlike the storm, he did not permit it to burst. Instead he gathered it within himself, holding it close to his breast like an infant, and let it take sustenance from the blood of his heart.

The physician gave the flask of urine an ostentatious swirl and held it up to the light glittering through the shutters.

Miriel watched him from the bed, her hand pressed to her aching stomach. She had been sick three times that morning and at the slightest provocation knew that she would have to dive for the slop pot again. She felt weakly, wretchedly ill. Perhaps she was dying. If she was, then she hoped it would be soon, today if possible.

'Well?' demanded Robert. 'Can you tell me what ails my wife, Master Andrew, or shall I dismiss you from my service?'

Master Andrew looked down the Roman curve of his nose at Robert. The size of the feature was emphasised by the stark linen physician's bonnet covering his hair and tied with strings beneath his chin. 'These things have to be studied,' he said in a supercilious tone. 'I cannot make a diagnosis until I have all the facts.' He swirled the urine again and then sniffed it. Miriel closed her eyes and turned her head to the wall.

'I would say that you have all the facts that you need,' Robert said irritably.

The Roman nose flared impressively. 'Allow me to be the judge of that.'

'Then allow me to show you the door and keep the coin in my pouch!'

Master Andrew drew himself to his full height and towered over Robert by almost a twelve-inch, the effect somewhat marred by the fact that he was as thin as a rake and Robert had the build of an ox. 'As far as I can tell without a more intimate examination, your wife is suffering from the natural condition of pregnancy, the symptoms exaggerated by the imbalance of her humours.' His tone suggested that he had been deeply insulted.

Miriel's eyes flew open. 'What?' She sat up and was overcome by another heaving surge of nausea. 'Do not be so foolish!' The last word disappeared in a bout of retching as she hung over the slop bowl.

The physician's head darted like a heron's. 'It is the common condition of breeding women to vomit and purge in the early months,' he said icily. 'You say that you cannot remember the time of your last flux except that it was more than two months ago, and that too is a sign of your condition.'

Miriel shook her head. 'No!' she gasped between heaves. 'It cannot be. I am barren, I know I am!'

'In seven months we shall see who is right. You have all the signs. Indeed, I would suggest that you engage the services of a good midwife to see you through the coming months and the ordeal of the birth.'

'I am not with child!' A note of hysteria entered Miriel's voice. The notion of becoming a mother terrified her. The word *ordeal* stuck in her mind, filling her with terror. She knew that she was bound to suffer terribly because she had sinned.

She heard him offering stilted congratulations, and Robert's gruff response as he paid the fee and saw him out. Exhausted, Miriel lay back on the bed and pressed the palms of her hands to her flat belly. It was impossible that a child was growing inside her. And yet she was aware of her ignorance on the subject of pregnancy and childbirth. With her grandfather as her mentor and her mother's reticence on the subject, she had grown up with scant knowledge of the matter. She understood that mating led to conception because she had often seen animals in the wool yard and her grandfather was forever at war with the local dogs when his mastiff bitch was in season. But there had never been enough contact with other women to learn the lore and lexicon of human symptoms. No friends when she was growing up to share their experiences as they became wives and mothers themselves, only her grandfather's business clients, and then nuns. She had never felt so frightened or alone.

Robert returned and sat on the bed. He put his hand on her

brow in a tender, sympathetic gesture, and then he sighed. There was an expression of deep sadness in his eyes and a downward curve to his lips. It occurred to Miriel that while most couples would be hugging themselves with joy at the prospect of an heir to their endeavours, she and Robert were acting as if they were at a wake.

'I thought I was barren,' she whispered again and clutched at him for support as she had done in the days following Gerbert's death. 'Do you think the physician could be wrong?'

Robert shook his head. 'Mayhap, but I doubt it. And, sweetheart, I am sorely afraid that you are mistaken.' He drew a deep breath, and held her away so that their eyes could meet with clarity. 'It is not you who is barren; it is I.'

A silence fell and stretched for eternity. Miriel swallowed. A great numbness flowed through her body. 'You?' Her lips formed the word soundlessly.

'Three wives and none of them has quickened by my seed,' he said, watching her intently. 'And nor have the women with whom I have lain for casual comfort between states of wedlock. I am not a man to doubt miracles, but neither am I one to believe in them without due cause. If you are with child, sweetheart, then I suspect the intervention of Nicholas de Caen, not God.'

The numbness spread, blinding her eyes and ears, stopping her breath. She had the sensation of falling down a long, dark tunnel into nothing, but before she could claim welcome oblivion, it was snatched from her as the numbness was shattered by a cold deluge that brought her gasping back into the light.

Robert sat over her, a pitcher in his hand, and she and the bedclothes were drenched. 'I'm sorry, sweetheart; it was all I could think to do.' Reaching out, he gently removed her dripping wimple and wiped water from her face on the palm of his hand.

Miriel stared at him, feeling like a small bird caught in the gaze of a hawk. He knew, dear God, he knew, and there was no point in denial. She had a sudden urge to laugh. The jest had been on her when she promised

Nicholas that she was barren, that he need not fear for her safety.

'Are you going to disown me?'

'It has crossed my mind.' He dragged off the wet bedclothes and cast them on the floor. 'But then I wondered why I should cut off my nose to spite my face. Whatever you have done, you are still my wife.'

'Oh Jesu Christ,' Miriel muttered and put her head in her hands, hiding her face, desperately seeking the dark path to nothing. It would be better if he lost his temper, bellowed at her like an enraged bull, struck her. This reasoned weariness was far more lacerating.

'Do you love him?'

'Yes,' she said through the cage of her fingers. 'To my cost. But whatever was between us is finished now.'

'It is not,' Robert answered in a soft voice, 'because you are carrying his seed.'

'I thought I was barren,' she repeated helplessly, knowing that it was no excuse. Like a child stealing sweetmeats, she had trusted not to be caught. And now she was, in a vicious trap of her own making. 'If I could undo the past, I would.'

He grabbed her wrists in one strong grip and pulled them down, leaving her naked to his gaze. 'And marry him instead of me? Look at me, Miriel. Stop hiding and at least have the honesty to meet me face to face.' And beyond the soft tone, the reasoning voice, she saw the anger, the hurt, the raw and naked jealousy that had been her expectation. 'And marry him instead of me?' he repeated.

'No, and stop my mother from falling for the silver tongue of a travelling minstrel,' Miriel cried. 'My grandfather used to say that I was like her. I didn't believe him then, but now I know I am, and I wish I'd never been born.' Robert's grip meant that she could neither hide herself again nor tear away, but still she tried.

His grip tightened. 'How long has this been going on beneath my nose? How long have I been wearing the horns of a cuckold?' he demanded. 'You knew him long before I brought him home to dine and you feigned not to know each other. Were you lovers then?'

Miriel gasped as he squeezed her flesh against bone. 'No, I swear we were not! On my soul we have lain together on no more than two occasions. I did not know you were using his ships; indeed, I did not even know that he had them until you brought him home that evening.'

'But you knew him in St Catherine's. The Abbess herself told me that you did.'

'Yes, as a patient in the infirmary. I saved his life, and in payment he brought me to Nottingham and gave me silver to begin a new life. We parted company, and I did not see him again until the night you brought him home. It's true, I swear it is true!'

Robert glared at her, his teeth making small grinding sounds behind his lips.

'You're hurting me.'

'Do I not have the right? What man would gainsay me if I took a stick to your faithless hide?'

Miriel had a sickening vision of her stepfather standing over her, his face crimson with rage, working himself up to the point where he was ready to strike. Last time that had happened, she had fought back with a fury and indignation as great as the man's and almost burned the house down around their ears. Now she had neither the vitality nor the strength to make a battle of the moment. If Robert chose to beat her, there was little she could do to prevent him. 'I doubt that any *man* would gainsay you,' she retorted. 'Strike me if you must, but it will not change anything.'

Robert went white. 'I ought to,' he muttered, but released his crushing grip and turned to pace across the room, his hands raking his thick hair. 'All the trust I had in you, all the faith and affection, you have betrayed it for a common lust.'

The way he said the words stabbed like a dagger because they were the truth and at the same time so far from the truth. 'No, it wasn't like that!'

'He filled your belly and turned straight away to another woman. If that is not common lust, I do not know what is,' Robert continued relentlessly. 'Nor if the truth is known do I really care except that you gave yourself to him when your love and duty was to me.'

He stopped pacing and looked blankly at the carved oak cupboard standing against the wall. With a sudden oath, he swung his fist and sent the salver and flagon upon it crashing to the floor and kicked the cupboard so hard that he shattered part of the fretwork on the door.

Miriel winced at the violence, fully aware that it could have been directed against her. Winced because it was her fault and she did not know how to set matters right. 'Do you want me to leave?'

Chest heaving, eyes aglitter, Robert turned to look at her. 'No,' he said huskily. 'The matter goes not beyond this door. If you went, then all of Lincoln would know that you have given me a cuckold's horns. Why should I suffer in public for your faithlessness?'

Miriel bowed her head and bit her lip. It had been a foolish thing to say. Where would she go? To Nicholas and his red-haired leman? Back to St Catherine's? As her husband, Robert had the right to all her property, and likely he would claim it if she went. All she would have were the hidden bags of silver from her hoard and the danger of Empress Mathilda's crown. Besides, sick and wretched as she was now, how would she care for herself or manage the birth of her child amongst strangers?

Robert folded his arms. 'We will patch together what we have left. Since I cannot father a child, I will acknowledge your bastard as my heir. At least we can salvage something from this ill deed of yours.'

'I wish you had never found out,' she said miserably, 'for your sake, not mine.'

Robert grunted. 'I wish it too, because although I can forgive you the world, trust is a different business. No more.' He raised a forefinger when she tried to speak. 'I will hear no more on the matter. It is finished. I'll summon Elfwen to change these wet sheets, and when you have rested, we will go hand in hand and announce to the world our joyful tidings.' And with a brisk nod to seal his decision, he left the room.

Miriel slumped on the bed and closed her eyes. They were dry and burning. Somewhere within her was an ocean of grief and terror, but there was a huge stone blocking its release. If she turned her head she would see the daylight through the open shutters, beckoning her to the window. She was still slim enough to fit into the aperture, no bulge of child yet to prevent her graceful progress. How easy it would be to leap out like a bird taking flight. Easy and stupid. The ground was not far enough distant to guarantee instant death. And if she killed herself, then she would be doubly damned for killing the child inside her too. Nicholas's child. She placed her hand on her belly in wondering fear. Lulled into complacence by the belief that she was barren, the thought of having a child had been a distant dream, sometimes wistful, frequently a nightmare. The ordeal of the bearing terrified her, and if she survived that, how would she deal with a screaming infant? In girlhood she had always fled from other women's babies, not wanting to know. Now she did not have a choice. Like her mother before, she was trapped.

Downstairs, Robert spoke briefly to Elfwen, then went into the yard to look at the sun glittering on the havoc wrought by last night's storm, the drunken angle of the wattle fences, the fallen fruit in the orchard, the torn leaves on the vines.

He had lied to Miriel in the bedchamber. It wasn't finished, but the decision he had deferred to the storm was made.

Chapter 26

Magdalene did not need a physician with a flask of urine to predict her own condition; with the life she had led, she was all too familiar with the signs. Despite prayers and precautions, it had been bound to happen. Unsure how Nicholas would react to the news, she kept it to herself until his keen sailor's eye and sensitive hands bared her secret during an afternoon's lovemaking in the loft of The Ship.

The shutters were open, admitting a mellow day, as rich and gold as fine mead – one of autumn's gifts before the winter darkness closed in. Lazing in the aftermath of pleasure, Nicholas caressed her body. Through half-closed lids, Magdalene watched his fingers track across her skin. Their brown, salt-scarred strength was tempered by the sensitivity of touch, by the masculine grace of tendon and sinew and wiry, sun-bleached hair on wrist and knuckle. Words of love swelled in her throat, but she held them back, not wanting to show him a cage lest he took flight like a wild sea-bird.

He traced the outline of her breasts, the delicate marbling of blue veins, the swollen outer curve and crown of dark-red nipple. Magdalene gave a sensuous little shiver and turned towards him, answering his touch with her own. He caressed the outline of her body, each ridge of rib, the curve of hip, and long thigh. Back up to her breasts, then slowly, slowly down. Quivering, Magdalene parted her thighs, but before his fingers found the magic place, he stopped. His palm quested gently over the mound of her belly and then remained there, warm and heavy. No longer pleasure-sated, his gaze was sharp and clear on hers.

'I hope you were going to tell me,' he said. 'And do not say tell me what or claim that you have been overeating. I am not a fool.'

A jolt of fear ran through Magdalene at being found out, but she was relieved too. The thought of broaching the matter had been weighing on her mind like a lead ingot. Now she would discover whether her fears were proven or groundless. 'I was going to do so, but I did not know how,' she said, and laid her hand over his on the full, creamy flesh of her belly.

'How does any woman tell her man? Surely it is a simple matter.'

Magdalene grimaced. In some ways she was a deal more experienced than he. Telling a man that you were going to bear his child was rarely a simple matter at all. She could remember her own parents' dismay at the thought of another mouth to feed, the worry, the arguments. There was the overwhelming pressure of expectation on the lady of the manor to be a good brood mare and produce several healthy sons, or the disgrace of the merchant's daughter who quickened out of wedlock. And there was the reformed whore who found herself at the mercy of love.

'But that is what I did not know,' she said. 'Are you mine? I could not bear you to turn away from me. I have bedded with other men in the past. What if you thought I was faithless now?'

'You insult my judgement and you insult yourself,' he said with narrowed eyes.

'No.' Magdalene shook her head and met his indignation squarely. 'If you had lived as I have done, you would know that my words are spoken out of fear, not insult. You would not be the first man to walk away from such news.'

He leaned over and kissed her hard on the lips. 'Not me,' he said. 'Christ, I have no living family. Why should I want to leave the new harbour I've found?'

Magdalene could think of several reasons, but kept them to herself and kissed him back.

For a moment he responded with enthusiasm, but then, despite his burgeoning erection, rolled away and frowned at the rafters.

'What's wrong?' Magdalene bit her lip.

He sat up and reached for his clothes, indicating that she should do the same.

'It seems to me,' he said, 'that the mother of my child should have my name too. Robe yourself as befitting a respectable matron, and we'll go and find a priest. I'll ask Martin and his wife to be witnesses.'

Magdalene gazed at him, her jaw slack. 'You want me to marry you?'

He struggled into his shirt and, emerging tousle-haired, returned her look. 'If you want to,' he said.

'If I want to!' It was too good to be true. With trembling hands she began to dress, feverish lest it all be a dream and she should suddenly awaken. She was shaking so much that she could not tie the lacing, nor see to attempt it, for her eyes were blinded by tears.

'Here,' Nicholas said gently, and performed the task for her, his fingers deft and his expression tender. He brushed his thumb across her wet face.

Magdalene threw her arms around his neck and gave him a tear-salt kiss. 'I have never wanted anything so much in my life,' she sniffed.

It was a freezing December day, with sleet in a wind that had a bite like a vicious dog. In the weaving sheds, the workers wore several layers of clothing and thick woollen hose. Charcoal braziers gave out a degree of localised heat, but did not reach the corners or banish the draughts that puffed through the shutters like the breath of ghosts.

Miriel rubbed her hands together and tucked them beneath her cloak where her palms encountered the swell of her belly. Last week she had felt the first delicate fluttering as the baby quickened within her. Since then she had been torn between wonder and panic, not to say indignation at the way the growing infant had taken over her body and her life. She was still being sick, although less than in the early months, and often was so tired that it was an effort to rise from her bed. The more she was told to rest, however, the less inclined she was to do so. She would not let her life be ruled by the dictates of others, and that included her unborn child. Besides, keeping busy prevented her from thinking about its father.

She went to the bales of cloth that had been piled up ready for transport to the fulling mill. The wool would be beaten in water and fuller's earth to thicken it before being stretched upon tenter hooks and then napped with teasels to give a soft finish. The cloth fetched a high price on the home market, especially the woad-blue. Nicholas had a tunic of that colour, woven and fulled in her workshops. If she closed her eyes she could see him wearing it, and even the diamond pattern on the braid at his corded brown throat. If she closed her eyes she could imagine the feel of him, the taste . . . With a sharp hiss of exasperation, she turned from the bales. Once dreaming had been a haven. Now she was not so sure.

The apprentice arrived from the fulling mill to take the bales of cloth and she made herself concentrate on the practical details and instructions. As he was leaving with his two laden pack ponies, Robert returned from visiting a customer. Above his beard, his face was weather-chapped and the age seams had deepened from etched lines to deep carvings between mouth and nose. But today his eyes held a gleam.

'Cold as a witch's tits out there,' he announced, his breath clouding the air. Removing his sheepskin mittens, he took the cup of hot cider that she handed to him and sipped with relish.

Miriel eyed him suspiciously. Of late his moods had been strange. The circumstances of her pregnancy had taken their toll on him, no matter that he professed to have forgiven and put it all in the past. The heavier lines in his flesh and the sudden flashes of temper were both a result. Good humour had been less forthcoming.

'How have you fared?' she asked out of duty, not really wanting to know.

He shrugged. 'Well enough. I've more negotiating to do yet.' He took another drink of the cider and rolled it appreciatively round his cheeks. Then he swallowed and fixed her with a predatory stare. 'I heard some amusing news though.'

Miriel arched her brows in question and knew from the look on his face that she probably did not want to hear it.

Robert glanced round at the busily occupied weavers and lowered his voice. 'Nicholas de Caen has married his leman, that red-haired whore.'

'And you think it amusing?' Miriel heard herself say in a voice filled with distaste, while inside her heart gave a great jolt of jealous pain.

'In the way that I think the antics of a madman amusing, aye.' He paused for effect, rubbing his beard. 'She is with child too, you know. About as many months as yourself, according to Master Wudecoc.'

Miriel turned away. 'I know that I have wronged you,' she said, her tone pitched even lower than his, 'but I had hoped you would be more merciful.'

'Merciful?' Robert gave her a look of quizzical surprise. 'Sweetheart, the thought never crossed my mind that you would not want to know.'

'Do not play me for a fool; surely it must have.'

'I swear it did not.' His voice rose with indignant innocence. 'I thought it would help you realise how much better off you are without him.'

Miriel clenched her fists. 'You are just tearing open old wounds,' she said with a glance at the weavers whose heads were bent diligently over their looms. 'How will they heal if you keep grinding salt into them?'

'Better open and salted than left to fester,' he muttered.

Miriel faced him, shaking her head. 'You are wrong. Every time you speak of Nicholas de Caen you make them worse. I do not understand why you don't find someone else to transport your wool. Ignore the fact that Nicholas even exists.'

He looked at her belly and she flushed. 'I can scarcely do that, sweetheart,' he said softly, 'and, as I have told you, his ships are the best I can hire. While I have no intention of dealing with him in person, I can come to amicable agreements with his agents.'

'Then do as you must, but do not bring your "news" home to me,' Miriel snapped.

Robert shrugged. 'As you wish,' he said, sucking the hot cider through his teeth, his look petulant.

Miriel turned to one of the looms and watched the weaver expertly change sheds and twine the shuttle through, creating a pattern of scarlet twill. Her eyes were burning and her heart ached so hard that she thought it might burst from longing and grief.

Most ships clung to inshore waters during the winter months, and although journeys were made across the high seas, they were of necessity, and the captains put a higher price on their hiring.

In Boston, Nicholas celebrated the Christmas season in port with Magdalene.

He had only himself to please, no family to be scandalised that his wife had once been a whore. Those who did not know would never have guessed. Except for their bed where she sported with the simple joy of a peasant, Magdalene conducted herself like a lady. He did not love her with the gut-wrenching pain that he loved Miriel, but he was fond of her and his affection was nurtured by the passage of days spent in her company and the shared wonder of the new life growing inside her.

'You did not have to wed me, you know that,' Magdalene murmured. They were sitting on a bench, sharing a cup of mead in the house that Nicholas had rented from an absent wine merchant. The firelight warmed them in undertones of gold and shadow. Her head upon Nicholas's shoulder, Magdalene's unbound hair was molten with the reflection of the flames.

'You set your worth too low. I tied this knot out of duty and concern for you and the child, but I tied it for love as well, of my own free will.' He stroked her hair, admiring the way it slid over his fingers like precious metal turned to silk. 'My only fear was that you would refuse to take me.'

Magdalene raised her head to stare at him. 'If I hesitated, it was because I could not believe you had asked me. What man of your means would look to a brothel for a wife?'

He snorted. 'Enough men of my means visit the places. It

is easy to breed loneliness and loveless power-matches out of wealth. I have seen it happen, I know the misery that grows.' He looked into the flames, his eyelids tense and narrow.

Magdalene watched him. 'You are thinking of her, aren't you?' she murmured.

He grimaced, knowing that to feign ignorance would not only be a waste of time but an insult to Magdalene. He had made her his wife and she had a right to pry. 'You know me too well,' he said ruefully.

'No,' she contradicted, 'for if I did, I would know the kernel of your thoughts and not just the shell you show to the world.'

'Is that what you want?' He ceased fire-gazing to look at her.

She gnawed her underlip and frowned. 'I do not know if I could bear what you had to say.'

He cupped her skull, bringing her mouth down to his, blocking the treachery of his wayward thoughts with the warm blessing of physical touch. 'You are my wife, and I love you,' he murmured. 'That is the kernel. Whatever happened in the past is naught but a husk.'

Magdalene was not to be so easily mollified and pulled away. 'If she came to you again, you would go with her,' she said with certainty.

Nicholas sighed. Her need for reassurance was palpable, and the words so hard to find, as much for himself as for Magdalene. 'I made the approach on the last occasion we were together,' he said at last. 'I thought . . .' He shook his head. 'I thought that I could change things, perhaps make her leave her husband and her life to come away with me.' Then he laughed bitterly. 'No, that's wrong. I didn't think at all, I just craved the way that some men crave wine so badly that they become its slave, and finally it kills them.'

'And you still have the craving.' Her voice was choked. 'I know you married me because I am with child, and because I ease your need a little. That is the kernel, whatever you might say.'

'Ah, sweetheart, no.' He smoothed her hair and caressed

her hot, suspicious face. 'I married you for yourself. I swear on my soul.'

He felt a small shudder ripple through her frame. 'And her?' Magdalene demanded. 'What of her?'

He frowned, striving to find a reply that was honest without further unsettling Magdalene. 'Miriel's a part of me,' he said at last. 'She always will be because I owe her my life and she owes me a private debt of her own, but I swear to you that she will have no place in our future.'

Magdalene gave a knowing nod. 'Mayhap not, but you will think of her often, and I would be desiring the impossible if I asked your mind not to wander.' She tightened and lifted her jaw. 'I came to this marriage with my eyes open. I do not want ever to close them and look away.'

'I'll never give you reason.' Filled with tenderness, desire and a feeling of poignant sadness, he kissed her again. She pressed against him, her grip suddenly fierce with possession, and he matched his response to hers. Soon, by mutual consent, they abandoned the bench for the softness of a feather mattress and an urgency of need as hot as the fire.

CHAPTER 27

SPRING 1221

Spring arrived with the joyousness of a tumbler, the wind cartwheeling the sky with blue and dragging ribbons of greenery and flowers through what had been a barren landscape. Sunlight sparkled on the sea, turning the grey waves a heavy, marbled green, dazzling their crests with silver lace. And men made ready to cross its wideness.

In Southampton, Nicholas was preparing his nef, the *Empress*, for a voyage to Normandy bearing officials from King Henry's court. He had made the crossing several times when the winter seas had been calm, but it was not his preferred time of year. Now that the season had turned, his enthusiasm was far greater.

Magdalene sat on a bench near the hold, watching the bustle as stores were laid in the hold and sails and equipment meticulously checked. The boisterous wind flattened her gown against her body, revealing her advanced state of pregnancy. She had enjoyed good health throughout the carrying. Her skin glowed and her eyes were luminous. A vast appetite had given her body the padded firmness of a new gambeson, and the graceful gait of nine months ago was now an awkward waddle. Nicholas had never loved her more. Cravings and memories still remained, but they had blurred a little at the edges. He had disciplined himself not to dwell on what had been, but to be content with what he had. Mostly he succeeded, and if he ever thought of Miriel, he was careful that Magdalene should not see the turn of his mind.

He took a brief respite from his endeavours and, sitting beside her, clasped her hand in his. The long, slim fingers had increased their girth too, and she had been forced to remove the vanity of her many gold rings before they had to be cut off.

'I'll buy you a new wedding ring in Normandy,' he promised. 'Big enough to fit your finger.'

Magdalene laughed. 'You had best measure it on the width of the ship's mast then!' Holding out her free hand, she waggled it and grimaced. 'The midwife says that once I've borne the babe, everything will become as it was, but I have my doubts.'

'You'll be beautiful whatever,' Nicholas said gallantly.

She laughed again and gave him a little push. 'Flatterer!'

'But it is the truth. I have never seen you look so . . . so radiant.' He brushed at a stray wisp of copper-red hair that had escaped her wimple.

'You have never seen me so fat either,' Magdalene said with a dismal look at her body.

Her need for reassurance was constant. Aware of the reasons, Nicholas gave it unstintingly. 'It makes not the slightest difference to me.'

She searched his face. 'Truly?'

'Truly,' he said, and kissed her.

A loudly cleared throat interrupted their embrace. Looking up, Nicholas encountered the sardonic gaze of Stephen Trabe, fellow ship-owner and veteran of the battle of Sandwich. Magdalene smoothed her gown and demurely folded her hands beneath her belly. Nicholas rose to his feet, his hand outstretched in greeting, but his eyes wary. He and Trabe were sufficiently acquainted to pass the time of day, but there was no deeper friendship. Nicholas could still see with too much clarity the moment when Trabe decapitated Eustace the Monk with no more conscience than beheading a chicken. Instinctively, he stepped in front of Magdalene, shielding her with his body.

If Trabe noticed the gesture, he gave no indication. Returning the handgrasp, he nodded his appreciation of the nef. 'A fine vessel,' he said, his gaze examining her with lupine thoroughness.

Nicholas agreed with him. 'We sail on the tide,' he added. 'Is there some business you wish to discuss?'

Trabe stroked his thumb along the golden beard at his jaw. 'Aye, there is, but you might want to hear it in private.' His eyes flickered eloquently towards Magdalene who was watching the men with curiosity. 'Nay, you *will* want to hear it in private,' he emphasised.

Nicholas glanced at Magdalene too, then, signalling that he would not be long, drew Trabe away to the prow of the vessel.

Trabe rested his forearm on the intricately carved and painted post and continued to thumb his beard. There was a gleam of relish in his expression. 'I thought you might be interested to know about a certain contract I was offered last month.'

Nicholas raised his brows in a question and waited.

'I might have accepted it in the old days before I had gainful employment from the King,' he said. 'I would not have you think that I have developed a soft underbelly with the passing years.'

'Of course not,' Nicholas said without expression. Gainful employment from the King for men such as Stephen Trabe was no more than a legitimate licence to play pirate. The notion that the man at his side possessed the smallest soft spot was untenable.

Trabe smiled darkly. 'But these days I'm selective about my "kills".'

Nicholas stiffened at the world 'kills'. 'The contract you were offered was for my life?'

'A man with a bright red beard and a common manner approached me on the matter,' Trabe said with a nod. 'I had never met him before, but I would know him again. He was acting on behalf of his employer, but of course he did not say who that was. The sum offered was high, and I was tempted to take it on.' He looked at Nicholas with shrewd, hard eyes. 'Someone wants you dead.'

There was a hollow sensation in Nicholas's gut. All the old memories flooded his mind. Surely after all these years the scene that he and his father had witnessed at Rouen was no longer a threat. It was John who had required their deaths, and now John himself was dead. 'Were you told why?'

'They never volunteer and I never ask. Once you start knowing things, the job begins to mean more than just money.'

'Conscience, you mean?'

Trabe snorted. 'You're treading on dangerous ground, de Caen. That is not a word I recognise.'

But nevertheless he possessed one, Nicholas thought. 'Then why come to me with this warning?'

Trabe shrugged and looked uncomfortable. 'We were part of the same group at that battle with the French. I know you and I know of you too well to do the job with an impartial mind.' He cleared his throat and ran his thumbnail along the contour of one of the carved dragon's heads. 'I was on the ship that sent your father's to the bottom of the sea. I do not want to be on the one that destroys you.'

The hollowness widened to encompass all of Nicholas's being. 'What?' he said stiffly. The old memories became as jagged as knives.

'I wasn't the captain,' Trabe said quickly. 'Jesu, I was only a lad of fifteen summers myself, but I was there.' He tensed his body. 'Strike me and I'll strike back twice as hard and you'll never hear the tale,' he warned as Nicholas clenched his fists.

'God's eyes, what do you expect me to do at such news, stand here with the calm of a monk at prayers!' Nicholas cried.

Below them, Magdalene struggled to her feet, her expression concerned. With a half-turn of his head and a wave of his hand, Trabe indicated her to stay where she was. 'I expect you to act like a madman,' he replied, 'but I am telling you for your own good to fetter yourself.'

Nicholas closed his eyes and drew several slow, deep breaths. 'Christ,' he muttered, digging his fingers into his palms, seeking the control not to leap at the other man's throat and not sure that he was going to succeed. At last, he raised his lids, and looked at Trabe. 'Tell me.'

'We had orders to take and sink the *Péronnelle*. Although

he acted through an agent, we knew those orders came from King John because our captain had dealt with him often before. Booty we could have, but there were to be no survivors. It was essential that their master, Alain de Caen, did not survive. We were paid to do the deed and keep our mouths shut.' Trabe paused for a moment to stare out over the water. Then he sucked a deep breath through his teeth and said without looking at Nicholas, 'We caught her in mid-Channel and rammed her through the bows. Then we swung grapnels across and before she sank we hauled off her cargo and killed her crew as we had been instructed.' His tone was emotionless. 'It was a duty and I've done the same a hundred times since and with more responsibility. What your father had done to encounter John's wrath, I do not know, even as I do not know the reason why someone seeks your death now.'

Nicholas sat down abruptly on the bench below the prow. 'I knew he was killed,' he said hoarsely. 'Some said that the *Péronnelle* went down because of bad seamanship or a sudden wave, but I knew my father better than that. He never made a single mistake on a ship in his life. He died for knowing things about King John that could have brought down the Kingdom.' He glared at Stephen Trabe. 'Now you have the gall to tell me that you were one of his murderers.'

Trabe spread his hands and returned Nicholas's look with eyes that were as hard as stone. 'Judging me will not bring your father back. He was an enemy of the King, that is all we were told and there was no reason for us to know more. I do what I do and make no excuses.'

'How do you sleep at night.'

Trabe gave a mirthless grin. 'Like the dead,' he said. 'God on the Cross, I came to warn you, not to chew over old bones and be made to justify myself. I am beginning to wish I had accepted that contract.'

'You expect me to thank you after what you have said?' Nicholas snarled.

'I expect nothing,' Trabe snarled back. He turned away. 'Just look to yourself and remember who warned you.'

Trabe had reached the wooden gangplank before Nicholas

caught up with him and, grabbing his arm, turned him round. The sailor's muscles tightened and one hand reached to the handy dagger at his hip.

'No,' Nicholas said urgently, 'I need to ask a boon of you.'

Trabe's eyebrows rose towards his hairline. 'A boon?'

'Yes, I . . .' Nicholas paused to rub his face. 'I am not ungrateful for the warning and I acknowledge the spirit in which it was given.' They were difficult words to say. There was a part of him that wanted to see Trabe's dagger flash and answer with similar violence, but he held it down because it was a response to what had happened in the past and the future was more important. 'If anything does happen to me, I ask you to ensure that Magdalene is brought safely to the house of my senior master, Martin Wudecoc, in Boston.'

Trabe glanced over his shoulder at Magdalene, who was standing again. 'I am not a nursemaid,' he growled.

'Not even for payment?'

Trabe drew himself up, his expression tightening.

'It's not an insult, it's an offer,' Nicholas said. 'A contract to preserve life, if you will. If my life is threatened, then hers could be too, and that of our unborn child.'

Trabe pursed his lips.

'I do not have time to make other provision; I sail with the tide.'

'As a boon then,' Trabe said reluctantly. 'But only until you make other provision.'

'Thank you. And if you should discover who seeks my death, I would pay well to know.'

Trabe smiled darkly. 'You might do better to put your money on a counter-contract of your own and see to whose lifeblood it leads,' he said and, without waiting for a reply, departed.

Nicholas watched him with troubled eyes and thought of what had been revealed. It was not as if a wrong had been righted, but there was a certain bleak relief in having his suspicions about his father's death confirmed. There was also the added worry of knowing that he might soon be joining him.

'Who was that?' Magdalene wrapped her arm around his and looked up at him, seeking explanation and reassurance.

'A friend,' Nicholas replied with slight misgiving at the use of the word.

'What did he want?'

Nicholas shook his head. 'To unburden the conscience he claims not to have,' he said. He turned to watch a labourer loading barrels of mead into the hold. He wondered if it was coincidence that a red-bearded man was apparently contracting for his death when it had been such a one who had struck down Maurice de la Pole outside a Boston alehouse. The notion was worrying. Perhaps he ought to have another word with Stephen Trabe after all.

The voyage to Normandy was smooth and without incident. There were no knives in dark corners, no cups of poisoned wine, and the only ships that hove into view during the passage were small fishing nefs and merchant craft. On edge, Nicholas studied the horizon, but it yielded nothing more sinister than a line of smudged blue joining a paler line of sky.

He tarried a night in Barfleur and made ready again to sail on the next high tide with a cargo of the superior Normandy cider in the nef's shallow hold. Barfleur itself was notorious as the port out of which the first King Henry's *White Ship* had sailed one winter evening, struck a rock as she cleared the harbour, and sank, taking half England's nobility with her, including the heir to the throne. Over a hundred years had passed since the happening, but it was still recalled with grim relish by the inhabitants. Every vessel that entered or left the harbour sailed close to the spot of the tragedy. Tales were told of a ghostly white ship that was seen each year in November, casting off to her doom.

A shiver ran down Nicholas's spine as the *Empress* sailed out of Barfleur on the evening tide. She was a white nef, just like the fated ship, and Nicholas already felt a dread affinity with the wreck fathoms below, for his own father had died at sea.

As the sun dissolved into flowing ribbons of purple and

gold, the *Empress* cleared the harbour; her bows sliced the spray of the open sea and her red sail developed a taut belly of wind. Tom, the lookout, kindled the lanterns at prow and stern, and she gleamed through the night like a ghost.

Nicholas listened to the hiss of the sea beneath her keel and, with his eyes on the lantern's swing, wondered afresh who was willing to pay for his death. It might be because of the past, but he thought not. If the instruction had come from the Crown, Trabe would not have warned him. And as far as he knew, his fellow sea-traders were friendly rivals rather than deadly enemies.

At the back of his mind was a notion that he did not want to explore, but nevertheless it niggled at him. If Robert Willoughby ever found out about himself and Miriel, there was no telling how the merchant would react. Willoughby was said to be ruthless in his trade dealings, and he had certainly set out to woo Miriel with single-minded purpose, but whether he had it in him, beneath that affable tawny exterior, to kill was difficult to judge. If he did, who could blame him? And if he didn't, then Nicholas had no inkling who might wish him sufficient ill to deprive him of his life.

Sighing heavily, he abandoned his thoughts and sought the company of his crew.

The attack came an hour later when the sky had lost all trace of light and the gathering clouds of a rain squall had obliterated stars and moon. Two ships, lanternless, dark of sail and hull, hove out of the night like birds of prey and, even as Nicholas's lookout bellowed a warning, the grapnel ropes hissed out and pronged iron claws chewed gouges in the *Empress*'s graceful white sides, slewing and stopping her in the water.

There was no time to break out the oars or make a run before the wind. Nicholas seized an axe and chopped through one of the grapnel ropes, but already more were being thrown like strands from the mouth parts of a spider. Arrows whined overhead and plummeted with devastating effect. As Nicholas chopped another rope, the crewman beside him screamed and fell, two feathered shafts quivering in his body. Nicholas cursed. The *Empress* was a sitting target, unable to move, bright as the moon.

He flattened himself against the deck, his heart thudding like a fist on a drum. A voice with a heavy French accent bellowed across the water, demanding surrender.

'Tell them to go to the devil,' gasped the wounded sailor sprawled beside him. He was bleeding heavily. 'They won't let us live, whatever we do.'

The *Empress* listed to one side as one of the French ships drew on the grapnel ropes and began pulling in for the kill. They weren't going to ram because they wanted the *Empress* intact, Nicholas surmised. They must have marked her as a target in Barfleur and then followed her out to sea at a stealthy distance. French pirates were as greedy for gain as English ones, and he was, after all, a marked man.

Beside him, the bleeding crewman groaned and then was silent. There was a bump of hulls as the first French ship secured alongside and the second one began to pull in. Nicholas rose from the deck. They would not use arrows now for fear of striking their own.

Nicholas's crew had been decimated and he knew there was no hope. Pirates, French or otherwise, did not take prisoners unless for an enormous ransom, and no ransom raised could be higher than the price of the *Empress*.

As the first raiders swarmed aboard, Nicholas stumbled to the prow and unhitched the lantern. Then, deliberately, he torched the rigging. There was another hard bump as the second French vessel came alongside and began disgorging her crew. A bearded Frenchman roared out of the darkness, steel flashing in his hand. Dropping the lantern, Nicholas ducked under the swing of the huge sword, chopped with his axe and leaped aside. The pirate writhed on the ground, clutching his splintered shin. Nicholas snatched the guttering lantern from the deck and set the sail alight.

'Get the bastard, get him!'

Nicholas was rushed from all sides. Abandoning lantern and axe, he leaped on to the wash strake and then dived into the sea. The water embraced him in icy black arms, closing over his head, drawing him down. The cold stunned him and made him want to gasp, but he held the spasm down in his lungs and kicked for the surface, breaking water like a seal.

Around him was the glittering darkness of the sea, illuminated by the sprinkled gold of a ship on fire. Men's voices bellowed with panic. The *Empress*'s mast and yard burned like a ragged crucifix, tatters of flame fluttering to entice the white deck and sides to join the dance of destruction. By the illumination of the fire, he could see men peering in the water, searching for him. One jabbed with a spear, as if harpooning fish.

'Leave it, the sea will deal with him soon enough,' a heavy French accent snapped. 'If we don't put out this fire, we'll lose our prize.'

Nicholas trod water, his teeth chattering. The sea was like liquid ice upon his flesh. When the pain of its embrace turned to numbness, he knew that he would die. Perhaps he had cheated his end, perhaps he had been meant to drown years ago on the Wellstream causeway. They were out in mid-Channel, much too far from land, even if he knew the direction without stars to help him.

A wave slapped over his face. He gulped and choked, his eyes stinging. Through sea-water tears, he watched the *Empress* continue to burn like a pagan offering, or a funeral pyre marking a hero's departure from the shores of the living. He began to succumb to the dreadful seduction of the cold, salt womb. The Widow-Maker, the Norse sailors called her in their fanciful way, only now that fancy was all too real. Without hope, and yet driven by his stubborn nature to fight on, Nicholas began swimming.

CHAPTER 28

Miriel pressed her hands into the small of her back and prayed that the gnawing ache would go away. For two days it had sawed at her loins. Seated or standing, no position was comfortable and she still had another four weeks of carrying to endure.

She was rapidly arriving at the conclusion that she should never have run away from St Catherine's. She should have attended studiously to her devotions, obeyed every command of Sister Euphemia no matter how petty or onerous, and she should have bided her time. Abbess Hillary had entertained great hopes for her, if not of her vocation, then of her practical abilities. One day she might have held the power of an abbess in her own hands.

Miriel sat down at her tablet frame, gave the squares of shaved antler a quarter turn and pulled through the weft thread. In the convent she might have chafed at the confinement, but at least she would have been safe from the hammers of the world. But then, the hammers of the world had been what she wanted, and to wield them to shape her own destiny.

Another quarter turn and she abandoned the braid loom, rising again to pace the room. She had made a disaster of that shaping. Now she was just as trapped as she had been in the convent, and in far greater danger. She cupped her hands either side of her mountainous belly and wondered with fear how something so enormous was going to squeeze out through the narrow passage between her legs. She had asked the midwife, who had said with the amusement of knowledge that the lump was not all baby. Much of the swelling was liquor, and the afterbirth. The information had eased Miriel's fear, but not dispelled it entirely. She was still half convinced that the midwife was wrong.

The room was too small to contain her restlessness and she wandered outside. Elfwen had been overseeing the washing of the bed linens and the huge wooden laundry barrel steamed in the yard. The line was draped with sheets, bolsters, and, more ominously, with long strips of linen to make swaddling bands for the baby and pads for the imminent mother.

Miriel looked at them and then looked away. Everywhere she went there were reminders of how quickly her time was running through the hourglass. Others burdened her with their advice and expectations. Elfwen was busy with her preparations the day long, singing as she toiled and thoroughly looking forward to the event. The women of the neighbourhood frequently called with gifts and wisdom garnered from their own experiences, none of which Miriel wanted to hear; yet, like a child with a ghost story, she could not help listening with pricked ears and horrified fascination. At mass the priest reminded her that because of Eve's sin she should expect to suffer, to bring forth her child in pain. And because her sin was worse than Eve's, being adulterous, Miriel knew that she would receive no mercy whatsoever from God.

Robert revelled in the sensuousness of her pregnancy. He would stroke and caress with fascination until Miriel was fit to slap his hands away. There was something distorted about his attentions. He was delighted by the enlargement of her breasts and liked nothing better than to fondle the swollen blue-veined globes, or take his satisfaction between them now that the size of her belly made ordinary copulation impossible. She was glad when his business took him away.

Rubbing her back, she moved towards the lush greenery of the orchard. The moist grass soaked the hem of her gown, changing the costly blue wool a darker, even more expensive shade. Apple blossom concealed the branches in clouds of scented pink and white, and beneath the trees three goats grazed voraciously.

It was a scene of pleasure and contentment, but the harder Miriel tried, the more difficult it was to feel a part of it. Instead, her mind wandered from a sea of grass to a wide, grey ocean. Where was Nicholas now? Did he ever think of her, or was all his attention taken up by his wife and the imminent birth of his other child? She looked down at her belly. He did not know that he had fathered this one. There had been no contact between them since that day in Boston. She had half hoped that he would seek her out, and within that half-hope was a dream that he would abduct her over his shoulder so that she could abjure all responsibility for the deed and yet still have her heart's desire.

Wicked and selfish, she thought with a grimace, and also impossible. Why should he seek her out when he had a wife at home, a red-haired wife who knew all the tricks of the brothel and was also carrying his child? Impatient with herself, she flounced from the orchard. There was to be no peace anywhere, for her thoughts went with her.

As she reached the yard, the ache in her spine pushed deeper, enclosing her loins. She stopped for a moment to absorb the sensation and as she did so, Robert came striding towards her, his expression smug. He had been meeting with fellow wool merchants in town, and had dressed prestigiously to suit. A fine new belt girded his tunic of Lincoln greyne, emphasising to all the wealth encompassed by his paunch. The unkind might have said that it was difficult to tell between him and his wife, which one was carrying the baby.

He greeted Miriel with a kiss and the present of a woman's girdle that was fashioned to match his belt. 'For when you are slim again,' he said, patting her belly. 'Thomas Thorngate made it for me.'

Miriel forced a smile and thanked him, for it was a handsome piece, if not entirely to her taste with its ostentatious tooling.

'Only the best for my wife.' Taking her arm, he steered her towards the house. She could feel the spring in his step, the coursing of pleasure and vitality, and wished that she felt the same. Her body was as heavy today as a lead ingot, matching her spirits.

Robert made her sit on a bench and bade Samuel bring a flagon of wine. Then he sat beside her and talked of this and that – the trivial details of his meeting, the price of fish in the market, the weather. The nagging ache in Miriel's spine intensified and her feeling of oppression became laced with dread. She knew this manner of Robert's. He was biding his time because he wanted to tell her something of moment, something that needed its build-up of suspense. The habit had always irritated her, but now she was afraid too, for although there was pleasure in his eyes, there was no gentleness.

Reaching for his wine, he took a deep swallow that left red droplets trembling on the ends of his moustache. 'Do you remember the time you asked me not to speak of Nicholas de Caen, and I agreed not to do so?'

Here was the crux of the matter, Miriel thought, realising that she should have known the subject. 'I remember it well,' she replied, 'but I suspect that you are going to break your word.'

Robert took another large gulp of wine, then bared his teeth. 'Believe me, sweetheart, I have little desire to speak of the man to you. There is enough of his presence in this room already.' He looked at her belly, then at her face. 'But speak I will, this once, and then nevermore. I swear it on my soul.'

Miriel's feeling of dread increased. She had an overwhelming urge to stuff her fingers in her ears and refuse to listen, for whatever Robert had to say was going to be unpleasant.

'He is dead,' Robert announced in a voice heavy with satisfaction. 'Drowned in mid-Channel between Barfleur and Dover when his ship caught fire. All his crew as well. I heard it from Geoffrey Packman who was recently in Boston. Martin Wudecoc's still at sea, but I suppose the news will filter to him soon enough.'

'I don't believe you.' Too late, Miriel did thrust her fingers in her ears, but the words were already out, the damage done.

'Nevertheless, it is true. I would not bring such a tale home unless I was sure.'

'And how can you be sure?' Miriel cried through the web

of disbelief and despair that was entangling all thought and motion. 'Rumour and gossip at merchant gatherings are never reliable!'

Robert sighed. 'I can understand that you want to think I am lying, but believe me, my sources are more reliable than mere merchant rumour and gossip. He is dead, sweetheart. Have a mass said for his soul if you wish, I am not without compassion, and then forget him.'

A bitter, distorted compassion, Miriel thought as she doubled over, the pain of loss rippling through her. How could it be true? Nicholas was too competent a sailor to fall victim to the mistake of a fire at sea. She had not saved his life out on the marsh for it to be squandered before his child was born. 'No!' she howled, as the pain redoubled and vicious pincers enclosed her loins.

Dimly, through the agony, she sensed Robert leaping to his feet, all patronising complacence flown and his voice loud with panic as he shouted for Elfwen. His sudden move sent the cups of wine crashing over and a splash of cold red liquid filled Miriel's lap and soaked through her gown to join the hot trickle of birthing fluid and blood between her thighs. Fire and water. She was drowning and burning at the same time and the only one who could help her was dead.

'Mistress Willoughby's hips are too narrow to allow for the passage of the child's head,' the senior midwife said, emerging from the birthing chamber to confront the pacing Robert. She made a nervous washing motion with her hands. 'If we do not act soon they will both die.'

Robert suppressed the urge to grab her by the throat, hold her against the wall and shake her. 'Then act,' he said through clenched teeth. Miriel had been in labour for almost two days. Her screams had stopped some time ago because she had lost her voice. Robert did not know which was worse, the sounds of suffering, or of silence. At least while she had been crying out he had known that she still had her strength. He balled his fists and hoped that Nicholas de Caen was in hell, then found himself wishing that the bastard was still alive so that a death less merciful could be devised for him.

The midwife still waited, washing her hands, dancing from one foot to the other as if in desperate need of the privy.

'Well?' he snapped.

'The difficulty is that we can save your wife, or save the child, but not both,' she said. 'She has not carried the babe for the full term, but there is still every chance for its survival . . .'

Robert looked at the frightened, white-faced woman. The decision was easy and he did not even pause for thought. 'Let the child die,' he said, a hint of triumph lurking in the rage of the last word. Neither sower nor seed would be left to gall him now.

She bit her lip. 'You are sure? It is likely that with the damage done, she will never bear you another one.'

Robert snorted with humourless laughter at the irony of that remark and the midwife recoiled from him with eyes full of shocked revulsion. 'It is of no consequence to me,' he said. 'Only a man who is unsure of himself needs the prop of an heir to bolster his importance. Go, do what you must to save my wife.'

The woman swallowed. 'I will do my best, Master Willoughby, but even so, the travail has been very difficult. It might be God's will that neither of them will live.'

Robert's eyes narrowed to slits. 'If my wife dies, Mistress Midwife, then I swear by all that is holy you will never practise in this town or anywhere again.'

She faced him bravely, although her body was trembling. 'I will do my best because it is my code to do so, not because in your overwrought state you threaten me,' she retorted with spirit, but sped back to the birthing chamber like a coney running back to its warren after a narrow escape from a stoat.

Robert cursed. He hated being helpless and dependent. All his life he had seized what he wanted. If at first it was unattainable, perseverance had always yielded its reward. He had wealth and influence, homes in the expensive quarters of Nottingham and Lincoln, a young and vivacious wife who had made him three times as rich as before . . . and then beggared him by her affair with a younger man. Now she threatened to leave him entirely destitute and he was enraged to know that he was as powerless as a straw in the wind. Arranging a death was a simple matter of spending enough silver. But he could not make the same bargain for a life.

There was pain that went beyond pain and continued for ever. Even when Miriel could bear no more, even when she had gone beyond the point of giving up, it shook her like a terrier shaking a rat, refusing to let her go. The midwife and her assistant murmured words of encouragement and urged her to drink their potions. They massaged her belly with fragrant oils and unbound her hair to prevent her braids from tying the child in her womb. To no avail. The time arrived when Miriel realised that she was going to die, and she found herself willing the moment to happen.

There came a point where she thought that it had, for suddenly she found herself rising out of her body and floating effortlessly above it, and the pain was gone. She could see herself upon the bed and the midwives bending over her. They murmured to each other, and she heard one of them say that it was a mercy. Though she no longer felt pain, there was a great deal of blood. And then she saw the baby, or what was left of it. A scream welled up inside her, but she had no voice. She tried to escape, but instead of floating away, she was drawn closer and closer to the scene. Darkness encroached, and suddenly the pain returned in a great, red gush. Hands pinned her to the bed and a cup was forced against her teeth.

''Tis all right, my lovely, over now,' murmured a soothing voice. 'Drink this, 'twill ease the pain.'

A bitter liquid stung her raw throat. She choked and swallowed. 'My baby,' she tried to say.

'Hush, you sleep now.' A maternal hand soothed her brow.

She fought against it, but she had no strength. All her limbs were as heavy as lead weights and every movement sent ripples of white fire through her groin. 'It's dead, isn't it?' A foolish question, since she knew the answer even without seeing the flicker of compassion in the woman's eyes.

'Don't think about it, loveday, just you rest. You've had a mortal hard time,' the midwife murmured.

How could she not think about it? Did they believe she was so out of her wits that she did not realise they had crushed its skull so that her narrow frame could expel it from her womb? Nicholas drowned, his child . . . their child dead. 'You should have taken me, not an innocent babe,' she whispered.

'Not in our hands, mistress, 'twas your husband made the decision.'

'He was the last one you should have asked,' Miriel gasped.

The midwife's hand continued to push Miriel's soaked tawny hair off her brow. 'He loves you very much, mistress,' she said in a tone that was meant to console, but only increased Miriel's sense of desolation.

'He loves himself,' she replied, and turned her face to the wall.

In the house of Martin Wudecoc, the loft shutters were open, admitting a stream of morning sunlight and the sounds of wharfside bustle. On the bed, Magdalene gave an almighty groan, her face red and contorted with effort, and then slumped, panting.

'A son, a fine little lad,' the midwife said with a smile as she lifted a bawling, bloodied scrap of life from between Magdalene's spread thighs.

The new mother reached frantic arms for him and clutched him to her, all wet and slippery as he was, and howled her anguish and joy with him. 'I want Nick to see him!' she sobbed. 'I want him.'

'Hush, it's all right, I know, I know,' Alyson Wudecoc wiped Magdalene's face with a cold cloth.

'No you don't!' Magdalene swatted her away. 'You still have a husband and a father for your children!'

Mistress Wudecoc recoiled, biting her lip. She exchanged glances with the midwife.

'Here, wrap him up before he catches cold.' The woman held out a square of linen and a blanket to Magdalene, offering practicality to dilute the concentration of volatile emotion.

Magdalene took the items, grateful for their respite. As she cleaned the birth fluid from her son with the linen, she examined each delicate, perfect feature. Nicholas's hands in miniature, the tiny nose that would one day be a masculine version of her own, the delicate eyelids lined with lashes of dark bronze-gold. Her heart filled with a pain so great that it almost tore her apart. Nicholas would never know their child, and their child would never know his father except by pictures made of words told by others.

Stephen Trabe had brought her the news of the *Empress*'s sinking, but he did not have to tell her. She had known the moment she saw him on her threshold a week ago that something had happened to Nicholas. Her first reaction had been to slam the door in his face and shut out his tidings. If she did not hear them then they couldn't be true. But he had hammered on the wood with the hilt of his sword and offered to bellow his business like a street crier, and so she had been forced to open up and let him destroy her world.

'Nick wouldn't let his ship catch fire, he was too good a sailor for that,' she had protested.

Trabe shrugged. 'It happens,' he said laconically, not meeting her eyes.

'And why were there no survivors? Why did they not abandon ship and take to the row boat?'

'Perhaps there was no time; perhaps they were overcome by smoke. Not being there, we cannot know, and it is pointless to speculate.' Closing the subject as firmly as his mouth, he had escorted her to the home of Martin and Alyson Wudecoc, clearly keen to be rid of his obligation. Ever since then she had lived in a world devoid of any feeling except despair. When she slept it went away and so she had spent most of her time courting slumber in the loft chamber, the shutters closed against the intrusion of the day. There was no one to whom she could talk. Alyson Wudecoc was a shoulder to cry on and they had shed tears together for Nicholas's loss, but Magdalene did not know her well enough to make of her a confidante. Martin was still at sea, so she could not talk to him of her doubts and fears or ask him to speculate with her as Stephen Trabe had refused to do.

Then, last night, her labour had started. She had welcomed the gripping, physical pain, had seen it almost as an extension of her suffering. Now, with her baby in her arms, and her womb still cramping as it strove to expel the afterbirth, her grief and joy were almost unbearable.

'How is the little one to be named?' enquired the midwife as she tugged gently on the cord, encouraging the afterbirth to descend from the womb.

'Nicholas, for his father and his father's memory,' Magdalene said in a cracked voice, and put the now warmly wrapped baby to suckle at her breast. As the tiny mouth tugged at her nipple, the pains gathered and cramped in her loins and rose to her heart.

Chapter 29

Nicholas knew that the cold would kill him before he could drown. He had seen it happen to men before; in the winter it was a matter of minutes. How long he had been in the water he did not know, but he could scarcely feel his limbs. He knew that he was pushing his arms and legs in the semblance of a swimmer's stroke, but he could no longer feel the sea against them, and each thrust of effort was more difficult than the last.

He thought about giving up, about letting the sea take him down into dark, green sleep. The idea grew seductively in his mind. Why fight? Then he became aware of his father swimming beside him, an enormous sea-washed gash in his ribs. The image matched him grimly, stroke for stroke, forcing Nicholas to battle on.

'You bastard, let me go,' Nicholas gasped weakly, and immediately coughed as he gulped yet another mouthful of sea-water.

'You wanted to die in your bed, did you not?'

Nicholas heard the words in his head and knew that they must be his own. His father was a vision, a trick played by his mind as he fought for his life.

He considered defying the spectre and just letting himself go under, but the even rhythm of its stroke, imagined or not, forced him to plough on.

'Good boy,' his father said in the same tone of patronising encouragement he had used in life to both his dogs and his son. 'Not much farther now.'

Farther to what? Nicholas wondered, not daring to open

his mouth and enquire lest he swallow more sea. Certainly not to shore. The attack had come in mid-Channel, more miles from land than he could swim. To death then, to becoming a mind-shadow like the image in the water at his side.

And then he heard it, the soft dip and plash of oars, the clunk of wood rotating in the rowlocks, and the muted sound of voices. Briefly he debated whether to cry out. Happen-chance he had swum in a circle and returned to his would-be killers. He reasoned that death by a single dagger thrust would be little different to death in the water. If both were imminent, he would take his chance. Drawing breath, he used the last of his strength to shout for aid.

The sound of oars stopped. He yelled again, choked, spluttered, shouted. There was a muttered debate, and then he was answered in rapid French. The oars splashed once more and out of the darkness rowed the dripping outline of a small nef, her strakes painted the colour of blood. A lantern gleamed on the low wash strake and by its light the pale ovals of bearded faces searched the water.

'Here!' Nicholas bellowed, waving his arms. 'Here!'

Someone cried and pointed. The small vessel came around and Nicholas swam the last few strokes to the extended oar. They hauled him aboard as if landing a large codfish and stooped over him in consternation. One of their number continued to search the water with the lantern, then swung back to address Nicholas.

'Was there anyone else with you?'

His cheek pressed to the cold planks of the deck, his body riven by shudders of cold, Nicholas spewed sea-water and weakly shook his head. 'No one.'

'I could have sworn I saw two of you . . .'

'If you did it was my father,' Nicholas croaked, 'but he's been dead twelve years.' He slumped. Dimly he was aware of them stripping him naked and swaddling him in coarse, dry blankets like an infant. Rigors shook him as if he were in the throes of a seizure. The oarsmen took up their places again and began steadily to row. Closing his eyes, Nicholas slept with an exhaustion so deep it was almost death.

It was dawn when he woke, his eyes opening on tangled

skeins of pink and grey cloud undershot by the fire of the rising sun. The prow of the small nef, rising and falling through shallow troughs of sea, was pointed towards a hummock of land on the horizon. Her sail had been broken out, and the bold green and gold stripes surged taut-bellied with wind. He stared up at the snapping canvas and licked his lips. The taste of dried salt burned his tongue and revived his memory. He had no idea who had rescued him or where he was, but they were the reason he was not dead.

Very gingerly, he eased himself to a sitting position. The nef was crewed by four men and a youth in early adolescence and they were going about their tasks with the cheerfulness of men who were not only homeward bound, but confident and at ease in each other's company.

It was the boy who noticed that Nicholas had stirred, and pointed it out to the tall, fair-haired sailor on the steering oar. The man nodded, gave care of the oar to the youth and stepped down into the well of the vessel with the rolling gait of an experienced seaman.

'You had a fortunate escape,' he addressed Nicholas, his flint-coloured eyes narrow and shrewd. 'Very few men are granted the grace of being plucked from the water if they are wrecked or fall overboard.' He spoke French but with a strange accent that Nicholas was unable to place.

'I know, and I am as grateful to you as I am to the Almighty,' Nicholas replied.

The man grunted. 'Don't count your blessings quite so soon,' he said. 'Not all of us wanted to pull you from your grave. Some said you were the sea's meat and the sea's meat you should remain.' He glanced over his shoulder at a couple of the sailors who were jesting together, their faces bright with the morning light and devoid of all malice.

'Then why am I not a corpse floating somewhere out there?' Nicholas huddled into the blankets. He still felt cold, as if the marrow of his bones had been replaced with ice.

'Because your clothes say that you might be worth keeping.' His saviour indicated the garments flapping on a rope attached to the mast. 'They say that you might be a rich man whose loved ones will pay a fine ransom to have you back.'

By which statement Nicholas immediately understood that he had been captured by pirates little different to those who had come upon him in the night and tried to take his life. He snorted with amusement at the irony of the situation. Sea-wolves had been paid to take his life, and now he was to pay similar men to restore it.

'And if my clothes lie?'

The man shrugged and smiled, exposing a huge grin marred by a missing front tooth. 'Then the fish feed well; but I don't believe that your clothes lie. It was God's will that you were saved, and His intention that we should be rewarded before we get to heaven.' There was a hint of self-mockery in the corners of the grin.

Nicholas returned it as best he could, aware that it was a poor travesty for his teeth were chattering. 'Then you had better hope that I live to write my ransom note,' he said, 'for just now I am not so sure that I will.'

'We're almost in port; you'll recover.' The man strode up the ship and returned with a small flask. 'Galwegian usquebaugh,' he said. 'To put the fire back into your belly.'

Nicholas knew all about Galwegian usquebaugh. He had fallen victim to its excoriating strength when the *Empress* had been commandeered by English barons for a diplomatic visit to the Scottish court. He took a tentative sip and felt the familiar burning sensation, followed by a warm numbness. 'Which port?' he asked to discover if his lips and voice still worked.

'Of St Peter on the Isles de Genesies,' said his captor. 'My name is Guichard le Pêcheur and I've lived here all my life.'

The Islands in mid-Channel then, and the former haunt of Eustace the Monk. Nicholas wondered if le Pêcheur had been a henchman of the latter and decided not to ask.

'And you are?' The sailor nudged Nicholas with his foot, plainly desiring a response since he had revealed his own name and place.

'Nicholas de Caen, ship's master of Boston and Southampton,' he replied.

Guichard le Pêcheur stroked his beard and looked thoughtful. 'Is that so?' he said softly. 'Is that so indeed?' And, turning from Nicholas, returned to the steer oar.

Nicholas was kept under house arrest in a stone dwelling not far from the jetty where his rescuer's small nef was moored. In full daylight and seen from without, she was not a vessel of prey, but one designed to slip in clandestine silence through the water. A ship for carrying men and messages in secret, as Nicholas suspected she had been doing when they picked him up. If she had been on her outward journey instead of on her way home, he knew he would certainly have been left to drown.

Nicholas was furnished with some of Guichard's spare clothes which hung on Nicholas's wiry frame like sacks. Guichard's wife, an outspoken woman almost as large as her husband, made him eat gargantuan meals as if she were feeding him up to be the main course of a feast. She also kept the household keys attached firmly to the ring at her belt and gave him no opportunity whatsoever to escape, being aided in her vigilance by a burly serving man. It was made clear to Nicholas that one step out of line would force his hostess to chain him to a barrel of salt fish in her undercroft.

Guichard set his ransom at one hundred marks, equivalent to eight sarples of the finest wool. 'You're worth more than that, but I'm feeling generous,' he said with a sarcastic grin. He set a sheet of vellum before Nicholas together with a pot of ink and a trimmed quill. 'Can you write, or do you want a scribe?'

'I can write,' Nicholas said, managing to keep the anger from his voice. He would hate to make le Pêcheur feel less than generous. He picked up the quill. 'My ship's master, Martin Wudecoc, will deal with the ransom. I will write to my wife also, and let her know I am safe. She is great with child and her time is very near.'

Guichard nodded. 'I've no quarrel with that,' he said gruffly and left the room, giving Nicholas once more into the custody of his giantess wife. Nicholas wondered how much force it would take to overpower her and decided not to try. Instead, he dipped the quill in the ink and started to write.

Soon after he had finished the letters Guichard returned from his outing. The smell of the tavern was on his breath, his colour was high, but he was far from drunk.

'I knew that I had heard your name mentioned before,' he announced triumphantly. 'There was a contract of five hundred marks for your life, but it's being claimed by a French crew. They're telling all who will stand them a drink that you drowned when your vessel caught fire in mid-crossing.'

The cold at Nicholas's core returned. 'Did they also say at whose behest?'

Guichard shook his head. 'Don't be a wood-wit. Such matters are always arranged through another party, but I tell you this' – he wagged a scarred forefinger – 'you must have a powerful enemy to warrant such a price.' Curiosity and fresh appraisal gleamed in his eyes.

Nicholas laughed bitterly. 'It's a family tradition. But if you ask me to name the man responsible for my price, then I must disappoint you, for I do not know.'

'Oh, come now, you must have an inkling.'

'Inklings are not facts.' Nicholas shrugged and eyed the two rolls of vellum before him on the trestle. 'Nor will I point a finger until I know the truth.'

Guichard nodded at the statement and rubbed the side of his jaw. He looked at his wife. 'A hundred marks is a paltry sum when held against five hundred,' he remarked in a voice devoid of expression.

'You cannot kill a man already dead,' Nicholas responded in a similar tone.

A wintry smile parted Guichard's fair beard. 'No, but I can resurrect one for that price,' he said.

Miriel was woken by the sound of an April squall blustering against the bedchamber shutters. It rattled the slats and shook the latches as if seeking entrance to the darkened room beyond.

She pulled herself up in the bed and stared dully around

the room whose walls had been the boundary of her world for the past three weeks while she recovered from the childbirth that had almost killed her. Most of the time she slept, if not naturally, then with the induced oblivion of poppy in wine for she could not bear to be awake with her thoughts. Her grief was a wave so huge that she had no notion of how to sail on it to survive. Nicholas and their child, murdered both. Although she knew that the baby had been taken from her, the blood that still stained the linen pad between her thighs was like a continuous accusation.

Two days ago she had begged Elfwen to put a powerful sleeping dose in her wine so that she might slumber for eternity. Shocked, the young woman had burst into tears and refused. The request had been reported and vigilance increased. Now she was scarce left alone for a moment lest she take it into her head to hang herself with a bedsheet, or tip over the brazier and set the room alight. She had contemplated both and decided against them since they were fallible, involved yet more suffering and would take too long. Death by sleep would have been easy and gentle.

She was alone, but not for long, she knew. Either Elfwen would appear, or Robert, or one of the women he had employed to tend her. Miriel stretched out her hand to the cup on the bedside. It was empty of all but sticky lees and the tantalising smell of the drug that would grant her oblivion. She licked her lips, feeling longing and nausea and disgust.

Footsteps sounded on the stairs, two sets, and she heard Elfwen's voice, bright and talkative. Miriel lay back and closed her eyes. She had no wish for visitors.

The door opened. Although her lids were shut, she saw with her ears. The click of the latch, the familiar thrusting sound as the wood caught slightly on the floor, the creak of the hinge.

'Of course, she may be asleep,' Elfwen said.

'Then wake her. I haven't come all this way just to listen to her snoring,' said Alice Leen in her peremptory voice. 'Small wonder if this is a sick room. It smells like one! Let's have these shutters opened!'

'But the light, it disturbs her!'

'Hah, then let her be disturbed. She can't lie there for the rest o' her life like a grub in a cabbage leaf.'

Miriel's irritable apathy was enlivened by a spark of indignation. Opening her eyes, she struggled up against the bolsters and was in time to see Alice Leen hobble over to the shutters and free the catches. A glorious, sun-washed spring day gusted into the room, flapping the wall hangings, fluttering the garments on the clothing pole and chasing away the cloying smell of poppy-seasoned wine.

'Better,' said Alice, sucking her teeth in approval, and turned round on her walking stick to stump over to the bed where Miriel was squinting at her, thoroughly bedazzled by the return of so much light.

'Didn't think you were asleep,' Alice commented, easing down on to the stool at the bedside.

'What are you doing here?' Miriel demanded, her tone less than welcoming.

Alice did not seem in the least put out; indeed, she grinned. 'Elfwen told her mam she was worried about you, and her mam told me. Said as you'd taken the loss of the babe hard and were refusing to leave your bed.'

'It is no concern of yours,' Miriel said with a furious look at Elfwen who was wringing her hands.

'I didn't build up my weaving trade to see you squander it,' Alice snapped. 'Only sold it to you because I thought you were a woman after my own heart – strong as sword steel and able to withstand the blows of the world. Now I find you malingering in bed feeling sorry for yourself instead of picking up the pieces of your life.'

Miriel pushed herself further up and back against the bolsters. Anger surged through her. 'If you knew anything about my life, you would not dare to come here and say such things,' she said furiously. 'My child is dead and I am in living death. Your paltry weaving weighs as nothing in the balance when compared to that. Go away and bother the monks with your tongue, not me.'

Alice too drew herself up to do battle. 'I know more than enough about your life,' she spat. 'God's eyes, I've lived more than the half of it myself, and most of the time I did not have your pampered advantages. Do you think I wallowed abed in misery when my babies died or when a childbirth went wrong and I was sick? I didn't have that luxury, my girl. Folk were depending on me. If my cloth wasn't sold, then my weavers didn't eat. And that weighs in the balance more than a child that never had the opportunity to know the gripes of starvation, or a wench who would rather turn her face to the wall than square up to her responsibilities!'

Biting her lip, looking frightened at the storm she had unwittingly unleashed, Elfwen fetched Alice a cup of wine.

Rendered speechless, Miriel stared at the old woman. Her tirade had been as effective as a bucket of winter water in the face. Poisonous old besom, was Miriel's instinctive response, but beneath that, beneath the defensive anger, was the shameful knowledge that Alice's savage words contained a shred of truth.

Alice downed the wine and it went straight to her cheeks, tinting the vellum hue of her skin with apple-crimson. 'You get out of that bed and on your feet. The past's for leaving behind,' she said with a vehement nod at her own wisdom.

The tart comment came to Miriel's lips that Alice did not practise what she preached in the matter of her former business where her nose was always intruding, but she bit it back. 'It is not always so simple to leave it behind,' she remarked instead.

'Never said it was.' Alice thrust the cup at Elfwen and walked on her stick to Miriel's dress pole. Her hands plucked and sorted. 'You could open a clothing stall with all these,' she said.

A memory came to Miriel, surfacing with all the clarity and brightness of the April day pouring into the room. Herself standing in a graveyard, consumed by a hideous, louse-infested grey dress with green embroidery; Nicholas laughing as she cursed him. The incident had been neither amusing nor pleasant at the time, but in hindsight it seemed both. If only she had known then what she knew now. If only she had stayed with him. Instead, she had trodden her own thorny path to disaster and cushioned it along the way with fine clothes and material goods. Now the rich dresses through which Alice was sorting might as well have been beggar's rags.

'Here.' Alice returned to the bed with a gown of deep rose-pink wool. 'Wear this, it'll give you some colour. I want to see those weaving sheds, and you can't show me from your bed.'

Miriel found herself being bullied into donning proper clothes for the first time in three weeks. Elfwen combed and dressed her mistress's hair, cross-gartering the plaits with strips of rose-coloured braid, her every movement anxious and swift as if at any moment she expected Miriel to sink back into her world of drowsy apathy.

Miriel submitted to her attentions with resignation. It was easier to swim with the tide than fight against it, and standing up to Alice had exhausted her reserves.

'Better,' Alice said as she viewed the maid's finished efforts. 'You don't look like a lost soul any more.'

Miriel grimaced. 'Appearances can be deceptive,' she said on a lingering echo of contrariness.

The act of leaving the bed and walking across the room made Miriel feel weak and dizzy, as if her soul had indeed been lost to her body and, newly reunited, had no concept of how to deal with a cage of flesh. She clutched the doorpost for support. Mouth firm with determination, Alice thrust her walking stick into Miriel's hand. 'Use this,' she said. 'You need it more than I do for the nonce.'

Miriel took the stick. Descending the loft stairs was an ordeal and there was sweat on her brow by the time she reached the main room. The smell of onion pottage wafted from the cooking pot and one of the spinsters was tending it in between twirling yarn from distaff to drop spindle. She looked astonished to see Miriel, and stammered words of welcome. Miriel managed a weak smile in return and progressed slowly outside.

The wind snatched at her garments and almost stunned her with its bright strength. Linen sheets hung on a rope to dry, snapped like the billowing sails of a ship. The sunlight dazzled her eyes which had been accustomed only to darkness for the past three weeks. For a moment Miriel was filled with panic and wanted nothing more than to turn tail and hide in the smallest, darkest corner she could find. As if sensing her mood, Alice took her arm in a firm grip and drew her forward.

'You've come this far,' she said. 'You can go a little further.'

And so Miriel crossed the yard, each step taking her from the dark cage of her sick-bed and into the world she had once known. In the weaving sheds she was greeted with pleasure. The clack of the looms as the sheds changed was like a heart-beat, the flow of the shuttle the pulse of blood. The scent of raw wool hit her like the aroma of cooking and she experienced a hollow hunger that she had not realised existed. Alice was right, life did go on, even if it was irrevocably altered.

The old woman was watching her with her sharp, miss-nothing eyes. 'Aye,' she said. 'This is what you need.'

Robert returned from an outlying hamlet two days later. Miriel had abjured the loft chamber for a cushioned bench in the weaving shed. Alice Leen had stayed to keep her company and was enjoying her role both as guest and unofficial supervisor of the weavers.

'Be a surprise for your husband to find you up and about,' she said as they heard the clatter of hooves in the yard and saw the stable lad go running.

Miriel murmured appropriately and rose to her feet. She was not looking forward to greeting him. He had watched over her in her illness and made sure that if he was not by then she was always well attended. He had been gentle and thoughtful, caring for her every need with a devotion that others perceived as selfless and which Miriel found cloying and self-seeking. He had what he wanted and he could afford to be magnanimous. It was as if she had leaned against a rock for support and discovered too late that its firm surface concealed a devouring mouth that was slowly engulfing her. Not once had he mentioned the dead child or acknowledged that she needed to grieve. It was a distasteful incident and now it was dead and buried – in an unmarked grave.

Slowly she went out into the yard. Robert stopped in the midst of dismounting and stared at her. Then his lips parted in a delighted grin. He took his foot from the stirrup and strode to greet her. 'Sweetheart, what a glad sight for road-sore eyes!' he declared and kissed her on either gaunt cheek and then full on the mouth.

She held herself stiffly under his embrace, the image of the engulfing rock so powerful in her mind that it was all she could do not to wrench away. The wet mouth, the fringed bristle of beard like a mollusc, the intrusion of his expanding merchant's belly against her own, empty and barren now. Nausea surged. She clenched her stomach.

'If Alice had not dragged me out, I would have stayed in my room until I died,' she said.

'Alice?' He looked round and as his eyes fell on the old woman watching him by the weaving sheds, his lids tensed. 'Not that interfering old sow.'

'If not for her, I would still be in my sick-bed instead of welcoming your return,' she defended, beginning to wonder if Alice's intervention had been a blessing or a curse. Without it, Miriel could have turned her face to the wall and feigned sleep to greet her husband's arrival.

'Then I will bear with her,' he said with a forced smile. 'But I hope she is not staying long.'

'I think not,' Miriel answered, knowing that Alice would likely depart with the morrow's dawn. Robert's antipathy was returned full measure where the old woman was concerned. And her own antipathy? Miriel went to fetch him a drink, falling into the customary habit of a wife and feeling as numb inside as an empty vessel. She could not fill herself with Robert's love, for it would be like drinking poison. Her sustenance, as before, would be her work. The fine bolts of cloth would be her offspring. The resolution caused an involuntary shudder to ripple up her spine as she looked at Alice, scowling on the bench, and saw herself in forty years' time.

Robert was in an expansive mood that evening. His business was flourishing. The death of Maurice de la Pole had been the turning point and he was amassing wealth as swiftly as the layer of fat around his waist. 'Who knows,' he said, in between taking decisive bites out of the chicken thigh in his fingers, 'by next year I could buy us a title. How would you like to be Lady Willoughby and a have a fine manor house to accompany your gowns?'

Miriel smiled so as not to cause confrontation. What would he say if he knew what lay under that old wooden coffer in the store room? She could have a fine manor house now if she wanted, would have jumped at the chance once, but now it seemed not to matter.

'Hah!' Alice sniffed from her end of the table. 'A beggar may put on the robes of a king, but he'll always be a beggar underneath.'

That did make Miriel smile, but it wiped the smug expression from Robert's countenance. 'And old hags are always old hags,' he snapped. 'You can smell them a mile off.'

'There's stinks far worse than old age,' Alice retorted and, wiping her hands on her napkin, took her drink and went to sit by the fire.

'If she doesn't leave tomorrow, I promise I will throw her out,' Robert said through clenched teeth.

Miriel shrugged. 'She does it deliberately, and you always rise to the bait.' She pushed her own trencher aside and rose. 'I'm going to retire, I'm weary.'

He looked at her from beneath his brows and bared his teeth to nibble the last shreds of meat from the bone. 'Aye, bound to be when you've so soon risen from your sick-bed.' He glanced over his shoulder at Alice, then turned back and lowered his voice. 'I wish I could retire with you. It's been too long since I've held your warmth in my arms.' He waved the bone at her as she recoiled in horror. 'Oh, I know it's too soon yet,' he said in an understanding voice. 'It wouldn't be decent or sensible, and I'm a patient man. The Church says a couple should abstain from the carnal act for forty days after a birthing.' From his pouch he produced a small tally stick scored with several notches. 'By my reckoning, this is the eve of the twenty-third day. A little more than two weeks. I can wait.' He gave her a slow, lustful smile, then wiped his lips on his napkin and hitched at his crotch where the thought of bedding with her had plainly caused a reaction. 'Excuse me, wife,' he said. 'I must visit the privy.'

'Glad I'm naught but a stinking old hag and past all that kind of attention,' Alice said from her corner.

Miriel swallowed and, without reply, climbed the stairs to the loft. Once within, she closed the shutters, barred the door, and curled up on the bed, arms crossed, knees bent like a child in the womb.

CHAPTER 30

Sitting at ease in the long barge, his arm around Miriel's shoulders, Robert watched the Boston wharves come up on either bank of the Witham. They passed the messuage plots and manse belonging to the great Crowland Abbey and sailed beneath the bridge that spanned the river and gave access to the market place, St Botolf's Church and the lands belonging to the Gilbertine monks of Malton Priory. The first quay was on the left bank, but the barge-master's destination was the wharves higher on the right bank beyond St Botolf's.

Numerous vessels were moored along the timber-shored river bank, some disgorging their cargo, others being loaded by hand and by crane. Others rolled at anchor in sleepy hiatus between journey's end and journey's beginning. Gulls circled and screamed over the rubbish heaps, or waited their opportunity perched above the cookstalls and taverns. Equally as raucous, the human populace went about its daily business, but without the gulls' saving grace of immaculate flight.

The barge in which Robert and Miriel travelled was laden with bales of cloth: lozenge-woven green and blue for the Norman market, plain tabbys that would be sold in London, and soft, napped scarlet for the Italians. All of it was produced from the wool he procured for Miriel's busy looms. They made a good partnership, a strong one. He reached for her hand and engulfed her narrow fingers within his possessive grip. As far as he was concerned, this journey was a repeat of the one they had made just after their wedding, and, as such, it reaffirmed their relationship with each other.

Since the churching ceremony yesterday which had purified

her body from the pollution of childbed and given them leave to have carnal knowledge of each other again, he had scarcely left her side. He could not get enough of her. Even in the supreme moment of pleasure he was greedy for more, could not wait to rise and fill again so that he could repeat his taking, claim her womb for his own and know that she was his equal now that she was barren. Truly they were two halves of a whole.

As they approached the higher quay, Robert saw several cogs lapping at anchor, amongst them *Pandora's Daughter*. Wudecoc was in port then, but only lately arrived, for the cog bore the signs of a hard sea voyage and her cargo was still aboard. Even now, Wudecoc was likely being told that he no longer had a master – only a mistress, a former whore with no more idea of the shipping trade than a baby had of politics. The business was doomed, but perhaps to seal its fate he could arrange the loss of another vessel. Half smiling at the thought, he looked at Miriel to see if she had registered the presence of the cog, but she was staring straight ahead, her eyes dry and blank. Robert leaned back and relaxed, the smile seams deepening around his eyes.

The barge-master punted beyond the spire and buildings of St Botolf's Church and pulled into a small mooring space on the higher quay close on the wool warehouses of Malton Priory. Another, larger cog, similar to *The Pandora* in size, was moored along the wharf. Her castle mast rippled with a banner of red silk, appliquéd in gold with mythical beasts that from a distance looked remarkably like the royal lions of England. But the crew bore no sign of the royal device upon their motley garments and no court officials or hangers-on cluttered the decks, just a fair-bearded man with a garish cloak of red and yellow vertical stripes that somewhat resembled a sail.

Robert pointed out the curiosity to Miriel. 'I wonder who that could be,' he said.

She nodded and looked with a dutiful murmur, but her eyes remained distant, and Robert was filled with the uneasy notion that despite the possessive grip in which he held her, she was inexorably slipping away from him.

* * *

Miriel listened to the sound of Robert whistling as he clumped away down the outer stairs of The Ship's loft chamber, and as the sounds faded, uttered a quiet sigh of relief. He was going to meet a prospective client and her time for the rest of the day was preciously her own.

She flapped aside the covers and left the bed with an alacrity caused by distaste at being there in the first place. Reaching for her clothes, she glanced down at her body. Although she had not suckled a child, her breasts were fuller and softer than before her pregnancy, with dark, reddish-brown nipples. Her belly, although taut, had a slight curve which gave the false impression of fecundity, and was marked with tiny silver striations. Robert seemed to find these changes in her body fascinating and had insisted on leaving all the candles burning when he claimed his right. While his eyes remained wide open, avidly absorbing every facet of the act, Miriel had kept hers tightly shut.

With a grimace at the memory, Miriel drew her chemise over her head and picked up her gown. As she freed her hair and shook it out, Elfwen tapped on the door and cautiously entered the room. Miriel knew that the young woman had been waiting below in the main room for Robert to leave. The girl was long accustomed to his morning routine, and knew when to stay away.

'The green dress, mistress?' she said and with cheerful efficiency took a gown of fine sage-coloured wool from the travelling coffer. She shook out the perfuming shreds of cinnamon bark and gathered up the yards of fabric in the full skirt so that she could drop the garment gently over Miriel's head. Will yapped around their feet, playing his usual game of grasping the hem in his teeth and tugging until Elfwen's foot shovelled him off and Miriel clapped her hands at him.

'I saw Master Wudecoc in the courtyard,' Elfwen added as she laced the back of the gown, her fingers working a brisk criss-cross of the green cords. 'He'll be hoping to see you or the master.'

Miriel inhaled sharply, and not because of Elfwen's lacing.

Martin Wudecoc was the closest link with Nicholas that she had. Perhaps he would know what had happened to the *Empress*; perhaps he could explain how Nicholas and his entire crew had come to die when they were such experienced sailors and their vessel one of the finest to sail in northern waters.

Her fingers were clumsy as she pinned her wimple and fastened the neck of her gown with a silver brooch.

'Mistress, are you all right?' Elfwen asked in concern. 'You're whiter than me mam's best sheet.'

Miriel gave her maid the travesty of a smile. 'No,' she said, 'I doubt I will ever be all right again in this world, but I cope. That is all any of us can do if we want to survive.' Straightening her shoulders, she drew a deep breath and went down the outer stairs, through the passage and into the tavern's main room.

Martin Wudecoc stood near the great hearth contemplating the flames as they helter-skeltered up the chimney's throat and vanished. His hands were clasped behind his back and his wind-burned features wore an expression of weariness and deep melancholy.

The sight of him filled Miriel with a flood of pain and grief too great to be dammed. As he turned towards her, she uttered his name in a breaking voice and ran into his arms. The salt tang of his tunic and beard filled her nostrils. He didn't smell exactly like Nicholas, but there was an echo and she clung to it with the desperation of a shipwrecked mariner clinging to a spar of wood in a tossing ocean.

With the aplomb that had earned him his place as Nicholas's most senior master, Martin did not push her away, but held her fast as if he was accustomed to such occurrences.

'My wife gave me the tidings as soon as I stepped ashore,' he said. 'We are all in deep mourning.'

'It can't be true.' Miriel raised her head from the comfort of his breast and searched his eyes. 'Nicholas would never have been caught out by fire.'

Gently Martin held her away. 'Nevertheless, it seems to be what happened. From what I have been told, the burned-out shell of the *Empress* was towed into St Peter Port on the night after it happened by a passing fisher craft. They searched the water for survivors, but there were none. My source is reliable; you can speak to him yourself if you want.'

Miriel wiped her eyes on her sleeve. Martin's gaze was shrewd and perceptive and it was too late for discretion. 'I would like that,' she said, recovering some of her composure. 'My husband only gave me the bare bones of the tale, and I was in no state to understand them at the time.' She signalled the hovering landlord to bring a flagon and sat down at the trestle against the fireplace.

'I love him,' she said as Martin seated himself across from her and poured the wine into two cups. It was Gascon, red as blood and strong. She shook her head. 'I could have had him once if I had listened to my heart and ignored my reason.'

'Yes, I know,' Martin said. 'I have heard the story from Nicholas's wife. She insisted that I seek you out and tell you what I know.'

Miriel's heart lurched with jealous pain. 'Magdalene – she is here in Boston?' She lifted her cup and took a long drink.

'She's staying with us during her confinement,' Martin said, looking at her, then away. 'Two nights ago she was safely delivered of a son. He has been christened Nicholas in memory and honour of his father.'

Miriel swallowed another mouthful of wine, forcing it downwards against the rising bile in her throat. She was disgusted with herself to feel a jealousy so strong that it was almost hatred. 'I bore a son too,' she said, the words pitched low, but filled with molten intensity. 'They christened him in the womb before they killed him and Robert said that they should call him Nicholas.'

That shook Martin's composure. She watched him blench and felt a small surge of satisfaction, followed by remorse. 'We were lovers,' she said wearily. 'Robert found out when I quickened with child. Nicholas never knew. When he married Magdalene, I shunned all contact.' She looked at him, her eyes quenched of light. 'Now it is too late to make amends or say all the things that lie heavily on my heart. What was between us is stretched like an unfinished piece of cloth on the loom with half the colours missing, and now it will never be completed.'

Martin cleared his throat. 'I am sorry,' he said.

Miriel laughed bleakly and finished her wine. 'So am I.' Abruptly she rose to her feet, knowing that if she sat there any longer, one cup of wine would not be enough. 'Take me to your source. Let me speak to him.'

Martin's eyes flickered. 'What about your husband?'

'He is gone for the entire day at least.' She pulled a face. 'Until tonight, my time is my own.'

Martin took her down to the quayside where the barge had moored yesterday. Everywhere there was vigorous activity. The process of loading and unloading, embarking and mooring, filled the morning with noise and colour. Miriel stepped over coils of rope and around cartloads of lead awaiting transport down the coast. The crane was busy this morning offloading great tree-trunks of Scandinavian timber from nef to barge.

Martin's destination was the cog moored next to the nef, a fine-looking vessel which Miriel recognised from the previous day as soon as she saw the red and gold banner rippling on its castle.

'Belongs to Stephen Trabe,' Martin said. 'Ever heard of him?'

Miriel shook her head. 'Should I have done?'

Martin shrugged. 'Not particularly, but he has had a notorious career. At the moment he is a respectable servant of our young King, but in the past he has made his living from unsanctioned piracy.'

'And he is your reliable source?'

'Trabe is intimate with haunts that others of us would fear to tread,' Martin said ruefully as he halted at the foot of the cog's gangplank in response to the challenge of two burly guards. One of them boarded the vessel with Martin's message, and moments later they were ushered on deck and brought into the presence of a fair-bearded man seated on a barrel.

He looked neither disreputable nor piratical to Miriel's

gaze, save perhaps for his loudly striped cloak. His hair and beard were neatly combed and his tunic and chausses were fashioned of the finest wool and linen.

Martin introduced Miriel and said, 'You have already told me what you know, but I would have you tell Mistress Willoughby too.'

Trabe sucked his teeth. 'And what would Mistress Willoughby's interest be in Nicholas de Caen?' he asked, his bluntness revealing that he was not as polished as he appeared.

'He was a dear friend of mine,' Miriel answered, 'and I owe it to him to know as much as possible.'

'You owe it to him?' Trabe raised an eyebrow.

Miriel flushed, but met him stare for stare. 'Yes, I do.'

Trabe's brow rose another fraction and so did the corresponding mouth corner in a sardonic smile. 'There is little enough to tell, mistress.' He spread his hands. 'In this trade it is very easy to make enemies. Someone wanted rid of him and offers were put about in certain quarters, including mine. A rich payment in return for ridding the world of Nicholas de Caen. I declined because I no longer swim in waters quite so murky, but there were others willing to take the bait.'

Miriel whitened and swayed. Martin reached an arm to support her but she pushed him aside as if swatting a fly. 'I thought as much,' she said huskily. 'I knew that his death was no accident; he was too good a sailor.' She swallowed, feeling sick, but filled with a renewed sense of determination. 'Do you know who put out those offers?'

Trabe shrugged. 'As to that, I have not an inkling, except that their agent was a tall man with red hair and beard and a bad French accent – English was his native tongue. The description would fit any of ten thousand men. I had never encountered him before.'

'And you are sure he gave nothing away about his paymaster?' Martin asked.

'I am sure. Jesu, I would like to know myself.' Trabe scooped his hands through his hair. 'I did warn de Caen on the eve of his departure for Normandy, but there was no time for him to take precautions. God rest his soul.' Trabe touched a gold cross at his throat and looked at Miriel. 'Do you have any thoughts, mistress, on who might have wished him enough ill to seek his death?'

Miriel locked her knees to stay on her feet. 'None,' she whispered, thinking of Robert. He had motive enough, and she knew the passion and cruelty that went sword in sheath with his smothering tenderness. But was he capable of murdering in cold blood? As Trabe said, theirs was a trade where it was easy to make enemies. There were likely as many candidates as there were red-bearded men . . . but some were more likely than others.

Magdalene leaned against the bolsters, seeking to quench the heat of her body against the coolness of the linen. A nagging headache throbbed at her temples, her breasts were tight and sore with milk and there was a dragging pain in the small of her back. The linen pad between her thighs was damp and uncomfortable with fluids from her draining womb, and she was aware of an underlying unpleasant smell. It irritated her nose and made her queasy. The ravenous appetite of the previous two days had vanished to leave her gagging even at the thought of bread and cheese, but her mouth was dry with thirst.

'There is nothing wrong with me,' she said aloud and was encouraged by the strength of her own voice. How could she be sick when her lungs still commanded such power? By her side, the swaddled baby gave a sudden start in his sleep and clenched his little fists, but she had only fed him an hour ago and he did not waken. Her heart filled with a great flood of love and her eyes with tears. 'Nick would have been so proud of you,' Magdalene whispered, 'so proud.' She pushed her forefinger gently through the curl of his fist and watched the miniature fingers tighten around her own, the nails like tiny shales of pink glass. 'I will make you into the man he would want you to be,' she said, the vow like an anchor, grounding her to life, giving them a future beyond this bedchamber and the bed upon which she had borne him.

She fell into an uneasy doze, patterned with strange colours, sludgy but violent, and dreams of wading through sucking mud towards a shoreline that came no closer. Exhaustion crept up on her and it became increasingly difficult to pull herself free of the mud's clinging embrace.

The sudden slam of the door on its hinges awakened her with a cry and a start. For a moment the colours and the mud persisted. As her vision slowly cleared, she drew a deep unfettered breath.

Alyson Wudecoc hastened to the bedside, her normally pale complexion flushed and her eyes as bright as if she had just drunk a quart of wine. Carried in her hand was an unrolled square of vellum inscribed with lines of erratic brown writing hung with a red seal. There was also another packet, as yet unopened.

'Wonderful news, Magdalene!' she cried, wafting the vellum at the new mother and handing her the packet. 'Nicholas is alive!'

'What?' Magdalene strove to sit up amongst the bolsters. A drum-roll of pain pulsed within the hollow of her skull. Alyson's words were difficult to understand, as if shouted from a distant shore.

'He's being held for ransom in St Peter Port on the Isles de Genesies by a fisherman who plucked him out of the water,' Alyson said breathlessly.

'Praise be to God!' Magdalene crossed herself. Scalding tears filled her eyes and brimmed over. She wiped them away on a corner of the sheet, her body shaking. Alyson's arms swept around her, and for a moment the two women clung to each other.

'That's a personal letter for you,' Alyson said at length, gently releasing Magdalene and pointing to the packet. There was a troubled frown on her face for Magdalene was as hot as a forge and there was a faint but unmistakable smell of tainted flesh.

Magdalene reclined against the bolsters. In the aftermath of her tears, everything was suddenly such an effort, and although she had but recently woken, she felt exhausted. 'I am not lettered,' she said to Alyson. 'You read it to me.'

'They want five hundred marks for him,' Alyson warned as she took the packet and broke the seal. 'Martin says he thinks we can raise it, but you'll have to sell the *St Maria* and the *Pandora.*'

Magdalene shook her head and then wished she had not as the pain knifed through her skull. 'I don't care,' she said. 'I'll pay any price to have him back . . . to see him again.' She looked at the sleeping baby, and new tears filled her eyes.

'Martin's raising the ransom even now,' Alyson murmured soothingly and began to read the letter. Magdalene closed her eyes.

> *My beloved wife, greetings. I hope this letter finds you in as good health as I am myself. I counsel you to be of stout heart, for although the* Empress *is lost, I am not and hope to be with you and our child very soon.*

The words continued, flowing over her like cooling water. How much he was thinking of her, how she must rest and not worry. All would be well. It was a peaceful notion and she clung to it, sinking ever deeper into its embrace.

Alyson finished the letter and looked at Magdalene. Very gently she laid her hand against the young woman's burning skin, then lifted the covers and sniffed. Hand over her mouth, she replaced the sheets and stood away from the bed. Then, on tiptoe so as not to wake the patient, she left the room and went in search of a physician.

After leaving Stephen Trabe, Miriel returned to The Ship in a daze. She had much to think upon. She knew that the easiest path was to be deaf to all that she had been told, to pretend that none of it had ever happened. Bury it deep and continue her life with the force of will not to look over her shoulder. It was probably the wisest path too, and the pragmatic side of her nature, the one her grandfather had fostered within her as a small child, said that she should follow it. But there were other sides of her character bequeathed by different elements, and they barred the way, turning her back on to a road that was narrow and difficult and strewn with thorns.

She chewed at the nail of her index finger which was already worn almost to the quick. If Robert had plotted Nicholas's death, then she was almost as much to blame, for without her adultery, Robert would never have been prompted to act. Yet she had no proof and could hardly ask Robert outright if he had paid someone blood money to murder his rival. It was likely that Nicholas had enemies of whom she did not even know. Which brought her back in a far from neat circle to the smooth, easy path, barred from her by conscience and guilt.

'God curse it!' she snapped and in sheer frustration snatched her small gilded mead horn from its stand and hurled it at the wall.

The horn struck and bounced off, splashing the white lime-wash with teardrops of pollen-yellow, and Will leaped in the air and began to bark. Miriel stared, thinking that the stain should be blood-red. She badly wanted to hurl something else, but she clenched her fists at her sides. Wrecking the room might ease the pressure of her frustration, but it would not solve her dilemma. Flinging from the table, she paced the length of the room like a caged animal, and ignored Will worrying at her skirts.

There was a knock on the door and Elfwen poked her head round. 'Master Wudecoc's below and asking to speak to you privately. Shall I send him up?' Her eyes travelled to the amber splashes trickling down the wall. Out of tidy habit she went to pick the mead horn from the floor.

'Leave it,' Miriel snapped. 'I'll do it myself. And yes, tell Master Wudecoc to come up.'

Elfwen nodded and, giving Miriel the slightest look askance, left the room.

Miriel stooped to the horn. A piece of the enamelling had broken off and its polished surface was scraped with chalky lime. She dusted it on her skirt. Like herself, it had been unfairly battered by life but, although bruised and damaged, was still intact. She smiled bleakly at the whimsy and lifted her eyes to the door as again it opened on a knock, and this time Martin Wudecoc stepped over her threshold.

'What can I do for you?' she asked. This morning they had parted in silence, each weighed down by the burdens laid on them, and neither able to talk. It had been difficult and uncomfortable, and she was surprised to see him now.

Surprised too, as she looked at him, to see fire in his eyes and hope imprinted on his dragged-down features.

'It is what we can do for each other, mistress,' he said. 'News came an hour ago that Nicholas is still alive. He was saved from drowning by a Genesies islander who is now demanding a ransom to protect him and send him home whole.' He waved a square of vellum at Miriel.

A shock of joy surged through Miriel. 'Say it again,' she commanded. 'Say it again so that I know I am not dreaming.'

Martin repeated his words and with a cry, all constraint forgotten, she flung herself into his arms, and once more used his breast as a support for overwhelming emotion.

'I knew he couldn't be dead; I knew it!' she laughed, and could not prevent a whoop of exultation. Will joined in, his yap rising to a howl in competition. Miriel sobered and, scolding the dog, wiped her eyes. 'I'm sorry,' she said, 'but I could not help myself, the news is so wonderful.'

Martin smiled briefly to show that he shared her sentiment, but added a word of caution. 'Indeed it is, mistress, but he is not safe yet, and to ransom him, we will have to sell at least two of the ships. With the *Empress* lost, it will leave him small hope of fulfilling his obligations unless he hires others vessels – and for that he will need money.'

Miriel drew a deep breath, and with it donned the mantle of hard-headed businesswoman. 'Is this the ransom demand?' She indicated the vellum.

Martin handed it to her and she studied it.

'Five hundred marks.' She frowned at Martin. 'He doesn't want a fortune, does he?'

Martin grimaced. 'This Guichard le Pêcheur knows that he has a golden goose in his hand. It may be that we can negotiate a lower sum, but with another price already on Nick's head, I do not believe it will be wise to tarry. Magdalene has given her permission for me to seek buyers for the *St Maria* and the *Pandora*.'

'No,' Miriel said forcefully. 'You cannot sell the ships.'

'We must. We can raise perhaps a hundred marks in coin, but not the sum demanded.'

'Will le Pêcheur accept instalments?'

'He might, but not small ones. Once Nicholas is free, he might not feel so inclined to pay up.'

Miriel bit her lip and turned away to pace the room, but this time in slow, measured thought. At the window she paused and looked out on the bustle of the courtyard below: a cartload of supplies arriving; a groom busy with a curry comb on a guest's mount; a woman collecting eggs from the hen boxes.

'Do not sell the ships,' she said without looking round. 'I will go surety for four hundred marks of the ransom. Only give me a week to raise the coin.'

'You can raise four hundred marks?' There was incredulity in Martin's voice.

Miriel gave a wintry smile and turned round. 'Yes, I can,' she said, 'otherwise I would not have offered. I may have been a fool over some parts of my life, but never where my wealth is concerned. All I have to do is find the right buyer for what I have to sell.' When he opened his mouth, she lifted a forefinger to silence him. 'My mind is made up, and when Nicholas knows what I have done, he will approve, I promise.' She returned the vellum letter to Martin's bemused hands. 'It is between him and me; call it the settling of an old debt. Within a week, you have my word.'

CHAPTER 31

'Leaving for Lincoln on the morrow?' Elfwen gazed at Miriel in surprise and doubt. 'What will Master Willoughby say when he returns here and finds you gone?'

Miriel fastened the straps on her travelling coffer and feigned nonchalance. 'Master Willoughby will say nothing. It is a matter of trade, and that he understands well enough.' *Even if he understands little else.* Although she was afraid, her need and her will were far greater than her fear of her husband. She would deal with the consequences later, if consequences there were. What Robert did not know would not trouble him.

Elfwen chewed her lip and looked worried. 'I did not mean to listen, but I overheard some of what you said to Master Wudecoc.'

Miriel flashed round. 'You mean you were eavesdropping on the stairs. How dare you!'

'No!' Elfwen cried, stretching her hand in supplication. 'I came to ask if you wanted wine and I saw you in Master Wudecoc's arms. I thought for a moment . . .' Her face flushed. 'I thought you were lovers,' she whispered, 'and then I realised you were speaking together of Master de Caen.'

Miriel thought frantically back over the conversation, but could recall nothing incriminating. 'What of it?' she snapped. 'He is a good friend and his trade causes ours to prosper. Why should I not help him all I can?'

Elfwen shook her head. 'Mistress, be careful,' she said. 'I may be your maid, but I am not simple. Four hundred marks is more than help. I do not believe that Master Willoughby will agree to it.'

'Master Willoughby is not going to know,' Miriel said curtly. 'Unless you tell him.'

'I won't say anything. I may hear things, but I can keep a close mouth,' Elfwen answered with an air of injured dignity. 'I am just warning you to have a care. I know Master Willoughby's never raised his hand to you or any of the servants, but that doesn't mean he's soft.'

Miriel left the packed chest and removed her wimple ready for sleep. 'Neither am I,' she said grimly.

To which Elfwen did not reply, although the maid privately thought that her mistress was wrong. Her toughness was no more than a protection of bone encircling a tender marrow.

Miriel slept restlessly and woke before sunrise for the fifth time, just as the sky was starting to lighten. The shutters were closed and the room still rested in pitch darkness, but her sense of time was good. When she quietly freed the catch and pushed the wooden screens wide, it was upon a grey-tinted world where all the colour had been strained into the scents of the cool early air: baking bread and dung; silver fading starlight and dew; the creamy sweetness of honeysuckle and the blue aroma of woodsmoke. She inhaled appreciatively, and then withdrew her face and used the morning grey to dress. On the town dungheaps the cockerels had started to crow their challenges, the sound blending with the melodic song of smaller birds and the husky cooing of pigeons in the tavern's large white cot.

On her pallet Elfwen stirred and turned over with a mumble, but did not waken, nor did Miriel seek to rouse her. It was too early to make their way to the travelling barges on the Witham but she was too restless to remain abed and wait for the light to strengthen and others to rise. As silently as she could, she unbarred the door, clicked the latch, and crept from the room.

Stepping into the cool, dawn air, she became a part of it, her charcoal-coloured cloak blending with the greyness, her hair tinted with the faintest hue of gold as the eastern sky continued to pale. She paced the perimeter of the courtyard, measuring her steps, controlling the urge to stride out. In the stable block, a horse turned its head from a manger of hay to snort at her. Further down the line a lantern had been kindled on a shelf and by its light she could see a saddled horse. The sound of voices came from within the stall, low and urgent.

Remembering her anger at Elfwen for listening on the stairs, she grimaced to herself and began to turn around, but the inflection in one of the voices caught her ear and held her fast, for it sounded like her husband's. Instead of walking quietly away, she tiptoed very softly forward and paused where she could see within the stall and not be seen herself.

Robert's mount was tethered to the bridle ring in the far wall and was champing hay out of the manger. Robert himself was standing to one side, arms folded, legs planted wide in a stance that Miriel had come to know and loathe. His expression was furious, face thrust slightly forward, complexion dusky and eyes staring. In the shadows, facing him, stood someone else whom Miriel could not see.

'Good Christ, what foolery led you to pursue me here?' Robert snarled. 'I pay you to keep your distance unless I call the tune.'

'You pay me for many things,' a gravelly voice replied, 'and I dance to no man's tune.'

'What do you want?' There was anger and perhaps just a hint of fear in Robert's tone.

'I followed you here with news, but plainly you don't want to hear it, so I'll take it elsewhere.' He began to thrust past Robert to the door, and as the wool merchant caught him and pushed him roughly back into the stable, Miriel received a clear view of the man's face. He had pox scars on cheek and brow, craggy bones and a bush of red hair, repeated in the thick curl of beard cupping the long jaw. Oh God, it was him; the one of whom Stephen Trabe had spoken. The go-between who had sought men willing to take Nicholas's life. Miriel stifled her shuddering breath against the back of her hand. It couldn't be coincidence. She sucked in her stomach muscles, binding her belly to her spine and forcing herself not to heave.

They would hear her and, whatever the depth of her horror and revulsion, there was still more to be learned.

'You'll go nowhere without my leave!' Robert hissed. 'I own you; don't you forget it. No one walks out on me!'

'And I own your soul as surely as you own mine,' Redbeard retorted, thrusting him off. 'I could sing ugly songs in certain quarters about a weaver who never came home from the tavern because you wanted him out of your way, or a wool merchant who died in an alley so that your territory would not be threatened.' There was a long pause and the ruffian's voice grew soft with menace. 'Or a sea-captain who overstepped the mark with your wife. Best pray that I don't choose to open my mouth. And it wouldn't do to pay someone to close it. Word gets around and there's more loyalty among thieves than there is among wool merchants like you with important fat bellies.'

There was a sudden scuffle. Miriel heard the sound of a blow, a solid punch like a fuller pounding a bale of felted cloth. Robert gave a strangled wheeze. Two more thuds followed in rapid succession, hard and deliberate, and the choking sounds increased. 'I don't like to see a job go unfinished, even for a bastard like you, so I'll tell you that you've been cheated,' Redbeard panted, and there was note of pleasurable triumph in his voice. 'Nicholas de Caen still lives. Some fishermen plucked him from the sea half drowned and now they're selling him back to his family. If you need my services you know where to find me. In the meantime, I'll pay myself for the information, shall I?' A grunt of effort accompanied the noise of leather purse strings being slashed from a belt.

Miriel ducked into an empty stall and just had time to crouch at the back before the red-bearded man came striding down the walkway. He was leading Robert's horse and tucking Robert's full purse into his own belt. As he reached the stable entrance he placed his foot in the stirrup and swung astride.

Miriel waited until she heard the disappearing clop of hooves in the yard, then stood up and went to the end stall. Robert's nose was bloody and one eye was rapidly swelling shut. A slick line of spittle tracked down his face and glistened in his beard. Miriel eyed the damage with pleasure. It was less than he deserved, much less, and it was fortunate that there was not a pitchfork to hand for she would have used it.

As it was, she drew back her foot and kicked him in the groin as hard as she could. As he doubled over with a choking sound of surprise, she tore her wedding ring from her finger and threw it at him. 'You murdering bastard!' she hissed. 'I curse the day I ever made my vows to you.'

'It's not what you think,' he groaned.

'No,' Miriel snapped. 'The truth is what *you* think, isn't it? All manipulated and twisted to seem so reasonable that only a madman would believe there was another way.'

'It's your fault. I did it for you.' Clutching his genitals, he looked at her like a small boy caught out for a misdemeanour and indignant at being taken to task.

'For me!' Miriel choked.

'You wouldn't get rid of that old weaver, your heart was too soft, so I had to do it for you,' he said in a tone that suggested he was being reasonable and she wasn't. 'And Maurice de la Pole would have stopped the supply of your wool or made the price unaffordable. I had to do something about him; anyone in my position would not have hesitated for a moment.' He held out a reasoning hand. 'Nicholas de Caen made fools of us both. I only ordered his killing for your own good.'

'You are mad!' Miriel said with revulsion. 'And if you are not mad, then you are truly evil.'

He eyed her in bewilderment. 'I am neither,' he said. 'I am just a man who has taken life by the horns and grappled it to the ground rather than let it trample me. Surely you understand that.'

Miriel did, and because she could see the glimmer of his warped reasoning, she felt sullied herself. Once, she too had taken life by the horns and grappled it to the ground, survival of her own needs all that mattered. It was easier to believe Robert mad or evil than to see the distorted reflection of her past in his reasoning. 'That does not make it right or mean that I can forgive you,' she said.

Robert straightened with an effort and wiped his knuckles

beneath his bloody nose. 'I am not seeking your forgiveness. I have told you, what I did was justified, and I would do it again a hundred times over to preserve what I hold dear.'

'Then what you hold dear is made naught but dross by your own hand,' Miriel said with contempt. 'I hope you fry in hell when the time comes.' Turning from him, she stalked away. He started after her and caught her by the arm, spinning her round, but as she turned, her free fist drove into his belly and he released her with a retching gasp. Miriel gathered her skirts and ran.

Clutching his stomach, Robert staggered to the stable door and watched helplessly as she vanished from the courtyard, her cloak billowing with her speed. He cursed and groaned, blood dribbling from his broken nose. Her fight and her spirit were what had made him want her in the first instance but, like training a wild mare, he had discovered that saddling was the easy part. Riding was a different matter entirely. Each time that he thought he had the mastery, she threw him and fled so that he had to begin all over again.

Perhaps in a way she was right. Perhaps he was paying a lifetime's ransom for something that was merely dross. He spat blood. Staggering back into the stall, he crouched on all fours and searched among the dung-soiled straw until he found the ring that Miriel had flung at him: a small circle of incised gold set with a single garnet and crafted by the same Lincoln goldsmith who made rings for the Archbishop of York. The circumference was too slender to fit on any of his fingers, but he could imagine it gleaming on Miriel's as she allowed another man to ride her loins and sow his seed in her womb. He could see her hands clenched upon de Caen's back, the gold of her wedding ring imprinting his naked flesh.

Robert closed his bloodied fist upon the token. 'If I cannot have you,' he said, 'then neither can he.'

Miriel banged her fist on Martin Wudecoc's door and looked impatiently up and down the street. Folk were about their early business now and the grey tints of night had been suffused with the clear colours of early morning. She banged on the door again. Surely someone must be stirring at this time; she knew enough about Martin himself to be sure that he was no slug-abed in the mornings. Biting her lip, hopping from one foot to another, Miriel rapped a third time and glanced up and down the street. The reasoning side of her mind told her that she would see nothing. Robert had been too winded to chase her and even if he did make a wild guess and realise that she was seeking succour here, he would be too late. But the superstitious dread remained. She could still see the violence in his eyes as he caught and spun her round, and he had been full of conviction, not remorse for his actions.

With what seemed like the crawling slowness of a castle gate being unbarred, she heard the bolts shooting back and the solid clump of the draw-bar as it was lifted from its brackets. The door opened and a heavy-eyed maid peered out at her.

'I have to see Master Wudecoc, is he here?' Miriel demanded. 'Tell him it is Mistress Willoughby and it is vitally important.'

The woman widened the door to usher her in, but her expression was doubtful. 'No, mistress, he has gone to fetch the priest.'

'The priest?' Miriel looked at her in surprise.

'Yes, mistress. We have a guest who was recently in childbed, and now she is very sick.' The maid glanced towards the loft stairs and made the sign of the Cross on her breast.

'You mean Magdalene de Caen?' Miriel too glanced at the stairs and her stomach lurched.

The woman nodded and, as she did so, Alyson Wudecoc shouted down from the loft opening, enquiring if the knock at the door had been the priest arriving.

'No, it's Miriel,' Miriel replied, and did not bother to use her married title. She was finished with the name Willoughby for ever. 'I need to speak with your husband when he returns. Is there anything I can do?' She climbed the stairs and joined Alyson Wudecoc in the bedchamber. The smell of candle wax and smouldering herbs on the brazier could not conceal the stink of putrefying flesh and Miriel's throat closed.

'You can pray,' murmured Alyson Wudecoc with the weariness of one who has sat in vigil the night through.

'She is beyond all other help. The birth itself went well, but the afterbirth was long in coming and the midwife had to reach deep inside and pull it out. When that happens, it often goes ill for the mother.'

Miriel thought of her own long struggle after being brought to bed. She had wanted to die, by rights should have done after the brutalities visited on her womb, but against the odds and her will, the strength of her body had resisted the final brink. She had no doubt that the woman on the bed was desperate to live, but was being failed by her own flesh.

Taking a deep breath, Miriel squared her shoulders and approached the bed. Sweetening herbs had been strewn among the sheets and perfumed oil burned in cresset lamps on the coffer at the bedside, but the smell of dying still overpowered them. Magdalene lay propped against the bolsters, her breathing swift and shallow. Sweat glistened on her forehead and her flesh carried the silvery-blue sheen of impending death. Against her skin, her braided copper hair blazed like new fire. Small shudders racked her body and her fingers gripped the top of the sheet, the knuckles showing a pressured gleam of bone. She was obviously in great pain. Death might be close, but it was not being merciful and letting her slip away in peace. Miriel bit her lip, feeling pangs of remorse and pity. Less than a year ago she had hated this woman. Filled with jealous rage, she had wished her to perdition.

Walking around the foot of the bed, intending to sit down on the empty curule chair by Magdalene's head, Miriel came upon the heavy cherry-wood cradle and its sleeping occupant. The candle-light fell across the baby's features and she saw Nicholas clearly in the slant of brow and eye and chin. The baby hair was pale gold and grew from the brow as Magdalene's did, and there was a hint of his mother too in the shape of his nose. Miriel stared. There was a great lump of love and longing in the pit of her belly and she felt her breasts tingle as if they still bulged with milk. Her own baby would have looked like this if he had been allowed to live. If she had not failed him and Robert had not— She closed that particular door in her mind and rammed the bolt across. That way lay grey madness.

'We have employed a wet-nurse,' Alyson murmured, 'and he is thriving well. We keep him by his mother. If she is awake and he is not by, it distresses her.'

'I can understand that,' Miriel said, remembering her own bewildered awakening from a haze of soporifics and wine to discover both womb and cradle empty. She sat on the chair and touched her own cool fingers to the burning ones of Magdalene de Caen. They were ringless, but there were fine, white bands of skin where each met the cushion of palm to show that they had recently been well adorned. 'Nicholas is coming home soon, I promise you,' she said. 'And he will live to see your son grow into fine manhood.'

Magdalene frowned and twitched, but her eyes remained closed. Miriel licked her lips. 'This is difficult for me to say, but perhaps it is the only opportunity I will have.' She bowed her head, seeking words that were deep and difficult. 'In the past I have been deeply jealous of you, have wished you ill in my heart for taking what I believed to be mine. I cannot make amends, but I can say that I am sorry. My loss was your gain, but rightfully so and I truly grieve to see you in such extremity. I know how much your baby means to you, and Nicholas too.'

Slowly, with tremendous effort, Magdalene raised fever-heavy lids and turned her head on the bolster to look at Miriel. 'You never lost him,' she said huskily. 'He took me to patch the wound of not having you, and even if I grew into his flesh and his into mine, the wound was still there beneath. In my turn, I too have been jealous.' A bleak smile crossed her parched lips. 'Never more than now.'

There was no reply to that. What could she say when the vitality of life was flowing through her veins and Magdalene's had almost burned dry. She squeezed the dying woman's hand in her own. 'I came here to speak to Martin about Nicholas's ransom,' she said, 'not to gloat at your bedside. I hope you know that.'

The smile had faded from Magdalene's face. She gave Miriel a long, steady look. 'Would you have the charity not to mind if your husband's former leman came in all her beauty and took your hand on your deathbed?'

Miriel bit her lip. 'No,' she said, 'I do not think I would.'

'Well then.'

Miriel released her grip on Magdalene's hand and rose to her feet. 'I'll leave,' she said quietly. 'I wanted there to be peace between us, but I can see that I am only hurting you.'

As she started to walk away, Magdalene's hoarse whisper called her to stop and turn back.

'I want peace too.'

In a flurry of skirts, Miriel returned to the bedside and once more took the burning, outstretched hand.

'I give him back to you.' Magdalene's voice was barely audible. 'With my blessing. Isn't that what you came for?' Her eyes closed, and tears trickled out from beneath the dark red lashes. Miriel brushed the back of her free hand impatiently across her own lids. It wasn't what she had come for, and yet perhaps it had been there at the back of her mind as she first sat down at the bedside. A dying woman's absolution and consent.

'I came to help and be helped,' she said.

For a short while there was silence between the two women, and into it, the baby woke and cried.

'Let me hold him,' Magdalene said. 'Let my flesh remember the feel of him before all feeling is lost to me.'

Miriel went to the cradle and bent to scoop the swaddled child from beneath his blanket. Although she had seldom held a baby before, her arm curved instinctively to support the tiny skull and her body tingled with poignancy and joy. The baby's eyes were open, following the contours of her face with myopic tenacity. They were a misty, sea-haze blue, as yet untinted with their true shade. Miriel wondered if her own child would have looked and felt like this. Gently she brought him to Magdalene and placed him in her arms.

Magdalene stroked the baby's cheek and kissed his brow. 'I'll be watching over you,' she whispered. 'Always, my heart, always.'

His cries increased, becoming the lusty bawl of thwarted hunger. 'See the life in him,' Magdalene murmured, the smile now back on her face, a smile in which grief and joy were inextricably and powerfully bound. 'Take him now,' she said to Miriel in a voice that shook. 'He's hungry and the wet-nurse will be waiting.'

Tenderly Miriel gathered the baby in her arms. 'I lost my own child a month ago,' she said. 'It was either him or me, and my husband chose to sacrifice the innocent. He said it was out of love for me, but I know he did it for vengeance too.' She compressed her lips. There was no point in saying any of this except to relieve the pressure of her own pain. Magdalene was watching her, but Miriel could tell that all her attention was for the baby, imprinting his image on her mind's eye before the fading of her life-force robbed her of sight.

'He will be cared for and deeply cherished, I promise you,' Miriel said, steadying herself.

'I know.' Magdalene gazed for a further moment, then closed her eyes and turned her head to the wall as she had been lying when Miriel first entered the room.

Cradling the baby in protective arms, Miriel bore him carefully down the stairs into the main room. His warmth, the infant smell of him washed over her in waves that sent gooseflesh shudders through her. It was almost more than she could bear to hand him over to the waiting wet-nurse and yield up the moment when she had imagined him all hers.

The woman cheerfully unfastened her gown and bared one large white breast crowned by a thumb-sized brown nipple. With casual expertise she put the baby to suck, and the hungry howls immediately changed to sounds of gratified gulping while the baby's complexion turned from dusky red to pale pink. Miriel watched with rapt fascination.

'Regular little toper,' said the wet-nurse with proud indulgence. 'Takes both sides too when he gets started. Heaven pity the alehouses roundabouts when he grows up.' She stroked the downy head nuzzled against her flesh. 'Shame about his mam though, poor wight.'

Miriel said nothing, for whatever reply she made would have seemed trite and banal in her own ears – the easing of a difficult situation with platitudes that came nowhere near the core of the tragedy.

The door opened on full, glorious daybreak to admit

Martin and a priest, both of them breathless with haste. Martin's glance flickered sidelong in surprise to Miriel and she made a beckoning gesture. With a nod, he showed the priest to the stairs and turned back to her.

'What's amiss?' If he had looked weary the previous day, the exhausted shadows on his face made him appear positively cadaverous this morning.

'I fear I must lay a yet greater burden on your shoulders than you already carry,' Miriel said. His broad chest was inviting, but she resisted the urge to run and cling to him yet again. Instead she drew herself up and clasped her hands, grip upon grip, to pull strength from within herself. Then she told him why she had come.

His expression remained as impassive as usual and he nodded thoughtfully.

'You knew about Robert, didn't you?' Miriel said, for she had seen not so much as a glimmer of surprise in his eyes.

Martin spread his hands. 'I suppose that I suspected, but a suspicion is far from being fact.'

'And it will never be proven because it is only my word against him,' Miriel said. 'Search as you might, I doubt you'll arrest his accomplice, because his confession to truth would be his undoing on a gibbet. I would have said that Robert's jealousy had unhinged him, and blame myself, had he not already secured the death of two others because they stood in his way.'

Martin brushed his silver-salted hair off his brow and shook his head. 'Yet he always seemed so good-hearted, as if he had not a cloud on his conscience.'

'He doesn't, Martin, and that's what makes him so dangerous. He sees no wrong in any of his actions. They have always been the fault of others – so he claims.' She unclasped her hands and spread them. 'I ran from him and came straight here, but I must to return to Lincoln to arrange the ransom money. I know you can't leave affairs as they are now, but could you spare a couple of men to escort me there and back?'

Martin rubbed his jaw and looked at her. 'I'll do better than that,' he said grimly. 'I'll give you half a dozen, and make sure they're armed with spears.' Beckoning to a manservant, he issued brief orders and sent the man out to summon crew members from *Pandora's Daughter*.

Miriel thanked him and sat down by the fire to wait.

'Want to hold him a while?' the wet-nurse enquired, and before Miriel could reply, she found the solid weight of a baby once more in her arms as the woman laced her chemise and pinned the neck of her gown.

Replete with milk, he was drowsy and watched her through heavy, half-closed lids lined with long, bronze-dark lashes. She inhaled his innocent, milky smell. His weight was warm in the bowl of her lap, filling the hollow space of her loss.

From the room above there came the sound of an indrawn breath, a stifled sob, and she heard the priest's voice quietly murmuring words of comfort. Moments later, Alyson descended the steep wooden stairs from the loft to the main room.

'Magdalene's dead,' she announced and turned to her husband's arms for solace.

Miriel held the baby close. She felt the rapid thud of his small heart and the soft swish of his sleepy breathing as it fanned her cheek. 'God rest her soul,' she murmured. 'And give me the grace not to feel like a thief in the night.'

CHAPTER 32

It was late afternoon and almost curfew when Miriel arrived in Lincoln. The sunset flamed behind the trees in the orchard, painting their sparse black outlines on a backdrop of hazy gold. White mist swathed around her ankles as she hastened up from the river to the house.

She was greeted by the permanent servants who were surprised but not alarmed by her sudden appearance and set about preparing a meal of bread and pottage for herself and her escort. A swift enquiry revealed that there had been no sign of Robert. If his intention was to return to Lincoln, he had not done so yet and she was ahead of him.

She had no notion of what Robert was going to do next. Pursue her? Let her go? Not the latter, she thought. He had fought too hard and immersed himself too deeply to draw back. It was a question of evading him and securing Nicholas's release. They were her most important goals for the nonce. She would struggle with all else when the time came.

While the men of her escort sat down to eat, she took a lantern and, keys in hand, crossed the cobbled courtyard to the weaving shed and counting house. The evening was cast with blue light from the rising moon. It slanted through the shutters in thin bars of illumination, aiding her lantern as she moved with the silent swiftness of familiarity between the looms, the tablet frames, the baskets filled with skeins of coloured yarn and the long bench where the bolts of cloth were smoothed and folded.

The lock and hinges of the counting-house door had been

recently oiled after the damp early spring. The key turned soundlessly and the door opened on a cool gust of air. Miriel stepped over the threshold and stood the lantern in a small aumbry set in the wall. On the trestle table stood a neat pile of counters and tally sticks and a set of scales with brass pans. Behind the trestle was a cushioned bench with a panelled back rest. To either side of that were the iron-bound chests that contained the rewards of Miriel's labours. And one chest in particular.

In her mind's eye she saw the gleam of its hidden secret. A ransom fit for royalty – or to reprieve the love of her soul. Miriel knelt on the floor at the side of the chest and freed the catch for a last look at the crown of the Empress Mathilda. Drawing the silk wrapping from the gleam of gold and pearls, she remembered the last time she had knelt here in darkness with Nicholas beside her as if in reverence at a shrine. Then the wild and tender fury of their lovemaking which had both sanctified and desecrated. Miriel touched the crown, absorbing the feel of the craftsman's skill into her fingertips. It was indeed an artefact without price and she would never finish paying the cost of the coveting. Her hand moved lightly down one of the gold fringes to the pearl trefoil trembling on its end while she recalled the pleasures and pains of the flesh.

At length, sighing, she restored the crown to its wrappings and its hiding place and rose to her feet, brushing dusty patches from her gown at the knees. A slight musty smell of damp warred with those of charcoal and the pervading aroma of wool. Miriel inhaled deeply, taking steadiness from such familiarity. Turning to the other chests, she set to work.

That night she slept uneasily on the barge, her cloak for a blanket and her pillow one of her gowns rolled up and thrust hard against the wooden chest. Two men from her escort had taken it from the counting-house and borne it down to the riverside. Now the same two men stood watch while their four companions slept like a row of fish in a barrel in the prow of the barge, leaving Miriel the mid-section.

The night deepened into a chill, dark silence broken only by the lapping of the river against the barge's strakes and the snores of the sleeping men. Miriel dreamed that she was alone at sea on a huge, white-painted nef with a mast of solid gold and a sail of billowing tawny silk bordered with outlandish writing. On the horizon a storm was brewing. Dazzles of lightning split the bank of purple cloud, illuminating it from within, and she could see the rain striking the surface of the sea in a wind-driven veil. The water beneath her grew choppy in anticipation of the storm and she knew that she did not have much time. She had to find Nicholas and rescue him before the lightning struck, but she had been searching for hours already without luck and she did not know what to do now except cling to the great golden mast and cry his name.

As the wind lifted her hair and blew it like a ragged banner across her vision, she thought she heard an answering shout. She ran to the side and looked over the wash strake at the deep, wind-ruffled sea. A dark head, sleek as a seal's, bobbed just beyond the distance of a grapnel rope. She screamed his name and although the sound was torn away across the heaving green whitecaps he heard her, for he looked up and shouted a reply, and began swimming towards her. Lightning split the world from firmament to sea and thunder echoed across the sky like an ogre roaring into the sockets of a skull. Miriel's eyes were blinded by a rush of liquid gold as the deck beneath her started to melt. Sobbing with fear and effort, she seized a coil of rope and succeeded in fastening it around her waist just as the ship dissolved completely and she was plunged into deep, green water.

It was cold and vast, salty as human essence, an enormous womb. Miriel was churned and tossed like an embryo in its vastness until suddenly she felt the umbilical cord of rope snag tight. She was pulled in sharp, hand-over-hand surges until the sea-coldness was replaced by the solid heat of another body and she found herself breast to breast, thigh to thigh with Nicholas. She opened her mouth to gasp his name, but he cupped her face and the heat of his lips took hers and his own love words filled her mouth and were absorbed through her body in waves of liquid heat.

The storm burst over them, flashing and roaring like a huge serpent. She clung to Nicholas, gripping him fiercely, determined that nothing should ever sunder them again. He took the rope and bound it about them, but instead of making her feel secure, its constriction began to burn her flesh and she screamed in pain.

Her dream eyes flashed open on a world of reality. Rain was slashing down, cold and unsavoured by salt, and she was indeed bound by a rope, a narrow length of hemp twine wrapped round and round her wrists. Instead of being bound to Nicholas, however, the other end of the cord was gripped by a mail-clad soldier with a sword at his hip. There were other soldiers with him, all armed to the teeth, the rivets of their mail gleaming as if fashioned of raindrops. Miriel's escort stood in a miserable huddle, held at sword-point.

Miriel struggled to sit up. 'What is the meaning of this?' she demanded in fury and fear. 'Who are you?'

'My name is Milo de Vere, mistress,' said her captor coldly, and there was a curl of scorn to his upper lip. 'I'm one of the sheriff's adjutants.'

'I've done nothing wrong!' Miriel spat. 'Release me at once!'

He inclined his head. 'Indeed I will, mistress, but only into the hands of your husband,' he said, and gave the rope he had been holding to the man who had been standing behind him. 'It is for him to decide what happens to you now. I know what I would do if you were my wife.'

'Robert!' Miriel almost choked on the word as she looked upon her husband. His battered face was ravaged by lack of sleep and his usually immaculate clothes were travel-stained and rumpled.

'Surprised to see me, sweetheart?' he asked with a grim smile that creased his eye-corners but did not light the eyes themselves. 'Well, it's less than I am to see you, and fortunate that I arrived when I did. A runaway wife who robs her husband's coffers to take the money to her lover deserves all that she gets.' He wound the cord around his fist and yanked. 'Get up.'

Miriel needed no prompting. All vestige of sleep had vanished and she was on her feet in a trice. 'The coin is mine!' she spat. 'I touched none of yours. Indeed, I would not want it, stained with murder three times over.' She pitched her voice so that Milo de Vere could hear every word. 'How many more before you shore your breaches? Where will you hide my corpse when you're done?'

Robert wearily shook his head. 'I can only put your persistence in these falsehoods down to an imbalance of your humours after losing your child,' he said. 'Indeed, it grieves me to see you like this.'

'Then let me go,' Miriel demanded, 'and you need never see me again.'

'Tempting, but it would be irresponsible of me in your present state, and I haven't moved heaven and earth to bar your path and then just step aside.' He chewed the inside of his mouth and looked her up and down. 'I'm here to save you from yourself, and, I admit, to preserve my dignity.' He looked over his shoulder to the impassive Milo de Vere. 'You can understand that, I hope, sir?'

The soldier nodded. 'Yes, sir, you can depend on my discretion.'

A look passed between them and, in the brightening dawn, Miriel recognised Milo de Vere. He was a member of the minor nobility, the younger son of a cadet house with but a small parcel of land to his name, land that was intensively grazed by sheep. Robert dealt with his wool clip and, in view of de Vere's connections with the sheriff, had always been disposed to treat him most generously. If Robert could buy death, then loyalty was a cinch.

'Of course he can,' Miriel sneered. 'How much did you pay him? Thirty pieces of silver?'

Robert's hand flashed out and cracked across her face. 'Enough!' he hissed. 'Keep that tongue of yours behind your teeth, or I will do it for you with a wad of your precious cloth!'

Miriel's eyes watered with tears of pain and fury. Her cheek was numb and her neck ached from the whiplash of the blow. The soldiers were watching in silence, but she saw not a single look of censure on any of their faces. Those who were not impassive obviously thought that Robert was totally justified.

He seized her roughly by the elbow and dragged her from the barge on to the towpath. 'We'll talk more about this at home,' he said, the implication being to the other men that once behind closed doors he was going to give her the thrashing of her life, which dignity prevented him from doing in public.

'I don't have a home with you,' Miriel said through her teeth.

His grip tightened on her arm. 'You do for tonight,' he growled and started to drag her along. She cast a glance over her shoulder and saw two of de Vere's men hefting the travelling chest off the barge. The others, on de Vere's instructions, were mustering around Martin Wudecoc's sailors.

'Don't worry,' Robert said with a tight grin. 'Your friends will be released once they've been given a taste of hospitality in gaol. A few good strokes of the lash should quell their eagerness for aiding and abetting theft.'

'You bastard,' Miriel hissed.

'It wasn't me who was born out of wedlock,' Robert answered with a lift of his shoulders, 'nor who bore one.'

Miriel launched herself at him, spitting and kicking, but was brought up short as Robert wound the end of her wrist rope around her neck and drew it tight. 'I hope I do not have to leash you like a dog,' he said with mild distaste.

Miriel choked and clawed, fighting for air. He slackened the pressure a little, enough to let breath tear down her windpipe. 'I'll do it every time you defy me,' he said. 'And yes, it will be for your own good.'

Wheezing, Miriel clutched her burning throat. Solicitous now, he uncoiled the rope from her neck and, wrapping his arm firmly around her elbow, drew her along with him.

'It doesn't matter,' she said, still defiant, if wise enough not to fight him physically. 'Even without my help, Martin will still raise the ransom. He knows that you are responsible for sinking the *Empress* and trying to arrange Nicholas's death. Your time is borrowed whatever you do.'

'Everyone's time is borrowed from God, sweetheart,' Robert replied with a shrug. 'And Martin Wudecoc and your lover do not appear to have got the better of me yet.'

They arrived at the house. Dismissing the goggling servants, Robert bade the soldiers leave the chest in the main room and paid them each a silver penny from his pouch. Will bounded forwards, yapping as usual, his tail awag.

Elfwen hovered on the threshold, staring with huge, dismayed eyes at the cord binding her mistress's wrists.

'Leave us!' Robert made an abrupt throwing motion. 'And take that mangy excuse of a rat with you!' His booted foot caught Will in the ribs and lifted and hurled the little dog across the room. The yaps became pathetic yelps. Elfwen grasped Will, tucked him beneath her arm, and fled.

'There was no need to do that,' Miriel said furiously.

'Christ, I've been wanting to kick the little shit-bag ever since I bought him,' Robert replied with satisfaction and not the slightest glimmer of remorse. 'It's a pleasure long overdue.' He pushed her up the loft stairs to their private chamber and then locked the door. 'We don't want any interruptions, do we?' he said pleasantly.

Miriel sat on the bed and wondered how easy it would be to draw the meat knife from his belt and ram it beneath his ribs. It would be a question of practicality, not conscience. As matters stood now, she could kill him without a shred of compunction. She pursed her lips. He was on his guard and twitchy with temper. It would be difficult, but she was perfectly prepared to try. Perhaps she could lure him to the bed under the pretence of being remorseful and submissive, and when he was in the throes of pleasure, take her revenge.

'I do not suppose that *you* want to be disturbed,' she said, her voice chill and remote in her own ears. It was as if she had carefully removed the emotions from her body and placed them on a shelf out of the way until it was safe to bring them down again. 'What is it you want of me? To prove your "manhood" on my body? To beat me into submission?'

Robert turned from the door and eyed her with a frown. 'Of course not,' he said. 'What kind of man abuses the sick?'

'The sick?' She stared at him.

He tapped the side of his head. 'Well, it is obvious to everyone but yourself that you are suffering from a malady of the mind. You were desperately ill when you lost the child and your grief has overset your wits, hence these preposterous tales of murder and conspiracy.'

'I see. You believe I am mad.' Miriel nodded slowly, thinking it a good thing that her emotions were well out of reach. Her eyes flickered to the knife on Robert's belt. Claiming insanity would be a good excuse for stabbing him in the heart.

'Not entirely out of your mind, but certainly touched by wood-wildness. A danger to yourself and others, and certainly not fit to carry on your trade.'

What a surprise, Miriel thought, and lay back on the bed, one knee raised, her breasts tautly outlined by the firm lacing of her gown. 'So you don't want to bed me.'

His face flushed and he rumpled his hands through his hair in an agitated gesture. 'I did not say that,' he growled.

'Well then, untie me.' She held out her hands and licked her lips.

Robert licked his lips too. He trod purposefully to the bed and gazed down at her. 'If you are out of your wits,' he said slowly, 'then I would be taking a great risk in untying you, for there is no telling what a madwoman will do in the throes of dementia, and I have heard it said that such an illness makes the victim fearsomely strong.' He unfastened his belt and draped it over the coffer, the scabbard still attached. Miriel tried her best not to look at the bone handle of the knife sticking out of the top of the cowhide sheath lest her glance draw Robert's attention.

'If you are not mad,' Robert continued, 'it still means that you believe me capable of murder, and it does not alter the fact that I caught you running away to your lover with a chestful of silver.' He gave a short, humourless laugh. 'I would be mad myself to untie you in those circumstances, you must agree.'

Miriel bit her lip. This was not going the way she intended. 'Please, Robert.' She extended her wrists to him in a gesture of supplication. 'The cord is chafing; I can't feel my fingers.'

'Mayhap not, but they haven't yet turned blue,' he said without compassion. Lifting his tunic, he unlaced the drawstring of his braies. 'Strange that you've never enticed me with your body before,' he mused. 'Either you want me to cut your bonds and it's a ruse – the minute you're free you'll kick me in the ballocks, or you're playing a game. Slave and master. Is that what you like?' He cocked his head to one side and his breathing grew swift as his words drove his arousal. 'Does de Caen tie you up when he fucks you? Is this what you want?' He threw himself on top of her, dragging up her skirts, bucking and plunging.

Miriel gave a single scream as he pierced her and then bit down on her lower lip. She did not fight him, but her body was as tense with the resistance of pain as a bent bow.

It didn't take him long. Desire and rage combined to create a lust so incandescent that it could not be sustained beyond the first bright burn and within moments he was shuddering in the throes of climax. Miriel gazed at the rafters, a sight she had seen a hundred times while Robert had his will of her. She was familiar with every knot and flaw in the beams, every dark shadow and crevice. Now she concentrated on them, holding herself together with their impassive wooden strength.

Gasping, Robert withdrew from her and eased his wilting penis back inside his braies. Then he drew her bunched skirts back over her legs and smoothed them down, not with any tenderness, but as if making a bed after a night's sleep. A task performed to make things neat and orderly.

'I'll untie you when we set out,' he said as he rebuckled his belt and hitched the scabbard until it was comfortable on his hip.

Miriel took her concentration from the rafters. 'When we set out?' she repeated.

He nodded. 'You don't think I am going to keep you here in Lincoln, do you?' he said. 'Not after the dance you have led me. Mad or not, you're an unfit wife. Small wonder that your stepfather wanted to put you in a convent.'

'Then why not just let me go.' She struggled to a sitting position and again held out her wrists to him. 'Cut my bonds and set me free.'

'Ah, sweetheart, that would be too easy, and I'm not the kind of man who lets a debt go unpaid. Besides, heaven knows the tales you might spread and the damage you might do the moment you were out of this door.'

'Then what do you intend?' Miriel asked huskily. She had a horrible vision of him taking her, still bound, to a quiet spot outside the city and disposing of her. He would tell folk that she had run away and no one would ever be any the wiser as to her fate.

'If a convent was the intention of your family, then I can only see fit to follow in their tradition,' he said. 'From St Catherine's you absconded, and to St Catherine's you shall return.'

'What!' The emotion that Miriel had thought safely out of the way on a shelf tumbled off and jolted through her body. 'You'll not put me in a nunnery!' In front of her face, her bound hands mocked her with their pose of dutiful prayer. She clenched them into fists.

'Not as an oblate nun, sweetheart, I agree,' he said with a bleak smile. 'That would be expecting too much of any respectable order of sisters. But there is naught to prevent you dwelling there as a guest. I shall pay a generous corrody to the abbey out of the profits from your weaving sheds, and the nuns will care for your bodily and spiritual needs.' He spread his hands. 'I could not wish for a more perfect answer to my dilemma.'

She tossed her head. 'And you think I will tamely remain as a boarder?'

Robert went to the door. 'Not tamely,' he said as he unfastened the bar and set his hand to the latch, 'but remain you will, I'll make sure of it.' He permitted himself a small, uncharitable smile. 'Or the nuns will.'

He went out, locking the door behind him.

Miriel glared in his wake, and swore like a footsoldier. If her hands had been free, she would have picked up the wooden fruit bowl on the coffer and hurled it at the door. As it was, she expended her rage in a furious, banshee shriek and flung herself from the bed to stamp up and down the room. And then, knowing that Robert would be listening, she compressed her lips and resorted to silent, swift pacing.

She glanced around the room, seeking a means to free her

own wrists. Perhaps she could smash the water jug and cut her bonds on a jagged edge, or somehow manipulate the shears in her sewing basket. The ideas kindled in her mind and then burned swiftly to ash as she acknowledged that the deed, small triumph though it might be, would be futile. The rooms below would be well guarded and Robert had locked the door to the outer stairs. The window was no use to her either. Even if she managed to free the catch on the shutters, the aperture was perilously narrow, and the drop too high.

'So you just go as a lamb to the slaughter,' she told herself scathingly, 'and so does Nicholas while his son grows up an orphan – if he grows up at all.' The thought rekindled the flame. She had to do something. The water jar was the better object for severing her bonds. The shears, sharp although they were, would be difficult to manipulate, and unless she could open and shut them with ease, she would be unable to cut the cord.

The water jar stood on a hip-height gaming table at the side of the room. Miriel stooped to the rim, tipped it slightly, and took a long drink. The pottery was glazed an attractive green-gold with an impressed decoration of wheat ears around the wide belly. It had been one of her mother's favourite pieces. Miriel could remember her filling it with flowers in the height of summer, could remember the perfume of honeysuckle and pink roses tumbling over the spout. For a moment she lingered to feel the cold, smooth glaze and the ridges of pattern. There were tears in her eyes as she curled her fingertips over the rim of the jar and prepared to swing it.

The key turned in the lock of the inner door and before Miriel could move, Robert pushed Elfwen into the room and shut her in with her mistress.

'Knock when you want to come out,' he said through the wood, turned the key again, and clumped away downstairs.

Torn between relief at the jar's reprieve, and disappointment that her intention had been thwarted, Miriel relinquished her weapon back on the trestle and let out a huge sigh of frustration. Then she looked at her white-faced maid.

'I do not suppose that you are permitted to untie me either,' she said.

'No, mistress,' Elfwen said with a swallow, 'although it is my greatest wish that I could.'

Miriel eyed her and then the window. Perhaps she could just squeeze out, and if she tied the bedsheets together, she would have a rope.

Elfwen appeared to guess what she was thinking. 'He has set an armed guard beneath the window,' she said. 'He says that you will try to run away again and that you are a danger to everyone, most of all yourself.'

Miriel's upper lip curled. 'The only danger I am is to him, and he knows it.' She jerked her head at the door. 'Why has he sent you?'

Elfwen pointed to the foot of the bed. 'He thought you might want to use the piss-pot and not manage without help.'

Miriel stared at the girl and began to laugh, the sound growing deep and harsh as the spasms ripped up from her core. 'How chivalrous of him!' she gasped, tears streaming down her face. She clutched her belly where there was a gnawing ache as she gave vent to her emotion. 'He p-plots murder and forces me to lie with him whilst my hands are tied, and yet he w-worries about how I'm to use a p-piss pot! Ah Jesu!' She threw herself on the bed, clutching her aching stomach. It was almost like being in labour again. Rolling over, she buried her face in the bolster and fought the spasms.

Elfwen tentatively touched her shoulder. 'Do you want a drink of water?'

'To aid me to use the piss-pot?' It almost set her off again, but the first impetus had been spent and she was too weak to bear another bout. Trembling, she sat up and gestured aside the cup that the frightened maid proffered.

'Jesu, I'm sorry. I've been holding it in for too long.'

'I told you to be careful, mistress.' Elfwen produced a kerchief and used it to wipe Miriel's puffy tear-streaked face. 'I knew when I woke up in The Ship and found you gone that there was going to be trouble. Then he brought us back late last night and gleaned what you had done from the other servants.'

Miriel clutched her stomach. 'He claims that I have lost my wits and he wants to shut me up in a nunnery. He's taking me to St Catherine's as soon as it's light enough and the town gates are open.' She drew back a little and looked at Elfwen. 'Do you think that I have lost my wits? The truth,' she added, as the girl lowered her eyes. 'Even if you offend me, there is little enough I can do about it.'

Elfwen frowned and plucked at her gown in thought. 'No mistress, I do not,' she said at length, 'but I think that you have walked straight into the mouth of danger.'

Miriel grimaced. 'After the first step was taken, I could do nothing else.' She looked down at her bound wrists. 'I know that you cannot untie me, and small good it would do anyway. The window splay is too narrow to squeeze through and, as you say, he has posted guards lest somehow I still manage to run. But you are not so constrained.'

The girl glanced over her shoulder.

'It's all right,' Miriel said. 'Even if my husband is listening at the door, he cannot hear what is being said.'

'What do you want me to do?' There was definite misgiving in Elfwen's eyes.

'Go to Martin and Alyson Wudecoc in Boston and tell them what has happened and what Robert intends to do with me. They are my only hope of freedom.' She held Elfwen's gaze with her own. 'And you are my only hope of their knowing where I am.'

After a moment, and to Miriel's weak relief, the girl nodded. 'I wasn't going to stay once you'd gone anyway, mistress,' she said. 'Not after the way Master Robert's treated you and kicked poor Will. 'Twill be me next, and I'm no man's scapegoat.'

'Bless you,' Miriel said. 'Jesu, you think I'd have no tears left to cry.' She wiped an impatient sleeve across the moisture welling in her eyes. 'Take Will with you as well,' she said. 'The way Robert is now, I know he would kill him for spite.'

'I will,' Elfwen nodded. 'I've put his basket out of sight in the store room and kept him quiet with a marrow bone.'

'There's one more boon I must ask of you,' Miriel said as the girl rose to leave.

Elfwen immediately looked wary again. 'Mistress?'

'I'm afraid I do need to use the piss-pot after all.'

Chapter 33

The fish lay on the thick wooden slab, its body still a fresh, bright silver, and its eyes as bright as amber and onyx discs. Madame le Pêcheur brought the knife down with a solid whack, separating head from body. Another practised motion slit the belly from red cavity to anal fin, and the finger following the knife hooked out the entrails and dropped them in a bucket with the head. The entire, brutal procedure was made graceful by Madame le Pêcheur's fluid skill. Nicholas eyed the knife and decided that she was too handy with the implement and the door too far to attempt an escape.

She saw him look, and a grim smile twitched beneath the dark moustache on her upper lip. 'My mother taught me, and her mother before that,' she said. 'We are the best in all the Isles of Genesies.' She tossed the gutted pollack in a basket to her left and reached for a fresh victim from the corresponding basket on her right.

Nicholas wondered if she was warming to him, or whether it was pride in her skill that had made her open her mouth. Whatever, it would do no harm to show interest. 'Yes, I've seen the fishwives at work in Rouen, but none as fast as you.'

'Hmph.' She gave him a warning look, telling him that flattery of any sort was completely out of order. 'I have to be,' she said. 'With a face like mine, what man would take me in marriage unless I had other skills?'

Nicholas shrugged. 'Perhaps you were beautiful in youth?' he said gallantly.

She snorted and chopped off the fish's head. 'I wasn't. My

father's wealth and my mother's skills handed down were what bought me a husband.'

'But Guichard is fond of you.'

'Oh aye,' she said. 'All cats are grey in the dark.' She looked at him from beneath her brows. 'You have a wife, no?'

Nicholas sighed. 'I do indeed, mistress. When I left her, she was less than a month away from bearing our first child.'

Madame le Pêcheur resumed gutting her fish. She tossed it in the basket and took a fresh one. 'What is she like, this wife of yours?'

'Tall,' he said, 'copper-haired, beautiful in my eyes.' He shifted uncomfortably on the bench. 'I married her because I could not have the woman I wanted, but Magdalene has come to dwell first in my heart. I hope that she knows it.'

'Hmph,' said Madame le Pêcheur again, her mouth pursed in disapproval. 'If you ask me, love's for minstrels' tales.'

'I know the difference between the confection of love as sung in a minstrel's tale and the sustaining bread of love in reality,' he defended himself. 'Both are to be savoured in their own way.'

The fishwife arched one eyebrow to show her suspicion of such thinking. Her red, chapped hands worked methodically through the catch. The knife slashed and a fine rime of silver scales adhered to the steel above the blade. 'This is love,' she said as she tossed the last fish into the left-hand basket. 'I wouldn't be doing it otherwise, skilled or not.'

'It's reality,' Nicholas argued, thereby earning himself a scowl.

The door banged open and Guichard strode into the room. He had been running, and a red flush mantled his leather-brown cheeks.

'Get your cloak,' he said to Nicholas without preamble. 'I'm letting you go. You're too dangerous to keep.'

Both Nicholas and Madame le Pêcheur gazed at him in astonishment.

'You can't!' said his wife, recovering first, her hands going to her hips in the age-old stance of argument. 'We've already fed and clothed him at our expense for a month. He's the means by which you'll never have to go to sea again, and I'll never have to gut another of these accursed fish!'

'No, because we'll likely be dead.' Her husband grabbed Nicholas's cloak off the back of the bench and thrust it at him. 'If I release you now, I want an undertaking that you will pay your ransom to me in full before Easter next year.' Darting into the main room, he returned with a scrap of vellum, an ink horn and quill.

'Guichard!' His wife's voice boomed as powerfully as a man's. 'Tell me why you are letting him go and let your reason be good!' She brandished the knife.

'Here, your promise.' Guichard pushed the quill into Nicholas's hand, and flattened out the vellum on the trestle.

Curious, more than a little apprehensive, but happy to cooperate if his freedom was imminent, Nicholas dipped the quill into the glutinous brown substance that passed for ink.

Guichard le Pêcheur turned to his simmering wife. 'His would-be killers have not been paid their full fee because they've been told he still lives and that his wife is negotiating with us for his release. The original price offered by the contractor has been put up to six hundred marks.'

Nicholas felt cold. The quill was split and the ink splattered everywhere as he tried to write. 'So why not do the deed yourself?' he asked.

Le Pêcheur's lip curled beneath his beard. 'Believe me, I have thought about it, lad. Six hundred marks is a fine sum – but when it comes to setting a man up for life, it's not much different to the five hundred already pledged to save your hide.' He parted his hands in a gesture that asked what else he could do. 'You have had my protection and hospitality for over a month. I cannot just throw them out of the window and cut your throat. Pledge me the ransom and you are free to make your own way home.'

'Free to go out and get my own throat cut, you mean,' Nicholas said with a grimace.

'I am counting on you not to, since then I won't see a single silver penny. At least this way I do not make my house a target for men in search of your death. Something tells me that they would not stop at your throat alone.'

Nicholas signed his name in a blot of ink and handed the vellum to le Pêcheur. A few greyish-silver fish scales adhered to the surface, and a smear of entrail blood. 'You will have your money, I promise,' he said, not without raising an ironic eyebrow that it was his would-be murderers who had secured his release. 'If I live, that is.' He held out his hand. 'Of course, you could improve my chances by giving me coin to pay my passage.'

Le Pêcheur rolled his eyes. 'If you die before you pay up,' he said, 'I will make a vow never again to put down an oar for a drowning sailor, and it will be your soul that carries the burden, not mine.' He unfastened the pouch from his belt and tossed it to Nicholas. 'I expect its return, filled with gold,' he said.

His wife wiped her gutting knife in a fold of her skirt and gave the weapon to Nicholas. 'You have more need of it than me if I'm to live in luxury one day,' she said.

Nicholas stowed the weapon in his belt. 'My thanks.' A wayward impulse made him take her moon face in his hands and kiss her on either vein-reddened cheek.

'Away with you!' She swatted at him crossly, but there was a gleam in her small blue eyes.

'Little wonder your life is sought if you go seducing other men's wives beneath their noses,' le Pêcheur said, pretending to be offended.

Nicholas pulled a face. Wondering how close to the truth the statement might be, he strode to the door and opened it.

'There are plenty of trading galleys headed for England,' said the fisherman. 'Just board the right one and you'll be in Southampton before the morrow's eve.'

'Board the wrong one and I'm dead.' Nicholas smiled grimly. 'You had best hope my instincts and luck runs true.'

He stepped out into the blustery morning and the door closed behind him. A stink of fish guts remained but was dissipated by the bracing salt wind. The scent of the sea and ships filled his lungs. He inhaled deeply and with the joy of freedom stretched his cramped muscles. Hand on the hilt of his knife, he moved through the narrow alleys to the dockside and paused at the wharves to view the harboured vessels. There were numerous small nefs, used as inshore fishing craft, with shallow sides and sails fashioned in all manner of colours, plain and striped.

Amid a pile of netted traps, a fisherman sat with his morning's catch of lobsters, mottled blue-grey like the sea, and rust-red crabs the same hue as his sail. Nicholas stepped over coils of rope and a ship's mast laid lengthwise along the quay. A group of sailors stood talking, and beyond them, out to sea, Nicholas saw a large cog tacking into the harbour, her banners flying red and gold. He narrowed his glance, thinking that she looked familiar, but then his attention was caught by another vessel moored up along the same line of vision as the cog. The sound of hammering echoed off her deck, and several workmen were industriously employed in what appeared to be a major refurbishment. Although she was no longer the gleaming beauty of a month ago, he would have recognised the *Empress* anywhere. He had commissioned her birth from Rohan on the Schelde and, by the same right, had tried to put her to death rather than see her taken. Obviously he had not quite succeeded, although she would never be the same again. They would patch her with different timber and it would change her spirit. In a way she was dead.

He studied the men working upon her, but could not tell if they were his would-be murderers or hired shipwrights. Whether the men were innocent or guilty, it was not a wise place for Nicholas to linger. He turned away to search the wharfside for other vessels with a look of deep ocean travel about them. The group of talking sailors had ceased their conversation and were eyeing him speculatively. One of their number, concealed from him by the angle of vision before, now came clearly into his sight and he found himself gazing in clear daylight at the red-bearded man who had stabbed Maurice de la Pole to the heart. Their eyes met. Even before Redbeard had set his hand to his knife, Nicholas read the man's intent in his expression. There was no way past the group that would not bring him too close. Nicholas spun back the way he had come and started to run.

With a shout they were after him like hounds after a buck. Nicholas knew he was at a serious disadvantage. He was unfamiliar with St Peter Port and unfit after a month confined in le Pêcheur's small dwelling. He knew that he would be unable to outrun them. Six against one and all of them with gutting knives as sharp as the one in his belt. It was inevitable. There was no point in bursting his heart and lungs in the effort to flee when they were going to be burst by a blade anyway, but still he ran.

Folk leaped out of the way. A woman screamed and clutched her small child to her skirts. Men and boys stared, but no one did anything to help. On an island where Eustace the Monk had recently held sway, people had learned to keep themselves to themselves where wharfside feuds were concerned.

Nicholas heard the sound of footsteps swift in pursuit, the hard panting of breath. Fear briefly lent his feet wings. He sprinted through a narrow alley between dwellings, turned a corner, found another entry leading back down to the wharfside. His pursuers spread out, cutting off his escape. One of them came close enough to rip at him with a knife and split his tunic, shirt and flesh in a single sharp flash. Pain seared down Nicholas's side and his feet faltered. His stagger caught his opponent off-balance and the second blow went wide, giving Nicholas an opportunity to use Madame le Pêcheur's gutting knife in the manner for which it had been intended. The man fell, his belly flooding red beneath his clutching hands.

Nicholas saw another dark opening and, with a last burst of speed, ran for its embrace in the manner of a wounded creature seeking a den. The darkness led to a fence of woven hazels at the back of someone's vegetable patch and it barred his way as effectively as a wall of stone. He turned at bay, his knife at the ready, prepared to sell his life at a high price.

They gathered around him like wolves, eyes glittering, teeth bared, each man measuring his likelihood of striking without being struck in return.

A sudden flurry of movement behind broke the terrible concentration. Men turned and their faces changed. Another blade flashed in the darkness, this time a sword of full length and cleaving power. In a single smooth motion, Stephen Trabe pinned Redbeard against the alley wall and sliced off his head as he had done to Eustace the Monk and with no more effort than beheading a pollack. There were some taut moments of vicious fighting as Trabe's crewmen took on Nicholas's attackers, and then there was silence. Three bodies, including Redbeard's, littered the alley. One man had made his escape at the expense of several fingers. Stephen Trabe gave a nod of satisfaction, wiped his reddened sword-edge on his victim's tunic, and sheathed his weapon.

'A moment later and you'd have been fish food,' he said to Nicholas, who was leaning against the withy blockade for support and clutching the bloody stripe in his side. His legs felt as if they had turned to curds.

'God's life!' he gasped. 'I never thought I'd be grateful to see you do that again!'

Trabe's teeth flashed. 'I like to make a clean job, which is more than he would have made of you.'

'What are you doing here?' Gingerly Nicholas straightened.

'Coming to bring you home. As we sailed into port, we saw you running along the dockside like a hare with the dogs on your scut.' His grin deepened. 'You owe me with interest, de Caen.'

'Gladly, and that's something else I never thought to admit with gratitude,' Nicholas said, and staggered.

Trabe reached a strong arm and bore him up. 'Come,' he said. 'Let's get you safe on board and bind up your wounds. There is much that you have to know.'

The convent rose out of the flat, fenland landscape, the ragged flint of its tower echoing the mottled sky and the thatched roofs of its outer buildings reflecting the surrounding reeds and lush grassland. Miriel sat in the well of the barge and watched its approach with feelings of oppression and inevitability. The runaway had been caught and was being returned to face her punishment. Robert informed all who enquired that he was taking her to St Catherine's to recuperate from the traumatic childbirth that had not only damaged her body but scarred her mind. She was in need of peace, he said, and he wanted to do all in his power to ensure that she had it.

Second only to the peace of the grave, she thought. St Catherine's was a two-day walk from the nearest town, as she had cause to know. Supplies came by barge, but only the cellaress and her most trusted subordinates dealt with the barge-men. Miriel knew that her own fate would likely be a bare cell and a locked door, her only outing to kneel in penitence in the chapel. Her one hope was that she could speak to Mother Hillary and persuade the old Abbess to set her free. Surely the nun's compassion would overcome the need for material gain in the circumstances?

In defiance of her journey to the convent, she had worn one of her most ornate gowns, a panelled affair of green tabby with gold braid encircling the wide hem and rich embroidery at the throat. Robert had eyed her choice with an expression of scornful amusement. 'I doubt the nuns will be impressed,' he said, 'and no one else is going to see your finery.'

'Except myself,' she had answered, lifting her chin at him. She did so now, giving him a cold look across the length of the barge. He had not allowed her to bring a travelling chest. He himself had put together what she needed and tied it in a linen bundle. As far as she knew, her worldly possessions consisted of a spare linen shift and hose, linen strips for her monthly bleed, a comb and another wimple. Empress Mathilda's crown remained in its hiding place, shut away and out of reach.

At least Nicholas would be safe, she thought. Martin Wudecoc could still raise the ransom despite her lack of contribution, and when Elfwen arrived in Boston, they would know where she was and why. She looked again at the approaching church. At least she could pray for Nicholas's deliverance – and her own.

The barge-master moored his craft at the small jetty where supplies were delivered to St Catherine's and leaped out to help his passengers ashore. His apprentice set about unloading several casks of wine from the supply barge they towed behind.

Miriel stepped on to the muddy path. The convent faced her and she saw how much it had grown in the years since her first imprisonment. Decorative stonework had been added to the porch and some of the buildings were faced with a chequerboard design of napped black flint.

More building work was being carried out, and a new church spire pushed forth from a skeleton turret of wooden scaffolding. Mother Hillary had been making the most of her profits. At the gatehouse, they were greeted by a nun whom Miriel did not know. Her manner was brisk and her habit immaculately brushed.

'Mother Abbess is expecting your arrival,' she said and, having ushered Miriel and Robert into the precincts, shot the bolt on the outside world with a resounding clang. 'I'll take you to her.'

'Thank you.' Robert inclined his head gravely.

A cold shiver had run through Miriel at the sound of the bolt ramming across. Prison. She had arrived in prison. 'Does Sister Winifred no longer hold this post?' she asked, remembering the shabby little nun with her wide, sunlit grin.

'No, my lady. She passed away last winter of a wasting sickness,' the woman answered politely.

'I am sorry, I was fond of her.'

'She rests in God's bosom now, my lady.'

Miriel murmured an appropriate reply. 'You were not here last time I visited,' she said.

'I came to my vows three years since.' The woman flickered her a look from her eye-corners, but there was no particular expression on her face. Miriel wondered how much the nuns had been told about their new lodger. How far had Robert twisted the details?

Miriel bit her lip and suppressed the urge to run screaming for that bolted gate. They would think her mad before she had even arrived. She must have full control of herself when she met Mother Hillary. Seeming to sense her hidden impulse, Robert took her arm in a bruising grip. The action looked solicitous, as if he were bearing her up, but Miriel knew that he was serving to remind her how tight his hold on her was.

The nun led them past the church and the small building that had been the Abbess's lodging in Miriel's time at the convent. Now Miriel saw that it had been converted into an extra guest house for passing travellers. She and Robert were brought to a new building further eastwards with a chequered stone panel above a handsome entrance way. Smoke twirled from a built-in chimney, and the dwelling was roofed with tile.

Miriel wondered if the comfort of the dorter had improved apace, or whether it was still a draughty room, smelling of the grave in the deepness of the winter night. And just where did Robert envisage her dwelling in this establishment? In well-appointed guest house, or freezing, dark cell?

The nun bade them wait inside the covered archway and went to knock on the door set into the right-hand side. Then she entered and there came the low murmur of voices.

'You will not shut me away in this place, you know that,' Miriel said with a glare at Robert's arm still possessively pincered around her own.

'No,' he agreed with a smile, 'I will not. It is the nuns who will see to your every comfort.'

Miriel felt uneasy. He was so sure of himself. It was as if he knew something that she did not.

'Mother Abbess will see you now,' said the porteress, emerging from the room and leaving the door ajar for Miriel and Robert. With a brief nod and even briefer smile, she clasped her hands before her and walked away in the direction of the gatehouse.

Robert ran his free hand over his beard in a smoothing gesture and drew Miriel forward into the Abbess's private chamber.

Although the lodging house was new, the old trestle desk and silver candle tree were exactly the same. So was the handsome olive-wood crucifix on the wall, and the carved vestment coffer. But no smoke-grey cat was curled purring upon the desk, and the woman who looked up at their entry was not thin and fine-boned with clear blue eyes, but as broad as a barrel with a face the hue of an enormous wheel of cheese. In place of the cat, a stick of polished willow lay across the dark wood of the trestle.

'Sister Euphemia!' Miriel's voice emerged on a rising note of horror.

'Mother Euphemia,' the nun corrected with a thin-lipped smile in which there was more than a hint of malice. 'Welcome back to St Catherine's . . . my daughter.'

Chapter 34

'Your son,' said Alyson Wudecoc and, with maternal ease, scooped little Nicholas out of the cradle and placed him in his father's arms.

Nicholas gazed down, surprised by the child's lightness which at the same time conveyed a solid warmth. Solemn, kitten-blue eyes gazed back. There was no indication of their final colour, but their shape and definition were his. The nose was going to be fine and thin like Magdalene's and the quiff of hair at his brow bore the merest suggestion of apricot-gold.

'He's thriving well,' Alyson added, driven to dilute the overpowering emotion of the moment by speech.

Nicholas engulfed one of the tiny hands in his closed palm and swallowed the lump constricting his throat. He had never felt such a depth of love and anguish, of joy and grief. 'She should be here,' he said, his voice cracking.

'I know.' Alyson laid her hand on his shoulder. 'It wasn't his birth that killed her; she weathered that well. It was the fever that came after, and there was nothing we could do.' She drew a shaky breath. 'It comforted her to know that you were still alive and that you would be here to see him grow up. I . . .' Her voice strangled on tears and she turned away to pace the room and recover her composure.

Nicholas sat down, the baby resting in the crook of his arm and across his knee. Stephen Trabe had given him the news of Magdalene's death while tending the long, shallow knife gash as the *Sainte-Foy* cast off for England. No details, just that she was dead but the child was alive and strong. Praise God for small mercies, Nicholas thought bitterly.

Trabe had also told him that Robert Willoughby had commanded his killing. 'Do you want to negotiate a contract of your own? It can be arranged,' Trabe had said as he completed the dressing and stood back.

Nicholas had declined with revulsion. Two wrongs were never going to make a right. He might not be innocent of sin, but he would not have murder reddening the hands that cradled his son.

Trabe had shrugged and, although he had not said anything, the implication was that he considered Nicholas a fool. At least he was not in Trabe's debt, and Trabe was not in his. The business of the past had been quit-claimed by Trabe's rescue on St Peter Port's wharfside. If not in peace, then Nicholas knew his father's spirit would sleep at least more easily. As to his own . . . He sighed and shifted the weight of the baby on his arm. It was sobering to think that a few moments of pleasure could have such far-reaching consequences. Magdalene, Miriel. God forfend that his son should make the same mistakes.

Alyson turned round, her eyes red but her composure in some measure restored. 'Do you want to see her grave?' she asked.

Nicholas nodded. 'I do not know if she will hear, but I want to tell her again that I loved her for herself and not as a substitute for someone I could not have.'

When they returned from their visit to the church, the wet-nurse was sitting by the hearth suckling the baby and Martin was waiting for them. Nicholas greeted his captain first with a handclasp and then, as emotion swept over him, a full embrace.

'It is good to see you alive and whole,' Martin said gruffly, the suspicion of moisture in his eyes.

'Nay, it is a miracle,' Nicholas stepped back. 'I owe you more than my tongue can ever find the words to utter for helping to bring me home.'

'You owe me nothing; you would have done the same for me.' Martin cleared his throat and scooped his hands through his hair in a grooming motion to settle himself. 'I'm sorry about Magdalene. We did what we could, but the fever was too strong.'

Nicholas nodded brusquely. 'I know you did your best for her.' He glanced at the contentedly suckling child. 'And for my son too.'

A maid entered bearing a flagon of hot wine and a platter of buttered griddle cakes. Trotting at her side, leaping now and again in a vain attempt to reach the platter, was a small black and white dog with enormous pricked ears and a great feathered curl of tail.

Nicholas looked and then looked again. 'Elfwen and Will?' he said on a rising note of question.

Hearing his name, the dog abandoned his attempts to get at the griddle cakes and assaulted Nicholas in a fury of wagging and barking.

'I was going to speak to you about that next,' Martin said, smiling despite the situation at Will's unbounded enthusiasm and Nicholas's vain attempts to defend himself. 'Trabe knew about Robert Willoughby's contract on you when he set sail, but not all the fine detail. We heard that later from Elfwen.' He beckoned to the maid. 'Come and tell Master Nicholas what you told me.'

The young woman set the flagon and griddle cakes well out of Will's reach and, wiping her hands on her gown, came to the men. Her height was diminutive and her dark eyes large and wide set beneath a broad brow, giving her the appearance of a young adolescent rather than a woman grown.

'Mistress Miriel left Master Robert when she realised the things he had done,' she said. 'But she had to go back to Lincoln to gather the coin she had promised Master Martin for your ransom.'

Nicholas blinked. 'She was going to ransom me?'

'Said she'd provide four hundred marks,' Martin said in a level voice. 'I was astonished that she could raise such a sum.'

Nicholas gnawed his lip and nodded. 'Believe me, she could, and more – a King's ransom in fact.'

Martin raised a questioning eyebrow but Nicholas did not elaborate, his attention given once more to Elfwen. 'What happened?'

'Master Robert stopped her at the barge wharf as she was preparing to leave. He brought soldiers from the castle garrison. Master Martin's men were arrested and thrown in gaol for the rest of the night, and my mistress was bound like a slave and brought back to the house.' Elfwen paused in the telling to wring her hands.

'Then what?' There was a dangerous edge to Nicholas's voice.

Elfwen's lip curled in disgust. 'Then he coupled with her, even bound as she was; we could hear him below stairs, and my mistress screamed. After that . . . after that he told her that he was taking her to St Catherine's to be nursed by the nuns. His excuse was that her mind had been deranged ever since she lost the baby.'

It was too much to absorb. Nicholas frowned and rubbed his forehead. 'What baby? I thought that she was barren?'

'She would have borne a son about a month before Magdalene was brought to bed,' Martin said, his voice and manner more wooden than ever. 'Robert's seed was barren, not her womb.'

'Christ on the Cross.' The hairs rose on Nicholas's nape. 'What do you mean "would have"?' he said hoarsely.

'Her hips were too narrow for the child to be born. The midwives christened it in the womb before they killed it so that Miriel might live.' A muscle bunched in Martin's jaw. 'Her husband told them to name the babe Nicholas.'

Prickles of heat flashed along Nicholas's spine and suddenly the air seemed too thick to breathe. Turning while he was still able to move, he slammed out of the room and stood in the yard, gulping at the soft spring air with its fragrance of greenery and new life. His belly heaved and he doubled over, retching.

Martin emerged and sat on the wooden bench set against the lime-washed wall. 'I'm sorry,' he said. 'I did think about not telling you, but the burden would have weighed on me too heavily.' The lines across his forehead deepened. 'I had to give it to you to shoulder too because it is yours by right.'

Slowly Nicholas straightened. His gut ached and the sickness was still with him, soul-deep. 'And you were right,' he said, 'but I cannot thank you for it.' With the slow care of a man three times his age, he sat down at Martin's side. 'I asked her to leave him before, but she would not – said that there was too much at stake. It was the hardest thing I have ever done, to let her go. If I had known what awaited, I'd have sailed away with her over the edge of the world.' He put his head in his hands.

'You would still have had to make the decision,' Martin murmured. 'Her or the child. Would you have chosen differently?'

His mind filled with the feel of his son in his arms, the weight of the tiny head in the crook of his elbow. And then he thought of Magdalene as he had last seen her, luminous and blooming with health. 'I do not know,' he said in a cracked voice. 'In God's name, I truly do not know.'

Martin said nothing, offering no comfort except his taciturn presence. Slowly Nicholas raised his head and leaned against the bench's solid oak back. 'So he has put her in St Catherine's?'

Martin nodded. 'She is not deranged,' he said. 'Her mind is as clear as my own. He has imprisoned her there as a punishment. I suppose it is a small mercy that he has chosen to put her out of sight and mind rather than adding her to his tally of victims – of which you are still likely to be one,' he added darkly.

Nicholas rubbed the healing slash in his side. 'I am not a vindictive man, Martin,' he said grimly. 'Always until this moment I have chosen to live and let live.' He rose to his feet. 'If Miriel once owed her husband allegiance, she has long since paid it back with interest. What he owes me, I will claim not in a dark, sea-port alley, but in the full glare of a town gibbet when the time comes.' His eyes narrowed with decision. 'First I must free her, and see her safe.'

'What are you going to do?'

Nicholas looked at Martin but without really seeing him. 'Go to St Catherine's, of course,' he said.

Spring rain was unpredictable. Sometimes it came as the transparent trail of a ghost's sleeve, leaving a whisper of moisture wherever it touched and the lingering scent of wet grass and woodsmoke. Outlines blurred, leaving the world washed in soft tints of green through which sunlight was swift to flash warm dapples of gold. On other occasions, the rain clouds came like galloping horses, whipped on by riders of storm-wild wind. The droplets slammed against shutters like clods flung from racing hooves; streets became glistening brown rivers and every object tore at its roots, foundations and moorings, striving to join the frantic race.

It was one of the latter days that called Robert to sit at the fire rather than go out amongst his clients. He huddled over the hearth in the Lincoln house that belonged to his wife, and through her to him. The fire lashed and guttered in the hearth like a speared dragon, now and then sending small clouds of smoke into the room. Robert shivered in his cloak, which was lined with the warm luxury of marten fur, but there was a chill in his bones that mere warmth alone could not displace.

He thought of Miriel in St Catherine's. This storm would be howling straight from the North Sea against the convent's walls. Was she suffering in her cold, damp cell, with naught but the contemplation of her sins to pass the time? He hoped so with a vehemence that almost made him weep. Part of that vehemence was because he missed her presence so much. He missed the sight of her poring over her tally sticks, her smooth, Madonna's face serious in concentration. He missed her mannerisms, her incisive wit, the honey-coloured eyes and the way they would suddenly light with a smile. Only the smile had been for another man, and at the end it had not been there at all because he had banished it from her face. He couldn't live with her, but he was beginning to wonder if he could live without her either.

'Bitch,' he said softly, his word overridden by another wild surge of wind and rain against the house. He rose and paced the room, unable to settle to his accounts, or to reading a copy of the tales of King Arthur, given to him in part payment by a Flemish merchant. The room was too dark, his eyesight no longer sharp enough to read the lettering, and his concentration nil. Soon even his pacing was not enough to contain his restlessness and, muttering grumpily, he went to the door and stepped out into the elements.

The fingers of wind became strong, malicious hands that snatched at his cloak and tried to push him back inside. He leaned forward into the vigour of the elements, determined as in all things not to be beaten. Rain slapped against his face almost hard enough to hurt. The courtyard was a soup of mud across which the weavers had thrown down sheaves of straw in a semi-successful attempt at making a causeway. Robert realised too late that he was not wearing his pattens, which would have lifted him above the mire, but must needs soil his good leather boots. He would not go back. Head down like a bull, he plodded on to the weaving shed and raised the latch.

The weavers had been laughing and chattering amongst themselves as they worked, but as Robert entered, they fell silent and looked covertly at each other before bowing to him.

'Carry on,' Robert said with a regal wave of his hand.

He prowled the shed, walking behind the weavers to look at the work in progress on the looms. As well as the usual Lincoln scarlet, a length of grey diamond twill was in progress for the making of chausses, and Walter was warping a loom with green and yellow wool to make striped cloth. The young man's fingers, never dextrous at the task, grew clumsier beneath Robert's frowning scrutiny.

'God knows,' Robert snarled, 'I should have removed you at the same time as the old man.'

'Sir?' Walter looked round, eyes widening, and Robert realised his mistake.

'I mean I would have removed the old man if he hadn't saved me the trouble,' he snapped. 'What's that supposed to be? I've seen better fishing nets!' He stumped off into the counting house, angry at Walter, even angrier at himself. There was a costrel of mead on the shelf. Lifting it down he removed the stopper and drank straight from the jar. The honey-sweet liquid slipped smoothly down his throat and warmed comfortingly in his belly. He kindled the ceramic lamp suspended on chains from a ceiling beam and gazed round the room where Miriel had spent so much of her time. Her presence was stronger here than in the house. Her quills, her inkhorn, her supply of vellum neatly held in place by a lump of polished amber the exact colour of her eyes. A leaf was captured in the middle of the stone, perfect in every detail. He picked it up. Stone should be cold, but amber was almost as warm as flesh to the touch.

As he fondled the weight, his eyes lit on the money chest she had been taking to her lover. It was made to be sturdy and functional and lacked the elegance of which Miriel was usually so particular. Robert glowered at the object. He could not understand her reason for taking it when she fled. It would have been far more practical to put the silver in a sack or satchel. Unless . . .

Leaving the amber, he went to the chest and threw back the lid. The bare interior gave nothing away. He felt along the base, but there was no cunningly hidden secret compartment; all was solid. A thin splinter drove into his finger for his pains. He withdrew, cursing, and glared at the coffer while he removed the sliver of wood with his teeth. 'Bitch,' he said again, softly, 'whoring bitch,' and looked at the blood oozing from the wound.

One last glimmer of a notion made him kneel and reach his good hand beneath the chest. He was not expecting to find anything, and when he discovered a vertical wooden peg, his heart lurched with sudden excitement. As he turned the peg to lie flat, he was as clumsy as Walter. A section of wood came away in his hand, exposing a hidden shelf. There was an object on the shelf; silk wrappings against the hardness of shaped metal.

Licking dry lips, Robert withdrew his find and brought it into the lamplight. Purple fabric shimmered, its border patterned with strange signs that he vaguely knew to be the writing of the lands beyond Constantinople. His breath came short as he unfolded the wrappings and drew forth the object they had been protecting; and then for a time he did not breathe at all.

'Suffering Christ,' he muttered at last, and sucked air into his deprived lungs. 'Where has this pretty bauble come from?'

He turned it in his hands, admiring the craftsmanship, the way it struck the light; the deep pools of the gemstones, the demure lustre of the pearls. Small wonder that Miriel had wanted to take the chest with her. With this, she could have bought the world.

Conscious of the weavers a mere door away, Robert replaced the crown in its hiding place, and stood back to contemplate the meaning of his find. His hands were sweating and he wiped them down his tunic. He took another long swallow of mead and rested his shaking legs against Miriel's writing trestle. Crowns belonged to royalty, and everyone knew the tale about King John's regalia being lost in the Wellstream. Young Prince Henry had gone to his coronation with the barest bones of majesty because most of the wealth was missing.

Robert rubbed his jaw. If Miriel had the crown, then she might know the whereabouts of other items. She could show him where to look, or at the very least explain how she came by this particular jewel. Whatever the outcome, he had the means to raise himself from being a rich and powerful man in his own world, to a status of wealth and influence at the highest level.

It was time to pay his wife a solicitous visit and see how she was faring under Mother Euphemia's benevolent rule.

CHAPTER 35

Miriel sat in her cell with a mutton-fat rush dip for light and a wall crucifix of Christ in suffering for company. She had a straw pallet upon a rope-framed bed with a coarse sheet and even coarser blanket for warmth, and a large pottery bowl in which to piss. A small square window hole let in little light, but was more than generous with cold draughts and spatters of rain when the wind was in the wrong direction – as it was tonight.

Miriel huddled in her cloak and her bed blanket, her teeth chattering. She suspected that not only had Robert put her here to keep her out of sight and mind, but in the hope that she would die. If she did, there would be no one to blame but her constitution, weakened by childbirth and the disordered state of her mind. Miriel glared at the crucifix. Well, she wasn't going to give him the satisfaction; she had every intention of living to be a thorn in his flesh until the day that *he* died.

She was kept apart from the other women boarders. Even when allowed into church to pray, she was flanked by two of Euphemia's minions who had authority to deal with any outburst or unruly behaviour. Miriel, thus far, had clung to her control. If she could lull them into thinking her spirit was cowed, they would relax their vigilance and an opportunity to escape was bound to arise.

The wind lashed outside like a wild beast and the square of oiled linen beat back and forth within the aperture. Rain spat through a gap where the cloth did not fit properly and glistened on the lime-washed wall. Miriel consoled herself with the knowledge that Abbess Euphemia hated storms and this unsettled weather had been raging for three days now. They were the one thing on God's earth that kept her from stalking the convent in search of miscreants, the dreaded switch in her hand. Miriel looked at the crucifix on the wall and prayed that the storm would be a bad one.

It was unfortunate but not unbelievable that Euphemia had become Abbess of St Catherine's. The woman had the right family connections and an ambition almost as large as her corpulent frame, advantages that weighed heavily in the balance when measured against spiritual suitability.

Miriel wondered what had become of Mother Hillary. Had her elderly body failed her indomitable will and razor-bright mind? Or had she chosen to retire to the habit of an ordinary nun? Miriel could not imagine the latter and made a gentler prayer to the crucifix for Mother Hillary's soul.

The wind surged again and fresh droplets gleamed on the lime-wash. Miriel thought she heard voices and turned her head to the door. It was full dark and the meagre supper of pease pudding and rye bread long finished. In the three weeks that Miriel had been incarcerated at St Catherine's, the routine had never altered. Food at dusk, then dark solitude until morning mass.

Hearing the thump of the draw-bar, Miriel stood up and clutched the blanket edges together at her throat. The door swung open to reveal two nuns dishevelled by the force of the wind. There was one of her usual gaolers, a dour-faced crony of Euphemia's called Sister Ignatia. Accompanying her was Sister Adela, whom Miriel had last seen as a timid oblate six years ago. Now the white wimple of her noviciate had been replaced by the black one of a fully fledged nun. In her hand she carried a guttering lantern.

'You've a visitor in the guest house,' said Ignatia, her frown exposing her disapproval. She plucked a loose pin from her head covering and rammed it firmly home. 'Mother Abbess has sent us to fetch you.'

'A visitor?' Miriel stared at the women. Her heart began to thump as her first thought was of Nicholas.

'Your husband,' Ignatia said. 'And the only reason Mother Abbess has consented to send for you this late into the evening.' She pursed her lips, indicating that if she had been Abbess, spouse or not, the man would have waited until morning.

'My husband?' Miriel's heart continued to pound. 'What does he want?'

Ignatia sniffed. 'I suppose he will tell you that himself,' she said sourly. Plainly she did not know and was irritated by the fact.

Miriel thought about sitting down on her pallet, crossing her arms and declaring that she did not want to see him, but that would just be cutting off her nose to spite her face. Any respite from this chill, dank cell was welcome, even if it involved her husband. He could have decided that she had learned her lesson and come to take her back. Or perhaps he had news of Nicholas, of a successful attempt to kill him this time, and he was here to gloat. A cell might be preferable after all, she thought; but her curiosity was whetted and she had to know.

The nuns led her from her corrody dwelling and up the cart track towards the main abbey buildings and the guest house. Harsh wind buffeted the women and tore at their habits and wimples; raindrops slanted like heavy darning needles and the flame in the lantern whipped and guttered. Miriel considered running off into the dark and immediately decided against it. She was chilled to the bone already and, without decent food or clothing, would soon die of exposure or stumble into a bog.

With relief, the women entered the shelter of the cloister arches and turned along the garden wall near the nuns' cemetery. The moon glimmered through the flying clouds and a figure blocked their path, its arms outstretched as if it had just stepped off a crucifix. Adela screamed, then stuffed her fists against her mouth. Sister Ignatia, who was made of sterner stuff, did not cry out, but still took a back-step like a skittish horse, her rump swiping Miriel who had to clutch the wall for support.

Sister Ignatia recovered almost immediately and grabbed the lantern from Adela. The flickering glow shadowed the face of the apparition, giving it the visage of a skull. Wisps of grey hair floated from its pate and its eyes held a stare that managed to be unnervingly blank yet piercing at the same time.

Adela whimpered and clung to Miriel, who was gazing in appalled pity at the sight.

'Mother Hillary?' she ventured.

The head turned fractionally and, within the gaunt sockets, the eyes narrowed. 'Have you seen my cat?' she asked. 'I can't find him.'

Sister Ignatia rolled her eyes. 'She's escaped from the infirmary again,' she said with more than a hint of irritation as her fear receded. 'Here.' She returned the lantern to Adela. 'Take Mistress Willoughby to the guest house. I'll deal with this.' Approaching the old woman, she took each of her outspread arms in turn and briskly lowered them. 'Come now,' she said authoritatively. 'We'll find your cat. He won't be outside on a night like this, will he? Just you follow me.'

Miriel removed her blanket and threw it around the old woman's shoulders. She was shocked to feel their fragility, the knobs of bone uncushioned by anything more than a thin waxing of skin.

Ignatia led Hillary away to heartbreaking cries of 'Puss, puss, puss!'

'Poor lady,' Miriel said, her own plight forgotten. 'What happened to her?'

Adela shrugged. 'The cat died last summer and, about the same time, her memory began to fail. By the feast of Stephen she no longer knew her own name, only that she had a cat and that it was lost to her. Sister Euphemia was appointed our Abbess at Candlemas.' She flickered a sidelong glance at Miriel and began to walk. 'She is not as bad an abbess as she was a novice mistress,' she said nervously.

Miriel raised a scornful brow. 'I can imagine that she relishes the power. Mother Hillary would never have agreed to lock me up in that damp cell.' She remained where she was and Adela turned, the beginnings of panic in her expression.

'It is for your own good,' Adela said. 'You have a malady of the spirit and you can only be cured by solitary communication with God.'

'Is that what she told you?'

Adela ignored the question and swallowed. 'You're not going to run away, are you?'

Miriel smiled. 'Why? Are you afraid that you'll have to pursue me across the marshes in the dark? Or perhaps you fear Mother Euphemia's willow switch?'

'Please, Miriel, please don't.' There was a note of near hysteria in Adela's voice.

Miriel made a disgusted sound. 'You need not fret. How far do you think I would get in weather like this, and now not even a blanket to my name? There are different degrees of madness. Ask my husband; he knows.' She joined the young nun and began walking in the direction of the guest house. Just for a moment she had indeed been tempted to run, but it would have been on a road to nowhere. And she had to know why Robert had come.

He was waiting for her in the main room, his back to the hearth while he warmed himself. Euphemia sat in an upright box chair to one side of the fire. Sweat gleamed on her brow and each time the wind gusted, she clicked her rosary beads through her fingers in agitation. Miriel almost felt sorry for her – almost, but not quite.

Robert looked unwell. His bulky frame had not diminished, but his flesh was the colour of dough and lacked its customary robust hue. Beneath his eyes there were dark circles as if he had not slept well. But within the eyes themselves, there was fire.

'Where's Sister Ignatia?' demanded Euphemia.

Adela bowed her head in deference. 'She's taken Sister Hillary back to the infirmary. She was out wandering again.'

Euphemia clucked her tongue in irritation.

Robert said, 'Thank you for waiting with me, Mother Abbess. I am sure that you and the good sister have other duties to attend to. I will let you know when my business with my wife is finished.'

Euphemia glared a little at being so summarily dismissed, but did not puff up with indignation. Miriel could tell that she was only too glad to have an excuse to leave so that she could go and hide from the storm.

She swept from the room, bestowing on Miriel a basilisk stare. Adela followed her out as nervy as a fluttering sparrow, and Miriel was alone with her husband.

Crossing the room, she took the chair that the Abbess had vacated, and folded her hands in her lap. Outwardly her movements were controlled, but her fingers were clammy and her stomach churned. 'I scarcely think this is a social visit to see how I am faring,' she said.

Robert cleared his throat and Miriel realised suddenly that he was as edgy as she. 'I've missed you,' he said.

The fire spat and crackled. Miriel gazed into its deep orange heart until her eyes burned. 'I hope you do not expect me to return the compliment.'

He clenched his fists. 'Mayhap I was a trifle hard on you,' he growled, 'but you drove me to it.'

'My own fault, I know.' Miriel nodded sarcastically and turned her gaze to his, the images of fire distorting her vision. 'So why have you come? To see if I have learned my lesson? To tell me that in your generosity you will allow me to return?'

Robert flushed. 'I may have missed you, but not your waspish tongue.'

'Then why visit, when you know it is all you will receive?'

He drew a deep breath. 'I had come in the hopes of forging a truce,' he said.

Miriel almost laughed aloud. Even now he did not understand what he had done. 'And what are to be the terms of this "truce"?' she enquired sweetly. 'What do you want of me that you have not already taken and destroyed?'

'I'm trying to be reasonable,' Robert said through gritted teeth.

'I know; it's all my fault again.' Miriel nodded, still smiling, although not with her eyes. 'In truth you have always had a reason for whatever action you have taken, be it a common business deal or murder in a dark alley.' She made a dismissive gesture. 'I am weary and I'd rather sleep in the chill of my prison than share a firelit room with you. Speak your piece and leave me alone.'

Robert eyed her narrowly. 'And wouldn't you rather have

your freedom above all else? To do as you choose without interference from me? To have a papal dispensation to dissolve our marriage so that you can mate again where you please?'

Whatever Miriel had been expecting, it was not this and she was unable to maintain her air of frosty contempt. 'Jesu God, Robert,' she spat, 'first you dump me in this hellish place, and then you come to me in the middle of the night to offer freedom. Why?' She shook her head. 'I truly do think that you are the one who has lost your wits!'

Wintry humour filled his eyes. 'I promise you, sweetheart, I haven't. My wits have never been more sound.'

'Then what do you want in exchange?' There had to be a catch, Miriel thought. Something so momentous that it was insurmountable and the offer of freedom only a taunt.

He shrugged. 'I would like to say nothing, but, as you know, I believe that debts must be paid. What I want is . . .' He turned to the carved oak sideboard along the guest-chamber wall. On top of it stood a small travelling chest that Miriel had not previously noticed. Robert took a key from his pouch, unlocked the lid, and withdrew a purple silk bundle.

Miriel suppressed a gasp of dismay.

'I see you recognise it,' Robert said as he delicately unwrapped the silk. 'Although I do not suppose for one moment that you are going to claim it is yours.'

Miriel put her hand to her breast. 'It belonged to the Empress Mathilda, our King's great-grandmother,' she said with a slight tremble in her voice despite her efforts to keep it steady.

'Ah, I see. And you were just keeping it safe?'

'What are you going to do with it?'

Robert pursed his lips. 'I haven't decided yet.' He turned the crown in his hands and the sight made Miriel feel sick. It was almost as if his touch were defiling the diadem's beauty and mystique.

'I could melt it down,' he mused, 'but that would destroy most of its value. Or I could sell it to someone who collects such things, but that would leave me open to the threat of arrest and the gibbet if I was ever found out.' To her relief he returned the crown to its wrappings and placed it in the travelling chest. 'But most likely, sweetheart, I will return it to King Henry in exchange for power and influence. That would suit me best.'

It would indeed, she thought, but at what expense to the peaceful dreams of others? 'So what do you want of me?' she shrugged. 'Scarcely my permission.'

Robert turned from the casket and fixed her with a stare that was almost feverish. She recognised the gleam, for she had been a sufferer too. 'I want to know how you came by the piece, where you found it. There must be more.'

Miriel smiled wryly. She was right; the barrier was insurmountable. She could not give him what she did not have. 'Assuredly there must,' she said, 'but if anyone finds it now, it will be a miracle. The sands have shifted and thousands of tides have washed over the place since.'

'But you can show me.'

Miriel sighed. 'I didn't find the Empress's crown; Nicholas rescued it at the time the baggage train was swept away . . . and I stole it from him.'

'You're lying; you must know something.' Robert's upper lip curled back from his teeth.

'No more than anyone else who vainly probes the sand in hope.'

Robert pointed his finger at her. The veins were starting to bulge in his throat. 'When you wed Gerbert, you claimed to be a widow, but you were a widow of means. You had more to your name than that bauble over there.'

'Stolen from Nicholas again. If you want royal jewels from me, then your journey has been wasted.' She opened her hands, showing him in gesture that she had nothing, and saw from the expression on his face that he still did not believe her for he was in the grip of gold-greed.

'If you had stolen from him, he would not have become your lover,' he said angrily. 'I may sell fleeces but you are not going to pull the wool over my eyes this time. On the morrow, we'll go down to the shore and you will show me where to search. If I find what I'm looking for, you can have your freedom.'

'I told you, I don't know!' Miriel stamped her foot.

'Then you can rot here for the rest of your life. The decision is yours, sweetheart.'

Perhaps on the morrow the storm would have abated. Perhaps on the morrow, outside the abbey walls, she could find a means to escape. She said nothing more.

'That's made you think, hasn't it?' Robert smiled and approached her. He stroked her face as he had stroked the gold and she had to swallow the urge to retch. 'Of course, I could always take you back to Lincoln,' he murmured. 'No one would know what has passed between us. Our neighbours believe that you're with the nuns for the good of your health. It could be like the first days. Spiced wine at the fireside and talking long into the night.'

Miriel jerked her chin off his forefinger. 'It is too late for that.' She gave a shudder of revulsion. 'I would rather sup with the devil himself. If you touch me again, I will scream.'

He looked hurt, and then the hurt became anger. 'You are my wife. Do you think the nuns will interfere?' he said scornfully. 'I could drag your skirts up and have you here on the guest-chamber floor and no one would come to your aid.'

'I don't need anyone's aid to defend myself.' Miriel backed to the fire and seized the iron poker. 'You come near me and I will ram this straight in that gross belly of yours.'

Robert stared at her, his complexion suffusing. His eyes flickered and she saw him weighing up the likelihood of disarming her against the chance of his being hurt.

'I mean it,' she said, raising the poker, and even if her insides had turned to jelly, her hand was perfectly steady. Robert might be ruthless but it was always someone else who fought his battles for him.

A pulse jumped in his cheek. 'You mad bitch,' he said with a revulsion as strong as her own. Turning on his heel, he strode to the door and flung it open. Ignatia and Adela were waiting outside.

'You may return my wife to her room,' he said coldly. 'Make sure you secure her tight. I fear that her behaviour has taken a turn for the worse.'

Miriel cast down the poker that the shocked nuns could see her holding and sailed out of the door, her head on high. 'Only in response to my husband's,' she said to the women.

Ignatia took Miriel's arm in a firm grip. Clearly, having dealt with one mad woman this evening, she was not going to take chances with a second. It was with relief that Miriel let herself be led away. Indeed, it was a boon to have the support of another to lean on, for her legs were weak in the aftermath of confrontation. Robert stared after her; she could feel his eyes boring into her spine.

She knew that on the morrow, on the sands, he was going to kill her.

Chapter 36

Nicholas beached the nef on the mud flats at high water. She was a shallow-draughted vessel well suited to inshore duties. A hundred and sixty years ago, Norman warriors had disembarked over her shallow freeboard on to the Pevensey shingle, the dawn rising in their faces. Now Nicholas leaped from her prow and waded ashore in the early grey light. Last night's wind had blown itself out. There was no sun, just a low, grey mist that swirled and eddied in patches like a dance of ghosts over the bleak fen landscape.

The crew settled down to wait, the cheer of fire rising from the portable firebox on deck, and the smell of frying fat-ham wafting on the air. Nicholas struck out across the sheep pasture towards St Catherine's. He wore a quilted gambeson against the chill of the day and as protection against any unforeseen assault. A long dagger lay snugly in the scabbard at his hip and his circular cloak was short so as not to impede his movements. Over his shoulder he carried a length of rope with an iron grapnel attached to one end.

The reeds were high; the grass was boggy – there had been no seasonal warmth as yet to dry it out. A heron took flight in front of him with a metallic cry, and he was close enough to see the fierce yellow beak with its white curlicue like an embroidered scroll.

It seemed a lifetime since he had staggered ashore not far from here, an enamelled wooden box in his possession. If he had known where it would lead, he wondered if he would have fought so hard to keep it, then decided that he would. Why else was he here now?

He paused to gain his breath but not because he had been walking hard. The thought of seeing Miriel and what he might have to do to free her from the nuns made his breath come short and his belly churn. The bleating of sheep drifted over the pasture, blending with the mist. He must be near the place where she had first found him, dying of cold and exposure. It came to him that life moved in circles like the ripples radiating from a stone cast into a pool. The stone had been his father's death, and now he was on the outer ring of the last ripple, journeying to fulfil the cycle. Or perhaps the cycle was already complete and he was about to cast another stone.

He shook his head to clear it of fanciful notions and continued on his way. By walking along the top of a dyke, he was able to see the abbey buildings rising clearly out of the fen. There were more of them than there had been six years ago, and the existing ones had been dressed with patterned stone and reroofed in tile. The prosperity of wool, he supposed, and a shrewd abbess. Sheep and cows grazed together in the home pasture. A walled enclosure held several large hay ricks, and beyond that, next to the kitchen buildings, was another enclosure for pigs. Near the abbey gatehouse, there was a row of buildings resembling the almshouses he had seen in the towns. These must be the dwellings of the women who had bought corrodies, he thought – or whose families had paid to put them here. Like Miriel. He wondered which dwelling was hers. The only way to find out, he supposed, was to knock on the doors and find out which one held a prisoner.

Descending the dyke, he started towards the boundary wall near the guest houses. As he threw the grapnel and started to climb, the alarm tocsin clanged out in frantic discord from the bell tower.

Hillary was looking for her cat again. Despite the assurances of the other nuns that he would return when he was ready, she knew that he was waiting for her to rescue him. She had seen their sidelong, pitying looks. They thought that she had lost her mind, but Hillary knew that she was as sane as daylight. Had she not been Abbess here for more than thirty years?

'Puss, puss, puss,' she called.

The response was a heavy sigh from Sister Godefe. From her eye-corner, Hillary saw the nun approaching with a cup of the horrible brew they kept forcing down her throat to make her sleep.

'Puss, puss, puss,' she said in a cracked, despairing voice and began to weep. Suddenly, through a blur of tears, she saw him staring at her from within the heart of the cooking fire, his eyes like two red coals. With a joyful cry she ran to the hearth and plunged her arm straight into the flames to draw him out. The fire seared her flesh and flashed upon her linen shift and the strings of her cap. She staggered backwards, screaming in pain and triumph, cradling her arms as if holding a child or an animal. Her body blazed like a white candle.

Before Godefe could throw a blanket over her and beat out the flames, Hillary fell against a pile of soiled bed linen waiting to be taken to the laundry, and the fire took hold and began to leap up the timber wall. Hillary paid no heed. There was no pain; the flames were cool as balm, and she could feel Puss in her arms as warm and solid as life.

As he heard the tocsin, Nicholas prepared himself for a confrontation, but no one came running. Doors opened in the almshouses, but, since they faced away from the boundary, he was not seen. From the top of the wall, however, he could observe the occupants hurrying or hobbling, depending on their state of health, towards the main buildings. And then he both saw and scented the smoke.

He shinned down the other side of the wall into the compound and ran round to the front of the corrody buildings. Immediately he knew which one was Miriel's, for a heavy draw-bar of wood had been fixed across the outside of the door. The sight of it filled him with rage and he hoped that the convent burned down to the ground. Heaving the oak beam out of its slots, he threw it aside and shouldered open the door.

Only the swiftness of his reaction saved him from being brained. A dark shape swung viciously towards him and caught him a glancing blow to the side of the head as he ducked. It was still enough to bring him to his knees and make him see stars.

'Christ,' he swore through pain-clenched teeth, not knowing how apt the oath was until he realised that the damage had been done by the solid wooden crucifix that Miriel was clutching in her fist with all the vigour and determination of a knight wielding a war club.

'Nicholas?' she gasped, and knelt hastily beside him. 'Holy Mary, why didn't you say it was you? Are you all right?' She touched his temple and he flinched. 'It's not too bad, only a little blood.'

'Thank heaven for small mercies,' he groaned sarcastically.

'I thought you were Robert.' She flung her arms around his neck and almost overbalanced him. The crucifix dropped to the floor behind them.

He grabbed her to steady himself and felt her frame, light as a bird's within his hands, but living, beating flesh and blood. The force of tears stung the back of his eyes. He closed them and swallowed the tightness in his throat. 'You need never fear Robert again,' he said hoarsely.

Miriel shook her head and drew out of their embrace. 'You don't understand,' she said. 'He's here. He found out about the crown and he thinks I know where there's more.' She looked at him with frightened, haunted eyes. 'He's taking me down to the shore today, and I know that when I can show him nothing, he will kill me.' She shuddered. 'When I heard you at the door, I thought it was him.'

Nicholas lurched to his feet, swayed slightly and steadied himself. He put his hand to his head and felt a bruise the size of a goose egg. 'The convent's on fire,' he said. 'I don't know if your hell-spawn husband is involved or whether it's the whim of God. Nor do I care, save that it gives us time to be gone.' He grasped her hand and together they ran out into the grey daylight. Clouds of yellow smoke were billowing from the heart of the buildings, obscuring vision, constricting breath. Thatch and wooden roof shingles were well alight. Nicholas hoped that Robert Willoughby was literally in the thick of it. He closed the door behind them, slotted the draw-bar back into place and pulled Miriel round the back of the pension houses to the wall and the dangling grapnel rope.

'Can you climb?'

'I can do anything,' she said. Against the pallor of her skin, her eyes were intense mead-gold and her mouth set in grim determination. A pang of love, sharp and strong, struck beneath his breastbone. On impulse, he cupped her face, kissed her once, fiercely, then took her hands in his and set them on the rope. 'Go,' he said.

It was not a high wall; Miriel had scaled it once herself with a ladder and, despite being hampered by her skirts, she reached the top easily enough. Nicholas followed, drew the rope up, and dropped it down the other side. As Miriel began her descent, he took a last look at the convent, and saw Robert Willoughby. Red-faced and coughing, he was running towards the pension houses. In a moment he was going to find out that his bird had flown the cage. Nicholas wished that he had a crossbow in his hands and, as he wished, Robert looked up as if drawn by the thread of thought. Their eyes met. The merchant's lips formed a curse that Nicholas was too far away to hear. He made an expressive gesture in response, shinned down the rope like a squirrel and shook the grapnel free.

'What is it?' Miriel searched his face.

'Robert knows,' Nicholas panted. 'He's seen me on the wall. Hitch up your skirts; I've a ship beached at the inlet if we can outrun him.'

In frantic haste Miriel dragged the folds of gown and undergown through her belt so that they bunched around her waist in bulky pleats and swags. Again Nicholas took her hand and they ran along the foreshore pony track until their lungs were bursting and their legs were like hot lead.

Nicholas stopped briefly to gain a moment's respite. The goose-egg lump on his head throbbed as if it were about to hatch and he could not breathe swiftly enough to supply his starving body. Beside him, Miriel clutched her side and collapsed to her knees, her breath sobbing. If Robert caught them now, he thought grimly, it would be the end of them. But they had covered the ground well and they were more than halfway to the ship. Another half-mile and they would be safe.

'Ready?' he gasped to Miriel.

She nodded, too breathless to answer, but staggered to her feet and gamely forced one leg in front of the other.

Through the sheep pasture they ran. Drifts of mist, as thick as the smoke, engulfed them, then suddenly parted, giving them brief glimpses of the reedy landscape punctuated by meres and pools. Once they stumbled over a dead sheep. Miriel screamed and stifled the sound against the back of her hand as Nicholas pulled her upright and lifted her over its decomposing corpse.

'Not far now,' he spared breath to encourage her. 'Safe soon.'

Almost as he uttered the words, he realised his error. In the mist he had mistaken one path for another, and although it had brought them to the shore, there was a treacherous expanse of mud and sand to cross to reach the beached nef. Quicksand or not, only a local would know.

'We have to turn back,' he panted to Miriel, who had collapsed retching at his feet. 'I missed the true path in the mist and we dare not risk crossing here. There should be another track further down.'

She nodded wordlessly. He stooped for a moment, hands braced upon his knees while he recovered his wind. He looked at her. 'It will be all right, I promise you,' he said.

Miriel nodded again and lunged to her feet. Clutching her side, she gazed out over the flat seascape. Fog was rolling in like a white tide, misty spray at its edges. It came as a friend in which to hide, and an enemy to hinder their progress. Beside her, Nicholas had turned round, intent on finding the right path. She started to turn with him when she saw a dim shape riding out of the fog and across the sands towards them.

A small, involuntary cry broke from her lips.

'What is it?' he said and then he too saw the rider. The grey of cloud yielded to the solid bay of a large cob, and astride it, bearing down on them at a mud-flinging canter, was Robert.

Running was futile. Neither Nicholas nor Miriel had the stamina remaining to outrun a horse, and Robert was too close to lose in the mist. Nicholas tugged Madame le Pêcheur's gutting knife from his belt and the light shivered icily along the steel.

Robert drew rein. The cob halted in a flurry of mud, but sidled and champed in response to its rider's agitation. The softness of muddy sand mired it beyond the hocks. Robert had a knife at his belt too, but instead of drawing it, he unlooped a wood chopping axe from behind his saddle.

'So you've come to take what you would not give to me,' Robert sneered. 'It's here, isn't it, you faithless slut.' He swung the axe by its haft.

His words immediately explained to Nicholas and Miriel how Robert had known to pursue them to the beach. He thought they were recovering royal loot, not merely putting distance between themselves and him.

'Yes, it's here,' Miriel retorted with a sweeping gesture that encompassed the entire foreshore. 'Take it if you can find it. Hunt like all the others with a spade and a pole. I don't know, I've never known!' She threw him a blazing glare, the fuel of fear rapidly burning into rage.

He licked his lips, his complexion dark with fury also. His gaze swept to Nicholas. 'Tell me and you can have her in exchange for the gold – pay for her like the whore she is.' He spat over the side of the saddle.

'The only whore I see is you.' Nicholas almost gagged on his words. 'You have paid your soul to gain your own ends through the foulest of back passages.'

The axe wove in Robert's hand and the gelding sidled, its eyes rolling to show their whites. It was working hard to pluck its hooves from the clinging mud. 'Enough clever words,' Robert snapped. 'Either show me where you have hidden the remainder, or I will kill you both.'

'All you will find is your own death.' Nicholas flourished the dagger. He tried to push Miriel behind him to protect her, but she flung him off, her eyes sparking with fury. Stooping, she seized fistfuls of foul-smelling mud and hurled them at Robert.

'There is no remainder except in your mind!' she shrieked. 'You see nothing but gold . . . you want nothing but power . . . you feel nothing but greed.' She punctuated each damning statement with another flung clod. 'In the end you are nothing!' The gelding, already unnerved by the sucking coldness around its hooves, took fright at the high-pitched screams and the slapping clods of mud. When the last one scored a direct hit on its eye, it whirled in panic and bolted across the foreshore.

Robert was flung back against the saddle's high cantle. His legs flailed at a comical angle as he struggled to right himself, tighten the reins and bring the horse under control. For an instant the gelding raced flat out, ears back, tail streaming, then its reaching hooves struck yielding, glutinous mud and it pitched, mane over tail. Robert cried out as he was flung from the animal's back. He did not land cleanly. One foot caught in the stirrup iron, and as the horse plunged and threshed, Robert too writhed, striving to free his foot while the mud took an inexorable grip. When he realised the full extent of his peril, he began to bellow for help like a stricken bull.

Heaving with emotion and effort, Miriel stared in horror. 'Dear Christ,' she whispered. Although she wanted to look away, to bury her face against Nicholas's chest, she forced herself to watch. There was nothing they could do. Nicholas had a rope, but it was too short, and besides, Robert was tangled up in the stirrup iron. Even if they could reach him, they would not be able to pull him free.

'Ripples in a pool,' Nicholas murmured, making the sign of the Cross. His expression was grim, but there was the faintest glimmer of satisfaction in his eyes. Justice, if brutal, was being done. His only regret was for the horse.

The quicksand was in a hungry mood and the swallowing did not take long. Robert was dead before he went under, suffocated by the crushing weight of mud and sand upon his corpulent torso.

As the cob had fallen, a small travelling chest had been thrown from the saddle pack. It had bounced along the ground two or three times and the hasp had broken, spilling Mathilda's crown and its wrappings like an exotic flower on to the mud. Now both casket and crown were sinking, but unobtrusively, their lighter weight making of their progress a stately, inevitable wake. Miriel had been going to ask

Nicholas what he meant about ripples in a pool, but suddenly, watching the crown, she knew.

In the silence a curlew called mournfully. The fog rolled in and covered the shore in a deep, white shroud. In silence, Nicholas and Miriel linked arms and turned inland to find the path that would bring them to safety.

That night they sailed into Boston and at the house of Martin Wudecoc were greeted with hot food, warm beds and no questions. If not dreamlessly, then Miriel slept deeply. When she woke a little after dawn, she did not, at first, know where she was. The room was warm and dry, the bed soft, with a feather mattress, and the surroundings were colourful with embroidered hangings on the walls and painted clothing coffers. There were other beds in the room, all empty, although several bore evidence of having been recently occupied.

While she was still gathering her wits, Elfwen entered bearing a hot honey and blackberry tisane.

'Feeling better this morn, mistress?' she asked.

Miriel nodded, although in truth she did not know what she felt at the moment. She took the tisane from Elfwen and gratefully sipped. Memory and obligation slipped into place, piece by little piece. 'I owe you a debt of gratitude, for reaching the Wudecocs',' she said to the girl. 'Name what you want, and it is yours.' She looked at the maid over the rim of the cup and found a smile. 'And do not say nothing, for I will not accept such an answer.'

Elfwen smiled too. 'Oh no, mistress, that would be foolish,' she said candidly and tilted her head in thought. 'I would like a bolt of scarlet diamond twill to make myself a fine dress for Holy days.'

'It is yours, and you need not make it yourself. I will have a sempstress sew it for you.'

Elfwen flushed with pleasure and Miriel was warmed by the sight of it. There had been no joy or warmth in her life of late, and now it was time to make amends. 'Where is— ?' she started to ask, but was prevented by a scrabbling on the steps, the rapid patter of paws, and then the sudden assault of a small, hairy body and frantic pink tongue. Elfwen made a grab for the tisane, rescuing it from Miriel's hand with no more than a few drips staining the bleached linen chemise.

'Will!' Miriel gasped with a mingling of delight and tears and clasped the little dog in her arms. He wagged and licked and fussed.

'Pined for you, he did,' Elfwen said. 'Kept looking for you whenever we went out.' The first frenzy of greeting over, she returned Miriel's tisane. Will settled among the covers, rolling on his back to have his tummy tickled.

'Is it true that Master Robert is dead?' Elfwen asked hesitantly.

'Yes, it's true.' Miriel folded her hands around the cup, seeking its warmth. An involuntary shudder rippled down her spine as her mind's eye relived those dreadful moments again. 'Drowned on the quicksand beyond the convent.'

The maid shuddered too, and crossed herself. 'God rest his soul, and I pity him,' she said, 'but I am not sorry that he is gone.'

'It is finished,' Miriel said, a finality in her tone that closed the subject with her maid. Setting her cup aside, she looked round for her clothes. 'I assume I am a slug-abed to judge from all these abandoned pallets.'

'Yes,' Elfwen said with a sidelong smile. 'They thought it was best to leave you. Mistress Alyson has gone to the market, and Master Martin and Master Nicholas went to the wharves.'

Miriel nodded. 'Am I to greet them in my shift when they return?' she asked.

'Mistress Alyson put your clothes to dry before the hearth, and then they'll need all the mud brushing out. She said to use these for now.' Elfwen took a bundle of clothing off a coffer and presented it to Miriel. There was a clean undergown of plain linen and a fine overgown of mulberry-coloured wool. A pair of woollen hose and a linen wimple completed the outfit together with a braid belt. Miriel donned the garments. The gown had to be gathered in several pleats before she tied the belt. Three weeks in St Catherine's had left her with precious little flesh on her bones, and Alyson was an ample woman. Still, Nicholas was accustomed to seeing her in less than flattering borrowed robes. A poignant smile touched her lips as she remembered the foulsome grey dress he had bought from the rag-and-bone stall in Stamford.

She finished the tisane, clicked her fingers to Will, and descended the loft stairs into the main room. The day was bright but cool. A sharp wind off the river was kept at bay by a good fire in the central hearth. The wet-nurse sat on a bench against the wall, spooning savoury frumenty into her mouth. She nodded to Miriel and indicated the cooking pot keeping warm on the side of the hearth. 'Fresh made,' she said. 'Warm your cockles nicely, it will.'

Miriel thanked her, and took an empty wooden bowl off the shelf. But before she filled it with frumenty, she went to the cradle against the bench and looked at Nicholas's namesake. He was awake and the blue eyes less kittenish and myopic than the last time she had seen him. They were going to be dark green-blue and their focus was intelligent. Leaning over him, she smiled. He seemed to puzzle briefly, and then, imitating her, he smiled back. Enchanted, Miriel found herself cooing at him.

'Aye, he's a good baby,' the woman said. Her eyes were shrewd. 'Pick him up. He's awake.'

Miriel set aside the bowl and stooped to the baby. He was heavier than last time too, but still small and vulnerable enough to fit into the crook of her arm as if he had been meant to do so. She walked him round the room, gently showing him the coloured hangings, the glint of light on the candelabra, and took comfort from his warm, tender weight. Just the act of holding him was cathartic.

The nurse smiled and nodded. 'Aye,' she said, 'you'll be a good mother for him.'

Miriel looked at her sharply, but the woman merely smiled, tapped the side of her nose, and continued with her frumenty.

The sound of masculine voices filled the street outside; the door opened, and Martin and Nicholas entered the room, bringing with them the tang of the sea.

Miriel met Nicholas's gaze and flushed. It was not as if

she was doing anything wrong by holding the child, and yet she felt awkward. It was on the tip of her tongue to blurt that she was not trying to take Magdalene's place, but to say so would only make the awkwardness worse.

'You'll have to watch the lad when he's older if he continues to attract women the way he does now,' Martin said with a grin at Nicholas and a nod at the baby.

Miriel gave Martin a look of gratitude for smoothing over the first difficult moment of contact. 'He takes after his father,' she said.

Nicholas gave a snort of amusement and, coming to her side, lifted his son gently in his arms. 'I hope he grows out of it, or at least learns to look before he leaps,' he said.

Miriel was intensely aware of his presence beside her: the brisk scent of outdoors on his garments; the warmth of his body; the paradox of closeness and distance that separated them.

She retrieved her bowl and sat down to break her fast on a portion of the hot frumenty. There had been no opportunity for her and Nicholas to be private, to talk and see if they could bridge that distance. She had tried to ransom him, he had come to St Catherine's for her, but that did not mean they would go on together from here.

Nicholas shook his head at the offer of hot frumenty. 'I broke my fast earlier,' he said, cradling the baby and rocking him lightly on his arm.

'You should have woken me.'

'You were so deep in slumber, I could have rung St Botolf's bells in your ears and you would not have roused,' he said with a smile. 'You didn't hear me trip on the hem of my cloak and curse, although it was nigh in your ear. I am glad you were able to sleep so well. Yesterday, when I found you, you looked like a lost ghost, so wan and gaunt.'

Miriel grimaced. 'Three weeks in Abbess Euphemia's tender care would turn anyone into a lost ghost,' she said. 'You don't know how good it is to be warm again – and well fed,' she added as she finished the last scrap of frumenty. 'They said that a diet of gruel and water would purge my mind of the evil humours affecting it.' She made a small gesture, as if casting something from her. 'It's finished now. I have sworn to myself that I will not brood.'

Looking at her, Nicholas said, 'Martin and I went down to the wharves this morning in search of news.'

She met his eyes. 'And was there any?'

'Only that St Catherine's will require much work to make it habitable again. More than half of it burned down to the ground. From what a barge-man told us, the fire was started by the old Abbess in a state of confusion. Apparently she was looking for her cat. For now, the nuns have dispersed to Sempringham Abbey. There was no mention of you, nor of Robert.'

'It would not matter if there was,' Miriel said. 'What happened was the will of God – the last ripple,' she said with a shiver.

There was a brief silence, the kind in which, given other circumstances, a prayer might have been said for the dead man. Nicholas broke it by placing his son in the wet-nurse's arms, and turning to Miriel.

'Walk with me,' he requested, and lifted Alyson's spare cloak from the wall peg.

Rising, Miriel shook out her skirts and swished the cloak around her shoulders.

Outside, the wind was as brisk as a knife and the sun lent only a small gentling of warmth. If summer was on the horizon, it was not yet visible. Miriel huddled into Alyson's cloak, glad of the double wool lining. Nicholas took the lead, sheltering her with his body, and headed again for the wharves.

'Martin told me that you had borne a child, and that it had died.' He glanced round at her as they walked. His eyes were narrowed against the wind, his expression taut, as if facing into a storm. 'I assume it was ours?'

Miriel bit her lip. 'I thought I was barren,' she said, 'but it was Robert who was unable to father children.'

'Why didn't you tell me?'

She shook her head. 'Because I was ignorant of the symptoms. I had to be told by a physician that I was with child. Besides,' she added with a spark of anger, 'what good would it have done? You were wedded to Magdalene, and she too had conceived. I saw her on the *St Maria* the morning after we returned from Bruges, and she was wearing naught but a sheet.' Her voice took on an accusing note, full of hurt and anger. 'You took her to a bed still warm from the print of my body. What kind of love is that?'

'It wasn't love,' he said savagely, 'it was despair.'

They emerged on to the wharfside and the full force of the wind attacked, no longer just a knife, but a full, slicing sword. Miriel clenched her teeth and put her head down. Nicholas took her arm and drew her at a half-run along the quay until they came to the *St Maria.* Her sail was furled and her decks bare. Nicholas dismissed the watchman with a brusque nod and led Miriel on board, drawing her to the deck shelter beneath the forecastle.

'I wanted you; I couldn't have you,' he said as he secured the flaps against the wind. 'Magdalene eased my pain.'

The watchman had left a small brazier burning. Miriel held out her hands to the glowing charcoal embers. 'You mean she took advantage of it?'

He shrugged. 'At first, perhaps, but not without my full consent. My eyes were wide open when I married her.' He frowned, seeking the right words. 'Sometimes love strikes like lightning, and its power is as blinding. Other times it comes gently, creeps up on you unawares and covers you like a blanket. Magdalene was my blanket, and I grieve deeply to have lost her.'

'I'm sorry.' Miriel looked at her hands outstretched to the warmth. Now that they had their moment of intimacy to speak, she wanted to tear open the shelter flaps and run for the safe haven of company. She did not want to speak of Magdalene, but knew that she must if she was to unburden her guilt.

'I saw her as my rival,' she said painfully. 'She took you when I thought she had no right . . . I even hated her for a time.' She raised her head and looked at him. His expression was impassive. She could not tell if he was loathing her for her confession. 'But when I thought beyond the jealousy, I knew that I was being unfair. I had chosen my road of my own free will, why should I begrudge you yours? You may not believe me, but I too grieved when she died. We spoke of you when she was sick, and it healed wounds on both sides. We made our peace.' She touched his arm. 'I would make my peace with you also.'

He raised his brows, questioning without speech.

'You still owe a ransom to the men who saved you from drowning. I was intending to pay it with Mathilda's crown. I can no longer do that, but I am a rich widow. I have all Robert's wealth at my disposal, and it would be fitting to use it for that purpose. Then you won't have to sell any of your ships.'

His lips curved with grim humour. 'Blood money, I believe it was once called,' he said. 'But you don't need to go so far to make your peace with me.'

'But I do.' She looked up at him and edged closer so that they were sharing the same space. 'We agreed to a truce that time in the counting house, not peace.'

The fine creases at his eye-corners deepened and a spark kindled in his eyes. 'So we did.' His arm suddenly curved around her waist, drawing her hip to hip against him. 'Fair enough. I pride myself upon being a reasonable man. I will consent to peace if you will stand before a priest with me.'

It was what Miriel wanted to hear, and yet she held back. It was only fair to warn him. 'If I was not barren before, then I am now,' she said. 'The birth was so difficult that the midwives said I would never carry a child again. I know you have Nicholas, but I cannot give him brothers or sisters.'

For a while he said nothing, and she braced herself for rejection. Then his arms tightened around her. 'We both have Nicholas,' he said. 'It is you I desire, not your abilities as a brood mare. You are my lightning.'

She made a sound that was half-laugh and half-sob because she was torn between the joy and the pain of the moment. All the futility of the past, all the broken dreams, which could have been hers from the start. 'You once offered to take me across the North Sea and up the Rhine,' she said. 'Does that offer still hold true?'

He tilted his head and pretended to consider. 'Will the morrow suffice?'

She laughed with delight and pulled his mouth down to hers. They embraced, until embracing was not enough, and their clothes an encumbrance.

The watchman's pallet was fortuitously to hand and they lay upon it and made love as wild and molten as the lightning.

In the aftermath, perspiration cooling on their bodies, breathing harsh and hearts pounding, they lay still joined. Miriel licked the sea-salt taste of sweat from the hollow of Nicholas's throat with the tip of her tongue. He stroked her breast, then his touch moved sideways to the cord of gold thread dangling in her shadowy cleavage. He lifted the necklace on his finger and studied the pearl trefoil attached by three links of gold chain.

He frowned. 'Isn't this part of . . . ?'

She silenced him with a swift palm across his lips. 'It's a reminder of our peace,' she murmured with a smile. 'Like a ring is a symbol of marriage.'

He looked at her and then he laughed and reached for his clothes. 'Let us go and find that priest,' he said.

AUTHOR'S NOTE

To this day no one knows what happened to King John's royal treasure. That it went missing between the accident to the baggage train and the coronation of John's son in 1220 is not in dispute. An inventory of regalia assembled for Henry III's crowning tallies very little with John's known possessions of four years earlier. The missing items include the imperial regalia of the Empress Mathilda. As a novelist, this was just too good an opportunity to pass up!

There are several theories about just what happened on the Wellstream estuary and the subject is still hotly debated in academic circles. The chroniclers of the time, rather like some tabloid journalists of today, were apt to make the facts as juicy as possible for the entertainment of the readers. I have chosen the dramatic paths of the chroniclers Roger of Wendover and Matthew Paris as a vehicle for my story, rather than the more prosaic version of Ralph of Coggeshall. There is also the possibility that John's regalia was looted from his body when he died at Newark Castle shortly after the accident to the baggage train. Unless the treasure turns up with its true story attached, no one will ever know.

Although characters such as Hubert de Burgh, Eustace the Monk and Stephen Trabe existed (Eustace the Monk really did come to the grisly end described in chapter 14), the major personalities in *The Marsh King's Daughter* are my own creations. I have, however, striven to take their circumstances from my research into their period. There was indeed cut-throat competition between wool merchants and many of them made their way to fame and fortune by deeds that would not look out of place among the Mafia today. The Prioress of the Benedictine nunnery of Rowney in Hertfordshire wrote to King Henry complaining of a runaway nun who was roaming abroad in secular dress, bringing disrepute upon the order.

THE CONQUEST

Elizabeth Chadwick

When a comet appears in the sky over England in the spring of 1066, it heralds a time of momentous change for Ailith, a young Saxon wife. Newly pregnant, she has developed a friendship with her Norman neighbour, Felice, who is also with child. But when Felice's countrymen come not as friends but as conquerors, they take all that Ailith holds dear.

Rescued from suicidal grief by Rolf, a handsome Norman horse-breeder, Ailith is persuaded to become nurse to Felice's son, Benedict, but the situation soon becomes fraught with tension. Ailith leaves Felice's household for Rolf's English lands and, as his mistress, bears him a daughter, Julitta. But the Battle of Hastings has left a savage legacy which has bitter repercussions, not only for Rolf and Ailith but for the next generation, Benedict and Julitta.

From bustling London streets to the windswept Yorkshire Dales, from green Norman farmland to the rugged mountains of the Pyrenees and the Spain of El Cid, this is an epic saga of love and loss, compassion and brutality, filled with unforgettable characters.

'An author who makes history come gloriously alive'
The Times

'The best writer of mediaeval fiction currently around'
Historical Novel Review